Warhorn

SONS OF IBERIA

Book 1

J. GLENN BAUER

First published 2013 by Bauer Photography and Media

This edition published 2019

ISBN: 978-1-9163312-0-4

DEDICATION

To my wife and son; I dreamed so long of writing this novel and now that I have, I realize that all these years it was you who believed that I could and myself that doubted.

Thank you for your unswerving loyalty.

CONTENTS

1

She would need to move despite having just given birth. The mountains were dangerous with winter-hungry wolves. The scent of afterbirth could easily draw the powerful hunters to her newborn. She was young and strong but no match for a pack.

She had a more pressing worry though. The sun would rise soon, and a greater danger stalked the hills. Warriors had passed within feet of her hiding place as she gave birth. Her golden eyes glinted as she watched them slip between rock and thorn, making their way downhill into the valley.

The lynx hissed as the first screams echoed through the pre-dawn gloom. The warriors were hunting and blood would flow. She nuzzled her cubs, her rasping tongue cleaning their matted fur and then effortlessly lifted them in her powerful jaws. On the rocks above, she paused to watch as flames flared among dwelling places of the humans.

The stonemason put the final seal on the tomb and turned from the granite rock. The day was still young and Caros knew Ugar had other tombs to seal. As the stonemason packed his tools into the heavy leather pack, Caros deliberately avoided looking at the tomb. Instead, his thoughts drifted to the vengeance he yearned. The warrior code was ingrained in all Bastetani and called strongly for retribution.

The stonemason hefted his pack over his broad shoulder. "It is done." Dusting his hands off on his tunic, he fixed Caros with a kind look.

"Thank you. It is a fitting resting place." Caros swallowed tightly and placed a pouch in Ugar's reluctant palm.

"You are not a warrior, Caros. If you join with Alugra in hunting the Arvenci, be sure to heed his advice." Sliding the pouch beneath his tunic, he set a hand on Caros' shoulder. "May the god of war strengthen your arm." Ugar patted Caros' shoulder, sighed, and set off down the rough track, leaving him alone to make his farewells. Caros appreciated the stonemason's departure. He hoped that the solitude of the mountainside could quell the imagined screams and cries he heard. At last, he turned to the cold granite of the tomb and stretched to touch the quartz-flecked rock. Bowing his head, he inhaled and pictured the face of each of his dead kin, while invoking the gods' protection of their shades.

His father, straight-backed and sharp-eyed. His mother, ever patient and kind, her long black hair fading to grey, tied at the nape of her neck. Ximo, his brother, whose massive hands were always doing good deeds and who was to take a wife in the coming summer. These were his kin; killed in the past day by raiding Arvenci warriors. Others had died in the raid too. Villagers and farmers slain as the Arvenci poured through the ancient forests and into the valley where the village of Orze nestled. His father would have seen the smoke from the family home at the end of the valley and known the cause. While his mother and her maids made for the hill fort to shelter behind its walls, his father and brother would have hastened on horseback to aid the villagers and farmers.

Caros found their battle-broken bodies on the road to the village they had never reached. About them were strewn men, women, and children. They would have met them as they fled toward the shelter of the hill fort and died together when the Arvenci overwhelmed them. Without the spears of the village men or farmers, the hill fort would hold the Arvenci back only for the time it took a pair of them to scale the walls and open the great gates. He remained astride his horse as he stared numbly at the bodies. After long heartbeats, he steeled himself and threaded his way through the scattered corpses. The urge to discover the fate of those who had fled to the hill fort was too powerful to ignore. There would be time to retrieve the dead and build the funeral pyres. Gaining open road, he edged his horse into a steady canter up the narrow trail.

The morning sun painted the bleached wooden walls in stark relief. His eyes remained fixed on them as he rode, but there was no movement to be seen. No indication that anyone watched from within the palisade. An ill sign. The lip of the rock outcrop on which the hill fort was built, hid the gates from view so he could not see if they were open. Cautiously he eyed the track ahead and the thick growth to either side. The Arvenci could easily be skulking among the ravines and thorn bush if they had failed to gain the fort. He unhooked the leather clasp from his sword's pommel so he could unsheathe it in a heartbeat. For now, he gripped his spear, ready to plunge it into the throat of any attackers.

Everyday objects lay scattered along the trail. A shawl, a torn sandal, a smashed clay jug and worse still as he gained the slope, the bloodied and disfigured body of a woman. His breath hitched at the sight and he cursed aloud before dragging his gaze away to continue sweeping the hillside for threats.

The top of the gates became visible and as he had feared; they hung open. He reined in his horse and in that moment, Caros knew with certainty that his mother too, was dead. A crushing ache at the death of his kin and fellow villagers forced the air from his chest and his chin dipped. Swallowed by grief, he sought the power of his parents, his people, the Bastetani. Their shades were with him, willing him to be strong.

After wiping his cheeks, he stared long at the walls, the hillside below him and the body. Anger threaded through his veins, his breath growing tight as he recognized the dead woman as one of his mother's close friends. With his gaze jumping from shadowy rock to rustling undergrowth, he rode up the trail that switched back towards the hill fort. Caros swiveled his neck, keeping the ominously hanging gates in sight until he was below the walls and heading directly towards them. The palisade above him, as tall as two men, was deserted. No watching faces, no sound other than the cries of carrion birds. Upon reaching the gates, he edged his mare warily through them.

The interior was open to the sky, allowing carrion birds to alight within the walls. Confronted by a heaving carpet of vultures and crows, he reined in the mare. Wings spread wide; they tore into the swollen flesh of the dead who were strewn over the ground. The presence of the birds feeding so freely reassured Caros that the killers were no longer here. Since discovering the bodies of the village men on the road, he had known the hill fort would not keep the women safe. If his mother had reached the walls, she too would be among the dead.

He hesitated inside the gates, unwilling to encroach upon this realm of the dead. The birds nearest the gates glanced briefly at him down gore-encrusted beaks before continuing to feed. The stench of the place caused his horse to stamp in agitation and she swatted at clouds of flies with her tail. Crooning to her in his deep voice, he dismounted and tied her reins to the gate. Birds hopped resentfully from his path as he approached, protesting with raucous cries. He stepped carefully between torn remains on stone and dirt thick with blood. His footing was precarious on the slick gore and bird shit. He veered away from the center and circled along the walls where the butchery had been less. Not more than forty paces from him was a lean-to built of timber and attached to the outer wall. The thatched roof was stove in and rotten thatch hung in ragged bundles from the walls and formed a mound within the lean-to. Something heavy had fallen through the roof. Reaching the doorway, he peered into the shadowy interior. The body which lay contorted in the shadows, untouched by the birds was that of Olia, the largest woman in the village by a considerable amount. Her immense girth was made even more so by the swelling of death. It was clear that she had been thrown from the wall and Caros hissed in fury and cursed the men who had done this. She had always been a generous and merry person who never missed an opportunity to throw her arms high and laugh aloud. She would never do so again.

Stepping away from the lean-to, Caros stared across the aftermath of the butchery. Overwhelmed by disgust, he stamped his foot and waved his spear wildly.

"Away! Filthy bastards!" Like an oily cloud, the birds slowly took to the wing. "Away!" he whispered; his sudden anger spent.

Weaving through bodies lying singly and in pathetic huddles, he at last sank to his knees beside a woman. Miraculously, his mother's eyes had not been plucked by the beaks of the carrion birds. Fumbling, he unclipped the copper brooch at his throat and drew his cloak across her body.

They found him there when the shadows were at their shortest. Forty Bastetani warriors from up and down the valleys had congregated at the gates beside his horse and watched as their leading man strode to the kneeling figure.

He approached Caros warily, his eyes flicking to the spear and falcata discarded to either side of Caros.

"Son? I know you, do I not?" Caros stirred and lifted his chin to see the man wince. "Your mother?" He nodded, looking about him at the scattered bodies. The shadows had grown longer and birds watched with glittering eyes from the walls. "I am Alugra of Tagilit." He made a sweeping gesture. "We will take the dead to the village. There are others coming to help. Come out of here with me; it is not healthy for you here."

Caros blinked and waved flies from his face. "I will carry my mother. The bodies of my father and brother lie on the road. I must take them home." Slipping his arms under his mother's knees and shoulders, he rose.

Alugra inclined his head and gestured to the waiting warriors who began filing into the hill fort to begin the dreaded task of wrapping the dead.

Caros took no notice of them as he strode to his mount. He settled his mother's body over the horse which stamped restlessly. Untying the reins, he mounted and looked at the Bastetani leading man.

"Thank you for coming. I am Caros. My father was Joaquim, my mother Mirand and my brother Ximo. What news of the raiders?"

Alugra lifted a hand, palm up.

"Greetings, Caros. They are of the Arvenci and have fled south, scattering as they flee. We captured a few and drew their tongues from their throats. We will do what we must here and then go after the rest."

Caros stared past Alugra for long heartbeats before his lips twisted into a semblance of a smile.

"Thank you. That you have exacted retribution gives me a measure of comfort. For that I am grateful."

He took her body to the family home. Much of it still stood despite hurried attempts by the Arvenci to torch the buildings. Caros rode his horse up to the front door that hung smashed on its hinges. He gently lifted his mother, and cradling her in his arms, walked into his home. The air reeked of smoke and ash and the cots and shelves had been burned. Caros laid his mother's body on the stone floor.

It took him until sunset to fetch the bodies of his father and brother from where they had fallen. With their bodies draped over the horse, he led it home on foot. When he arrived, he started at the sight of a woman running toward him from the house. With a sob, she fell against him, burying her face in his chest, tears dampening his tunic. When he could pry her free, he sat her down.

"Julene, what are you doing here? Where are your kin?"

She was the daughter of their neighbor and promised to his brother.

Julene was a pretty girl who matched Ximo's bright mood with a joyful demeanor, although that was absent now. Her eyes were red and her face blotched. She had clearly not slept since the day before. Working her fingers through the torn hem of her chiton, she took a hiccupping breath.

"They passed right by our home, Caros. They must not have known we were there for they came before our fire was lit. We only knew they had come when those fleeing from them, stopped to warn us. Father found their tracks. They had stalked so close that a single murmur while we slept would have betrayed us to them."

Her face paled and her breath came fast and shallow. Caros held her and shushed her the way a father would a frightened child.

"Endovex, god of all, shielded you and you are safe, as is your family. Did your father try to take shelter at the fort?"

She shook her head. "Brent said they were between the fort and us. He said we would be better off hiding in the high forest and led us into the hills. Many others did the same."

Caros said nothing about what had happened at the hill fort. He rose on tired legs and crossed to the well. Once again, the Arvenci had not wreaked as much havoc as they could have for the water was untainted. No butchered animal heads or innards polluted the well. After dousing himself with cold water and drinking, he drew a bucket and gave it to Julene to take indoors. She took the container wordlessly and as she passed the mare, looked mournfully at the two bodies draped over its back.

He dragged off his tunic and drew another pail of water. A good drenching helped clear his head and with the sun just set, the evening breeze made him shiver. He would need to cremate his family and entomb the ashes the next day. His father had long ago prepared a tomb in the hills, converted from a disused mine. Caros needed the stonemason to close the tomb and put the necessary seal and mark on it. Others would need the stonemason's skilled hand too, although many would simply inter the ashes of their kin in clay urns. He planned to ride to the stonemason that same evening and secure his services for the morning. Once his family was entombed, he would join Alugra's warriors in hunting the Arvenci raiders.

Julene had lit a fire in the hearth and its flickering flames cast an orange glow over her cheeks. Caros crouched beside her. Using his tunic, he dried his face and then wrung the garment and set it before the fire.

"I am going to see Ugar, the old stonemason."

She looked up from the fire. "Now? It is dark and he may have been slain."

He turned the steaming tunic to allow the other side to dry.

"Perhaps, but his dwelling is well hidden. I am certain he is well. I will see you to your kin." He needed time alone to sort out his plans.

"You wish to see your kin sent to the ancestors in the proper way. I understand, but there are things that need to be done first." She gestured to the bodies of his kin.

Caros had shied away from thoughts of preparing the bodies and he was grateful for Julene's practical thinking.

"You want to do this?" She frowned at him. "Apologies, I meant did you want to do that now?"

"I loved your parents like they were my own kin and Ximo…" Choking back a half-sob, she raised her chin. "When they have been sent to their ancestors, what will you do?"

Looking into her eyes he could tell she already knew what he intended.

"Alugra, the Bastetani champion, has brought his warriors. They will go after the Arvenci and I am going with them."

She lifted his right hand in both of hers, gripping it tightly. "With this hand you will slay them. Do this please. For your kin and clan. For Ximo." Her words brimmed with the ferocity of a wounded lynx.

"I will." He took her into a close embrace. "I must go now. The stonemason might be generous and provide us with a little bread and cheese as well."

Night made the ride hazardous and, eyes heavy with fatigue, he strained to guide his mount safely along the rocky path. Blinking hard, he pushed on until at last the welcoming site of a fire burning at the stonemason's hearth appeared. As he approached, he called out greetings loudly, not wanting to alarm the stonemason or his wife. They lived on a secluded spur above the valley and beside a quarry where he cut and dressed stone. They would not be used to receiving visitors in the dark and in the aftermath of the bloodshed, would be nervous. Ugar appeared swiftly at the door and Caros noticed an arrow already nocked in his bow.

"Ugar, it is Caros, Joaquim's son." Caros kept the pace of the horse steady and tried to tell what the stonemason was doing with the bow. It worried him, especially as the stonemason usually won all the archery contests held in these parts.

"How goes it, Caros? These are dangerous times to be out after dark."

Caros slowed the horse and stopped within the glow emanating from the doorway. "You have heard then?" He guessed the stonemason had heard of the attacks from some fleeing clan member.

"I have heard. We saw the fires as dwellings were raised. The raiders were between us and the fort." He shrugged. "I could not join the fight, so we stayed here."

Caros swung down from his mount and embraced the powerful old man briefly in greeting. "That is why I am here, Ugar. My parents and brother were amongst those killed. My mother made it to the fort, but few of our warriors reached there. There were not enough men to hold the walls. Everyone inside was put to the blade." A part of Caros was disturbed that he could talk of their deaths in such a calm tone.

Ugar grunted and spat at the evil news. His eyes fixed on Caros for a long heartbeat before he bellowed over his shoulder.

"Suls, pour some ale, we have a guest."

Caros wanted to object, he did not want to stay, just come to an arrangement and then return home. He said nothing though, not wishing to appear ungrateful.

"Have you eaten anything, son? Sit and have some stew. Slaughtered a goat two days past. Meat is as stringy as a witch, but tastier." He beckoned him indoors and Caros followed, stooping to avoid the lintel of the low doorway. It was pleasantly warm inside and Ugar's wife was already ladling a watery stew into a clay bowl.

"Greetings, Caros. Sorry times these. What is the news from the village?"

"Bad. Many of our kin were killed trying to reach the fort. Those that did make it were slaughtered within." Suls dropped the ladle with an exclamation, both hands covering her mouth. "That is why I have come so late."

Ugar cut him off. "Not now. Sit and eat first. Suls, get some ale into the lad. All his kin were lost. From the look of him, I am surprised he got all the way up here."

Suls pushed the bowl of stew across the table. "Sit, Caros. Such evil news cannot be faced on an empty belly."

Caros sat gratefully. The kind sympathy had triggered the feelings of loss he was trying to bury, the horror of the day and the bitterness he felt. It flooded through him and he hung his head, blinking back tears and willing himself to be stronger.

Ugar laid his bow and quiver aside and sat. He splashed ale into a cup and set it next to Caros' bowl.

"Cursed goat was the stringiest one in the flock! Fill your belly."

Caros smiled dutifully at Ugar's attempted levity. The stew was good and the ale better. Caros mopped up the last dregs of sauce with a lump of bread. Remembering Julene, he looked at Suls who sat quietly at the fireside working a sheet of new leather.

"Julene is at our farm. You know her?" Ugar grunted noncommittally while Suls nodded. "She came to see Ximo and remained to tend the bodies. May I take bread for her? Everything has been robbed from our stores." Suls was back on her feet in an instant and while she was packing a basket, Caros spoke to Ugar.

"I am joining Alugra's column tomorrow. We are going after the Arvenci." Ugar frowned deeply but said nothing. "Before I go, my family must be entombed. My father had a tomb cut summers back. Will you seal it for me tomorrow, Ugar?"

"Yes, of course. Where?" Caros explained how to find the tomb and Ugar confirmed he knew the place. "I will be there at first light to prepare it. Your father chose that spot well."

"Thank you, Ugar. I am sorry to have disturbed you so late, but I cannot let the deaths of my kin go unpunished and Alugra leaves early tomorrow."

"I know, lad. Alugra is a dangerous one to have hunting you. If the Arvenci see him on their trail, they will scatter and flee. You take care because a cornered lynx is especially vicious in a fight."

Caros left shortly after with a basket of provisions. He hefted it appreciatively; Suls must have packed a feast fit for a champion. He let the mare choose her pace off the hill and back home. Julene awoke when Caros entered the dwelling and scrambled bleary eyed and terrified, into a corner.

"It is I, Caros. Do not fear."

The fire had burned down to glowing coals and their orange glow was enough to light the three wrapped bodies. He was impressed at how fast she had worked. Ximo was as big if not bigger than he or his father. His respect for her increased a hundredfold, and he was glad he could at least offer her food. He placed the basket on the table and laid more wood on the fire.

"Suls packed a meal. From the weight of it I reckon it would feed an army." He smiled at her while she opened the basket. Her hands trembled as she fumbled at the knotted cord holding the lid on. "Your parents will be worried that you have not returned home."

She paused the untying and pulled her cloak tighter. "They sent two men to check. I had them help me with the bindings."

That explained how she had managed to lift the bodies. Caros stared now at those bodies. It was unnatural. This was their home. They should be sitting here at the table finishing their evening meal, planning the next day's business or discussing village news. Laughing, joking, talking, living. Now he sat there while they lay shrouded in scorched blankets on the cold floor. He shook his head. It was too much to think on so it was best to just shut it out and deal with things as they happened.

Julene succeeded in opening the basket and gasped. "Oh! I hope Suls has left something in the larder for Ugar. Look at all this food!"

They both laughed and spent a few moments unpacking it all onto the table before them. The thought occurred to Caros and Julene at the same time. Most of the provisions were of the kind you could take on a long trip; dried meat, fruit and nuts, hard bread and wrapped cheese.

Julene began repacking the basket. "Suls packed this for you to take when you go hunting the Arvenci."

Caros had not even considered taking food with him. His heart pounding as he wondered what else he had not thought of. To mask his fears, he gestured at the spread.

"There is plenty, so eat, please."

"Caros, when did you discover your father and Ximo? Were you not with them?"

"No, I was away in Tagilit and arrived home by the northeast road this morning. Balic's place had burned to the ground and was smoldering still. There was no sign of battle and yet neither he nor his kin were there. At the bridge, a dog lay speared to death and as I neared the village road, I found the bodies of those that had been killed there." He stared into the fire, fists clenching and unclenching. "That was where I found my father and brother. The Arvenci must have come at the village from different directions because they passed your place before sunrise. They knew everyone would flee to the hill fort and trapped them before they reached its walls. Only those living on that side of the valley reached it. Ugar and Suls saw they were cut off, so they hid up in the rocks above their home. Nobody would ever catch the stonemason up there." Caros fell silent, picturing how the Arvenci had stalked his people.

Julene startled him with a hand on his shoulder, rousing him as his chin edged towards his chest.

"I filled a cot with new hay and there is a blanket too. Go find sleep."

He nodded and stood, eyes burning as she hugged him briefly, fiercely, in shared grief.

2

Caros rose before sunup and began laying the pyre. There was a large pile of wood left from their winter stocks and to this he added piles of dry kindling gathered from the hillside behind the house. When satisfied that there was enough to burn away the bodies and free their shades, he placed them on the pyre. Two amphora of rancid olive oil lay untouched beside the midden heap where they had been discarded. They were each as long as he was tall and he dragged them to the pyre one at a time. Cracking the neck of the first; he filled a wooden pail with the thick oil and began to douse the shrouded bodies and wood. He continued until oil pooled below the pyre and the air was bitter with the stink of the stuff. It would be a large fire.

He closed his eyes and called on Saur, god of the underworld, to grant his kin passage through the dead lands and then to Endovex to receive them in his domain. While Caros offered his prayers, Brent together with his wife and son, arrived and stood with Julene. Caros opened his eyes to see Julene's family along with two other neighbouring farmers.

"Thank you for coming. It is ready."

The men broke away from their families and approached, each bearing an offering which they placed beside the bodies. Small blades, strings of beads, dried meats and fruit all formed a pile. Caros stepped forward and placed a nugget of silver on top of the pile of gifts. Next, he lit a torch with a deft crack of flint and once that was burning well, he circled the pyre, lighting the tinder as he went. Thick smoke poured from the oil-doused kindling until a gust of wind lifted the flames with a whoosh. The pyre began to crackle furiously as the flames grew, forcing Caros to back away.

By noon the fire had burned away and Caros had placed the ashes within the sacred clay urns. Ugar was as good as his word and had already prepared the tomb. In truth a crew of slaves who had carved the benches from the granite rock had completed most of the work years before. Ugar had only needed to put the finishing touches to the walls and then carve the inscriptions for the dead into the face of the stone that would seal the entrance. With the urns stowed in the tomb together with further offerings, Ugar closed and sealed the tomb. Now Caros could leave with Alugra's warriors. They would most likely have moved from the hill fort to the village. He would seek them there and if they had already left, he would follow. Most of Alugra's warriors were on foot and Caros was confident he would soon catch up to the column.

Caros descended the mountainside under the hot, afternoon sun to where he had tethered his horse. Already Ugar had disappeared into the valley on his way home. Walking his mare, he came across villagers and farmers who had survived the raid and were now out seeing to the needs of their kin and neighbors. This was a close community and such devastating losses would scar them for a long time. Once he was done with the raiders, he would return to aid his clan. As the eldest son he had been groomed by his father to take over the trading when Joaquim became too old to travel. For the past two years he had steadily been doing more and more negotiating and trading on behalf of his father. He was confident he could rebuild the home, restock the stables and continue trading.

The family business was trading the tin and iron mined in the mountains and recently they had also bought and sold a shipment of arms and armor. There was war in the air with the new Carthaginian Commander pushing north and west, subjugating those tribes living there. While many villagers would not know much of Carthage or the Barcas, Caros had learned the histories of Greece, Rome and of course Carthage. His father had even had the foresight to purchase a slave from Carthage who had been instructed to teach Caros and Ximo that city's dialect. On trips to the port town of Baria, Caros had met with Carthaginian traders. He winced as he recalled the first meeting where he had traded five talents of tin to a Carthaginian and had been comprehensively out bartered. He resolved never to make that mistake again and on the next occasion; fixed his price at more than double what the goods were worth. He had let the apoplectic Carthaginian walk away from him no less than three times before a fair price was struck. No sooner was the deal made than the Carthaginian's demeanor changed from outrage to amused respect. Laughing and slapping Caros' shoulder, the bearded man had asked if Caros liked masquerading as an illiterate Iberian, for he must surely be a Phoenician or Greek to trade so skillfully.

The Bastetani village of Orze appeared at the end of the valley and he was heartened to see many more people between the buildings than he had expected. Most people he passed knew and greeted him although here and there were huddles of people too grief-stricken to even glance at him as he passed by. The village had also been fired and while many of the building's roofs had burned through, the fires had not been hot enough to crack and destroy the walls.

Caros reined in at the village well. From the homes about him came the wails of the bereaved. The community was as broken and fractured in spirit as in property. Caros dismounted and tied the mare up at a trough from which the beasts drank and then drew water from the well alongside. He drank then rinsed his face of the cloying smell left from the funeral pyre. The two village elders had noticed him and were making their way over. After each man had embraced him and offered their condolences, Hunar eyed Caros' sword.

"Alugra has taken his men south after the Arvenci. Some others of the village have accompanied him. They will cut the enemy down where they find them, Caros. We have need of you here."

Caros slapped the hilt of his sheathed blade, his eyes dark beneath his knotted eyebrows.

"My place is with the warriors seeking those who slew my kin. There is a blood debt owed for what they have done." Caros replied firmly.

Luan placed a restraining hand on Hunar's arm and threw a frown at Caros.

"This is your choice and we cannot hold it against you. You must return though, Caros." He gestured about him at the surviving villagers. "They have suffered a great tragedy. Many are afraid and talk of returning north to Tagilit. They say it was foolish to think that the Carthaginians would prevent such raids. Soon there will not be enough people here to keep our village alive."

Caros eyed the desperate and despondent as they carried their remaining possessions with them on the road north.

"I am pleased you respect my obligation in this. Once done, I will return. My grandfather's family established this community and it has been peaceful and prosperous, but it was a mistake thinking we were safe from raids. I will sponsor the building of solid walls around the village." He gestured at the low hill the village had been built upon in the wider valley floor. Most villages were built on hilltops for defense and in addition had a stout wall of rock and post encircling them. They smiled at his words, but he noted a trace of doubt in their eyes. He suspected their biggest concern was losing the family of the most prosperous trader in the valley. The rest of the villagers made fine wares that sold well enough, but it was his grandfather and his father who had become wealthy trading in metals mined from the mountains. Riding on his family's successes in trade, the villagers had been able to expand the market for their cereals and flax.

Hunar gestured south. "Alugra left at sunrise. He expects the Arvenci to splinter, some taking their plunder back to their homes and other perhaps heading to the coast to sell it to the Greek and Carthaginians. He hopes to gain them before then."

"The Arvenci took all our livestock. I have not seen a cow or horse in the entire valley. That will slow them down." Caros drew a leather satchel from his baggage on the horse. "Ugar has sealed the tomb of my parents and brother. Please accept these gifts and call on Endovex to guide the shades of my kin through the lands of death to our ancestors. The homestead is burned, not destroyed. If I may request, please employ craftsmen from among the villagers to begin rebuilding the house." Caros offered the satchel with both hands. Hunar accepted it and surprise showed on his face when he felt its weight. Caros had included enough silver to employ men and women to restore the dwelling as well as a generous compensation for the elders. As much as he enjoyed trading with miners and sea captains, his greatest passion was horses and he dreamed of breeding a herd of his own. To that end, perhaps he would even recover the stolen livestock. Luan embraced Caros once more.

"Go then and do this thing. We will hold a proper ceremony for the dead once you return."

Caros nodded a farewell to Hunar before mounting his mare and striking south, past the village to where he intended to avenge his slain kin.

3

Caros found Alugra's column late in the afternoon, strung out and trotting briskly south on a local trail. Alugra and his leading men set the pace for the men on foot. A shout from the column at the sight of Caros brought the riders at the front to a halt. Caros trotted his mare past sweat-stained warriors taking the opportunity to catch their breath.

"Greetings, Alugra." Caros called upon reaching the Bastetani leading man. "I hope I have not missed any fighting?" He doubted he had, as the Arvenci would still be at least a day ahead of them.

"Caros! Welcome! I had hoped you would reach us before we taught those murderous crows a lesson in Bastetani hospitality!"

Alugra was a popular leading man among the Bastetani people and his village near Tagilit had grown and seeded several outlying villages through his skillful leadership. Not many leading men could raise a column of sixty warriors. Alugra's skill in war was well known and his reputation as a fierce enemy went a long way to preventing those small, strength-sapping raids that were the bane of so many settlements. Caros hoped Alugra would pursue the Arvenci with a vengeance, not just to avenge the attack against a friendly neighbouring settlement, but in the interests of protecting his reputation.

"I have buried my kin and settled affairs with the elders. Now my falcata hangs at my side thirsting for a taste of their blood." Caros gave the leading man a grim look to reinforce the ancient warrior mantra. Alugra motioned to him to ride beside him.

"Come, we need to keep a good pace. I hope to receive news of the Arvenci before nightfall." He flicked his rein and set his horse to trot along the trail with Caros alongside.

"Have they been sighted?"

"The only people who have seen them are a couple of shepherds. Seems they have all the plunder they can manage. They are avoiding settlements now in the hopes of making good their escape."

"Murdering thieves!" Caros spat into the undergrowth beside the trail. "They will stop at some point. They have to as they are at least five or more days journey from their lands."

"Stop? They are fleeing. My concern is that they will scatter into still smaller groups as each makes their way to their clan settlements."

"You think they are more than a band from a single village?"

"I reckon there are more than two hundred of them. Not many leading men that can boast such numbers so they must have joined forces." Caros sneaked a glance back at the seventy men in the column and Alugra barked a laugh. "What do you see there, Caros?"

He blushed in consternation, hoping Alugra would not think him afraid. "Err, your warriors. They number less than half the numbers of Arvenci."

"Good, a merchant that can count." He chuckled at his joke. "Why did you think I was so glad to see you?"

Caros' mouth dropped open in surprise, prompting more laughter from Alugra. The riders behind him joined in the laughter and Caros was forced to smile. He assumed a nonchalant expression.

"Well, I am known to have a half-decent sword arm and there are few men who can launch a javelin as far and true as I." He shrugged, enjoying the look of surprise that grew on Alugra's face. The Bastetani leading man glanced back at his rough-hewn companions who looked equally surprised. Now he could enjoy the joke more and did so, laughing out loud. Alugra shook his head and laughed with him.

"You young bullock!"

Caros realized this was what made Alugra the accomplished leader he was. He could lift his men's morale when it flagged and ease tensions before they escalated. They rode on south while the sun cut the western sky and the land rose and fell steeply about them. In the far distance, they could occasionally see the darker blue of the sea between hazy, grey hills.

Towards dusk the scouts ranging ahead began reappearing. These did not ride back to the column; instead they simply waited alongside the trail for Alugra to reach them. This was not a good sign for if they had news, they would have come galloping back. Alugra greeted each and the scouts shrugged and told the same tale. The Arvenci were moving at speed, always south. Alugra decided to set camp at a watercourse identified by the darker green vegetation that mimicked the stream's sinuous course through the hills. Caros was disappointed but knew that it could take days to overtake the Arvenci if they were no longer stopping to plunder and especially if they suspected they were being pursued. Alugra had explained why he was not concerned about the numerical superiority of the enemy during the afternoon's ride. Many of the raiders were most probably youths just coming into manhood. As a fighting force they would be fickle. The experienced warriors among the Arvenci would allocate the young and inexperienced to guarding the booty and livestock they had rustled. That would free fewer than half of their spears to fight. Additionally, they would have been on the trail for days and were not as fresh as Alugra's men. Finally, their primary focus was to escape and any fighting they did would be just enough to allow them to flee. Caros was not sure of the logic of the last reason, but someone of Alugra's experience in war would surely understand better than he.

A murmur from the column dispelled his musing and he looked back when a yell went up from the men. A smudge of dust on a near hillside gave away a rider scrabbling his mount downhill. The man was teetering on his horse and everyone drew a breath as rider and mount twisted, slid and leaped down the hillside. Alugra spurred his horse forward as did Caros and the rest, and they rode to intercept the man who reached the foot of the hill and jumped his mount over a tangle of thorn bush before galloping across a rocky field towards them, yelling. He reined in the lathered mount to a skidding halt amongst Alugra and his leading men.

"The Arvenci! I spotted them making their way west just beyond that hill!"

A growl rose from the throats of the warriors on the road and they surged and rippled.

"Hold!" Alugra snapped at them. He turned narrowed eyes on the scout. "How many and what was their nature?"

"I counted a score, maybe a score and a half. Hard to be sure as they were in the trees and brush. They had maybe sixty horse and cattle with them so there was plenty of dust."

Caros nodded, thinking it would be difficult to count an exact number in those conditions and Alugra was of the same opinion.

"What of their nature? Warriors?"

"All warriors, quite a few are young. They are moving fast and quiet. No yelling and little talking. These are men that do not want to be found."

Caros felt his heart racing at the thought of catching this first breakaway band of raiders. He glanced at the lowering sun, estimating the time till sunset. They could take them as they were setting camp, lighting fires and readying their meals. His hopes were dashed when Alugra ordered them to keep heading south to the tree line. Caros quickly dragged his horse around and caught up with Alugra, furious at this development. The Arvenci were there and while they may not be the whole force, they would be easily wiped out and by tomorrow Alugra's warriors would be ready for the next day. Alugra did not wait for him to speak.

"You want us to attack them now. Today. Tonight even. Yes? Just thirty of them. Kill them as they eat and regain all the stolen livestock. In and out. Am I right?" He glanced at Caros who swallowed back pretty much those words. "Ah, I was. I do not need to explain my decisions Caros, but the gray in my beard is a testament to the virtues of caution. We will see what we see tomorrow." He spurred his horse ahead and joined several of his leading men as they approached the designated overnight camp. Caros sighed, frustrated. He had a lot to learn about the ways of warriors. It all sounded like action and glory. So far what he had seen was the horrifying aftermath, the victims and the toil, just to watch the enemy slip away. He wondered where the rest of the raiders had gone and why this group had broken west so early in their flight. Maybe this was what Alugra was thinking. It was possible this was a trap. Too many thoughts were tumbling through his head and the afternoon was waning fast as the sun sank. Somewhere out there his enemy hid.

The camp was a boisterous one for the most part as Alugra's men gathered firewood from the nearby creek. Past summer floods had left large piles of broken trees in drifts at the flood mark on the steep banks. There they had dried and whitened like skeletal remains. The men broke and snapped off all they needed and soon had several large fires burning in the dusk. Caros took his time grooming his mare. He was fortunate that he had taken her on the trip to Tagilit that had seen him absent from his home when the Arvenci attacked. She was a beautiful roan mare with a startling black mane. His father had overseen her training and presented her to Caros just two years ago on his sixteenth birthday. Caros still remembered the joy and pride he had felt when he saw her colors and form. This was one of those fine horses his father had been able to breed from their herd of handpicked stallions and mares. He was glad of the mare's company now as the grief he had kept in check all day gripped his heart at thoughts of his father. The mare must have sensed the sadness in him and nickered quietly and turned her deep brown eyes to him. He held her cheeks, breathed in her breath and felt his sadness lessened somehow. "Good girl. I will bring your friends home too. How would you like that, eh! That handsome desert stallion as well. I have seen you making eyes at him." By way of reply the mare nickered and snorted. Caros laughed out loud.

Feeling better, he made his way to where the creek flowed quietly from one shallow pool to the next. He filled his waterskin and then washed the day's dust from his face. Darkness was settling in and the fires were bright as Caros returned. Fowl was roasting on more than one campfire and the aroma reminded Caros that he needed to eat, although he felt no hunger. At one fire, a handful of men sat subdued and apart from Alugra's warriors. They said little and ate nothing. Caros recognized them as men from the village and surrounding farms. Farmers and craftsmen whom he knew only by sight. He made his way over to them.

"Do you mind if I share my meal with you? It is not much, but please help yourselves. I am Caros, the son of Joaquim." He laid the food Suls had packed for him next to the fire. The men murmured appreciatively as they shifted to give Caros a place to sit and began to break off chunks of heavy bread and salted goat. They ate in silence until a warrior from a nearby fire strolled over. He was a tall, lanky man with sun-browned skin and a crooked nose that leaned to the left. Ale sloshed in the skin he hefted in his hand.

"Fellows, it has been a long, dusty day. I have some ale here if you wish. It is cut so do not get too excited." He grinned as he handed the skin over to Caros who thanked him and introduced himself. "Greetings, Caros, I am Neugen. I noticed that horse of yours. She is worth her weight in silver that one." Caros passed the ale to the man on his left and invited Neugen to sit. "Thanks, I will not stay too long, the bird's nearly done and those bastards will guzzle the lot!" He raised his voice so the men at the near fire could hear and they laughed and agreed. Neugen chuckled and shook his head. "They are good fellows. I grew up with them and we have been on three campaigns together."

"Do you ride then, Neugen?" Caros asked.

"Not I. My feet do all my carrying, but I would." He patted his belt. "Just not enough silver to get my own mount!" Neugen laughed. "One day though. Just one good campaign with rich pickings. I hear rumors this new Carthaginian general, the Barca son, is levying thousands for a big campaign in the north again, maybe against the Ilerget of Athanagia. That will be a campaign worth fighting in. Loot and spoils in abundance." Caros winced and Neugen paled as he realized he was talking to a group of men whose homes had been pillaged. "By the gods, my big mouth. Do not take offence, I beg."

"None taken. We are just thankful you fellows have come to our aid."

The warrior smiled with relief. "Best get back and claim some fowl before I am left with just feathers and bones for a meal." He rose smoothly. "Until tomorrow then. Keep an eye on me; I will show you why the Arvenci fear the Bastetani." He patted the sword at his hip confidently.

A cool breeze blowing off the northern mountains woke Caros just before dawn. It had dewed heavily during the night and despite his youth, he woke with stiff hips. The cold ground had leached the warmth from him. Grimacing at the dampness and cold, he sat up. He had slept with the village men and like them; had only a cloak and tunic to wrap in. They lay slumbering, hoping for someone else to light the fire. Caros rose and walked sleepily into the nearby bracken to relieve himself. Warriors from Alugra's column were up as well and had small fires crackling. He considered lighting a fire before opting instead to find Alugra and learn what his plans were. He strapped on his falcata and loaded his travel bag onto the mare tethered with the other horses. Leaving her there, he strode down to the stream to fill his water skin. Although still early spring, if this day was like yesterday, the rising sun would soon burn off the ground cold and the dust of the road would thicken the men's saliva. He nodded greetings to others at the stream doing the same.

"Caros!" Neugen came up beside him. "Good sleep? Are you ready to use that sword of yours?" The man's high spirits were contagious.

"Do you know something I do not?" He did not expect the reply he received.

"I do not know what you know, but we will do some circling this morning."

"Circling?" Caros was mystified.

"Ah, those Arvenci the scout spotted; they are either a diversion or bait. Either way, Alugra is planning to find out and fifteen of us are going to circle their camp and see which. Fancy coming along?"

"I would, but I am not leaving my horse."

Neugen laughed. "We will all be mounted. We are using the leading men's spare mounts."

Caros was elated at the news and happily accompanied Neugen to where the warriors were rallying. The men were eager to move and he was grateful he had readied his mare earlier.

Alugra saw Caros and came over to him. "You are certain you want to go with these men, Caros?" He shot Neugen a glare, but the young warrior was staring north innocently.

"Could not be more certain. I will not slow anybody up and the mare is good too."

The leading man smiled. "That is the spirit. Keep up with Neugen here and do what he says. If there is a fight, let my men take the sting out of them. That is what they are good at."

Caros felt a bite of annoyance. It was true he was no warrior though and so he nodded reluctantly.

One of Alugra's leading men, a stocky man with piercing black eyes, trotted his horse past them and grunted to Neugen. "Keep to the rear and off the ridgeline. I do not want them seeing us before we see them."

Caros smiled at Neugen who shrugged. They both knew the advice was for Caros. The dark-eyed leading man met the scout who had discovered the Arvenci at the head of the column.

Neugen shifted his shield where it hung at his knee. "That is Alfren. He is not Bastetani, but fights like a cornered lynx, so we tolerate him."

"Oh? Where is he from?" Caros had thought he looked out of place among the taller Bastetani.

"West. He is Luistani. Kissed the wrong girl as the rumor goes. Has a bug up his ass most of the time, but he is alright. Anyway, I reckon we will hear the warrior songs tonight. Alfren gets bored when he is not hacking off arms and legs."

Caros prayed that was true and that Alfren would lead them into the Arvenci. Bait or decoy, he did not particularly mind which. The sun was struggling over the eastern horizon when they rode north. They struck off the regular track and edged their mounts out along a game trail that wound north through the hills. The breeze had dropped, and the sun cleared the lingering mist from the hillsides, leaving just the steeper, shaded valleys still misty.

Neugen nudged him. "See?" Smoke, smudged by the earlier breeze, lingered in the air over the valleys west of them. "We are going to come at them from the north, the west if we make good time. We may hit them about noon. By then Alugra will have the main body up behind them."

"We will drive them into his men?" Caros asked.

Neugen snorted. "We are scary bastards, but not that scary. They will come at us rather than run. We call them cowards, but the truth is the Arvenci are tough as old hide and usually give as good as they get. We are playing them at their own game and will be decoys. Most of our men are on foot, so need to get in as close as possible. We are just a distraction. When they realize they have an enemy at their backs, it will be too late to flee and they will have to fight."

Caros wondered why they would fight if they were not trapped. Neugen's confidence made him wonder if he would be up to the task. He knew how to swing a blade and throw a javelin, but had never fought in anger. He had not even competed in contest bouts. They rode on, keeping to the hillsides and off the ridgelines on which they would be silhouetted, making them easy to spot. Caros examined the riders ahead of him. All wore sheathed swords and carried a trio of javelins. They wore armor of bronze plates on their chests and on their heads, dome-shaped iron helmets with heavy leather hanging over their necks and ears. The wealthier warriors, including Alfren, wore greaves on their forearms and lower legs. They looked formidable and experienced. He trusted they would live up to the reputation Alugra had built.

They were making steady time despite the winding trails they followed over rocky terrain and at mid-morning rounded a hillside to see a heavily wooded valley running due west. They were approaching the western end of the valley from the north. He glanced at Neugen. "That is probably a great place to make good time without being seen."

Neugen slapped a biting fly at his neck. "I wager they are in there somewhere and heading west like we guessed."

"Straight towards us."

"Hope so." He grinned widely as he flicked the crushed fly away.

Alfren led the column downhill, off the open hillside and toward the tree line. The sun had long burned off the mist in the valley and the heat was beginning to rise off the ground, so Caros was glad when they entered the trees and the shade they offered. Undergrowth was sparse. This was an old wood and the trees well-spaced, leaving plenty of room for the men to meander their horses between the trunks. Occasional large clearings were thick with dry meadow grasses and spring flowers. Alfren brought his mount to a stop in the deep shade of the trees at the edge of one such meadow. They were at its western end and roughly in the center of the valley floor. The men gathered in a line facing west, all keeping well within the shadows of the woods. Two men peeled off and began circling the meadow from either side. Neugen leaned towards Caros.

"Now we find the Arvenci. You ready for a fight?" He had a wicked gleam in his eye and looked every bit the warrior Caros wished he could be at that moment.

"Never more ready." He lied.

"If they came up this valley, which makes sense if that smoke we saw this morning was theirs, then they have not yet passed this point."

"What makes you so sure?"

"Have you seen any tracks? They have cattle and horse and that meadow has not seen anything larger than a deer. The grass would have been trampled to shit."

Alfren walked his horse down the line of men to where Neugen and Caros sat their mounts. He halted behind them and ignoring Caros, spoke to Neugen.

"Keep to the left of the valley. When we attack, hit their flank and stay on it. If they make for the woods they are probably alone, but if they fight back, it will mean they are the bait just as we thought." Without waiting for a response, he pulled his horse round to head back to the center of the line. Caros stared at the bright sunlit meadow, the thick grass reached to the height of a horse's chest. He imagined charging his horse through that and attacking the Arvenci from horseback. He had done little training in fighting from horseback. He expected that it would be fast and furious. Swing strike and parry. He patted his horse who rocked her head up and down, aggravated by the tension that was suddenly stifling him. The air had become too still. He glanced up the line and saw graybeards drinking deeply. Realizing how dry his mouth had become, he did the same, but then found he needed to relieve himself. He thought about putting it off, but the need got more urgent.

He glanced sheepishly at Neugen. "I need a piss."

"Hurry." Neugen continued to scan the field ahead, eyes narrowed in an effort to see into the woods on the far side.

Caros quickly swung from the horse and hurried a few paces towards the nearest tree. He urinated quickly, desperately. He did not want to be caught on foot if they charged. He finished, dropped his tunic and adjusted the belt while looking around the woods. Shadow figures darted from tree to tree and he gasped in shock as a man on horseback loomed in front of him. The rider urged his mount right past the shocked Caros, who stood arms at his sides and mouth agape. It finally sank in. The rider was one of the scouts who had ridden off earlier. He flung himself onto his horse and watched the returned scout conferring urgently with Alfren who was smiling and nodding. He caught Caros' eyes and smiled wider as he issued orders to the men beside him. Word quickly spread down the line. The Arvenci were heading down the valley towards them.

Caros began drawing his falcata from its sheepskin sheath, but Neugen leaned over scowling. "Too soon. They catch a glimpse of sunlight off that shiny toy and they will be away like fleas off a dead dog."

Caros cursed himself. He could not act more like a novice if he tried. The sun baked them through the thick foliage of the trees under which they hid. Time stretched and then suddenly there was movement ahead, the shimmering heat waves parted thickly to reveal contorted figures that coalesced into the heads of beasts. Cattle and horse trotted out of the distant tree line and into the sun. Caros felt his heart hammering and gulped. He clenched the reins and strained higher to see further. A figure emerged carrying a shield and spear and then another appeared at his back. The Arvenci were flanking the herd. The animals came on, eating up the ground and filling the open field while the flanking Arvenci kept them going straight down the valley. Directly towards the waiting Bastetani. Neugen eyes never strayed from the Arvenci as they strode alongside the herd.

"Now Caros, see your enemy. We strike hard and fast. They will try getting the herd to stampede and block us. Keep to the left and reach them before they get to the tree line." He grinned, but his eyes had hardened. "Oh, stay behind me."

Caros grunted, staring fixedly at the men who had killed his kin.

The herd sensed them. Horses nickered and cattle lowed. The leading bull stopped dead in his tracks, rucked the grassy loam with a foreleg and swung his horned head from side to side. In that moment, Alfren roared his battle cry and his horse flew from the tree line. Warhorns bellowed through the valley and rolled up and over the hillsides. Caros started and then furiously whipped his mare after Neugen who, charging from cover, let loose a shrill war cry. Like so many wild lynx, the Bastetani warriors burst with blood-curdling screams from the tree line and hurtled towards the stunned Arvenci.

Cattle and horses milled frightened and confused in the valley and in moments a great dust cloud rose billowing from hundreds of hooves. Shadowing Neugen, Caros watched the warrior curl his spear arm and unleash the missile. The Arvenci targeted, flung his shield up at the last moment and deflected the weapon from piercing his chest to merely striking him under his eye. Caros saw the gout of blood as the spear tore into the man's face, knocking him senseless and bleeding to the earth. Behind the fallen man other Arvenci warriors had time to raise their shields to fend off the hurtling missiles thrown by the Bastetani. Caros suddenly realized he was unarmed and snatched for his falcata, dragging it out in one fluid motion as he flew towards the enemy warriors. Lightning fast, Neugen hurled two more javelins and scored two more hits. Neither strike killed, the Arvenci having had time to cover their vitals, but one man was hit solidly in his right shoulder while another dropped with a javelin pinned through his upper thigh. Caros tore towards the warriors and swung his falcata overhand and down. Shock jarred through his arm. An Arvenci had sidestepped Neugen's barreling charge and stumbled right under Caros' blow. Without glancing back, Caros charged on. The Arvenci lunged their spears at the galloping horsemen, snarling their challenges. Caros heard nothing, but thundering hooves and his roar of rage. He hacked at a spearhead and then nimbly dragged his blade backhanded through the attacker's face.

Then they were past the Arvenci and hauling on their reins to bring their horses around. Caros pulled his mount to the left and tore about in an arc, judging that the surviving Arvenci would hare for the tree line. Seven were left uninjured and as he had guessed, they were belting uphill towards the nearest brush and trees. His path intersected theirs and as he bore down on them, they glanced around in horror at him. Three turned and hurled their spears. Caros ignored the missiles and swept over the men, pummeling one man into the ground under his horse while striking another with his swinging falcata. He tore on toward the four escaping warriors and reached them mere paces from the trees they desperately sought. Behind him, Neugen and two others kept pace and within moments the remaining Arvenci had been smashed to the ground. Caros spun his horse, prancing on its hind legs, to face the enemy fallen. Neugen and his comrades were already off their horses and dispatching the wounded Arvenci. Although bloodied and reeling, the Arvenci still had plenty of fight, but no advantage and they died quickly under the merciless blows of the Bastetani falcata.

Caros saw a group of limping and staggering Arvenci fleeing back up the valley. With an animal growl he turned his horse after them. Within heartbeats he clattered over the rearmost of these, a thick chested warrior with blood-soaked hair plastered to his face. The man screamed in defiance as Caros drove him under his horse. The next two warriors ran together and ducked and weaved apart as Caros charged them, his falcata whistling harmlessly through the air. Cursing he charged on leaving them to his companions. The next warrior turned at the approaching drumbeat of hooves and snarled. Caros felt the exuberance of victory and with his right arm stretched beside him readied for the killing blow. Without warning, the warrior hurled his shield, which flew straight at Caros' mount. The shield spun and as it did so, it whistled like a falcon. Caros stared in shock as the missile slammed into his horse. The mare reared, screaming in fright and he felt himself go airborne before crashing into the valley floor. Stars burst and pain blackened his vision. His breath blew from his chest and he clawed the ground in pain. He watched in horror as the warrior strode towards him, axe swinging to cleave him. The man's face was all but peeled from his skull, which just made the hate that Caros saw there all the more horrifying. He fumbled blindly for his weapon. It was nowhere to be found in the long dry grass. Runeovex! He wanted to throw up, to get a breath into his body, but could not. His horse drummed past him and as it did, it trod his outstretched hand into the ground. Shrieking, Caros found the strength he needed in that fresh bolt of pain and shot to his feet. The warrior swung the heavy war axe powerfully, meaning to cleave Caros in two. The blow was hurried; the warrior surprised that Caros had managed to lunge to his feet so quickly. Caros followed the swinging axe head and struck the warrior in the center of his bloodied face. Bone and teeth crunched and the warrior sprayed blood from his mouth and disfigured nose. Caros kept striking as the warrior backed away. The man turned his back on Caros as he tried to shield his tortured face from the blows. At once, Caros grabbed the axe at both ends and jerked it back towards the injured man's throat. The warrior was powerful, but he was determined that this fight have only one outcome. Caros used the axe's thick handle to choke the man. They grappled like that until the Arvenci warrior finally slumped. Caros tore the axe from his blooded grip and swung once. The warrior toppled from his knees onto the dirt. Caros stood gasping for air in the dust filled valley. He stared ahead unblinking, spittle spraying from his slack lips. There in the tree line, a figure moved furtively through the shadows. Caros narrowed his eyes and for a heartbeat, glimpsed a flash of color and a familiar shape. Then it was hidden by horses milling through the field before him.

Alfren and Neugen reached him at the same time. The former was smiling triumphantly down from his horse. The bastard had not broken a sweat and yet his gore encrusted falcata told its own tale. Neugen was nursing a swollen elbow, but his face was full of concern at seeing Caros. The young warrior leapt from his horse and approached, "Ho, Caros! You look like carrion. Best you find shade and swallow some water. This fight is done."

Caros responded with a nod and fearful of toppling over, took a pace toward where his horse milled with the other mounted horsemen. Pain and fatigue washed over him and he felt a spasm shudder through his body. He would not lose his stomach now he vowed to himself, not before these seasoned warriors. He had woken with revenge in his heart that morning, never having killed a man and now he had killed a handful. He was no longer a man-boy, but a blooded warrior. He clutched that thought tight while fighting the welling nausea. Neugen was suddenly right beside him and passing his mount's reins to him. He hauled himself weakly onto his mare and they trotted through the chaos on the valley floor to where the other Bastetani were congregating. Warriors had dismounted and were drinking deeply from waterskins or whooping at their victory. Just two of the warriors had any telling injuries and while obviously in pain, they still beamed with pride.

The men cheered Caros as he reached them. Confusion at their sudden friendly demeanor quickly turned to joy. The slick feeling of nausea gave way to the warmth of comradeship. He had experienced friendship and family before, but this feeling was something new. He felt invigorated and a special closeness with these warriors who had risked their lives with him. He grinned at Neugen who threw his head back and released a huge whoop that echoed back off the valley walls. In moments, all the men were whooping their triumph and Caros joined in with a cry of victory. Hoof beats drummed and he twisted about to see who approached. Alfren and two other riders came galloping towards them from the east end of the valley. He looked grimmer than usual and Caros wondered why. Their fifteen warriors had killed easily the same number of Arvenci and by first estimates, recovered much of the stolen livestock. He reined his horse to a halt and slid to the ground. Even with armor, his movement were lithe. Caros knew instinctively that this man was one of those breeds of men that could dance through blade and fire without harm. Alfren raised his voice to address the gathered warriors.

"The Arvenci have broken into bands now, most even smaller than this one. We were wrong. These were neither decoy nor bait. Alugra caught some stragglers still at the night camp, injured men I expect. A few more fled back east after we attacked and ran straight into his men. We need to round this herd up and get them heading home; the hunt is over."

The men cheered and laughed in delight, but Caros was ambivalent. He was pleased they had been successful, but something nagged at his memory.

The men rounded up the scattered cattle and horses. Caros guessed that most of the community's livestock had been regained. That would make it easier for the villagers who had suffered so much. The Arvenci dead were stripped of everything of value. Neugen found the deadly battle-axe that had so nearly ended Caros' life and offered it to him.

"No thanks, you keep that lump of iron. I would lose my foot trying to swing that monster!"

The Bastetani warrior grinned. "Thanks. Do not often see these on the battlefield, but it will fetch a nice little sum from some weapon smith."

The dead were covered hastily, but respectfully and by mid-afternoon the men were urging the recaptured herd back up the valley to rendezvous with the main body of Bastetani. The Bastetani camp was alive with laughter, singing and the bellow of warhorns. Men drank from skins of ale and with Alugra's permission, had slaughtered a bullock from the herd and were roasting the fresh meat on numerous fires. The camp was festive. Alugra was listening to Neugen tell of the battle in the valley while Caros chewed on a lump of greasy meat. Alfren sat alongside Alugra, drinking deeply from a skin.

"The way Neugen tells it, you acquitted yourself well today, Caros." The Bastetani leading man beamed at Caros who flushed with pride.

"I just listened to Neugen's advice. Not a lot of time to think once it all started."

"The stolen livestock, did we retrieve many head then?" Alugra asked.

"I reckon we managed to recover the greater part. The village will be overjoyed to have this many returned. The elders will reward you greatly Alugra and I am certainly most grateful to you and your men."

Alugra smiled warmly. "This is what being a Bastetani means, Caros. We stick together and help one another out when things get rough." The old warrior frowned and then, "I see a lot changing here closer to the coast. The old Greeks and Phoenicians, they came and went; just trade. Good for everyone. Now?" He shook his head. "Now the Barcas have come to stay. They send their desert warriors to conquer the tribes." He went quiet, chewing slowly, spat out a piece of grey gristle and swallowed. "I do not like it. The tribes grow restless and few have any love for this young Barca."

Alugra looked to Alfren, who stirred. "Hannibal Barca. Hamilcar's son."

Caros knew of the Barcas who had come as traders for Carthage and then become conquerors, led by Hamilcar Barca. His father had met with Hamilcar's son-in-law, Hasdrubal, or as people called him, Hasdrubal the Fair. The eastern tribes along the coast were strong and made stronger through trade and Hasdrubal had made treaties with them that benefited the people greatly. The wealth produced was a magnet for the raiding, warlike tribes of the Olcades, Arvenci and Carpetani.

Alugra grunted. "Yes, Hannibal. He is stirring a wasp nest. I preferred his brother-in-law. Your father and I signed a good treaty with Hasdrubal." The warrior drained the last of the ale in his skin and then grunted and turned onto his back, settling himself for the night before raising his head for one last comment. "I am too old for what is coming, but warriors like Alfren here and maybe you Caros, can do great things in the times ahead. Now make your thanks to Runeovex for a good fight, fellow." With that he promptly fell asleep.

Alfren stared hard at Caros who stared back. The warrior grinned. "Great things. Alugra is right. It is a matter of choosing the winning side, eh?"

With that, he too rolled into his cloak to sleep. Caros felt his eyes droop. Most of the talking and yelling beside the fires was dying away to snores and mutters.

Neugen threw a bone on the embers and farted. "Cursed elbow is going to be a bitch tomorrow." He had wrapped the swollen joint in steaming linens and was favoring the swollen joint. "Have you traded with the Carthaginians, Caros?"

"Yes. Greeks, Gauls and Romans too. My father knew many of the most prominent traders at the ports and was toying with moving our business to Qart Hadasht or Sagunt."

"Truly! I have heard of these cities but not yet visited either."

"From here, Qart Hadasht must be three days ride. Sagunt is well over a week to the north."

Neugen lay back and gnawed another burnt piece of beef with a distant look. Caros thought back to the days his father took him to the ports to visit and trade when he was just a boy and how in the past year he had visited as a representative for his father's lucrative business. All that history vanished within the space of two days. He wished he could sob as the mourning in him grew. Those few Arvenci slain in retaliation did nothing to numb the pain. Sighing he pulled his cloak tighter and lay down beside the glowing embers to try to sleep. His mind darted from event to event though, from the bodies of loved ones to screams of war. He tried to blot the recent events with happier memories and was beginning to drift off when his mind suddenly fixed on the battle in the valley. Something he had seen. A shape and color. He knew it was important and worried at the memory like a loose tooth. He fought and killed the axeman and was staring far tree line. A figure appeared for a heartbeat. A man on foot disappearing into the trees, a circular object dangling from his back. Crimson with a flash of white.

His eyes snapped open. His father had fought in two campaigns before he had become a merchant and long before Caros was born. It was the plunder he had won in those campaigns upon which he had built his trading business. In the second campaign, against the Carpetani, his father had taken a warhorn from a renowned Carpetani champion after a brutal battle. It was painted crimson and had an uncommon, white lynx tail fastened to it with silver braid.

Caros sat up. He had stared at that warhorn for hours as a boy; lost in dreams of battle. He cursed himself for not remembering earlier. Now the camp was quietly asleep under a blue velvet night. Even Neugen had fallen asleep, dreaming of horses and silver no doubt.

He stood and paced restlessly. Alugra's men had run down the Arvenci who survived the battle, but all told, there were just twenty-five Arvenci killed. They knew the Arvenci numbered closer to two hundred spears. There were a lot unaccounted for and Alugra had scouts out in all directions, searching for larger bands.

The man Caros had seen among the trees, had been fleeing east. Away from Arvenci lands. He sighed and rubbed his knuckles, wincing at the bruises they bore. This was hopeless. In the morning he would establish with Alfren if any of the men had come across the warhorn when dealing with the dead. If not, then he would know an Arvenci warrior had escaped with it. Neugen could track; he had regularly pointed out spoor all morning as he rode ahead of Caros. Even in the hard, stony ground of the hills. Caros lay back, hands cupped behind his head. The warhorn symbolized the memory of his father and his family. It was likely that the Arvenci who carried it had torched his home, maybe even killed his father and brother. He gritted his teeth and forced his heart to harden once again as the pain of loss threatened.

4

The Bastetani warriors were eager to break camp when the dawn sun rose. Cooking fires were small and men hurried to pack their belongings, eat and be away. The few men that had accompanied them from the valley took responsibility for the regained herd of horse and cattle. Alugra was bellowing out orders to his men and ever cautious, already had his riders out to scout their way back to the valley.

Caros ate hastily prepared hard bread and cold beef, remnants of the steer slaughtered the evening before. Beside him, Neugen flexed his elbow, which was not as seriously injured as he had thought. He gave Caros a grin.

"Looks less swollen. That is good because I have not finished hunting the Arvenci."

Neugen was startled. "Why? We killed plenty of them and retrieved most of the herds. What more do you want?"

"I saw something that belonged to my father yesterday. After I killed the axeman. I did not recognize it for what it was, but last night I recognized what I had seen." He went on to tell Neugen of the warhorn, its distinctive shape and coloring and how he had seen someone escape into the forest with it. Neugen looked skeptical but did not say anything. "I want it back, but most of all, I want the bastard carrying it to know who he took it from and the cost. He most likely tore it from my father's wall, maybe even killed him and my brother."

Neugen slapped his thigh weakly. "Caros, what is done is done. You could go on to the end of time trying to revenge your family and villagers, but you have other things to do."

"Like what?" Caros spat. "Right now, there is a chance I could confront the Arvenci responsible. What other things need doing more than that?"

Neugen was exasperated. "This Arvenci; he could be anywhere by now. How do you plan to catch up with him? You surely would not chase him all the way back to his land?"

Caros pursed his lips. "That is where I could use some help. I watched you yesterday; you are able to read tracks like they were carved in stone. Help me track him down."

Neugen was shaking his head before Caros had finished asking. "I must remain with the column. You heard Alugra last night; war is looming. Not just raids upon isolated villages. This is the wrong time for me to leave my fellows."

Caros had one more arrow to fire. "Look, I did not expect you to do this for nothing. You ride well yet you still fight on foot. I will give you two of my mounts in exchange. We will make good time and be done with this inside of two or three days. Do not tell me you cannot track a warrior in that time? You could be back with Alugra by the time the rest of the warriors reach home."

Neugen lips thinned in anger for a heartbeat before the possibility of gaining not one, but two horses, set his mind spinning at his enhanced status and better share of spoils. The young warrior flexed his arm, his face betraying little. Caros prayed to Runeovex that the warrior would accept the offer while remaining silent and let the offer work on the warrior. His father had taught him a good deal could often be made fewer words spoken. Finally, Neugen smiled at him, his dark eyes glinting.

"You are a good trader. Your offer is a fine one and I will accept!" Caros beamed at him as he went on. "However, you will have to weave that magic again on Alugra. My spear is his and I will only accompany you if he allows it."

"I am glad. Very glad! I will talk to him as soon as he has finished barking at everyone!" Both men laughed.

Alugra contemplated the proposal with a deep frown. "I can see you are determined and determined people usually find a way of doing what they set their minds to." The Bastetani graybeard drummed his sword hilt with his fingers. "Your proposal is sound while you hunt just one man. It is possible the Arvenci have prearranged places where scattered warriors will gather before reaching their lands. If you discover more than one or two men, send word and we will come." He glanced to where his leading men waited for him on their horses and then beckoned to Neugen. The young warrior came over, looking from Alugra to Caros with a raised eyebrow. "Caros has spoken to you and you are willing I understand?"

"Yes. I am confident if we backtrack and scour the valley where the battle took place, I will be able to pick up this man's spoor. After that it is up to the gods."

Alugra grunted and spat into the dirt. "Your spear will be missed. May Runeovex guide you." He looked at Caros. "You too. This is something you must do, but do not take more risks than you need to and when it is done, put these days behind you. It is easy to become obsessed by revenge." He glanced at Alfren who sat alone on his mount, staring west. "It rarely leads to peace."

Caros was elated. His respect for the battle-hardened champion had grown in the three days they had marched together. He would be fortunate to have the same wisdom and gravity when he reached his fortieth year.

They said farewell to the ranks of warriors who marched off behind their leading man. Many of them called Caros by name as they passed, and he felt a wave of emotion that surprised him. In three short days, he had gone from wealthy merchant's son to part of a column of warriors. Beside him, Neugen was brimming with eagerness. He had in his hands the reins of the two mounts that Caros had selected from the herd of horses recovered from the Arvenci. Both good mares, they were worth a purse of silver staters each.

Caros had outfitted himself with greaves for his shins and forearms as well as a simple iron helmet and importantly a shield. He also boasted seven iron-tipped javelins. He had purchased the armor and weapons from those of the warriors who had brought extras or who had plundered them from the dead Arvenci. Neugen had quickly acquired the items for him from amongst his fellow warriors for just a fraction of their value. Caros was immensely grateful and reveled in strapping it all on.

"Yesterday I had a just my sword and my mare and you allowed me to join you in battle. I feel like I was naked in comparison to how I feel now." He rapped his knuckles on the iron helmet.

Neugen grinned sheepishly. "No one expected you to go charging like a lynx into battle wearing just a tunic. It was all I could do to stay ahead of you!"

Caros stared at him in horror. "You mean…"

Neugen shrugged. "No insult intended Caros, but you did not exactly look like a fighter with your brushed locks and perfumed tunic. Alfren all but pissed himself when Alugra ordered him to allow you along." Caros turned blood red. They had all thought he was some rich boy along to claim bragging rights after they had done all the fighting. Neugen slapped him on the shoulder. "Like I said, you proved us wrong. Alugra must have seen something the rest of us did not."

Caros glared at Neugen and snarled. "Now I feel a real fool. Imagine what those Arvenci thought when they saw me." They looked at each other with wide eyes for a heartbeat before breaking into fits of laughter.

The two young warriors rode west till they reached the valley in which they had ambushed the Arvenci the day before. At this point Caros led the two extra mounts that were loaded with their few possessions. Neugen forged ahead and began casting about for tracks. The sun was already high, but they had made better time than they had yesterday, as they knew the most direct route there. They had agreed the Arvenci who had slipped away from the battle would have broken north. This would take them on the most direct route back to Arvenci lands and strongholds. For this reason, Neugen began casting for tracks along the valley's northern flank. It was slow, hot work. Caros had every faith in the man's abilities though. He kept behind and stayed on Neugen's trail so as not to foul any of the enemy's spoor. By afternoon, they had worked their way up from a point adjacent to where they had ambushed the Arvenci and back east along the valley perimeter. Finally, Neugen snorted in disgust and gestured to Caros who brought up the mounts.

"Nothing. Nobody but us has passed this way heading north. Anybody fleeing the battle would have reached Alugra's lines at this point." He waved south into the valley.

Caros grunted with disappointment. "If not north, he must have gone south before running into Alugra's men."

"Right. Except he would be traveling further from his people and safety."

"The coast is filled with travelers, traders and the like. Once he reaches there, he will not stand out." Neugen squinted south and removed his iron helmet to wring sweat from his hair. Since the Carthaginians had arrived some years earlier and begun trading then occupying the ports and villages, the coastal plain south of them was an open corridor. Caros slapped Neugen's shoulder. "I know the southern lands well. I have traded up and down it with my father since I was ten years old."

They dismounted for a short meal of cold beef and hard bread. The sun was baking hot even in the shade and there was no breeze today. The unfamiliar armor had chafed his skin under the leather strapping and sweat stung the raw spots. He barely felt the discomfort though and washed the light meal down with tepid water from the water bag. After eating the men mounted up and crossed the valley keeping to the east of the line Alugra's men had held to trap fleeing Arvenci. Quickly reaching the southern flank of the valley they cast west along that flank. Caros admired Neugen's confidence as he broke ahead and leaned forward to scan the ground and vegetation, for any sign that would betray their quarry. Caros kept a guarded eye out for lurking warriors preparing to spring upon them. They passed various trails, most made by wildlife, others forged by shepherds and their flocks of sheep. At each of these Caros would cast along the path for some distance looking to find fresh tracks that could have been made by their quarry. The afternoon wore by and Caros had his first doubts. They had already passed the point in the valley where they had slain the Arvenci. The forest trails dwindled and the trees and undergrowth became dense and the air thin. The pair were forced to backtrack often to find passable trails down the south flank of the valley. In the near distance on their left, breaking from the dense growth, rose a rocky hill. It marked the western end of the valley.

Caros lost sight of Neugen ahead of him on the winding trail. He felt like he was plunging into ever-denser undergrowth before he broke free of the bush and found himself under a canopy of tall pines on the northern face of the hill he had seen. The dappled shade and breeze an instant relief. It was a splendid, restful hillside. Neugen sat his horse under the trees and he walked the horses over him, their steps muffled by years of accumulated pine needles on the forest floor. Caros gazed about appreciatively, before noticing the triumphant smile on his friend's face.

"Do you have something? What?"

Neugen pointed to the forest floor. Caros saw pine needles, the odd pinecone and a scattering of bird shit. Nothing struck him as out of place or disturbed. Neugen laughed at his expression. "You traders. If it was dipped in silver, you would notice it quick enough!" He pointed out a series of depressions, the scuff of dry needles visible through the needles still green.

Caros squinted at the signs Neugen pointed out to him. "What makes you think this is the trail of the Arvenci? Or even a man?" The faint trail failed to impress or excite him and his skepticism was clear.

Neugen snorted. "This is he, or I should say them." He smiled at Caros' confused expression. "Three men came up the hillside. They were moving fast, but quietly and they were careful. That last clue makes me think these were Arvenci. They were breaking out of the valley and did not want to be discovered." This made sense and Caros was once again grateful he had Neugen's help.

"This was yesterday evening. They probably climbed that hill and hid there overnight."

Neugen looked up the hill. "Yes, that would make sense. They would have had the high ground in case they were attacked."

"Right, so we should go up there and find their tracks." Caros was keenly aware the Arvenci had already gained a day as the sun was heading to the western horizon at speed.

Neugen had other ideas. "Waste of time. They would have had to come down off the hill. We will just skirt it at this height and find their tracks leading away. Come on."

Caros saw the intelligence in the plan and he was thrilled by this hunt. It was obvious that Neugen was in his element and thoroughly enjoying it. Sticking to the plan they circled the hill, fully expecting the Arvenci to come off the north face of the hill and head for their tribal lands.

The sun was touching the western hills when Neugen finally found the tracks. Except they were heading southeast. Their eyes followed the direction the tracks led. The faint blue smudge of ocean was visible in the distance. Caros was surprised, but as the implications set in that surprise changed to confidence. They were heading into lands he knew well. Had they headed northwards, they would have soon encountered Oretani and Carpetani lands and then the Arvenci homeland. They had followed the tracks only a short while before Neugen halted.

"It is no use. It is too dark; we will sleep here and make an early start at dawn."

Caros was impatient to make up that time, but it was obviously too dark to see the tracks and they needed the rest.

"Fine. I will get some firewood and we can shelter against those rocks." He said, thrusting his chin towards a granite outcrop that formed a nice little shelter. Neugen hobbled the horses while Caros dragged up some dried boughs. Before long they had a fire burning and had some flatbread roasting on a rock next to the hot flames.

Neugen searched for more food once they had eaten the hot bread. "Curses. Nothing to eat in the morning." He pronounced after scratching through every fold in his pack.

Caros was not concerned. "We will find something tomorrow. I thought I heard a goat bleating earlier. I wager we come across a shepherd or a village tomorrow. This area is good farmland." He settled down to sleep.

"Err, I expect I will take first watch then." Neugen stated.

Caros groaned. "What is there to guard against? We are in the wilderness!"

"So are the Arvenci. They are out there, not to mention wolves, bears and even hill warriors."

Caros sighed. "You are right, of course. Take first watch then and wake me when you need to sleep." He rolled over; his eyelids heavy with sleep.

The night passed into a brisk dawn. Song thrush began calling while it was still dark and a distant wolf cried for the dying night. The two men blew the embers awake and fed the fire to heat some water in which they steeped leaves for a meagre breakfast. While they sipped the bitter tea, they watched the day slowly brighten.

Caros had noted that the contents of their packs rattled as the horses walked and he repacked his belongings more tightly, ensuring there would be no sound.

Neugen smiled. "You learn fast. I had meant to mention that, but I forgot. Since we are tracking three men, the last thing we need is for them to hear us coming and ambush us."

Caros worried at this thought and realized that this was a contest that left little margin for error. They were hunting experienced warriors, not deer or mountain goat. He would need to be constantly alert, covering Neugen whose attention would be on the ground.

"Is there any way we can get the jump on them instead?" He asked once they were mounted.

Neugen shrugged. "I guess it depends on the lay of the land. We do not know their destination so I cannot see how."

"How far ahead do you reckon they are? A full day?"

"I cannot tell from the tracks, but yes, a day or more. They may have kept going through the night."

"Shit. How about if we pick up their trail then leapfrog and pick it up where we most likely think their tracks are leading? That will save time will it not?" He was grasping for ideas as something needed to be done to whittle away the lead the Arvenci had. Neugen nodded slowly and then more enthusiastically.

"It may be possible. It is not easily done, but I have heard of trackers doing this when chasing down horse or deer."

"Excellent, since you are the point man I will follow on the established tracks while you head off to where you best judge they are heading. If you lose them, you pick up again from where I am and try again."

The two young riders moved out at first light following the trail as it sloped down towards the distant sea. They put their plan into action once the sun had lifted clear of the eastern horizon and daylight was established. Neugen gave Caros some pointers on tracking and then headed for a distant junction between two low, rocky hills. They lay like long mounds to the southeast and the junction bisected them neatly in the center. It was feasible the Arvenci had made for that intersection to avoid climbing over the hills. Caros walked his mare alongside the faint tracks; no more than intermittent depressions, turned stones, and occasionally, the partial imprint of a foot. He kept an eye on the surrounding landscape as well, trying to second-guess the Arvenci warriors. In the distance, Neugen reach the junction and begin casting for tracks. Caros grinned with relief when he immediately straightened up and waved. He had found the tracks again. Caros spurred his mare forward, bringing the other two horses along at a canter to catch up with Neugen who was already trotting through the short valley between the two hills.

"That went well!" He said in delight when he reached Neugen.

"Better than I had hoped!" He pointed southeast. "They are still heading that way so I will cut ahead again."

He headed off to repeat the process. By early afternoon the two men had covered a great distance and had only once been unsuccessful at cutting the tracks left by the Arvenci warriors. Backtracking a little, they had found where, instead of continuing on the southeasterly route, the Arvenci had veered east. They were heading for the coast; that was now certain. The men could already scent brine in the air, but they were still a day's ride from any coastal town or port even. Neugen estimated they had closed the gap down half a day at the rate they had cut the tracks and confessed the system worked better than he would have dreamed.

The pair became more alert than ever as they closed the distance with their quarry. Caros wore his new armor and his shield hung at his left leg, ready to be lifted in a moment. In his right hand he held a deadly iron-tipped javelin that would easily drive through light armor when well thrown. Their path brought them to a main road that ran parallel to the coast. Caros thought the port town of Baria lay to the north with minor villages all along the road. Neugen was casting for tracks up the road while Caros watched disconsolately. He was concerned the Arvenci would be able to disguise their tracks amongst the many others on the road. Added to this, his gut was rumbling with hunger. They had had little to eat in the past three days and none today. Deciding that doing something would take his mind off the hunger, he hobbled the two spare mounts at the roadside and trotted his mare in the opposite direction Neugen was tracking. A javelin rested across his thighs, ready to be used. He sought out any sign that the Arvenci had passed this way. A fresh sandal print, warm campfire, fresh turds, anything! The dusty road threaded past open glades and stands of trees. Ahead, a spur of rocky hill sprouting sun-dried grass, prodded the beaten road, forcing it to curl out of sight around it. Caros scanned the spur for movement and saw a flock of sheep, wearing their ragged tan fleece loosely. They were languid in the afternoon sun and lay panting in the sparse shade of the occasional bush. Beyond the spur, the land opened into a wide glade.

Caros spotted a wisp of smoke on the far side of the glade. It was almost too little to see having been broken up in its ascent through the canopy of a copse of oak. Caros thought he detected the barest scent of roasting mutton. Perhaps it was just hunger causing him to imagine the smell. He swept his eyes around the glade, but otherwise did not show any signs of his suspicion. Before him the road curled up and over a low hill. No travelers in sight. Yet in this deserted corner, he sensed eyes upon him. He cursed the spur that hid him from Neugen's view. He glanced at the road, but tracks on it were meaningless on the hard, bare ground. He deliberately gazed to his left where the country fell away to the azure sea in the distance. The breeze had shifted and the smell of sea air was strong. He still felt the hairs on his nape rise. He was certain there were people in the shadows of the copse. He urged the mare to a slow trot climbing the hill out of the glade. He scanned the glade while trying to appear relaxed and disinterested in the surroundings. He crested the hill and left the glade. He trotted the horse downhill until certain he could not be seen, then brought her to a halt. What could he do? Ride back to Neugen or wait here for him. In either scenario the Arvenci, if it was in fact them, would realize they were hunting them. They could take flight again into the broken hills behind them and again Neugen and he would be forced to track them. Only then the advantage would be with the Arvenci as they could easily ambush the riders in the hills. Caros was not going to let them escape. This would end here today. There was another option and the more he thought it through the better it seemed.

He loosened the falcata in its wool-lined sheath. He had one javelin; the rest were on the packhorses. He knotted his brow briefly at the mistake. He closed his eyes and pictured the glade before him. It was crescent shaped with a steep hill on the right and to the rear. The hill behind which he sat ran along the left and was the easiest of the three to climb. The glade itself was covered in tall yellow grass and seemed to be relatively flat. The copse of trees lay in the left rear corner. He could reach them in a short and furious gallop if needed, but did not think that would be necessary. He took a deep breath and hooked his left forearm into the shield straps, tightened his helmet and then with reins in his left hand and spear held upright he turned the mare and cantered back over the hill and down towards the glade. Instead of remaining on the road, he nudged the mare into the grass kept her cantering diagonally into the center of the glade.

The copse of oak trees stood dark and heavy with presence on his left. He rode calmly into the glade without looking at the trees until he was a javelin's throw from them when he reined in the mare. Restlessly, the mare stamped the ground, sensing peril. The Arvenci had slaughtered a goat and had risked a cooking fire beneath the leafy trees. They must have been starved and having a hard time being on foot. They should have made for a village instead, there were many along the road.

Caros rose tall on his mount. "Arvenci! I am Caros! You have killed my kin and stolen my property. Come out so I can avenge my family!" He glared at the trees as his pulse quickened and rage built. He fed it, relying on it. If Neugen was right, he faced three warriors and he would need the rage. He danced the mare from side to side, using his knees to keep her moving. Lifting the javelin skywards, he raised his voice. "I am here as a killer of Arvenci cowards. I, just one warrior. You cannot run forever so fight me like true warriors!"

Sound faded in the glade and the mare's snorts came from far away. Shadows deepened beneath the oak trees. Caros trotted the horse into the range of a javelin throw then turned and walked her back; taunting the Arvenci. As he turned the mare to the left, he deftly changed his grip on the javelin so he could lift and hurl it in the blink of an eye.

The shadows beneath the trees resolved into three warriors who stepped into the sunlight. They kept apart, leaving room to wield their spears and shields. These were no first bloods; rather they were seasoned warriors who knew their craft. Their tunics were well padded beneath leather armor and they wore shields on their left arms and greaves on their limbs. Each man wielded a war spear and from their waists hung swords. Caros eyed their weapons and armor and then lifted his gaze to the faces of the Arvenci warriors. Their long, dark hair was plaited and tied with leather and their beards were similarly long and plaited. Above their beards and moustaches their faces were painted red. They exuded menace. They strode forward purposefully, surefooted as lynx on the hunt. They spread apart still further as they stalked, forming a battle crescent.

Caros grunted, his anger and hate chewing up the fear that should have been flooding through him. Instead, his senses sharpened. Here was death and at his neck he felt the breath of his ancestors. No surprise ambush and injured, bloodied axeman. These were champions among the Arvenci; graybeards that had raided and fought for a score of years. Caros clenched the javelin with white knuckles as his mare rolled her eyes and snorted at the closing warriors. On the beast, Caros' inexperience in fighting was largely nullified by his skill at riding and he sent an invocation to Runeovex, god of war, to strengthen his arm.

The Arvenci closed the gap silently. The warrior approaching the front of the mare held his shield close to his chin, his spear at his shoulder; ready to let fly. He was prepared for Caros' charge. Caros held the mare so his spear hand was shielded from the Arvenci. He looked the middle warrior in the eye.

"I am Caros, son of Joaquim." He smiled coldly at the warrior who continued forward without pause. An eagle screamed far above them and Caros moved. He pressed with his knee, clicking his tongue and the mare leaped to the left, not at the warrior most expecting the assault, but at the warrior in the center.

Horse and rider burst into motion raising a cloud of dust. Caros had his javelin up and flying in a heartbeat, using the horse under him to add momentum to his throw. The iron head would punch through shield and leather if thrown well from a galloping horse. The warrior in the center froze as the mare leaped towards him, then cursed aloud. He lifted his shield to cover his throat and chest. The javelin scored the shield rim before punching into the warrior. The Arvenci's curse turned shrill as the javelin tore like fire through his gut just above his hip. When it hit his spine, his knees buckled.

Caros saw a flicker of a smile on the warrior's face as the man dropped to his knees and lifted his face. Then the mare slammed into him and her hooves broke his body.

Like a lynx, Caros twisted his mare to charge the warrior on his left. Certain of an easy kill a heartbeat ago, the warrior cursed as his spear brother of twenty years died without landing a blow. Where another might have turned and run, he howled his fury and charged. In response, Caros screamed a wordless battle cry, his falcata already in his hand. He drove the mare in a single leap at the enraged warrior and leaning far forward, hacked at the Arvenci. The warrior thrust his spear at Caros' face with a howl that sent spittle flying.

Caros was leaning low over the horse, armed only with a sword. The spearhead loomed sharp and just as it seemed it would bury itself in his throat, his blade struck the spear shaft and sent the spearhead spinning under his arm.

Determined to finish the warrior, Caros twisted his arm as he passed the man so that the falcata struck his face in a backhand swing. The chopping blade broke bone and sent shattered teeth flying. The warrior's howl was cut short and he hit the ground senseless. Caros tore forward, leaning low over the mare's shoulder and brought her around in a wide circle. He was out of range of a spear throw from the remaining warrior and slowed the blowing mare, trampling dry grass and dirt. He crabbed-walked her while watching the remaining warrior who hunched behind his round shield. His face was hideous in rage as he glared across the grass at Caros astride his mount. The warrior still held his spear. Caros had hoped the man would have hurled it at him while he was attacking the man's fellows. That he had not fled after the second warrior had been felled alerted Caros to the man's danger. Besting him would take some considerable skill or intervention by the gods.

The warrior held his shield at the ready, his right arm stretched behind him at an angle that suggested he would strike hard when he threw. Caros did not doubt what the man had in mind and he cleared his throat and spat. The Arvenci warrior would send his spear flying at the horse, hoping to remove Caros' single advantage.

Caros trotted his horse in a wide circle beyond the reach of his foe's spear. His breath came in gulps and his heart hammered at his ribs. The bloodied sword in his hand shook and Caros feared he had no strength to finish the fight. He closed his eyes and confronted the horror that had awaited him on his return home. With a groan, he snapped open his eyes and gritted his teeth, determined to avenge the butchery inflicted on his kin. The sun now hung low so that his shadow reached out across the trampled grass to where the man crouched behind his shield.

Caros could see the Arvenci tracking his mare with the point of his spear. His patted the mare's neck and turned her away from the fight so that he had to watch the warrior over his shoulder. The man licked his lips and rolled his shoulders. He would not allow the Arvenci his kill. He turned the horse towards the warrior at a hundred paces and raking his heels along her ribs charged the Arvenci who drew back his spear.

The mare's speed increased and Caros watched the ground whip past. The Arvenci was on the point of throwing his spear when Caros leapt from the mare's back, rolled and came up, running. Behind him, the startled horse rose on her hind legs and thrashed the air.

Caros screamed the same war cry he had first used just two days earlier. His shield held before him, he battered long grass and thorn from his path, his eyes fixed on the Arvenci. His shadow fell on the warrior who spat and rose to his full height.

Caros' blood roared in his ears and he bellowed his war cry ceaselessly as he sprinted, his falcata held low. The Arvenci's mouth opened wide as he screamed his challenge, but Caros heard nothing other than his own voice and pounding blood. He dropped his left shoulder into his shield in the final strides and drove it, like a battering ram, into the Arvenci's shield. Carried by momentum and his powerful thighs, Caros rammed the warrior's shield up, revealing his torso and knocking his spear aside. At the same time, he punched his falcata up from his thigh.

The Arvenci regained his footing with a hiss, holding Caros stationary so that the two men stood panting chest to chest. Caros glared into the other's yellowed eyes for strained heartbeats until the spark in the man's eyes faded. His ancestors were calling to him.

The Arvenci brought his shield down on Caros' head and it glanced harmlessly off his helmet and slid down his back to hang limp at his side. He clamped his spear hand around Caros' throat, but his fingers lacked the strength to crush. Caros shoved the man's arm away, ignoring the smile that flickered over the warrior's ashen face.

"I thought you had fallen from your horse and was glad." The Arvenci grunted in pain and sweat squeezed from his skin. "Glad that I did not have to end its life."

"I seek my father's warhorn. Where is it?"

The warrior shook from his bloody feet to the crown of his head and pushed away from Caros, his guts unsheathing the sword Caros had driven into them. The warrior looked down at his wound and sank to his knees in the gore collecting about his sandals.

5

A thousand horsemen thundered north along the coastal road from Abdera. These were horsemen the likes of which had never been seen by the local inhabitants. They thundered north, appearing in moments and just as quickly disappearing in an all-encompassing cloud of dust. The drumming of their hoofbeats gradually dying away, leaving the villagers wide-eyed with surprise.

At the vanguard rode a complement of two hundred Iberian horsemen. Behind them were a further eight hundred African riders. These men on their rangy ponies, dressed in identical tunics and headdresses. That they were expert horsemen was evident as they used no reins to guide their mounts, controlling the animals by twisting their manes and exerting pressure with their knees and ankles. The host of riders rode with the sun on their backs as they neared the port town of Baria. They had been riding hard for two days and had made excellent time, but their Iberian leader was eager to get to their destination. They crested a low rise and started down the road on the other side when he caught a flash of movement. Ever alert for an ambush, he signaled the men behind him and they came to a halt. It quickly became clear that no enemy lay in wait.

"The gods!" His leading man gaped in astonishment moving only as he walked his horse downhill, the men behind followed, fanning out along the ridgeline. With the arrival of the African horsemen, a thousand riders sat their mounts and watched as a horseman ran down an armored spearman and best him with just a sword. That rider turned his attention to yet another warrior wielding a spear. The watchers muttered and pointed; eyes glued to the lone horseman who deftly maneuvered his mount.

"Well, this is an interesting diversion!" The leader smiled, his impatience to reach his destination suddenly forgotten.

"The spearman is an Arvenci warrior. He is a long way from home." The second rider remarked, taking in the spectacle with interest.

"I wager he is about to get a free ride home. That horseman was fortunate to defeat a spearman with just a short sword." The leader commented wryly. He was a veteran and knew the advantage a spearman had over a rider armed with a sword.

His leading man spotted another corpse in the trampled grass. Knowing the leader's eyesight was failing he did not mention it and instead offered a wager.

"I wager a silver piece on the rider!"

The leading man raised an eyebrow at the wager. It was long odds for a silver piece. With a gruff laugh he accepted.

"It seems you have silver to spare. I will gladly take it."

As he spoke the words, a murmur rippled through the watching horsemen.

"Whoa, I thought he had fallen. Did you see him dismount!" The second rider beamed as he watched the rider dive from his horse, roll to his feet and charge the Arvenci warrior. The host of horsemen on the hill shouted in excitement at the daring stunt. Two days of hard riding were suddenly being rewarded with a fine treat. Men began yelling encouragement to one or other of the combatants and jeering one another's choices. The leading man remained silent; the wager gone from his mind as he appraised the now dismounted warrior who attacked his foe fearlessly. Yes, this was honor and battle as told of in the legends. The hair on his neck rose as battle fever coursed through his body. The body of horsemen were shuffling down the hill, their horses prancing to the excitement of their riders.

The fighters met in a clash the riders heard over their own shouts. A great roar went up as they all recognized the signal. This was the moment of blood. One combatant would triumph; the other would die.

The column leader squinted. "What is happening? Come on, come on." Again, the hillside rang with cries as the two combatants stepped apart.

"By Runeovex! See that?" His second was beside himself.

Even the leader could see the Arvenci was done for. The man's guts were ribbons and as he winced at the sight, the Arvenci fell. The victorious warrior's right arm was crimson with blood as he raised a bloodied falcata and swept it down. The Arvenci's head toppled from his neck and blood pumped briefly skyward.

"Now that was a sight!"

Even his usually brash second in charge sounded awestruck. Across the hillside, the Iberians whooped their excitement while the African horsemen's whispers grew into a chant that swelled in volume, drowning out the others.

The Iberians glanced nervously at each other and their leader raised his eyebrows questioningly.

"What are the Africans going on about?"

His second knew the language and cocked his head to hear the chant better.

"They have just given the victor a war name." He looked at the leader of the column who stared at the lone warrior standing over his dead opponent. "They are a vicious lot when it comes to war. Once they have proven themselves in battle, they are given a second name, a war name. Unusual to bestow a war name on an unknown warrior though."

The leader shook his head and grunted. "A war name, eh? What is it?

"It translates as Claw of the Lion."

"Hmm, Claw of the Lion. Come, we should go meet this Claw of the Lion."

His second held out his hand, palm down, their sign to pause. His keen eyes had noticed a rider approaching from around a distant spur of rock. Daylight was fading fast, but he could make out that the horseman led two mounts.

"Over there. Another horseman."

The column's leader peered at the approaching rider. "Probably a trader. Come, the light is fading. I want to meet this warrior before we push on." He shouted to another of his leading men. "Have this lot move on. I want to be on the outskirts of Baria tonight. We will camp there, so set up my fire, and bloody leave something for me to eat!"

The Iberians grinned and set off up the road. The rest of the horsemen followed at a canter.

Caros stood still on trembling legs. His heart beat as never before while his lungs burned for air. At his feet, the Arvenci warrior gurgled and choked until at last, his eyes closed and his shade fled into the twilight. Caros drew a breath and lifted his chin to see Neugen, eyes wide and mouth agape.

He reined in before Caros. "Oh gods, who is he?"

Caros offered a grim smile and Neugen felt apprehension roll through him at his friend's cold expression.

"We found them. Without you I could never have."

"Them?" Neugen croaked. He gestured at a column of horsemen coming from the near hillside. "I hope he was not one of their friends."

Caros frowned; he had not noticed the horsemen. He breathed deeply, struggling to recall the last moments and shrugged at Neugen's bewildered look. Turning, he spied two warriors break from the column.

"I do not know who they are. They must have only just arrived."

Neugen cursed. "I was not gone long enough to take a comfortable shit and suddenly the whole world is here!" He jumped as beside him, Caros whistled sharply. His mare had been grazing near the copse and her head came up at the sound of Caros' whistle. She whinnied and trotted over. Caros patted her affectionately as he swung up onto her back. He grimaced at the ache that rolled through his strained muscles.

"Come, we should greet these fellows." He walked his horse toward the oncoming riders and lifted his hand to greet them. The sight of his bloody hand caused him to recoil and he quickly lowered it. It seemed inappropriate to greet strangers with an arm covered in blood. "Gods, I need a wash." Neugen rolled his eyes. The riders were big men and their horses were equally large. "Greetings. I am Caros of the Bastetani and this is my companion, Neugen of Alugra's clan."

The two pairs of riders halted, their horses snorting their own equine greeting. The column's leader studied Caros a heartbeat before replying.

"Greetings, Caros." He nodded to Neugen. "Neugen. I am Gualam of the Turdetani at Malaka." He gestured to his second. "Drasal is my leading man." He smiled through his gray beard. "We saw your encounter." He glanced towards the darkened grass and shadowy corpses strewn in the field. "Good fight. I am heartened to see that Bastetani warriors still hold such skills."

"They were Arvenci raiders. My village suffered greatly and many of my kin and clan were killed by them and their fellows." Caros flinched as his shoulder cramped. "I am no warrior; just a trader. My father was a prosperous merchant before these raiders attacked and killed him and the rest of my kin."

The Turdetani graybeard nodded. "If you trade as well as you fight, then I am doubly glad you Bastetani are our friends." He ran a hand through his beard and shrugged. "We are riding as far as Baria tonight. Come along with us; I should like to hear more about you."

"Thank you. That is appreciated for truly we have ridden far these last days trailing the raiders and a good meal will not go amiss if you are offering?"

The Turdetani patted his gut. "I will be honored to share a meal with you!"

"Thank you. We will catch up with you in a moment. The Arvenci were camped in those trees and I want to recover any property they plundered."

The Turdetani eyed the cluster of trees. "We will ride along. With a bit of luck, there will be more of them waiting in the dark, if you know what I mean." He grinned wolfishly.

They rode slowly into the trees under which it was practically night already. Within the trees, the smell of burned meat was strong on wafts of campfire smoke. Embers from the cookfire still glowed a fiery orange though a layer of ash and were easy to spot in the gloom. A haunch of mutton had fallen into the coals and Caros' gut rumbled hungrily. Ignoring the meat and his stomach, he dismounted stiffly. Neugen joined him and stirred the embers, prompting a greater glow from them before tossing on a brittle twigs and a handful of dry brush. These flared into flames and in the flickering light Caros spotted the raiders' belongings. They had travelled light and there were just two packs perched against a fallen tree. Caros strode over and nudged each with the toe of his sandal. There was no sign of the warhorn.

Then he spotted it; laying on the old tree trunk itself and partially obscured in jumping shadows. The Arvenci had stashed the warhorn into an old water skin made from the belly of a pig. Gratefully, he retrieved it, leaving it in the makeshift pouch. It was better protected that way. "This is it." He kicked at the other two bundles again before dumping their meagre contents on the ground. The Turdetani graybeard grunted with disappointment and turned his horse away.

"You done, Caros? We have a way to travel yet tonight."

"Yes. There is nothing more here."

Neugen smiled happily and kicked dirt over the fire. "Thank Runeovex. Any longer and I would have been happy to eat this shit." The mood lightened and the men exchanged grins and nods.

Caros and Neugen followed silently behind their new travelling companions. Nobody spoke as they rode north to Baria. He felt a weight had been lifted from his shoulders with the retrieval of the warhorn. It was a gesture of respect to his murdered kin, especially his father. He would mourn them for a long time but felt some measure of justice had been meted out.

He wondered at the appearance of the Turdetani graybeard leading this large column of horsemen. The Turdetani, the southernmost Iberian people, were a wealthy people, more numerous and powerful than the Bastetani. He was curious as to why the Turdetani rode north. Baria did not seem to be their destination and yet the riders were travelling with provisions for just a day or two. These men were surely going to battle. Who were their enemies? He shook his head and instantly regretted it. He was lightheaded as it was and his neck stiff with bruises.

He looked forward to arriving at Baria. There, he would hire a room, wash, eat and sleep. His tunic had stiffened with blood and would need to be soaked and scrubbed. Vainly, he tried to rub the dried gore from his arm while longing to encounter a stream in which he could wash.

Neugen interrupted his thoughts. "Ah, I never thought I would be so happy to see a camp!" Caros raised his head with a start, realizing he had been on the verge of falling asleep. He sighed at the sight of a hundred flickering campfires.

The Turdetani leader bellowed over his shoulder. "There we go! Almost there."

Caros shared a smile with Neugen.

The camp was vast, but one of the leading men had left two riders to escort their column leader to where a fire had been banked for him. They dismounted at the fireside and others took the horses to be watered and rubbed down before being tethered for the night. Caros followed stiffly after the horses and upstream from where they sucked at the water thirstily, he stepped into the shallow stream. He tore off the bloodied tunic and wearing just his smallclothes, sank up to his waist in the cool water. He used a fistful of sand to scrub his body, arms and legs. Once the dirt was gone from his skin, he dipped his head below the water and scrubbed his face and hair. Next, he rubbed down the tunic, especially the dark patches visible in the glow of a quarter moon. Shivering, he emerged from the stream and donned the sodden garment.

Neugen trudged past him, hollow-eyed. "What a day, eh! You look better already. I thought you might never wash clean."

"Something to eat would make my day complete. My gut thinks my throat has been cut."

"Save me some of whatever they are cooking." Neugen turned and fell backwards into the water. Caros smiled at his friend's antics and headed for the fireside to dry and eat.

They ate silently; Caros and Neugen chewing every mouthful delicately, savoring the flesh of the spitted fowl. From an iron cauldron they pulled wedges of porridge to dip into a pot of stewed leaves. Hunger sated, the men wiped their hands on their tunics and reclined on their cloaks beside the fire. Drasal, Gualam's second, produced a skin of ale and passed it to Gualam and then began asking Caros and Neugen about the Arvenci raid and the subsequent chase led by Alugra.

As he told of the raid and the hunt for the Arvenci, Caros got the feeling that these men had heard the tale before. He capped off his account by describing events after he discovered the three Arvenci warriors.

Drasal hawked and spat into the shadow beyond the firelight and laughed. "We saw that part, the end anyway. You are too modest."

Caros shook his head. "I was lucky. I should have waited for Neugen."

"You knew they were there and lured them out of the trees. From that moment, you had the advantage and you used it to win. That is the way to win fights, even wars." The column leader looked hard at Caros. "Some learn these things over many seasons of campaigns. Others know them intuitively. I think I know which you are."

Caros shrugged. "I am a merchant though. My father has holdings in many of our ports including Baria and Malaka. Now that this thing is done, I will continue life as a merchant."

"Who would not want to be a wealthy merchant? I think you may be at a crossroads and you should know that a man with your abilities could also make a good life as a warrior. Return home. Tie up your affairs there, then come and ride with me." The Turdetani leader watched Caros closely, while his second nodded, his expression earnest.

Flustered at the attention of these men of status, his thoughts flew wildly over what had happened these past few days and his uncertain future. What he had said of his father's holdings was true and he could easily take up the reins as a merchant in his own right. He knew the traders and markets thanks to his father's training and did not doubt that he could become wealthy. He even envisaged extending trade north, to the green islands, although right now the demand for silver dug from the hinterland of Iberia was rising. There was so much else he could do as a merchant. That he was a blooded warrior now could even count in his favor, one less guard needed to protect the merchandise at least, he thought wryly.

The idea of being a career soldier held a definite allure. There were so many small wars and Alugra seemed to think something larger was brewing. He chided himself, of course there was! He was at a campfire amidst a host of warriors who had more than guarding merchandise or raiding a village or two on their minds. A good merchant always kept an ear to the ground for any gossip or information that could affect business. His father proved this often and gathering such information was sometimes as simple as just asking the right people.

"Your offer is tempting, Gualam. I never knew such a strong bond formed so quickly between warriors." He looked at Neugen whose eyes were wide with excitement. He had liked the tracker from the first moment and now he knew they would always be as sword brothers, yet Neugen was a warrior first and last. It was his ambition to go on long, bountiful campaigns and grow rich through conquest. "If I may ask; where are you heading with such a large body of warriors?"

"Ah, what a question!" The Turdetani graybeard exclaimed. "As you can see, most of the riders are strangers to these lands. My king has hired these men to bolster our defenses and we ride north to get a feel for commanding them and to learn their abilities." He leaned back and wiped his already washed hands over his cloak. Caros nodded, but he suspected what he had heard was a half-truth. The man's lips said one thing and his body another. He had distanced himself from his words by leaning back and then unconsciously wiped the lie from his hands. A few years trading with crusty Greeks and Carthaginians had taught Caros to look beyond the words.

"Where do these horsemen come from?" He nodded in the direction of the many campfires from where the babble of a foreign tongue could be heard.

Drasal gestured southwards. "Mauritania, they are Masulians. I was lucky enough to be captured ten years ago by a raiding vessel from that coast. An old Phoenician turned pirate. Set himself up as a king at a little oasis on the coast and then came looking for plunder. I made myself useful and he elevated me to a leading man of his household guard where I learned the local people's language and customs. Two years ago, he killed himself servicing one of his new young wives. What a way to go, eh!" The men chuckled, imagining the scene. Drasal continued after a moment's reminiscing. "After that, the place fell apart quickly. He had no sons to take his place. A local champion rode in one day and carried off everything of value before torching the place." Drasal grinned. "I, of course, saw that coming and was halfway to the Pillars of Hercules by then."

The column leader nodded as though confirming the tale. "Drasal mentioned that the warriors from across the sea would make half decent horsemen when our King wanted to increase our forces." He scowled at Drasal. "So far, I am just happy we have larger numbers. As far as actual fighting ability, frankly, I will need convincing."

Caros was intrigued that these men had come here to fight for the king of Malaka, and why did the king of Malaka require such a force? Before he could consider the question any deeper, the Turdetani rose.

"Think on my offer, Caros. You would join the ranks, but I would wager you would be a leading man within a season or two. Greater share of the spoils and there will be plenty of that soon." He paused, trying to gauge Caros' mind, before continuing. "I am going to check on how deeply our guards sleep before I chance my throat and close my eyes to sleep." Drasal joined him and the pair disappeared into the night.

Caros lay back and settled his head on his pack with his cloak pulled up to his chin. Neugen stirred the dying fire, watching as sparks flowed in a river to the stars.

"So, are you going to join them?"

Caros looked over at him where he hunched over the fire. "No. There is something that they have not told us. We ride to Baria tomorrow. My father has a warehouse there and I need to let the foreman there know what has happened. Then I want to get some decent clothes and food before heading back home."

"Did you never consider his offer then?" Neugen asked, sounding a little bewildered.

"Would you, Neugen? Would you join this host?"

Neugen poked the fire for a moment. "I might have. Except he never made me the offer." He sounded a little aggrieved by this. "I suppose I would not have either. I fight for Alugra after all and that is my place and his men are my spear brothers." He sighed in frustration and tossed the smoldering stick into the fire before slumping onto his back to stare into the smoky, night sky.

Caros rolled onto his side and propped up his chin. "Hey, cheer up. Five days ago, you were slogging up and down mountains on foot. Now you are a horseman with a spare mount. Not the least prosperous campaign for you lately I wager."

"You are right." Neugen laughed, his positive attitude reasserting itself.

"I will stay with you until you reach home and then return to Tagilit and see what Alugra and my fellow warriors are up to. He is growing old and is less and less likely to go campaigning these days."

Caros nodded in understanding. No campaigns left a warrior little to look forward to by way of plunder. "Still, there is Alfren." Caros thought of the surly champion, his fierce attitude and hunger for battle. "Alugra will most likely use Alfren more and more to lead campaigns and from what I saw, Alfren will not tolerate a season with no campaigning."

Neugen grunted in agreement. "You tell it right, I think. Alfren is hungry for battle. I could do worse than stick close by him."

The following morning, Caros and Neugen rose quietly amidst the clatter of the waking camp. The Iberian leading men were up and urging on the Masulian warriors with their early morning meals and ablutions. Both Gualam and Drasal were bawling out to warriors throughout the camp to shit and ride. Neugen and Caros looked at one another meekly. Already they felt like outsiders. They hustled down to the stream where they had washed the night before. The water was muddy from watering the horses and the ablutions of the hundreds of men. They eyed it suspiciously before deciding to forego a wash.

"Gods, my mouth tastes like one of these fellows took a dump in it last night." Neugen complained.

Caros hitched a thumb over his shoulder at the sewage-filled stream. "Hair of the dog is right there then." Neugen mock heaved and they exchanged a laugh. "To Baria then. Let us bid farewell to the Turdetani first." Caros was feeling good and looking forward to the day ahead.

6

Caros found the column leader chivvying along the Masulians who moved unhurriedly as they broke camp. The Turdetani looked in exasperation at Caros.

"I swear they would sleep here till they turned to turds rather than get mounted. So, you are off, are you? Set on becoming a merchant. I guessed you might. Anytime you change your mind, come find me. I will be wherever there are a lot of lazy Masulians lounging about." He directed the last remark at a group of four riders who stared impassively at him while kicking dirt over their cooking fire.

Once they had bade Gualam farewell, he and Neugen left the camp and turned north. As they reached the road that led to Baria, the drumming of hoofs made them glance back. Drasal was approaching with two accompanying riders. Masulians. Curious, Caros waited for the Turdetani.

"Ho, Caros! You decided against Gualam's offer. A pity that. We could always use good men like you!" His gaze included Neugen, which made the tracker sit straighter. The two Masulians drew up, clicking their tongues and twisting their hands in the shaggy manes of their ponies. Caros had not had the chance to study the Masulians up close; wiry with a coppery, sun-dried appearance, they dressed in tunics of coarse fabric with colorful cloth tied about their waists. On their heads, they wore a scarf of sorts, wrapped to form a head covering. The older of the two Masulians edged his horse towards Caros. The skin of his face, where it showed under a wispy beard, was deeply lined and his black hair was silvering above his ears. His piercing green eyes fastened on Caros. Drasal began to speak and to Caros' surprise, the Masulian threw up a hand, silencing the Turdetani. Neugen edged his horse closer to Caros, his hand gripping the spear on his lap with white knuckles. It was clear from the way he carried himself that the Masulian was a leading man.

"It is good we meet. I am told your name is Caros." It was not a question. "I am Massibaka. I am also told you fought to honor a blood debt. My clan brothers and I were there to witness your revenge. It was as it should be." The man spoke the Greek patois commonly used among traders. Caros nodded, his brows furrowed. The Masulian paused, his eyes boring into Caros' own while his companion passed a wrapped object to him.

"We wish to offer you a gift. It is a thing of honor amongst our people." He presented the object to Caros with his right hand while holding the wrist of that hand with his left hand in a show of respect. Caros accepted it, gauging its weight and form before carefully unwrapping the soft leather. The object was a piece of polished obsidian the size of an eagle's egg. The black rock was hollowed to form a miniature bowl and a white figurine was fixed in the depression; a carving of a beast that resembled a lynx. Caros had seen many amazing carvings, but the lines of this beast were exceptional. Attached to the amulet was a silver chain. He looked from the amulet to the Masulian who dipped his chin. "We of the Baka'Masulians offer you a war-name." Beyond Massibaka, a host of Masulians had gathered. "You shall be known amongst the Baka'Masulians as Claw of the lion."

Caros was speechless. It was the custom in Iberian tribes to bestow a war name on a warrior if they performed a great feat. He had never imagined he would receive such an honor and that from a graybeard of a different tribe.

"Claw of the lion." He whispered the words and as he did, a cold breath stalked across his neck. Shrugging aside the premonition, he smiled. He did rather like the strength and prowess the name implied, but was vague on what a lion was. As he considered the name, he heard a rising hiss. The Masulians had grown in number and they cupped hands over their mouths and hissed through their teeth. The sound ended abruptly and as one they shouted.

"Claw of the Lion!"

The town of Baria was set on a low rise north of the Zakarra River whose estuary mouth fed into the Inland Sea. The town was encircled by sturdy walls of stone and overlooked the harbor. Within the defenses were the dwellings of the rich, the merchants and the artisans. The walls also enclosed a barracks that housed a score of spearmen. Beyond the walled city lay scattered settlements and most importantly, the harbor with its single pier. Warehouses, cantinas and an open square that served as a market for local traders also served the galleys that visited. Caros and Neugen bypassed the walled city and rode to the harbor.

Caros was still fingering the amulet hanging from his neck when they entered the narrow streets around the small pier. Here they encountered the usual early morning traders unloading their wares in the square. Farmers hawking produce straight off deep-sided wagons. Fishermen bartering with boisterous fishmongers over the early morning's catch. Gulls floated on the breeze blowing to sea and screamed raucously as they dived to eat their fill of entrails gutted from freshly caught fish. The town guards walked rutted streets doggedly, killing time until they were relieved.

Caros knew the area and walked his horse down a narrow street to an adobe and wood warehouse on the northern side of the harbor. The sun cast a golden aura over the structure. Outside the barred doors, two guards sat on a wooden bench, leaning their backs against the wall. They looked to be asleep, legs stretched out before them and feet crossed at the ankles. At the sound of the horses on the road, their eyes snapped open and they rose.

"Greetings. I am here to see Marc."

The door of the warehouse was closed and chained. One of the guards gestured at it with his thumb. "He will be here later. Are you not Joaquim's son?"

Caros gritted his teeth. "I am and I wish to see him now."

The man sucked his teeth before cocking his head to his silent companion. "I will take him up to Marc's home. Will you be alright here alone?

The silent guard shrugged and returned to the bench. "It is daylight. Nothing happens when the sun watches."

They followed the guard through narrow lanes created haphazardly between leaning buildings. Ascending from the harbor to the walls of Baria, they arrived at the town gate and after an exchange with the guards there, were permitted to enter the town. The guard stopped outside a mud and stone dwelling and gestured to it.

"This is his home. He was up late so you will need to kick in his door to wake him."

Caros thanked the guard whose attention had moved on to a maid with an armload of laundry exiting a nearby dwelling. The man waved farewell to Caros over his shoulder as he sauntered after the girl.

"This Marc is a merchant that knew your father?" Neugen slapped his tunic to rid it of dust and burrs.

"He was my father's foreman and manages the warehouse. He is like family." Caros drew a deep breath and knocked at the door to the dwelling, rapping insistently on the thick wood. Along the street, shutters cracked opened and frightened faces peered out.

Neugen grabbed his arm. "Caros, stop. Look how afraid these people are." Shutters banged shut again as Caros turned to look. "Something has these citizens scared, Caros."

Caros backed away from the door and saw the shutter above it was ajar. "Marc, it is Caros, Joaquim's son. I have grave news."

The shutters flew open and a hairy face followed by a set of shoulders fit for a bull, leaned from the window. "Caros! You scared the shades out of us! I will be down in a moment."

Caros smiled as the brute of a man withdrew into the room behind the tiny window. Marc was a man who lived large, lived hard and did not dance around issues. The door crashed open and Marc strode from it. He had rounded out as age grew on him and was breathing hard.

"Caros! Curses man, come here!" He spread his arms wide and gave him a fatherly embrace. Releasing Caros, he stepped back and looked him up and down. "You look as bad as you smell."

Caros was acutely aware of how he looked. "I know it, Marc. Here, this is Neugen, from Tagilit."

"Greetings, an equally smelly Neugen of Tagilit." Marc clapped Neugen on the shoulder, before turning back to Caros. "Grave news you said? Is it your father? Is he ill?" Caros swallowed, surprised at how hard his breathing had become. Marc's hand was on his shoulder, squeezing. "Do not speak here. I see in your face that you have dire news." The old man looked about and nodded to himself. "Come along. You can tell me once we are off the street."

Marc hustled the two men through streets still free of people at this time of day. Children could be heard laughing and chattering behind walls and livestock was herded from those places that housed them during the night. Other than those few servants that were out, the citizens were still in their dwellings.

Upon reaching a wooden door set in an adobe wall, he turned the latch and shoved it open. The men stepped into a cramped courtyard into which the early morning sun streamed. Marc looked about proudly. "I own this place. It is a bathhouse." Remembering why they were here; his face grew somber. "Come, sit. Tell me your news, Caros."

"I have ill tidings, Marc. My family have been killed in a raid by the Arvenci."

The big man shot up straight with a roar. "What! When? I just sent a messenger to your father late yesterday."

"It happened a few days ago. I thought you might have already received a message."

Marc shook his head. "No, nothing."

Caros leaned his elbows on his knees. "Alugra of Tagilit came to our aid. His warriors combed the hills for the raiders and I rode with. We hunted them down and recovered much of the livestock they had stolen."

"This is terrible news, Caros. It is some measure of comfort to know that you struck back, but such a loss. Your father and I have been friends for many years." He shook his head sadly.

"Alugra had to return to Tagilit, so with Neugen's help, I tracked down three more of the raiders. We caught up with them south of Baria yesterday." Talking of the past days seemed unreal. His anger had dissipated leaving him feeling only raw grief.

Neugen spoke from where he sat on his haunches. "Caros matched them single-handedly and sent them to their ancestors."

Marc blinked at Neugen before looking at Caros. "Your kin will know of how you avenged them, Caros." He patted him on the shoulder, eyes misty. "I always warned your father the village needed a stronger wall. He was a shrewd merchant but thought the world was much safer than it is." The old man smiled sadly at some memory and then shook himself and clapped his hands. "You must want to wash and eat. Wait here one moment." He pushed himself upright and disappeared into a gloomy doorway leading from the courtyard and his deep voice echoed from beyond. Moments later, he popped his head out and pointed to a second doorway.

"Go in that way, my girls will meet you."

Neugen gave Caros a sympathetic smile. "The news has wounded him. It is good it was you who broke it to him." Caros rose with a sigh and nod. Neugen's face took on his most innocent look. "Did he say 'girls'?"

Caros elbowed him with a laugh. "Fool!"

They found themselves in a large room, the likes of which Caros had rarely seen and then only in Greece and Utica. Four rectangular bays lined the length of the room. Between each was a low wooden bench. At either end of the room was a large fire pit over which hung two steaming cauldrons. "This is a bathhouse."

Neugen frowned and scratched his ass. "Where is the water?"

A scuff of a foot heralded the entrance of two women. They approached with shy smiles.

"Greetings. Marc would have us bathe you." The taller of the two spoke. Her long hair was tied at her neck and she had the nut-brown complexion and dark eyes typical of the people of the region. Young and attractive, when she smiled, Caros' heart lurched. In a blink, she went from pretty to beautiful. "My name is Ilimic. Please disrobe and sit here."

Caros glanced at Neugen who was already fumbling at the strings of his garment, a wide smile on his face. He shrugged, undid his belt and dragged his tunic over his head. Ilimic took the clothing, frowning at the bloodstained fabric while Caros took a seat on the bench wearing just his smallclothes. He found that his lower back rested comfortably on the fired clay wall. The girls exited with their garments and returned moments later carrying jugs. Ilimic placed the jug beside Caros and then nimbly perched on the wall of the pit right behind him. Her smooth calves hung either side of his body, brushing against his arms. She stripped the wax seal and unplugged the jug, releasing a perfumed scent. Just then, Marc appeared with two men and a third woman.

"Ah! Apologies, I had to get things moving along. We are not usually open for business so early in the day." He disrobed and sat in a vacant bay and the third woman took up a position behind him. The women began to rub the scented oils into the men's skin and knead their shoulders and neck. Caros felt the knots and bruises keenly. Neugen sighed happily and Marc laughed. "I have been planning this little enterprise ever since I made a trip to Utica. Of course, I do not have their fancy systems, but I have worked around our limitations. I am certain you will enjoy it and not a day too soon."

The woman used her strong hands to work the knots in Caros' muscles loose, while every fiber of his body was aware of her smooth legs and sweet breath on his neck as she worked. Slowly, her hands reduced his tension and he enjoyed a wave of bliss as he relaxed.

"What of the shipment of ore my father stored here? I see you have just two men guarding it."

Marc turned his head to Caros. "Just like your father, cannot relax for a moment." He grinned at Caros. "No point guarding merchandise that is no longer there. We have sold the lot. There is not an ingot of iron or bronze pin left. A merchant from Syracuse took all the copper. The iron was divided between the Barca's and a buyer from Sucro. The bronze was split among them all. They would have bought the nails out of the beams if I had offered them."

Caros was amazed. They had filled the warehouse at the beginning of spring and had expected to sell the ore in consignments over the summer.

"That is fortunate. Why all the interest in ore?"

"Have you heard what happened in Sagunt?"

"No, we have been hunting Arvenci in the hills and not had news for days. What news?" Caros enquired lazily, his head lolling as the woman worked his neck.

"From the rumors, it seems a revolt has taken place there with Carthaginians and Greeks murdered and their property confiscated. A galley fleeing Sagunt, limped in day before yesterday, barely afloat under the number of women and children onboard. Many of the rowers were injured and we learned of the murders from them."

Caros was horrified; he knew merchants with families in Sagunt. "There is a connection between the sale of the ore and Sagunt?" Caros quizzed Marc.

The old man beckoned to the two men stoking a fire under a bronze basin. The women shuffled aside as the men hauled the basin to the bays. They slowly tipped the warm water over each of them, making sure to drench them from crown to toe.

Sighing, Marc winked at Caros. "I think so. Once we are done here, I will explain."

After the three men had been scrubbed and dowsed, Marc insisted they lay on the padded benches while the women dried and oiled them again. Caros smiled gently at Ilimic as she caressed the oil into his chest, back, arms and legs. She caught his eye and blushed, but stared back for a moment until a loud gurgle emanated from Caros' gut. She burst out laughing and Caros smiled weakly.

Neugen snorted. "Yesterday we rode with Masulian horsemen from Africa. They gave Caros a war name. I would now like to bestow on my hungry friend his bath name. Thunder in the Bath!"

Caros threw a towel at Neugen and Marc laughed. "Well named! I think we can remedy the problem. We need food and I know just the place."

"What? I am surprised you do not have food laid on here for your guests?" Caros cried in dismay. He was famished. Marc pursed his lips in thought. "I was jesting!" Caros laughed.

"It is not a bad idea." Marc nodded as he rolled off the bench to dress. He had thoughtfully also had new tunics, smallclothes and sandals brought for Caros and Neugen. They gratefully slipped these on, happy to never have to see their blood-stained garments again.

The three men were soon tucking hungrily into a breakfast of cured hams, cheese and fruits with plenty of vinegar water and diluted wine to wash it down with.

Neugen belched and thumped his chest. "By the gods, I needed that! I have been hungry before, but I was sure my stomach was beginning to gnaw on my liver."

Caros, still chewing on sour raisins, nodded. "Fine warriors we two are; not even properly provisioned before setting off."

"Seems to me we were on a rocky hill in the middle of the wilderness when you decided to set off." He mimicked Caros' words of two days before. "*I know this area. We will find a village or shepherd and get food there.*"

Marc pushed aside his eating board. "You mentioned Masulians?"

Neugen described their encounter with the horsemen. When he had finished Marc looked troubled.

"There has been a lot of turmoil of late." Marc shrugged. "You know the Greeks in Sagunt, the wealthy Edetani too, were pro-Roman. They have been pushing for closer ties with the Latins for some time. With the young Barca crushing the Vaccaei in battle last summer, this faction in Sagunt has become even more hostile towards Carthage."

"Why?" Neugen rubbed a hand through his freshly washed hair.

"They are hemmed in by territories and tribes who answer to the Barcas of Carthage or are allied to them. They fear their fine city will find less and less trade coming their way from the hinterland." This made sense to Caros whose father had become increasingly reluctant to invest in Sagunt. This was why so much ore had been stored in the Baria warehouse. "I do not have all the facts, but what I heard came direct from a Carthaginian merchant on a galley that limped into the harbor yesterday." Marc greeted two craftsmen who appeared and set themselves down beneath an olive tree to break their fast. Turning back to Caros he went on. "He said tension had been growing between the two sides; Carthaginians versus the Pro-Roman faction. The pro-Romans include the oligarchy who rule the city. This man said he had been concerned for some time and had recently taken the precaution, expensive as it was, of keeping a small galley anchored in the bay near Sagunt. He said he was selling off his property in the city when the tension escalated and overnight the pro-Roman citizens turned on the pro-Carthaginian population."

Caros was puzzled. "He did not say what caused this uprising? Some action or declaration?"

Marc shrugged. "It could have been anything I suppose. There is always a danger that people will turn on those they hate if they feel they can escape judgement. They saw an opportunity to rob and pillage the warehouses and homes of more prosperous citizens without being held accountable."

"How did this Carthaginian escape and what of the rest?"

"The man was a sight. As I said, he had taken precautions to keep a galley on hand. He had also hired additional guards and made sure they were Carthaginians or trustworthy locals at least. On that day there had been some stoning on the city streets. Petty stuff, but seeing no action taken against the criminals, more people began to join the mob. In the early evening they started to loot warehouses which belonged to Carthaginians. The merchant said that he would have left then except the mob was at its worst at the western gate and he was warned the eastern gate was being watched. He had his guards out to keep an eye on the mob. Once the warehouses had been picked over and burned, they streamed into the inner city. The Carthaginian guessed they were coming for the family homes where they would find rich pickings. He got his family out their home and circled the city, keeping away from the mob and staying as inconspicuous as possible. Carthaginians are, if nothing else, wily people. Before he knew it, there were a dozen families like his making for the harbor. Unfortunately, the looters spotted the larger group and their escape became a race for the galley." Marc wiped a hand over his face. "He says what he witnessed that night will haunt him to his death."

Caros shook his head. He could all too easily sympathize with the Carthaginian merchant. It seemed there was no end to those who would kill families out of pure malice. His blood boiled at the thought of all the families murdered in their homes in a civilized city, all so that some already wealthy bastards could get even wealthier. Neugen's face was grim, his lips pursed in anger and Marc looked weary at the telling of the tale.

Another thought occurred to Caros. "Marc, how safe is Baria? Sagunt is close."

"Bah! Close as one rides maybe, but we are a world apart. Yes, there is some fear and apprehension here, but we are allied to the Barcas and have no pro-Roman faction. There is the potential of a city war, I guess. Sagunt has a large standing militia and can call on thousands of Edetani warriors if it came to that."

Neugen's eyes narrowed. "If it did, what provisions have been made here?"

Marc looked uncomfortable at the question and chose not to answer. Caros exchanged a worried look with Neugen.

"This explains where the Turdetani is taking his column of horsemen. He tried to explain it away as a training excursion, but I never believed him."

Marc sat up straight. "Who? The Turdetani from Malak?"

"Yes. Like we said, he was riding north with a thousand horsemen. Timing seems a little suspicious."

Marc thumped a huge fist on the table. "That is your reason!" Caros and Neugen looked at him; both had jumped at the explosion. "You asked what sparked the riot. The Barcas are moving against Sagunt. If the city elders at Sagunt heard…"

Caros completed the thought. "That the Barcas were planning to overthrow them, they would want to rid the city of sympathizers and spies. Or maybe, Hannibal is moving against them because of the killings?"

Neugen took up the thread. "I expect the horsemen are an advance guard. There may already be other columns converging on Sagunt."

The men digested the idea in silence until Marc shrugged his shoulders. "Well, if all this conjecture is right, there will be war soon and I do not mean between the Barca and Sagunt. It will be war with Rome."

Caros knuckled his eyes thinking. Where was his place in all this? War between this Barca general's mercenary army and Rome! War meant provisions and iron, men and bread. He had heard it said that when trade was poor, merchants prayed for war. That was the heart of it. War made wealth. He had the coin to invest in the goods an army would need. His thoughts drifted to his family, to the villagers slain for a few coins and their livestock. Their lives were forfeit for another's gain. There was another side to the coin though. Could he remain a merchant after his recent experiences? Aside from his brother, he had not had friends his age. His father had taught them to read and write Greek letters from an early age. They had always lived on the property beyond the village and once he could ride and contribute in the business, he had begun the journeys from the inland mines to the harbor markets. There had never been time to develop relationships with peers. His life had been so easy with no real decisions to make. It was as though he had been set on a narrow path and there had been precious few junctions at which to choose a different direction. Now he was at a fork in the road and he had to choose a new course. He shifted on the bench, uncomfortable with his thoughts.

Neugen mistook this for a sign that he was preparing to leave. "Are we going to get some provisions before heading back?" He smiled. "I plan to avoid going hungry again for at least a fortnight."

"I will arrange provisions for you. We need to discuss the business commitments your father made before you go, Caros. Meet me down at the warehouse just after midday. In the meantime, you are welcome to stay here or at the baths if you wish."

"Thank you, Marc." Caros said earnestly. "There is much for me to think on." Then he grinned. "I may just go to the baths again before midday!"

Marc laughed, as did Neugen. "Ah, she is a pretty one. Curves in all the right places and such inviting eyes! You should know she is my niece." Grinning at Caros' surprise, he paid the man who ran the cantina and left.

Caros and Neugen left the cantina feeling better than they had for days. They had no plan and wandered the streets of the walled town, enjoying the morning sun. The town's citizens were out; going about their daily work and trade. Most were Bastetani. Their way of life had changed dramatically over the last four generations as the Inland Sea, acting like a highway, had brought Greeks and Phoenicians to their lands here on the Iberian coast. With ever-increasing numbers of these foreign traders and adventurers arriving and settling, the Bastetani had learned and incorporated many new ways into their lives. They were a proud people, but they quickly accepted and mastered improved techniques in building, trade and metalwork. Towns like Baria had been little more than backwater fishing villages. Dotted all along the eastern and southern coast, they now thrived and grew prosperous through trade with a dozen kingdoms on the shores of the Inland Sea. Merchant buyers came in their fat-bellied galleys to buy all manner of produce from flax to sea snails. By far the most valuable commodity was the silver dug from the mountains inland. Bastetani, tired of the grueling life of farmers working the land, had come to the coastal towns like Baria to claim a share of the wealth this trade brought. Along streets of hard-packed soil and rock, were all manner of stores and craftsmen. They passed leather workers sewing sandals, belts and bags, their finished goods displayed on hooks. Beyond them was a potter's store. A tall Bastetani woman, dressed in a colorful chiton, tended to a customer while from the rear came the whirling of the potter's wheel and slap of wet clay. Two women brushed past them to join the woman at the potter's stall. Their voices fell and they turned to watch Caros and Neugen, exchanging comments from behind their hands. Grinning at one another, they strolled on, leaving the women tittering as only excited women could. The aroma of fresh-baked breads and other delicacies was a pleasure and they brushed shoulders with Bastetani, Greek and Gyptos. They walked a full circuit of the walls, taking in the everyday scenes of life in a peaceful town. Caros grew quiet as he watched friends laughing and children playing. The fear and pain of loss he had experienced had changed him. He accepted that now and knew he would ever be a different man from the one that rode home seven days past to find his kin dead.

The sun edged towards its zenith and Neugen remembered his horses were in need of new bridles. He turned back the way they had come to visit a leather craftsman they had glimpsed working in a stone alley piled with all manner of leather wear for riding. They agreed to meet again at Marc's bathhouse.

Caros found himself strolling in the shade of the town wall. It was a solid wall of rock up to the height of a mounted man. On top of the rock, a further wall of stout timbers had been erected, giving the wall a height of well over three times a man's height. Along the inside of this wooden palisade, a walkway allowed guardsmen to patrol or in times of war; archers, slingers and javelin throwers to stand and fight. Tall stone towers rose up, sentinel like, at intervals along the wall, further reinforcing the strength of the town's defenses.

Caros approached a tower, looking with interest at the solid structure. It seemed to him that all his life he had taken such things for granted. He had never examined why they were there, how they worked or even his part in them. He had just assumed all would be there the next day and the next. The tower drew him and he found himself climbing the stone stairs that led to the battlement above. There was a rectangular room on each level of the tower. Pausing at the doorway of the first, he realized it created an additional firing platform for archers. Rough wooden beams caked in bird droppings and other debris led to two narrow windows. He contemplated entering but the cloying smell of pigeon shit turned him back. He passed the second room and the sudden furious flapping of wings startled him. He swore as two plump rock pigeons tore out the doorway, their wings causing his hair to lift. He continued up, enjoying the spectacle of the town from this different perspective.

The sun hit his face at the top of the stairs and he looked down only to experience a disconcerting spell of dizziness. He quickly stepped onto the top of the tower and lifted his gaze. A figure sat on the edge of the tower, overlooking the bay below the town. Caros expected a lookout, but the figure was unmistakably female. Her chiton rode low on one shoulder revealing smooth, sun-kissed skin. Long hair tied in a wide braid, streamed down the center of her back to where her hips flared. He marveled at how the sun shone from the russet colors; as though in motion. He stood unmoving, just drinking in the loveliness of the woman's figure as she sat looking out to sea. He had been with women on occasion since he had become a man at the arrival of his thirteenth summer. Usually brief, lusty encounters when at a feast or gathering after he had drunk copious amounts of ale and wine.

He had once thought he was in love with a girl from the village of Helike, the eldest daughter of a merchant there. He had bedded her at every opportunity for a fortnight and day and night, he had thought of little else. Coming early one evening to Helike from the Balearic port of Ebusos where he had expected to be for a few days longer, he had glimpsed a familiar silhouette as he walked past a cantina. The merchant's daughter was sitting on a burly guardsman's knee, laughing merrily. Caros had thought he would be angered, but instead felt relief. He had never seen the girl again.

Caros cleared his throat politely and approached the outer wall where the woman sat. She turned to glance over her shoulder at him. Caros was overjoyed to see the woman was none other than Ilimic. She smiled widely at him and patted the wall beside her. Caros hopped onto the wall and sat down lightly, his legs dangling beside hers. He noticed again how smooth and well-shaped they were.

"This is a pleasant surprise!" He greeted her. She flashed a smile at him, her teeth white between dusky red lips. Strands of hair, loosened from her braid, blew across her face and framed her brown eyes. She leaned towards him silently and placed a slow kiss on the corner of his lips. Caros felt an intoxicating lust sweep through him. He traced a finger down her cheek, drawing her hair back behind her delicate ear.

She stroked the back of his hand. "I am glad you found me. I come here often, before the midday meals, to see what the world brings to our lives." She looked across the sea to the distant smudge of sails on the hazy horizon.

He glanced that way, but his eyes were instantly drawn back to her. She held his hand now between both of hers on her firm thigh. He took in her form beneath the light fabric of her chiton. Her nipples pushed like copper coins against the fabric which dropped away to her slender waist where it was cinched with a soft leather belt.

"Has the world brought anything interesting lately?"

She tilted her head in thought and then a slow, playful smile lifted the corners of her full lips. Caros felt the effect of her smile rush to his head. "Oh, odds and ends. Perhaps." She flicked a glance his way and laughed softly at his expression. "Caros. Hmm… a strong name." She lifted his hand to her cheek and held it there closing her eyes briefly.

He wanted to hold her to him, ached to do so, and disengaged his hand to draw her close. Shifting closer, her thigh rubbed against his as she leaned into his chest and rested her cheek on his shoulder.

"It was a good day the day Marc built that strange bathhouse of his." He said softly. She smiled at him; her breath sweet on his cheek. He lowered his lips to taste her and his tongue caressed her lips and then explored deeper. Her tongue met and parried his playfully. Her breasts pushed against his chest, the thin-woven fabric allowing him to feel her swollen nipples. With his free hand, he caressed her thigh and cupped her breast, his thumb flicked over her nipple. She groaned and moved her hand down his chest. Caros felt he could never tire of her sweet taste. His blood was high and becoming more so as she stroked under the edge of the belt at his waist. Breathing fast, they broke off their kiss. Her hand remained at his belt as she gazed at him while his hand gently cupped her breast.

"Mmm, a strong name for a strong warrior. I can taste your victories. Share more with me." Her words were an age-old invitation, as old as the

Bastetani themselves.

Caros nodded. "My victories will be your victories." They closed to kiss passionately.

Neugen was already at the bathhouse, stretched out and being rubbed down with a rough sea sponge.

"Eh, Caros. Is this the life or is this the life? I am going to enjoy describing it to the graybeards back at Tagilit!" He cocked his head at the girl rubbing him down and winked. "Not *all* about it though." She slapped the sponge over his head. "Ow, watch it with that thing; it is hard."

She laughed. "So *you* say!"

Ilimic joined them and after Caros had enjoyed another wash and massage under her skillful hands, they all four decided to eat together at the same cantina they had breakfasted in. It was clear that the girls were sad to see Caros and Neugen leave when they had finished their meals. Caros turned at the door to look back at Ilimic; she was intently picking apart a crust of bread, her face wistful. He nodded to himself and exited to the heat of the day. He was keen to get to the warehouse and make business plans with Marc.

7

Marc pointed at the provisions he had purchased for them. "There you go. Plenty of food and a spare set of clothes each, including cloaks. A couple extra water skins. Have a look and let me know if you need anything else."

The items were piled on a cured oxhide. Caros smiled at the sight of a bedroll for each. That was a luxury they had not had on the journey here either. It seemed everything they needed for the three-day ride up to Orze was there. Marc had also supplied two heavy-duty, leather packs that could be loaded behind a rider or on a spare mount. These were useful for journeys where there were greater distances between friendly villages.

Neugen knelt and rifled through the goods. "Aha, this looks like plenty. Thank you, Marc. There is more than enough here. I have never been this well supplied before." Neugen sat back and looked up at Marc. "This is all worth a lot. I am not sure I can afford it as I have only three staters?"

Caros laughed and Marc waved Neugen's words away. "It is a gift! You did us a service helping Caros find the Arvenci. Keep your coin my friend."

Looking relieved, Neugen set about packing the items into the packs supplied. "Hey Caros, do you want me to pack your provisions?"

"No, I will do that when Marc and I are done. Go have a good time in the town in the meantime." He winked at Marc who grinned widely.

"Oh, that is a fine idea. Do not be too long; we will be at the cantina." Neugen looked up.

"Us?"

He winked at Caros. "That is right, my friend. I am never lonely when I am in town. It is my crooked nose that women adore!"

Leaving Neugen humming happily to himself as he packed, Caros and Marc climbed a set of stairs to a second level at the rear of the warehouse. The air was stifling hot this close to the roof. Marc threw open the shutters barring a large window. It did not overlook the seaside, but at least created a flow of air that drew out the heat.

"So Caros, what are your plans?"

Caros appreciated Marc's directness. "I want to restock with ore. Iron, but also silver and tin. Whatever we can buy up from the mines. If war breaks out, I want to be able to supply the needs of the army."

"Armies do not always pay the best prices." Marc rubbed a big hand through his beard. "If we can buy up all the reserves, we could force a better price per talent."

"If this all dies down and there is no war, there will still be a demand for the ore. It may take longer to sell, but we will double our coin."

Marc nodded, impressed. "Agreed. The sooner I get to the mines and start buying the better."

Caros grunted. In the past, his father had always hauled the ore using hired wagons and men. It was expensive and took a lot of time to organize, something Caros did not want to get bogged down with. He felt that speed was important in securing deals with the mines.

"We will pay the mines to arrange the shipments and deliver the ore. I know father always did it himself, but it was time consuming. I would rather spend that time dealing with buyers."

Marc smiled slowly at Caros. "You are right; I hated organizing those bloody wagons and mules. Drovers are all alike, stubborn as the beasts they drive. The miners will not like it, but we give them a bonus on top of the price of the ore and they will do it."

By late afternoon, both Caros and Marc were ready to get out of the building and get some refreshments. They had covered a lot of the planning, but it was clear to Caros that it would take many more days to arrange the purchases and receive the shipments. He thought about Orze and his promise to the villagers there to return and help rebuild. It was his duty and he would make sure that if ever they were attacked again, they would have safe walls to protect them.

Marc's words broke through his thoughts. "Have you thought about a place to stay while you arrange this, Caros?"

It had not even occurred to Caros. He remembered that his father used to own a building in the town, but it had been destroyed in a gale the previous winter. "Ah, the old place is a wreck! I forgot about that! Do you have a room I could use, Marc?"

"Not anymore. The wife's mother is in there now." He said unhappily. Caros grinned at him and the older man smiled back sheepishly. "She is fine, but curses man, she puts me to shame when she breaks wind!"

Caros snorted. "I see. Maybe I will set up a place in the warehouse then."

"No! It is awful in there after dark. I know a man whose wife runs him and a cantina. They have rooms they will accept a coin for."

Dusk was already stealing across the port where fishermen mended nets and cleaned their catches. Two trading vessels were berthed on the shingle beach outside the port and men wearing only undergarments were lighting fires on the beach as the crews relaxed. The stench blowing off the galleys was sour and earthy. Marc stopped at the four spearmen sitting inside the door of the warehouse, playing dice and preparing their meals.

"You know why Caros wants four men on guard? That bloody business up in Sagunt. Keep your eyes open and mind that fire when the wind shifts. I do not want the place burning down."

Caros found Neugen at the cantina they had lunched in. He was at a table with two strangers, talking and laughing. He signaled to the owner as he strode over to the bench.

Neugen jumped up. "Ho! Caros! I was just telling these men about the Arvenci." His eyes were watery from the strong ale and he slapped Caros on the shoulder. "This is the champion."

The two men smiled through their beards and clasped Caros in a brotherly embrace in turn. The older man released him and cleared his throat.

"Bad business; Arvenci attacking Bastetani villages. Your friend here told us you fought them. I wish I had been there." His tone was wistful.

The younger fellow was eager for details. "Is it true you charge them wearing no breastplate?"

Caros smiled awkwardly. "I did, but I will not be doing that again anytime soon." They laughed and had barely sat and begun talking again when Caros felt a hand brush his neck. Glancing around, he found Ilimic standing behind him and he smiled widely. "Ilimic! Have a seat. You finished at the bathhouse for the day?"

"Yes, fortunately it is quiet when there are few merchants in town. Marc charges three staters, so only the wealthy use the facility."

She sat down close beside Caros; their thighs rubbing and sending fire through their bodies. Her friend, Nerea, took the space beside Neugen. The two men finished their drinks and with knowing winks at Caros and Neugen, took their leave.

Nerea and Neugen were talking quietly to one another and Caros smiled happily at Ilimic. "I have some happy tidings. I will be staying in Baria for longer than I had thought."

"That is good news! For how long?"

"Till early summer, I expect. I must go back to Orze to settle some affairs there before then, but just for a few days."

"Oh Caros, that is fantastic! You will visit me in the bathhouse every day, will you not?"

"I shall be there every chance I get."

Neugen looked over. "Did you say you were staying in Baria?"

Caros nodded. "Yes, Marc and I have some business with the miners. It will be easier to handle from here."

Neugen looked a little crestfallen for a heartbeat and then brightened.

"I suppose I can stay a few more days." He looked pointedly at Nerea who blushed and giggled.

"I have arranged two rooms at a cantina near the warehouse. We can stay there. In fact, the owner has promised us a fine feast tonight, so we should head over there soon. Nerea, Ilimic are you able to join us?"

As the four companions approached the cantina, the smell of food and sounds of conversation from inside was inviting. It was still noisier inside and Caros noticed it was filled with all manner of sailor, merchant and trader. They spied a good spot at a low table occupied by two of the off-duty town guards. These two greeted them politely and invited them to share the table. Neugen quickly got the attention of one of the serving boys.

"Bring us a flagon of ale son and not the sour stuff." Before the boy could leave Caros added. "Tell your master that Caros and Neugen are here with two friends and we are hungry."

The boy nodded and darted off to come back shortly with the ale and take the required bronze coins from Neugen before running off to the kitchen again. Neugen offered ale to the guardsmen who nodded their thanks.

"Busy in here. Is it always?" Neugen asked.

"Yup, just the faces and moods that differ. Last night it was full of Carthaginians and tonight it is all Greek and Sicilian. Oh, and a table of Romans, least they look grumpy enough to be Romans." One of the guardsmen answered.

Caros could tell the different nationalities apart easily enough, but Neugen was nonplussed. "My friend here is from Tagilit and has never seen a Roman, but he could track a lynx through a flood."

The guardsmen nodded approval and Nerea rubbed Neugen's arm proudly.

"Right then, who is who?" Neugen took a long swallow of ale from a red clay cup.

Caros lifted his own and tipped it in thanks to the buyer. "See the six sitting there nearest the door? They are Greeks."

"I see. Big lads. Odd looking noses though, eh? Makes you wonder what else about them is oddly shaped."

The two guardsmen guffawed at the innuendo and Ilimic and Nerea smirked. Caros felt the cool ale kindle a warm glow in his gut. It was a strong brew and he settled forward contentedly. "Oh, and the men from Syracuse are easy enough to tell apart."

"Wait, do not tell me." Neugen gazed about and lifted his cup to gesture. "Those chaps over there?" He pointed at three men in the far corner. "The ones who look like they are drinking vinegar and dog piss?"

Caros eyed the men. He could not tell where they were from, but Neugen's description was as accurate as a slingshot. "Nope, the Sicilians are on the opposite side all dressed in white linen and green capes. Prosperous looking buggers too." He looked at the guardsmen. "Who are the sour-looking chaps then, Romans?"

The guardsmen looked at one another and laughed. "How did you guess? What is it about the Latins, eh?"

Caros took another long swallow of ale while eyeing the Romans. Dressed in drab tunics and leather sandals, they were as unhappy a trio as he had ever seen.

Neugen eyed them speculatively over the rim of his cup. "I hear the Romans consider anyone who wears braccae to be a barbarian, so I expect a lifetime of freezing your sack off would make anyone sour." The guardsmen sniggered and dug their elbows into one another.

While the men laughed and exchanged remarks about Romans, Caros turned and leaned close to Ilimic. "Is it true you are Marc's kin?"

"He is my uncle. My mother died two winters past. The coughing sickness."

Caros took her hand and rubbed it, feeling her distress keenly. "Marc is as an uncle to me as well. He saved my life when I was just a little rat."

The serving boy returned bearing a board piled with bread, olives and cheese. Behind him an older girl followed, carrying two smaller boards with crisp pork strips and stewed apples. Caros sat up straighter. The food looked and smelled enticing. The guardsmen downed their cups and said thanks and farewell. Neugen already had a handful of succulent meat in his mouth, so he just grunted, juices dripping through his beard. Caros bade them well and then also attacked the food. When the meats were gone and the serving boy had brought them another flagon of ale, their pace relented. They sipped and picked at the remains of the meal slowly while talking. The crowded room had emptied while the noise had increased as the remaining patrons drank deeply and became more boisterous. Caros noticed the looks thrown at the two women and caught Neugen's eye.

"I think it is a good time to take our visitors home. This lot are getting rowdy."

Outdoors, a swathe of stars that sparkled in the sea and glowed off the whitewashed buildings, lit the night. With his cloak over Ilimic's shoulders and her in his arm, they walked slowly towards the walls of Baria, enjoying the closeness of their bodies. Caros looked forward to many days here in Baria with Ilimic at his side. In time, she may even wish to become his wife. His heart drummed with excitement at the prospect and he whispered a prayer to Cabar, goddess of love to make it so.

Four days of planning the purchase of the ore and getting permission from the local elders and leading men, in whose territory the mines were, sped by. This was just the first phase. They would then need to negotiate the price and convince the miners to deliver. Caros rubbed his head to clear his thoughts and the nagging ache behind his eyes. He would have struggled without Marc's knowledge of the various leading men and what their price was. He stood and stretched the kinks from his shoulders and Ilimic sprang to mind. He was blessed to find her for she had a similar sense of humor and they laughed often. He felt buoyed by her presence and was becoming more and more certain she would become his wife if he asked. He had enquired with Marc why she was not yet someone's wife at the age of sixteen years. Most girls were wed at fourteen and at sixteen were with their first child.

Marc had nodded sadly. "Her mother, my sister died young and left Ilimic to grow up with my boys. She got it in her head she would only wed when she received a sign."

"What sign?" Caros asked with a falling heart.

"How would I know? It is a womanly idea I am sure, so why try understanding it, yes?"

"Hmm." Caros responded, wondering if Nerea might know.

Night had fallen and Caros and Neugen were enjoying their cups at the cantina. Caros managed to get the serving boy's attention and soon enough they had a third cup. Neugen was talking about the ambush on the Arvenci. "Always the same pattern, that is their downfall. I wonder why they bother. Raid, plunder, make off with too much and a day or two later, whoosh, we catch up with them and it is off to feed Saur's dogs."

"What would you do? The whole point is to get as much plunder as possible is it not?" Caros asked.

"Aha! What good is it if you cannot get away with it quick enough though, eh? Me? I would go after the rich stuff. Gold, silver and gemstones. Once I had a bag full, I would be off and nobody would be able to catch me."

Caros shrugged. "Not much of that around in the villages. Livestock is what counts for wealth in the country."

"That is why I want to campaign in a real war where we sack enemy cities. Plenty of riches in a city." Neugen stared away dreamily.

Caros wondered what would happen if the Barcas did make war on Sagunt. He had been there and seen the defenses. It was an old city, so old it had three walls, well; two walls and a hill fort. The outer wall ran along the edges of a rocky promontory. Towers rose at intervals along the wall and the defenders were able to fire all manner of missiles down on any attackers grim enough to come close. Even if the outer wall was breached, there was a similar wall to overcome before reaching the hill fort built on the east side of the hill. It would take tens of thousands to breach the walls and the hill fort. It did not seem possible and yet cities had fallen before, many times. What manner of leader would it take to order men to attack such a fortress? He fingered the amulet he had received from Massibaka. Would he be able to charge a sheer wall under a rain of javelins, arrows and slingshot? He shuddered. Would that he was never in such a battle and yet there was a quality to the moments before and after a fight that enhanced his senses. Made him feel powerful.

Neugen was losing his battle with a fourth cup of ale. It was their final night in Baria and on the morrow they would set off for Orze. From there, Neugen would continue to Tagilit and rejoin Alugra's column. Caros blinked blearily, wondering where the fourth ale had come from. He sat up and peered around. Many of the patrons were slumped across or between the tables. A trio of Greeks still sat hunched about theirs, talking animatedly. The fire was burning low. He rose and staggered, almost toppling headfirst across the table. Neugen snorted.

"Saur's dogs, this place has some strong ale." He needed to empty his bladder badly and staggered determinedly to the door which burst inwards just as he reached it, narrowly missing him. A party of Turdetani horsemen surged in, bringing with them the smell of horse and trail. Caros backed up unsteadily as they glared at him and marched over to a table.

The unfortunate sailors sitting there, glared drunkenly at the Turdetani. The warriors said nothing as they kicked the sailors from the benches and took their places. One sailor remained slumped forward on the table, hand clutching his cup. A warrior sat down in the newly vacated spot next to the oblivious man and smiled at his fellow warriors. He pulled the cup out of the man's hand and emptied the ale over his head causing him to sit up unsteadily, coughing and spluttering. Before he could react, a powerful hand gripped him by the neck and tossed him onto the floor. The warriors roared with laughter and began to shout for ale.

Caros smiled and shook his head then his bladder reminded him that he had urgent business outside. When he returned the sailors had regrouped and were on the way out. As Caros stepped through the door, he collided with the first of them. With a growled curse, the man shoved Caros backwards. Seeing an opportunity to vent his anger at being kicked off his seat, the sailor threw a roundhouse punch at Caros who saw it coming and easily dodged the blow. The other sailors crowded forward and Caros kicked out, catching a man between the legs. As the man choked and doubled over, a flurry of blows struck Caros, forcing him to cover his face with his forearms. A fist struck him in the armpit, sending a flare of pain through his ribs. The agony lifted the ale fog from his mind and he lashed out. Three powerful blows, all delivered to the center of a sailor's weathered face. The man's lips and nose split. A flagon shattered and another of the sailors dropped to his knees, eyes rolling into his head. Neugen had noticed Caros' plight and broken a flagon on the man's head. Caros yelled in glee, as did Neugen. Next, they were punching and kicking for all they were worth. They had the upper hand for a moment, catching the sailors by surprise. However, they were outnumbered and soon out of breath. A blow from the largest of the sailors sent Caros tumbling. He slammed into one of the seated Turdetani, knocking the man's cup from his hand, before slumping to the floor.

"Shit!" Caros spat, sitting up and rubbing his jaw, eyes rolling. The Turdetani growled and stood. Shit, shit, shit. The big sailor charged towards Caros like a maddened bull. As he passed the Turdetani, the horseman slammed his elbow into the sailor's throat, stopping the onrushing man in his tracks. Wheezing and clutching his throat, he staggered out of the inn with the rest of the sailors backing off and following. Neugen rose unsteadily from where he had gone to ground in a corner and slumped onto a bench that had somehow escaped being upended in the fighting. A growl focused Caros' eyes on the Turdetani who stood above him.

"My apologies and my thanks. Let me buy you another drink." Caros was doubtful the warrior cared for apologies or spilled ale, yet it was worth a try. The warrior stared hard at Caros and then sent a lightning fast kick at his head. Caros dodged it and rolled below an unoccupied table and out the other side. As quick as a lynx, the horseman hopped onto the table, kicking cups and scraps aside. Caros managed to stagger to his knees just as the man pounced. Again, Caros dodged and this time he rolled to his feet. He was sober now, but he was also growing tired of being punched and beaten. The horseman roared and swung a massive fist at him. Caros bent his left arm and swung his elbow at the oncoming fist, timing it so that the point of his elbow struck the warrior's wrist. It did not break, but the impact numbed the man's arm. The Turdetani grunted, his only concession to the pain, and threw a punch with his other hand. Caros stepped inside the punch and swiftly head-butted the horseman in the center of the face. The warrior's nose snapped with a crunch, and he staggered backwards before dropping to a knee to throw up.

"I apologized. You should have left it at that." Caros growled as he stepped forward to deliver a kick. A shout stayed his leg.

"Enough!" A bench was bowled over and a figure loomed into Caros' narrowed vision. Tensing, he turned to the new threat. "I said enough. Strike my man again and I will eat your liver." A grizzled warrior strode to the side of the kneeling man and grabbed him under the arm, hauling him to his feet and shoving him back to their table.

Neugen staggered up to Caros and stood beside him, but the grizzled warrior just smiled and stalked back to the table, shouting for more ale. The rest of his men glared balefully at Caros and Neugen.

"Come on." Caros mumbled, his jaw swollen. "I do not like the stink in here."

Neugen grinned and spat blood onto the rushes at his feet, never taking his eyes off the Turdetani as he followed Caros to the rear of the building. At the entrance to a passage at the back of the room, a tall, thin man stood twisting a club nervously in his hands.

"Are you alright, Caros?" The man's eyes flicked over Caros' bruises.

"We are good. Sorry about the mess."

"Never mind that. I own a cantina at a harbor side, these things are part of the business." The thin man turned and stalked down the gloomy passage admonishing the serving boy on the way. "Back to your tasks and get that room cleaned up. Where is your sister? She should be helping." A fresh bout of gruff laughter from the newly arrived warriors had him thinking better of sending the serving girl among them. "In the kitchen! Make sure she stays in the kitchen. Out of sight, hear!"

Caros thought that was a wise decision. "Who are those fellows? That old one is a real son of a bitch."

The owner of the place gave a thin smile. "I have not seen them before." He sighed. "At least they are allies. I see strangers visiting from all across the world and of late many more are warriors such as these." He shook his head in consternation. "It is all this warring by Hannibal. He rides against tribe after tribe. First the Olcades, then the Vaccaei. Have you heard the tidings from Sagunt? Madness! The whole Edetani people are rising against Hannibal."

"Why would they wish for war?" Caros asked. His father had taught him the value of information supplied by men like this innkeeper. Men and women who heard every rumor from across great distances thanks to the travelers that visited their establishments. While much of what was said was hearsay, there were often nuggets of information that could be leveraged.

"Ga, they have grown strong on trade with Rome and the islands. Their strength has made them boisterous. Now they want more. It is said they have made peace and pacts with the tribes to the north and west. They will not rest while a Barca lays claim to trade rights with any of the Iberian people." The innkeeper shrugged and looked guilty. "I am keeping you from your rest." He surprised them with a wink and smile before returning to the front room.

Neugen had stripped to his undergarments and stood soaking wet, examining his newly acquired bruises. "I tell you Caros, your company is great, but it is hard on the body, my friend." He flexed his still swollen elbow. "I do not think that little tussle did this any good."

Caros snorted and gave Neugen's back a resounding slap with the flat of his hand.

"Ah, curses, that stung. Thank you!"

Caros laughed and then began hauling off his clothes, also stripping down to just his smallclothes. He threw cool water over his head and rubbed his face vigorously. His body ached from the battering, but he felt good. The ale fog was gone and he looked forward to a good night's rest and an early start.

Neugen yawned and belched. "Time to sleep. Up with the sparrows tomorrow, or should that be the gulls?" He grabbed up his clothing and climbed the ladder to his room.

Caros pulled another bucket of water from the well. It was good water considering how close to the shore the inn was. Must be tapped into an underground stream flowing down from the hills. He upended the water over his head and chugged a good swallow. He wanted to be clear-headed and fresh in the morning. He rubbed the water out of his eyes and when he opened them, jumped in surprise. Standing before him was Ilimic, wearing her beautiful smile.

"You know," she said, "That is a good look for you, mouth wide open and eyes staring. I would close my mouth though, there is likely to be a big old moth about with all these torches burning."

His mouth snapped shut and she giggled. "Yes, a good man. Mother always said they were few and far between."

He laughed, his surprise turning to joy. "Ilimic! What are you doing here?"

"Why Caros, it is good to see you too!" She laughed again as he flushed. She stepped close to him, her body just a film of well water away from his. He could feel her warmth against his skin. "You will never guess what I found today." She whispered quietly into his ear.

His eyes popped wide open. With all the ale he had consumed he had forgotten the gift he had purchased for Ilimic. He had commissioned the town's only silver smith to make a moon amulet to hang on a fine silver chain around Ilimic's neck. He had just this morning collected the gift from the smith and had decided to leave it among her belongings at the bathhouse as a surprise for her to find.

Caros laughed. "I am not sure, let me see. Is it bright and shiny?"

Ilimic giggled again.

8

Berenger shifted on his mount to eye the sun. There was still daylight left. He grunted, satisfied the caravan would arrive before nightfall. Not that they knew he was here. One of his scouts had spied the column just before noon, trundling slowly south along the old road and had nearly killed his horse to get back to Berenger's makeshift camp with the word. Three wagons, heavily loaded, some women and children. Two score mounted warriors escorting it. Berenger reasoned they likely came from the mines up in Turboli lands. Allies of the Barcas, they made fine targets. Hopefully, they had a shipment of ore, maybe some silver, perhaps even gold. The fact was it did not matter if the wagons were carrying Turboli shit; his orders were to carry war far and wide. Any friend of the Barcas was a target and even some who were not. He had told the shifty Olcades scout to take a fresh horse and a second rider and find the caravan to keep him informed of its progress.

He led two hundred horsemen. Most were Edetani warriors, men Berenger had made war with since he could wield a sword. Olcades, Carpetani and some others from the far west made up the numbers. He was not picky. As long as they followed orders and killed Bastetani, Turdetani and Carthaginians, they could come from the slums of Rome for all he cared. His scouts kept him informed of the column's progress and, importantly, kept out of sight. His men were now ranged among a copse of trees and bush in an elbow of the road. He wanted this one last trophy before he turned back to Sagunt. His men were happy to fight and raid for as long as it took, but their depredations were starting to attract the Barcas' attention and soon the countryside would be teeming with enemy warriors.

A horse snorted and stamped amongst the thick, dry foliage. Berenger snarled for silence. He expected total obedience from his men and that meant their mounts as well. Few disobeyed him more than once or twice before they learned the hard lesson. He was a tall, broad shouldered man with a narrow waist and powerful thighs. His black hair shone midnight blue in the sun and was tied in an intricate knot in the nape of his neck. Thick black eyebrows above dark eyes underlined his broad forehead. If a man cared to look into his eyes, he would notice they were deep blue. Most men glanced away before they registered the color. His nose was prominent and hooked over thin lips encircled by a coarse moustache and thick beard, now flecked with grey. His beard was braided, each braid finished with silver ringlets.

Berenger saw a rag of yellow linen flutter on the hill across from his position. A thin smile formed on his lips. The van of the escort was now in the elbow of the road. Soon enough, the wagons themselves would come squealing and creaking into view on their massive wooden wheels. Berenger could hear the horses of the vanguard now on the road below. He had close to eighty horsemen hidden in the crook in the road. Two of them had swept the track of telltale signs of their presence before they had secreted themselves in the foliage on the hillside opposite to give signal once the column appeared. Berenger was meticulous and had ordered that none of the men with him were to even crane their necks to look for the column. Movement would be the first thing any horseman would see, even the less alert ones. Once the column was in the killing field proper, the lookouts on the hill opposite would signal with a yellow linen fragment. He remembered the woman they had torn it off only two days earlier.

Berenger tightened the grip on his mount's reins. As he moved, the horned-bull motif, painted blood red, seemed to stir and come alive on the black shield fastened to his left arm. His right hand gripped the pommel of his broad sword. He had had it made two fingers broader than most and a hand longer. It was all the heavier for the extra width and length, but to Berenger it weighed little once it was singing in circles and scything his foes down. When the enemy saw the blade their eyes grew wide, they grew still wider once they tasted the metal.

Berenger cocked his head. Yes, he could hear them now. A constant squeal of poorly greased axels and the rumble of those giant wooden wheels. The low of oxen was almost drowned out by the grinding rumble of the wagons. He suspected that his entire force could explode howling from their position and the poor buggers riding beside those things would never even hear them. A flutter of yellow appeared on the hill opposite as the lookout signaled. Berenger drew his sword, lifting it above his helmeted head. His men had seen the lookout and he could feel their anticipation. He thrust the point of the sword high into the air.

"Now!" He dug his heels viciously into the ribs of his night-black steed. The mount screamed as it exploded from the foliage, taking the rider in a wild charge down the rocky slope. The trees and shrubbery rippled and twisted as a frenzy of horsemen took up the charge behind him. They broke from cover like a wave of iron and horse and in mere moments struck the first of the horsemen escorting the wagons. Berenger was at the forefront of the wave. Screaming his war cry, he drove into a hapless warrior, knocking man and mount sprawling into the dust. The escort was thinly scattered and Berenger led his men up the line of wagons slashing drovers and followers as he passed. There would be time enough to deal with them properly, but right now he wanted to engage the main force of horsemen escorting the column.

Scattered riders reacted in alarm at the sudden onslaught and fled the wagons knowing they were too few to withstand the charge. They had reached the lead horsemen who had halted and were quickly forming into a line. Berenger racing toward them, watched their leader, who stared back. The man was inordinately calm considering the surprise attack and the overwhelming numbers attacking. Berenger admired courage and professionalism and this man displayed both.

The distance between them closed rapidly and the leader of the escort calmly lifted his falcata and pointed it forward for the charge. Berenger's lips thinned as he leaned over his steed's shoulder, his huge sword pointing at the leading man like a spear. Many of the escorting warriors carried javelins and as the distance between the two forces closed, they launched their missiles. He snarled as one whistled past his ear. Screams erupted from men and horses behind him. The enemy knew this was a fight to the death and they targeted the horses to try even the odds. He would have done the same. Sometimes the only rule in battle was ruthlessness wins all.

The world narrowed until the enemy leader was the only thing before him. He braced himself and then their horses were upon one another. The man slashed at Berenger's sword arm, but he easily avoided the blow and in the next breath drove his sword through the man's thigh. He felt the blade eat through muscle and scrape bone. Then Berenger was past, snarling in victory. In such a charge many would have tried to kill their enemy outright, but that was for the fools told of in children's tales. His first cut had just deprived the enemy leader of his ability to ride and in the time it took to nock an arrow, the man's blood would drain.

Berenger blocked a spear thrust from a passing warrior, parried a few swinging swords and then he pulled his steed into a spin. The animal knew the move and rose on its hind legs and lashed with its forelegs. Like a thundercloud, horse and rider unleashed a storm. He swung and stabbed, swung and stabbed; every move precise. The size of the sword gave him a great advantage. He could block even occasional blows by a war axe, he could outreach other swordsmen and he could cleave the heads off offending spears. In moments, he had killed three horsemen while his horse had maimed the mounts of two others, smashing forelegs or kicking flesh from heads. His men overran the horsemen of the escort in a cloud of grey dust and red spray. A wild melee played to the tune of battle. Swords rung high on iron, men screamed and cursed and the beat of hooves drummed the pace.

In the midst of it, Berenger danced and killed.

The battle was done. The sounds of killing ended with a last scream of a dying horse. The battlefield was strewn with riders and mounts seen faintly though the clouds of dust which smothered everything.

Berenger shouted for his leading man. "Josa!"

From nearby in the eerie grey murk a rough voice answered. "I am here!"

"Take thirty men south down the road. Kill anybody that tried to escape that way then return."

"At once." The man answered from the murk and with a hoarse voice, he gathered men from the dust and rode away in a thunder of hooves. Berenger ordered the rest to take the wagons.

"Prisoners?" A voice called.

Berenger thought a moment. A slave could be a valuable commodity and there looked like maybe ten or twenty women and children amongst the wagons.

"No. No prisoners." He could not be burdened with the bother of captives right now. They were four or maybe five days ride from any lands safe from the Barcas and their allies.

"As you say." The man's voice was already thick with lust.

Berenger hawked and spat a wad of dust-thickened phlegm into the muck at his steed's hooves. He threaded his way between the carcasses of horses and over dead men, friend and foe alike. Under their mantle of grey dirt and blood, they were all the same to him. The first screams started ahead through the fog. Fools, had they thought their men would drive him off? They should have run as fast as their legs could take them to the hills. His men would have found most of them, but one or two might have escaped the horror that was to be their end.

He emerged from the dust cloud at the head of the column of three wagons. There he had to pull up sharply to avoid a group of his warriors. They were clustered around one or more of the women who appeared to still be kicking and clawing, all while begging for mercy. Berenger rode around them to inspect the cargo on the wagons. He reined in again. The same scene he had just passed was being played out all around the wagons. He stared in disbelief. Did none of them run? He shook his head in disgust at the stupidity of people. Three of his men sat apart from the butchery. Berenger rode over to them. They sat straighter on their mounts as he approached. He noted that they were bloodstained, and gore dripped from the rims of their sheaths.

"A good fight." Their leading man, a graybeard, greeted him.

He did not know their names, only that they came from the west; wild Lusitanians.

"You do not want the spoils?" He asked, jerking his thumb in the direction of the screams.

The graybeard spat into the dirt. "Not that kind."

As gaunt a warrior as Berenger had ever seen, the man looked him in the eyes for longer than most before letting his gaze wander north. Berenger followed his gaze. The wagons had come from that direction. He glanced back to where his men were tearing apart bodies and looting the wagons. If even a small troop of horsemen came upon them now, they would be slaughtered. The message from the Lusitanian was clear.

Berenger narrowed his eyes and looked back at the warrior. "Your name?"

"I am named Rudax, of Tarapa."

"Take your riders north. Ensure that we are not surprised by anyone from that direction."

"Very well." The man hauled his mount's head around and led his men north.

He shook his head; the screams were dying down now and coarse laughter and banter rising as the men's heads cleared. Still, it was beginning to rankle him. Josa had not yet returned so Berenger rode over to the wagons to bring order to the chaos. Most of the women and children were dead. Their pale, bloodied bodies sprawled in obscene postures. A commotion was growing on the far side of the rear wagon. Putting it aside, Berenger ordered the nearest men to get the dead off and out of the wagons and get them moving. Three of the oxen lay dead so their carcasses would need to be dragged clear of the traces. If needs be, he would torch a wagon and the men could burn their dead on it if they wished. Or let them rot beside the victims. It was all the same to Berenger.

Once he had barked out his orders, those men nearest jumped to see them done. He watched a man cut a woman free from one of the great wheels to which she had been strapped spread-eagled. She had not died easily and as her head flopped, her staring eyes fixed on Berenger's. He stared back with a smile. It will take more than your evil eye to put the fear in me, he thought. The commotion he had heard earlier caught his attention again. He rode his steed over the dead and around the wagons. A snarl and pained exclamation followed by a roar of laughter came from beyond the last wagon. He rounded it to find a group of his men circled around a young woman. She had her back to a wagon wheel and held a wicked looking dagger before her. Behind her skirts an infant of a few years hid in terror. The men were baiting the woman. She must have been well hidden to escape the calamity that had befallen her fellows. Until now.

"Finish your sport. Now." Berenger commanded the men.

They stopped and looked at him in disappointment. "Kill her?"

"No, marry her. Make her queen of Sagunt. Yes of course kill her. We have wagons to move!"

"I wish to keep her?" One of the men pushed forward holding a blood-drenched rag to his right hand. "I would not need any of the other plunder.

Just her and her child."

The others laughed when they heard his request and the woman's face tightened, proving she understood their tongue. Surrounded by seven men, had she expected to fight her way free with a skirt-lice attached? He looked at her again and realized why the man had asked to keep her. He had rarely seen a woman as attractive, despite the dust and tears. Her hair was an extraordinary yellow, not a color often seen in these hills.

"No. We are warriors, not slavers. If you wanted her so bad you should have sliced her already." He looked at the man's bloodied hand. "Seems she got the better of you. Let the scar remind you even a dormouse fights when cornered."

The men laughed and most began to move away to prepare the wagons and treat injuries. The bleeding man stood his ground. Young, just the first flush of hair covering his upper lip, he was just a boy and had probably never had a woman before as a prize. Berenger prodded his horse back toward the woman. She glared at him and shuffled back, keeping the infant behind her skirts with one hand. Her other hand shook from fear and fatigue. Berenger loosened his sword with his right hand. She could not see past the shield on his left arm and so did not know what he was doing.

"She is pretty. Did you find out her name?"

Hope flared on the young man's face. "No. Not yet, but I can and anything else she knows."

Berenger rolled his eyes, unseen by the young warrior. Those few who had stayed to watch looked at one another and their faces grew somber. One man spat and stepped forward.

"He is my nephew and new at this. I will teach him."

The young warrior looked from Berenger to his uncle and his jaw dropped as realization struck. Berenger drew his sword with a hiss and drove the wide blade through the woman's slender throat. With a deft flick of his wrist, he sent her head tumbling to the road while her lifeless body crumpled to the ground, knocking the infant sprawling.

"You owe your uncle your life, boy. Now finish the skirt-louse and get to work." With hurried thanks, the men fled to the wagons and traces to prepare them.

Berenger was pleased at the haul of goods on the three wagons. Ingots of iron ore were loaded on all three along with a chest containing silver. There were bales of raw flax, linen and other produce that he was not concerned with. The ore was the primary treasure here and he would be rewarded for it in the city of Sagunt.

Josa returned just as the big wagons began to roll forward. In the end, they had enough oxen left to haul all three, although it would be slow going over the steeper hills. The big wheels shuddered as the oxen bent into their yokes and hauled. With whips cracking above their shoulders, they lurched forward. The warriors had not bothered to clear away the dead and the wagons cut through the corpses of men, women and children as they moved off into the dusk.

"We caught up with three of their men. They were the only ones who tried to flee."

"Good. I sent the Lusitanian north to guard against more escorts from that way."

Josa grunted. "Maybe, but the scout said forty were escorting it this morning."

Berenger remembered the scout's estimates. Still, with Barca's allies everywhere it was best to be cautious. "See that we have outriders flanking the column as well as riding ahead and behind. It is a long haul from here to Sagunt and if it comes to it, I would prefer to burn the wagons and lose the ore than die for it."

Josa nodded. He had fought with Berenger long enough to admire his pragmatism. In the seven-year run with him, Josa had become wealthy in comparison to many warriors his age and was wise enough to accord the wealth to Berenger's uncanny knack of taking the richest of prizes with a minimal cost in life.

"How about the other bands we have out? Should we recall them?"

"Yes, they must have pillaged Bastetani villages throughout these hills by now. Have them burn their way back to us. We could do with their numbers to guard the wagons."

9

Morning came swiftly as it always did here on the coast of the Inland Sea. Stars dimmed and faded along with the deepest darkness of night. Light flooded into the world from the east. Songbirds began to sound the arrival of the dawn. Competing with them came the raucous cries of gulls as they rose to the sky to begin their wheeling and feeding. The breeze blew gently in fits and starts from the highlands of the interior, bringing with it the smell of sun-dried earth and resinous cedars. Bringing also the warmth of yesterday's sun and a promise of the heat of a new day.

Caros stirred when a gull had the effrontery to caw from the roof of the adjoining building. He grimaced at the sour taste of old ale on his fur-coated tongue. Turning his head slowly, he was relieved that the headache he felt was minor, no doubt thanks to the copious amounts of well water he had drunk before sleeping. His eyes snapped open. Ilimic. She lay asleep on her stomach. One arm up under her breasts with her long fingers curled beneath her chin. He watched her eyelids tremble as she dreamed. Maybe she dreamed of their lovemaking. He gazed at her beauty which grew by the day in his eyes. Her lower lip showed a hint of a quiver as she exhaled slowly and deeply. His gaze flowed down her body, travelling over the graceful arc of her shoulder to where ribs showed below a firm breast. Every curve his eyes found, they retraced. His gaze moved lower. Her trim waist and shapely hips. Back again to take in the fine hairs just catching the first light of morning, like finest silk threads.

Morning light. They were supposed to be getting an early start to Orze this morning. Caros would miss his friend's good humor once Neugen had gone on to Tagilit, but he had plenty to keep him busy and besides Ilimic had accepted his proposal last night. He grinned happily. He would wed her and in time they would build a happy family in Orze. He trailed a finger through her hair and curled it back from her cheek. Of their own accord, his fingers trailed over her shoulder and upper arm. Her skin was cool to touch.

"That tickles."

He smiled as she shifted closer and buried her face in his shoulder, laying her hand on his stomach. He felt himself stir. Maybe there was time, although the day was growing brighter with each breath he took.

"It is light already. As much as I would like to stay right here, we have to rise."

"Hmm, yes, some of us seem to have done so already." Her hand moved lower and he groaned. Her breath came hot in his ear, further inflaming him. Deftly she swung over his hips and settled on him. He sat up as she moved, drawing him out in waves. He gripped her around her shoulder and kissed her throat as she tossed her head back. Their motion was liquid smooth and flowed together in an ancient rhythm until Ilimic bucked and shook with her climax. Her eyes were like liquid pools as she stared into Caros' own. He let himself go and was lost in moments of bliss, deep within her. He flopped onto his back and she kissed him lingeringly, still holding him within her.

"My victor." She whispered as at last she lifted her honeyed lips from his.

A loud bump shook the wall beside their bed. From the room next to theirs another thud sounded. Curses followed and a moment later Neugen hollered out the window at the screeching seagull. "Wait there you little bastard, I am coming to roast your drumsticks you winged rat!"

Ilimic stifled a giggle. "At least it was not us that woke him."

"Hmm, seems we are not the only ones late to wake. Now I need breakfast. Preferably not gull."

They dressed hurriedly and left the room quietly, leaving Neugen still thumping and mumbling in his. Ilimic darted down the stairs and out the back gate as Caros ambled to the well and sluiced cold water into the trough. He would have preferred another hot bath, but this would do. The sky was pale blue and the sun about to lift over the flat horizon that was the Inland Sea. More than just roosters and gulls were stirring now. Caros could smell cook fires burning and hear pots been clanged about in the cantina's kitchens. A baby wailed from a nearby home. Many people lived outside the walls of the city. The less fortunate for one, but also traders and workers who had grown used to the years of peace that endured on the coast. The Bastetani had learned that trading with the foreign merchants brought many rewards including peace.

Freshly washed and clothed, Caros entered the inn. Its thick adobe walls and tiny, rectangular ground floor windows ensured it was gloomy in the passage, but the kitchen was another matter. A large fire crackled in the spit hearth. An iron cauldron hung above it, bubbling with thick porridge. A large, round clay oven held an eye of glowing embers from which a boy was drawing out freshly baked bread. Caros was surprised at all the activity, but on consideration it made sense. Sailors and merchants, guardsmen and traders, they would all want a full belly to start the day on.

Marc was waiting in the front hall. He lifted his eyebrows when he saw Caros' swollen jaw. "I was going to ask if you rested well, but it looks like you had some fun first."

Caros prodded the swelling gingerly. "Fun. Yes, come to think of it, it was fun."

"Did you ask her then?"

Caros smiled. "I did. I am glad to say she accepted."

"Ah. Good then. Her father and I were friendly and on occasion dabbled in some trade or other. He was lost at sea when she was a babe and her mother, my cousin, died of the cough. She is a daughter to me that one, so I am glad she has chosen you, Caros." The big man had a misty look in his eye as he enfolded Caros in an embrace.

"She wants to travel with me to Orze. She is keen to meet the villagers and see her new home."

Marc frowned. "It is dangerous on the roads these days. The only swords will be those of yourself and Neugen."

"I thought about that too, but it is just three days to Orze and we will be riding fast."

Marc did not look convinced, but nodded his assent. "Talking of swords, one seems to be markedly absent considering first light has come, gone and almost returned? I recall something about you leaving early?"

Neugen stomped into the hall at that moment. "What? Miss all the food? That would be wrong. It is a desolate waste out there beyond the walls. We almost starved getting here, just ask Caros." He tossed his pack onto the packed clay floor beside the bench, swung a leg over it and sat heavily.

"Alugra was more cunning than I realized. He let you come along with me to save himself the food of three men."

"Yup. And how long have you been up and yet there is not a morsel on the table?" He shook his head in mock regret. "Caros, Caros, Caros. Fortunately, I have instructed the kitchens to send food to follow swiftly!"

"What took you so long to come down anyway? We heard you yelling at the gull before we were even out of bed." He cursed himself as he closed his mouth.

"Hmm, did you make friends with that mean Turdetani bastard after I left? Oh, no! It was that sailor. He even left a mark of affection there on your jaw."

Marc laughed and Caros glared at him. "Do not laugh, it only encourages him!"

Their horses were waiting outside when they left the inn. Three of the horses carried packs only. Ilimic was sitting a grey mare and talking with the stable boy as he tied on the packs he had collected from Caros and Neugen while they breakfasted. Caros gave her a broad smile that she interpreted quickly.

"Morning, Uncle Marc. Thank you!"

Marc waved her thanks aside. "No need to thank me, girl."

Ilimic sidled her mare up alongside Marc and gave him a peck on the cheek. The big man smiled happily. Caros knew that beneath the rugged, bear-like exterior, Marc was a gentle man who cherished his family. A fleeting knot of pain and longing for his dead kin rose in Caros' chest as he swung up onto his horse and led the party off with a farewell wave.

The road to Orze ran due north into the interior. The land outside Baria was well tended with many villages within a single day's ride of the gates. They passed farmers heading into town with carts and wagons loaded with the first spring produce; fresh greens, flax, hides and wares crafted over winter. Others had wicker cages filled with cackling geese. Young boys drove herds of cattle and sheep for slaughter. All going to the market in Baria, which not only serviced the needs of the townspeople there, but also of the galleys putting into the harbor, hungry for fresh foods. This was Bastetani land and the people of the Bastetani had grown stronger with the ever-increasing trade that came to their coast. In generations past, villages here would have only traded surplus goods between one another and the occasional adventurous Greek or Phoenician galley. They had relied entirely on their crops and herds for survival. Lean times would have seen their warriors travel to the lands of neighbouring tribes to sack their villages. In some instances, even raiding distant Bastetani villages; their own people. This was why settlements were built on top of hills with earthen or wooden walls encircling them.

The sun climbed along with the temperature as they rode. The traffic they had met around the outskirts of Baria dwindled and died. The villagers were hard at work in the fields, preparing for the summer and autumn ahead. They rode until after noon, making good time. Caros had spent a lot of the time riding beside Ilimic, chattering about his life and learning about her. It was exactly what he needed to help him relax and enjoy the day. Her laughter often tinkled merrily down the road as he jested with her. Caros found himself staring at her at times as she looked at distant mountains or the sea that lay blurry behind them. Every little thing about her mesmerized him, from the little silver jewel drops of perspiration along her brow to the tantalizing curve of her buttocks on her mount. She knew how to ride, and it was plain that she loved the horses. She often leaned forward to stroke her mount's neck, sighing contentedly as she did.

Caros sensed she was becoming uncomfortable on her mount. They had been on the road a long while and were already deep into the hills. He decided they should stop soon to rest and stretch their legs. They had been riding all morning and while he was used to long hours on horseback, neither of the others were. If his recollection was accurate, there was a pleasant village not far ahead. It was a place his father had occasionally rested at when making the same journey. His memory was not wrong as they soon began passing cultivated fields and orchards, a sure sign of a community nearby. Neugen was grumbling that they should stop and eat. The road took them through a cutting made by a stream, which they crossed by way of a precarious wooden bridge, which swayed alarmingly under their mounts. Just beyond the stream they rounded a bend to see the village on the hillside before them. A thick adobe wall with the usual wooden palisade bristling along the top, encircled the village. Smoke rose lazily from cook fires and the village forge.

It was as Caros remembered and he smiled at Ilimic. "We can rest here until the worst of the day's heat passes."

"Great! I need to stretch. I did not realize how sore you could get riding like this."

"You get used to it. Unfortunately, it takes longer than a couple of days, so you should expect to be even more uncomfortable tomorrow."

Neugen lifted his head and took a long breath. "Hmm, I smell lunch!"

Ilimic laughed and Caros shook his head with a wry smile. They easily found the cantina where they all dismounted somewhat stiffly. A couple of boys, brothers judging from their looks, came trotting up.

"For a bronze we will water the horses for you." One of the boys addressed Caros, who was stretching his legs.

He smiled at the boys. "A bronze it is, but I will come along as I need to walk this stiffness off." He plucked a bonze coin from a hidden purse and flicked it expertly into the air. It winked in the sun for a moment before a little hand snatched it from sight. Caros laughed. "Good reflexes lad, now we should water the horses." The boys were a blur of energy as they took the reins from the riders and with clicks and whistles, led them off with Caros following.

Ilimic called after them. "We will have some ale and bread for you when you return!"

Three large cedar trees grew in front of the cantina and the ground at their feet was packed hard by years of use. Rough-hewn benches and wooden tables were set out in the shade of the trees. They made for an ideal place to rest when the worst of the day's heat lay oppressively over the village. The innkeeper brought them cool ale to drink as they sat gratefully at one of the tables, enjoying the slightest of breezes as it visited the shade below the trees. Another party of four travelers had arrived before them and had eaten already. They were four men and had the look of traders or farmers who were making a decent living. Two of them slept below a tree while a third sat on the ground and whittled a lump of wood. The fourth man smiled at them and waved a good afternoon from the bench he sat on. They waved back politely.

The cool ale refreshed Caros as he sipped. Ilimic sat beside him, her knee against his thigh. Neugen smiled happily when the innkeeper arrived with olives, honey and fresh bread. He immediately tore a piece off the loaf and set to loading it with the chunky white cheese.

Passing the honey to Ilimic, he nodded. "We made good time this morning. We can do a fair bit before dark, although I fear you will feel worse by this evening." He squeezed her hand. "I think we will be able to get to Flat Cave before nightfall." He referred to a place beside a good stream commonly used by travelers on this road. There was no inn or any kind of dwelling, but a shallow cave in the side of the cliff face, overlooking the stream.

After eating, Caros unfurled his cloak at the base of one of the trees. It was still too hot to ride, so they would sleep in the dappled shade until the heat lessened. Neugen was already snoring, flat on his back beside the table he had eaten at. Ilimic stretched out on the cloak. Caros stood looking around and wondered if he should sleep too. The innkeeper was in a basket chair; feet out before him and fast asleep, as were the other travelers. Children laughed gaily somewhere in the village and a dove cooed softly in the branches above them. It was beyond peaceful. He looked down at Ilimic and found she was looking up at him tenderly. His breath caught at those beautiful eyes shining up at him. He smiled gently and she patted the space beside her and unbuckled his belt and dropped it along with the sheathed falcata before settling down beside his woman.

Caros slept lightly, every time he dipped into sleep, visions of the days past appeared. Like an unseen river of thought, flowing just below his conscience, the visions threatened to drag him into their world. Just as they became too vivid, he would pull hurriedly away and surface to feel Ilimic's arm resting lightly on his own, her breath sweet on his cheek. After a time, he would doze again only for the visions to reappear. Finally, after jerking awake a fourth time to avoid the dreams, he had had enough. Ilimic slept soundly, as did the others. The innkeeper was nowhere to be seen. Caros sensed that it was nearly time to depart. The breeze was stronger and the heat of the day had dissipated a little. He rose without disturbing Ilimic and buckled on his falcata to head for the village well and draw a pail of cool water. He did not bother using the stone trough. Instead, he sluiced the water, straight from the wooden pail, over his head and face. The water refreshed him and he drew another to drink. A clatter of hooves and a bark of laughter echoed from the village gates. Two strangers were riding up the street, geese dispersing with squawks from before them. The men were warriors, armed with spears, short swords and shields. They wore leather armor over linen and wool tunics and their iron helmets hung beside their shields at their knees. The men stopped talking when they saw Caros and glared at him. He gave them a friendly nod as they passed, but neither man responded, unless hawking and spitting out the side of the mouth could be considered such. Too many men with sharp iron and little honor were about these days. The pair rounded the corner, clearly heading for the inn. Caros glanced back down the road they had come up. It was empty. He felt his gut tighten with tension and again he wondered about bringing Ilimic with them. He returned to the others to find them awake. Neugen was fussing beside the horses, checking the packs were well secured. Caros smiled at Ilimic who was seated at the table, her cheeks blushed from sleep. She looked lovely, even as she yawned the afternoon sleep away.

"Rest well?"

"Hmm. My butt hurts." She groaned and stretched.

"Did you see two horsemen?"

Ilimic shook her head, but Neugen nodded. "Woke me up, the bastards."

"The water in the well behind the cantina is good. Why not freshen up and then we can be on our way?"

Caros turned as one of the four travelers; the one who had greeted them, came across. His three companions were readying their mounts.

"Greetings. We are from near Tagilit."

Caros eyed the man. Tall, gangly with big, calloused hands. His tunic was good quality flax and someone had done a good job of dying the linen. Yes, a wealthy farmer. He had the look of someone who worked hard outdoors. A good farmer could become wealthy these days with markets always hungry for fresh produce. Caros greeted him coolly.

"We are travelling to Baria and were hoping you would ride with us if you are going that way?"

Caros shook his head. "Thank you, we came from there and are heading in the opposite direction."

The man looked glum for a heartbeat. "Ah well, I thought I might ask. Is the road good to Baria? I do not mind admitting that we are a little nervous after our trip here."

Caros frowned. "Yes, the road is good. You should be able to reach Baria before nightfall. What do you mean you are nervous after your trip?"

"I do not wish to alarm you my friend, but the road from Tagilit is not as safe as you would hope." He looked back at his companions who were waiting with their horses. "We are just farmers so have little of value, but still we were set upon twice by armed men. The first time they stopped us and demanded all our goods and horses." The farmer shook his head sheepishly. "Fortunately, they were on foot and we were able to outrun them. I think they would have killed us if we had not run."

"This is Bastetani land. Who were these men?" Caros had a deep hatred for the type of outcasts that preyed on travelers.

The farmer shrugged. "I do not think so. The second time we did not let them get close enough to hear what tongue they spoke. We were lucky enough to see them before they saw us, especially as they were mounted. They did chase us for half a day, but we escaped into the hills until we could rejoin the road further south."

Caros was desperately worried at this news. How could the road be this dangerous? He had travelled on it many times with his father and alone and had never encountered bandits.

"I see I have caused you much concern. I apologize my friend, but that is why I asked if you were going to Baria."

"No need to apologize. It is probably the best thing you could have done for us. Without your warning, we may have blundered right into these men and we are only three."

"I fear the trip back home once our business in Baria is done. The gods have favored us these last few seasons, but we cannot afford to hire swordsmen."

Caros could see the worry in the man's eyes. These men were not warriors, they were armed and healthy, yet they looked frightened.

"How many men in each of these bands?"

"Maybe ten or so on foot. The horsemen were fewer. I counted six."

Small groups, but dangerous if they took you unawares. This was bad news and Caros would ask Neugen to speak to Alugra about the matter. This was a peaceful land and such banditry on high roads would break down that peace quickly.

"Thank you for the warning and we will be extra vigilant for it. What business do you have in Baria?"

"We had heard that prices for raw and woven flax were good there. We will have a large crop this autumn, the gods willing, and are sounding out possible buyers."

That made sense to Caros. Flax crops produced the fibers woven to make linen and linens of all qualities were much in demand.

"Maybe this meeting was good fortune for both of us. I may be interested in becoming a buyer myself."

Arckat's face showed his astonishment. "You? That is fortunate. I had taken you for a warrior perhaps, not a merchant."

Caros laughed. "Yes, I own a warehouse in Baria and another in Malaka and have good connections with Greek and Carthaginian buyers, even some Gyptos."

"Then you will truly consider buying from us?"

"Certainly. I shall be pleased to inspect the bales and make an offer. If not I, then my colleague, Marc. Look him up when you reach Baria and mention me to him." They concluded arrangements to meet again in late autumn, once the flax had been harvested, before parting, happy at their chance encounter.

Neugen and Ilimic returned from the well looking wide awake and ready to travel. Caros was deeply concerned about the dangers of travelling the road north and told them of the news the farmer had given him.

Neugen frowned at him. "A few hill warriors will not stop us, Caros. I am going to Tagilit alone if necessary."

"Neugen, it is not whether we continue or not. It is how we go."

Ilimic and Neugen simultaneously asked, "How?"

"You are right, Neugen, I am not going to allow outcasts to stop us, but I am not going to walk into an ambush either. We need to play this carefully."

Neugen caught on. "Oh, that is good. I was worried you were going to go back to Baria." He smiled sheepishly.

Ilimic asked the obvious question. "What do you plan to do, or how rather?"

"We know one group is mounted and number six riders and those on foot are ten spears strong. Either way, we are outnumbered. We must see them before they see us, so Neugen and I will take turns riding out front. If we spot them first, we can do as the farmers did and skirt them."

Neugen looked skeptical. "They will have lookouts and this is hilly country. They will see our dust long before we see them, if we ever do."

Caros smiled grimly. Neugen was right; the inevitable dust might betray them. "Then we must ride fast or ride by night." There was silence at this. No one liked riding the hill roads by night, not even warriors.

Neugen shrugged and patted his falcata. "We have blades and horses. Two mounts each. I say we ride hard and change mounts often to keep them fresh." It was a good suggestion.

"We do that then. Flat Cave or further by nightfall and then we rise early and start out before sunrise again tomorrow."

Neugen laughed. "Sure, before sunrise, just like this morning!"

Caros punched his shoulder. "We were waiting on you as I recall."

"Watch it, that is my spear arm, I may need to be using that again soon."

Caros helped Ilimic onto her horse although she could cope on her own. "We will be fine." He reassured her. "It will be a tough ride, but I will be beside you all the way."

She settled onto the mount with a wince. "That will be nice and with my victorious warrior beside me, I will be fine." She gave him her most wicked smile; the one that sent arrows of excitement of a different kind through his body. "I cannot say the same for my behind or thighs. I may need a rubbing down after this ride."

Caros grinned. "Every owner of a good filly knows how important that is. I will not forget." He slapped her horse's rump. "Off we go now."

She laughed gaily as the horse started off and then groaned. "Oh gods, that is sore."

They spent the afternoon keeping up a good pace along the ever-climbing road. They passed two other people, a young boy herding a flock of goats to a grassy hillside and a surly blacksmith on the way back from a funeral. On both occasions, Caros stopped to ask of the road ahead. The shepherd boy knew nothing of bandits and was clearly terrified at the prospect. He had shooed his family's few goats off the road the moment Caros rode away and in the blink of an eye had disappeared, goats and all. A useful quality, Caros mused wryly. He regretted scaring the boy. The blacksmith had heard nothing of bandits either. Judging from the wafts of odor exuding from the man's skin, he had consumed flagons of ale at the funeral the previous day and Caros was surprised he could remember he had been to a funeral at all.

The sun sank beyond the western mountain ranges. They were as weary a trio that had ever camped at Flat Cave. Caros had hoped they would be far past the well-known rest spot, but Ilimic was not used to riding and even Neugen was struggling by the time they reached it. Reluctantly he led them off the road to a green patch beside the stream that flowed from the mountains. They were all coated in dust from the road, a fine grey powder that reached into every fold of cloth and skin. The cold waters of the mountain made short work of washing away this film, but left them shivering in the early evening cool. Caros was tempted to light a fire, but on consideration decided that darkness served them best.

Neugen took first watch and Caros was glad to have Ilimic curl up in his arms. There would be no mischief though for she winced in pain as she lay beside him. He fell asleep breathing in her rich scent, touched with a lingering smell of their dusty ride. Caros woke in the dead hours to take the final watch and he uncurled Ilimic's arms from his chest gently before rising.

"All quiet then I take it?" He asked quietly.

"Nothing other than owls and mice moving."

Neugen fell swiftly asleep, leaving Caros to watch over their sleeping forms in the faint glow of the starlight.

Caros woke them before first light with cheese and bread. A skin of ale served to wash their breakfast down and add some warmth to their bellies. The men packed the horses while Ilimic washed. When all were ready and Caros and Neugen had donned their armor, they took to the road again. The sun had not risen yet, but the birds were wide-awake and singing through the hills. It would be a long morning, but by the time it was too hot to ride they would have broken the back of the trip to Orze.

Caros spent the better part of the morning ahead of the other two, spying out the road ahead for signs of bandits. He wore his shield on his left arm rather than have it dangle as usual at his knee. He had three javelins quivered on his back and held one more in his throwing hand. Neugen, riding beside Ilimic, was similarly prepared and alert. By noon, the sun had so heated the road that Caros often thought he saw figures in the distance that were only waves of heat dissipating into the already warm air. Neugen rode up not long after the sun had passed its zenith.

"We are going to have to rest, Caros." He shifted in pain on his mount. "My ass is on fire, but it is Ilimic who is struggling."

Caros regretted the harsh pace he had set and the discomfort it had caused them. He reasoned it was better to suffer a few travel sores than to fall prey to bandits on this lonely stretch of road. He vowed to get Alugra to bring warriors down the road to sweep the bandits away.

"Sure, there is a cutting not far ahead with good water. We will rest up there." He sent Neugen back to let Ilimic know they could rest soon.

The cutting was a steep-sided ravine torn into the hillside by countless floods. The stream that tumbled along the rocky bottom was nothing like the raging waters that stormed down the ravine after heavy rains in the high hills. They all climbed stiffly from their horses and while Ilimic lay in the shade of a strawberry tree, Caros and Neugen changed the reins to the fresher horses as they had planned. When that was done Caros lopped from rock to rock down to the stream below and filled their water skins with fresh, cold water. He removed his helmet and breastplate so that he could wash. At this pace they would be at Orze before this time on the morrow. He had secretly hoped they would be there this evening, but Ilimic was already too sore to ride any harder. At least they would only have to spend one more night on the road, although he was not sure where they would camp. He was struggling to judge where they might find themselves on the road come sunset. They would need to find water for the horses and it would be another night without warm food. Unfortunately, there was no village between here and Orze where they could rest in comfort and security.

He finished washing and was reaching for his armor when he noticed the footprint. There was little mud on the rocky streambed due to the fast-flowing water, but in the lee of a boulder was a little sliver of washed sand, just large enough to accommodate a single footprint. Neugen was the tracker and would possibly be able to tell more, but it looked fresh enough to Caros. Suddenly alert, he quickly donned his armor and grabbed the water skins. Climbing out of the arroyo, he strode over to Ilimic, eyes tracing the hillside and foliage around them.

"Here we go. Get some of this inside you before you sleep." He offered the skins to Ilimic who looked done in. "Neugen come have a look here." He scanned the hillside above them and then the road in both directions.

Neugen grimaced and rose stiffly. "What do you see?"

"Not here, in the ravine. I spotted a footprint."

"Ha. You have learned. I make a great teacher if I say so myself."

They returned to the ravine and the little patch of sand. Neugen gestured to Caros to stay back and hopped to the boulder sheltering the sand. He crouched there briefly, examining the footprint and then started to scan the rocks and streambed. His silence frustrated Caros.

"What do you see?"

"A footprint. A man's and freshly set."

"Well?"

"I see just one set of tracks."

"One man?" Caros felt relief.

"The bad news is he is a warrior."

"What?"

"It is as I say. Some warriors have taken to studding the soles of their sandals and boots. It is said that they stand firmer when swinging a shield and sword, walk hills better and roads faster." He shrugged. "I do not know about all that, but it is what some do and the owner of this footprint has these studs."

"Still, he is only one man."

"One pair of feet sent to fetch water for five others?"

"Curses. Right, we get Ilimic mounted and move on." Caros felt awful urging Ilimic on at such a pace and her face fell when he broke the news to her.

"It was just one man though. Surely even if he is a hill-warrior, he would not attack us?" Ilimic sat up, her eyes imploring him. "Can we at least rest for a little while longer? Honestly, the skin on my legs is close to breaking." She pleaded. Caros wavered and Neugen spoke instead.

"We need to put some distance between us and this stream. Just in case this fellow has companions up in the hills here."

Caros stared up at the hills. Nothing moved beyond a vulture floating high above them in the thermals.

"Neugen is right. It makes no sense to risk remaining here. In any case, we would get no rest if we stayed here now for worrying." Mounting up, Caros sensed even his mare was reluctant to continue so soon after stopping and in the worst of the day's heat. He steeled himself and led them back onto the road. They did not go fast or much further. The road twisted and turned along the hillside and after passing through two wide turns and leaving the arroyo two hills behind, he spotted a likely looking shady spot to rest up. There was even a stream here, although the water barely trickled between the sun-warmed rocks along its bed. At least the horses could reach the water here and they would not have to haul it to them.

"Neugen, before we dismount, have a look around and see if you can spy any tracks." Caros thought this would be better than dismounting only to have to bolt a second time. Neugen tracked from left to right on foot along the stream and just beyond and then waved the all clear. Ilimic heaved a sigh of relief. Caros had to help her off the horse as her legs cramped.

"I am sorry. I promise I will take care of you once we are at my home."

"It is not your fault I have cheeks as soft as a babe's." She smiled gamely at him. He kissed her deeply, tasting the sweetness of her mouth. "Hmmm. That was good. Now go away, I need to sleep and I am hot and sweaty."

He feigned a look of hurt. "I thought I was your victorious warrior?"

"You have a lot to learn about me, for instance, I do not like being hot and sweaty."

"You win." He laughed. "I will keep a watch over you, sleep now." She mouthed a kiss at him and shut her eyes. Caros smiled down protectively at the sleeping woman. Not long now and you will be safe he promised her silently. He turned away with a heavy sigh. Neugen had hobbled the horses and was casting about on the near side of the stream. Caros made his way through the scrub.

"See anything?"

Neugen shrugged. "To many tracks. Not surprising as we are right beside the road. Nothing that should worry us though."

"Good. Go get some food and take a rest while I keep watch."

"You sure? You have been pushing as hard as us."

"What? You volunteering?"

"Haha, nope, just being polite." Neugen laughed and slapped Caros as he limped back to the shade of the trees.

Caros climbed the slope of the hill. It was hard work in the heat. When he reached out to catch his balance, the rock he leaned on burned hot against his skin. He stopped halfway to the summit and looking south, watched the road they had travelled for any sign of movement. Nothing moved nor were there any tell-tale plumes of dust. To the north it was equally still. No travelers, no bandits, no warriors. The road was deserted as far as he could tell. He made his way to the scant shade of an ancient oak where he sat and removed his helmet. Sweat dripped from his sodden hair and he wiped the salty liquid from his eyes. He squinted across the landscape, the bleak hillsides that hid the occasional verdant valleys.

He wondered what was happening back in Orze. Had the villagers begun rebuilding or had they moved to the hill fort? A small part of him felt guilty for leaving the village just as it reeled from the ravage and chaos of the raiders, but he knew what he had done was the right thing. There were things a man had to do at times and what he had chosen to do was the right path. That they had managed to recover most of the herds and slay some of the raiders was incidental. Rebuilding and mourning had their own season.

He hoped Ilimic would find life in Orze pleasant. Surely she would come to love the natural beauty of the valley and the peaceful nature of the villagers there? Once the homestead was rebuilt, they would build a family and bring joy to the shadows beneath the oak and cedar of the valley. He caught himself dozing and jerked awake. He had not brought any water. He must have some he knew, or he would be sick. He had once felt the sun sickness when as a boy, he and Ximo had gone searching for eagle's eggs in their high fastness. The wind had blown cool across their brows all day, but they had not thought to take water and by afternoon were parched. That evening Caros could not see from the pain in his fevered head and for three days his mother had had to nurse him as he shivered and sweated. Somehow Ximo had not become ill. He shook his head at the memory. They had never found the eagle's nests either. He scrambled back down the slope and crossed the road to the shady spot in which Ilimic and Neugen lay.

Neugen opened an eye and closed it again. "Rest, Caros. It is quiet on the road. Not even a hill warrior would be idiot enough to travel in this heat. It is early summer and already so hot."

Caros slaked his thirst and splashed some water over his head. He reckoned Neugen was right. The horses would signal if anybody approached. He flopped down on the thin grass; Ilimic lay sprawled on his cloak and he did not want to disturb her. For once he fell into a dreamless sleep.

He felt a hand on his shoulder shaking him. He wondered why somebody was disturbing him, could they not leave him to sleep? Asleep! He should not be asleep! He woke frantically, rising and groping for his falcata.

"Caros! Time to move on. Whoa, you were fast asleep there!"

His eyes focused on Neugen's face. He looked about and noticed the length of the shadows. The bright road that he last saw now lay swathed in the shadows of the hills.

"Gods, I slept too long. Look how late it is!"

"You needed it. We can still make a fair distance before last light." Neugen smiled again and patted him on the shoulder. Caros was not placated and cursed himself silently. He should have been pressing them to speed along, not lie sleeping like an old hound in the sun. He grabbed his helmet from the grass and rose, dusting himself off. Donning the helmet quickly, he did not bother tying the strap; instead he slung the javelin quiver across his shoulders and stalked over to the stream.

Ilimic turned at his approach. "Nearly done here sleepy one." She said brightly as she filled the skins.

"There is plenty of water, come we must get going." He snapped.

"Why look who woke all grumpy!" She scooped the waterskin out of the stream and tossed it to him without bothering to cork it. He snatched it from the air and water spurted from the spout, splashing him. He caught the curse at his teeth. Ilimic was staring at him, eyes burning with anger. By the gods, she looked beautiful. The lowering sun lit sparks in her hair and turned her skin soft and golden.

"Sorry. I did not mean to snap. I just feel bad about sleeping away good daylight."

The anger faded from Ilimic's eyes and her face softened. "Do not be so hard on yourself. You needed the rest and you have been through so much." She went to him and hugged him tightly to her bosom. He wrapped his arms about her and they swayed gently in the afternoon sun.

After a moment, he pulled away. "Thank you. You are so beautiful and kind, but now we must set that bruised rump of yours on a mount I am afraid."

Caros judged they had enough daylight left to take them far enough that they could still make Orze by early afternoon the following day. He rode ahead, setting the pace, the worry in his chest causing him to ride fast. He felt bad at pushing them so, but he could not shake the disquiet he felt. This feeling had only grown since he had seen the footprint at the arroyo.

Cresting a rise, he surveyed the road ahead. He had expected to see more travelers since leaving the village yesterday afternoon. He reined in the mare he had swapped to for the afternoon leg of the journey. He had gotten too far ahead of Neugen and Ilimic, so paused at the crest in the road, eyeing the road to the north and south. He rubbed his eyes clear of sweat and squinted at wisps of smoke, only it was not smoke, but dust. A plume swirled above the road to the south, caught in the afternoon sun as it grew steadily closer. His heartbeat drummed and his palms grew clammy. Those were horsemen coming north. When Neugen and Ilimic caught up, they could tell at once he was tense and he immediately told them why.

"Looks like we finally have company." He pointed back the way they had just come. From the crest of the rise they had a good view of the dust eddying into the air in the distance, but due to the hilly terrain, they could not yet see the riders.

"Seems they are making good time. Better than us. I think they will be with us before nightfall." Neugen estimated.

"No reason we need to wait for them. They are probably regular travelers like us."

"Maybe even the farmers returning."

Caros did not care for the approaching company. The ominously empty road now seemed a much better option than one with approaching riders.

"Come on then, I will ride out front." He flashed an encouraging grin at Ilimic and began to urge his mount on.

"Hang on. I will take the point; I am tired of eating all your dust and besides you ride too far ahead." Neugen called.

Caros reined in. He could do with riding beside Ilimic and cheering her up or the other way around. He still felt bad at snapping at her. He turned his mount and let Neugen pass. Thump! He was looking at Ilimic when he heard the impact followed by a strangled cry and curse. Ilimic's eyes widened in horror and he spun around to see Neugen staring at a javelin thrumming in his shield.

Ilimic gave voice to a piercing wail that snapped through Caros like lightning. He spun around again and a spear struck his shield. The hillside above suddenly seemed filled with hoarse cries and movement. Neugen was yelling and Caros realized they had to flee. He shouted to Ilimic who stared, paralyzed with fear, at the warriors leaping towards her.

"Ride, Ilimic! Ride!" He brought his javelin down hard on her horse's rump, sending it plunging ahead. A spear passed a hand's breadth from his head and a packhorse screamed behind him. The beast had taken the point meant for him. Charging through the brush towards him were their attackers. Their faces twisted in battle fury as they hurtled down the hill. Caros leapt his mount forward, eyeing the foremost warrior, a lean man wearing a conical iron helmet and leather armor. He launched his javelin, which whipped through the air to bite deep into the man's throat. The impact lifted the warrior off his feet, throwing him onto his back in the brush. The attackers threw their own javelins. They were so close that he caught only the briefest flicker of sun on their wicked barbs as they flew at him. He blocked two simultaneously with his shield, the force rocking him onto his horse's rump. The third flashed over his head. They did not want to hit the mount and were aiming at a higher mark. It would make no difference in a moment as they were just strides away from him.

He drew another javelin from the quiver on his back while checking his companions. Neugen was a short distance away and yelling at him. Ilimic had flown to safety down the road, clinging in terror to her mount as it raced away. The javelin balanced expertly over his hand and he hurled it, not needing to line up his target as the attackers were so close. As it left his hand, he drew his falcata and spun his horse to follow after Ilimic. His javelin had torn through the leather vest of a bandit who reeled, teeth gritted in pain. Clear of the sheath, he slashed his blade down, only to have it deflect off the shield of an attacker who sprang at him. A javelin flashed past him and he heard a snarl of pain from behind. Neugen had struck. Caros cleared the attackers and passed Neugen who had drawn his sword, his javelins spent. His friend spun his horse and urged it into a gallop beside him. Caros leaned low, his cheek beside the bobbing neck of his mount. He twisted his left arm up around his back. A javelin in the kidney would be just the parting gift he would prefer to avoid. Down the road they bolted, as fast as their mounts could run. Behind them they left the packhorse on its side, thrashing and blowing blood from its nostrils. The bandits disappeared in a wake of dust, only their shouted curses chasing after them.

The trio fled as fast as they could, pain and bruises forgotten. Beside them, their remounts kept pace and a smile crossed Caros' face when his mare drew close beside the mount he rode. They crossed the ford of a river and splashed to a breathless halt. They had left the scene of the ambush far behind in their dash. The ford was only hock deep on the horses and the water flowed sedately. On the far side, they reined in, riders panting and horses lathered. They all looked like specters, covered as they were in fine, grey dust from head to hoof.

"We have outdistanced them." Neugen frowned, staring back over the water.

Ilimic sobbed in shock, tears tracking through the dust on her cheeks, leaving her skin looking pale in their wake. She slid off the mount and, in a heartbeat, Caros was beside her on the ground where she huddled sobbing. He wrapped her in his arms, his vision blurred by sweat and anger. How close they had come to taking her. He rocked together with her while gently murmuring.

Neugen hobbled the horses and then drew the last two javelins from a spare quiver. From where he sheltered Ilimic in his arms, he watched him ride back across the ford.

"Where are you going? Do not go after them."

"I am not. I want to be sure they are not coming after us on horses."

The words terrified Ilimic. He could feel her gasp and shudder in his arms.

"I am so sorry my love. I could not imagine they were hiding there." He stroked her hair, hating the dust for hiding its beauty. "You must be strong. We cannot stay here. We must ride on and reach the village." She sniffed and nodded but remained huddled. "I was a fool. We should have turned back when the farmers warned us." He cursed himself. At his words, Ilimic raised a tear-filled face to him, a spark growing in her eye, animating her.

"Do not blame yourself! You fought them off and saved us."

"Yes, but now you must ride again." He rose with her in his arms. "You will need to lead the spare mounts."

"Where are you going?" She clutched his arm.

"To fetch Neugen back so we can follow. Go on, mount up and start ahead. It will be safe that way and we will be back in a moment." Caros saw Ilimic off, leading the two remaining packhorses. She kept glancing back uncertainly as though he might be going back to attack the bandits. He might have as well, but the relief he felt was draining him and he did not want to leave Ilimic now. He crossed after Neugen and rode out of the ford to the lip of the shallow depression down which the river flowed. Neugen was just over the lip; watching the road beyond.

"See anything?"

The man hawked and spat into the road. "Nothing, thank the gods. That was a total cock-up back there!"

Caros winced. He had been on point and the bandits had attacked their party right where he had sat. He should have seen them.

"It was. They chose that place well and I was not paying attention." He had been watching the oncoming dust from the riders behind them.

Neugen glanced at him. "You were watching the distant riders. They will ride right into the bastards, the poor sods."

"I am thinking they may be in with the hill warriors."

Neugen hissed, startled at the thought. "How so?"

"The farmers warned us that they encountered two groups. One on foot and one mounted. We have seen no other travelers, so where are the horsemen they spoke of?"

Neugen hawked and spat. "This is a pig's mess. If you are right, we had best keep moving." They turned their horses as one and headed north, quickly catching up with Ilimic who wore an anxious look.

"Are they following, Caros?"

He shook his head firmly, determined not to concern her with his worries. "Not that we could tell. All the same, I think it is best that we ride as far as we can through the night. The sooner we are in Orze, the better."

Neugen agreed and Ilimic nodded her head heavily. They rode on all afternoon with Caros occasionally leaning over to stroke Ilimic's shoulder or cheek. At each rise, Neugen would hang back to check the road behind and all afternoon it remained clear of dust. Evening fell and they stopped briefly to pull some fare from the packs and eat before riding on. A crescent moon rose and with it a bright entourage of stars filled the void above them. The pale light lit their way eerily on the road. The hills around them crouched silent and watchful as they glanced fearfully about. Finally, they could go no further. The moon had slipped across the night sky and was sinking in the west when Ilimic almost slipped from the mount in exhaustion.

Caros called to Neugen who was ranging ahead. Together they hobbled the horses right there on the road and set down their cloaks to sleep upon. Ilimic protested that she could still ride, but in truth she could not. Caros insisted she sleep and Neugen too. He would wake them before dawn and by noon, they would be safe in Orze.

"You need to sleep too, Caros. Wake me soon and I will take the last watch."

"Thanks." He had no intention of waking Neugen. He was tired yes, but he doubted he would sleep.

They came before dawn. He was pacing beside the horses, listening to the night sounds dwindling and the birds of the day beginning to stir. His mare whinnied and stamped a foreleg. He looked her way, thinking of quietening her when he went cold with dread, realizing she had sensed strangers. He swiftly drew his falcata and backed towards his sleeping companions. Kneeling, he roused Neugen, shaking him roughly and placing his palm over the man's mouth when he woke with a start.

"They have come." He hissed.

Neugen's eyes widened and he quickly rose and drew his falcata, the blade glinting in the feeble light of the last stars.

"What do we do?"

"Run. Untie the horses and I will wake Ilimic. We need to flee as fast as we can." Neugen nodded his understanding. They had left the horses with packs on in case of just such a situation. Caros quickly untethered the horses, which were restlessly snorting and stamping. He signaled to Neugen who stood, pulling Ilimic along with him. Silently they darted to their horses and mounted. Caros leaped onto his mare and slammed his helmet onto his head. Digging his heels in, he gave a yell and led his two friends in a charge up the road.

Horses appeared out of the dark, carrying silent riders who slashed their blades at them. His mare was struck by one of the charging horses so violently that she was sent crashing onto her rump. Caros desperately clung on, urging her up. She complied and suddenly Neugen was yelling and iron struck iron. Ilimic screamed and Caros' heart lurched into his throat. He roared and savagely kicked his mare into a charge. A shadow figure swept at him on thundering hooves and he swung his falcata. His blow missed and his blade hissed harmlessly past the attacker. There was a confusion of dark shapes ahead and Ilimic screamed again. Frantic, he cursed, unable to tell where she was in the chaos.

He charged straight into the mass of riders, striking out left and right. A glancing blow to a rider drew a pained curse. The mass of horses broke and he made out Ilimic leaning away from a rider beside her. Caros charged at them and to his horror, saw the rider lift his sword and bring it down on Ilimic's back. A scream tore from her as the blade struck her across the shoulders and she slipped from her mount. Caros cried out in despair as he bore down on the rider. He jumped his mare over Ilimic, who lay curled on the road. As the horse touched down, he drove his falcata into Ilimic's attacker. His blade tore through leather and flesh before the mare's momentum carried him away. He turned the mare, intent on reaching Ilimic when a shadowy figure loomed beside him, dawn light reflected off a sword blade that slashed towards his face. He had no time to react and it struck his unfastened helmet, knocking it from his head. Bright colors filled his sight and a roar his ears. Shaking his head to clear his vision, he lifted his chin in time to see the blade swinging at him a second time. The blow whipped his head backwards and a pain like nothing he had ever known flared through his head. In agony, he flicked the reins and gave the mare her head. He had failed. He had failed Ilimic and his despair turned dark.

10

A beast chewed and clawed at Caros, its fangs grinding his skull, its saliva poisoning his blood. Darkness burned him like fire and he groaned, tried to fend it off, but lacked the power to do more than pant. It was as though Orko, the mountain god himself, was pounding on his head. His body began to slide and then he was falling. He landed roughly, blinding pain searing through his body as he rolled over rocks and brush.

Opening his eyes, he found he could see only from the left eye. He reached for the throbbing wound that seemed to bear a life of its own. Gingerly, he touched his scalp and his fingers found dried, sticky lumps of blood and dirt. He traced a gash that reached from his right brow to behind his ear. The injury was bad. His head was ringing and his stomach kept turning. He tried to rise, but slumped when a wave of dizziness and pain washed over him. His mare cropped at the sparse foliage nearby. There was no telling how far he had ridden or if Ilimic and Neugen had survived the attack to escape. He reached for his falcata and found the sheath empty. Shuddering, he could only imagine what Ilimic's fate was. He had been able to avenge his family, but now he was done. He had been a fool. He should have stayed with Gualam, taken up his offer and joined his riders. He would never have met Ilimic and she would be safe in Baria. He had caused her death and probably Neugen's too.

He balled his fists and tried to rise. He could not. Cursing, he tried again and got to his knees before retching. The motion caused the pain in his head to erupt with renewed fury before merciful darkness swallowed him.

When next he came to, he sensed a presence nearby. He opened his eyes slowly, afraid to waken the beast that brought such pain to his head. He struggled to focus and was forced to close his right eye to see with any clarity.

Neugen was sitting hunched under the same tree in whose shade Caros now lay. He appeared to be sleeping, but something was wrong. The shape of his body was somehow strange. He tried to speak, but only managed a rasping sound through lips like clay. He grunted instead and tried to clear his burning throat. Neugen stirred and slowly lifted his head. His face was gaunt and pale. Sweat hung from his nose and dripped from his brow. His bloodshot eyes were sunken, the skin around them dark. Neugen slowly reached for a waterskin and lifted it to Caros' lips. It was difficult to drink, but he managed to swallow a little while a good portion spilled over his chest. He did not mind; it helped quench the burn in his throat.

"Ilimic? Where is she?" He croaked, looking around in vain for her.

Neugen let the waterskin fall and slumped back. "No, my friend. I saw her struck from her horse." He faltered and a pained sob tore from his throat.

Tears tracked down Caros' cheeks and he groaned as the truth struck him. They had killed or captured her. He needed to find her. He had to save the woman he loved.

"At daybreak I saw blood and tracks, guessed it might be you." Neugen's voice was strained and had a whispering quality.

"You are injured? Badly?"

"Chest." Neugen pulled aside his cloak, revealing a broken shaft embedded in his upper chest. Caros shut his eyes tightly and whispered a prayer to Endovex, god of healing. His friend was dying, that was clear. That he had survived the injury this long was a wonder. Was this the end then? Here under a stunted cedar on a hill in the wilderness. A fool and a tracker. The thought brought a wry smile to his bloodied face. He may be a fool, but he did not have a javelin impaling him. He could still get them to Orze. They would have been there by midday today, with Ilimic. He just needed to make it to an outlying farm. He breathed deeply and steeled himself to overcome the pain and rise. It took him three attempts. Neugen muttered that he was being a fool. Angrily, he levered himself to his hands and knees, Neugen's face just a hand's breadth from his.

"Oh, I am a fool. I admit it. Too stupid to lie down and die. We must alert the village and Alugra. I must find Ilimic!"

"Go. I do not think I can rise. Go, find your woman and make the bastards pay." Neugen stared in pain and exhaustion at Caros, his breath coming in short bursts.

"By the gods, Neugen. I am not going to Orze without you. I will not be able to lift you so get up and get on the bloody horse."

A spark of anger flashed in Neugen's eyes. "I am all but dead. Leave me and go find Ilimic."

Caros was desperate to find her, but he would never leave Neugen to die alone like that. Somehow, he had to get to his feet, and the beast was already stirring in his head. He rose slowly and painfully. Every move planned until finally, he stood on legs as weak as those of a newborn foal. He whistled with difficulty and was rewarded by his mare's nicker. He smiled in gratitude and nuzzled her when she came to him.

"There now. We are going home. You will take us there, will you not?"

Neugen coughed. "Curses. I suppose I cannot let you go off by yourself with half your brains missing." He used the humor to cover his pain and added hoarsely, "I do not know how long my senses will remain, but give me a hand up."

Both men were drenched in sweat and parched when they finally struggled onto their horses and began their way back to Orze. The ride was agony for Caros and nausea made him throw up as he rode. Every gasp for air inflamed his head wound and every bout of vomiting brought him closer to oblivion. The sun burned both men mercilessly as their mounts plodded through the hills. Caros led, knowing that even if he lost his senses, his horse would take them home.

He watched in helpless despair as Neugen's breathing grew more and more ragged. He had little experience with such severe injuries, but knew he was looking at a man whose ancestors were a heartbeat away from welcoming him to them.

For a long while Caros blacked out and when he came to, Neugen was slumped forward on his horse, blood dripping from his lower lip, eyes closed. If he fell from his mare's back, Caros knew his friend would die where he fell for there was no way he would be able to lift him back onto the horse. Caros himself was rapidly succumbing to his wound and the nightmarish pain in his head had forced his right eye closed. He tried to focus on his surroundings in the harsh afternoon light. They were on a slope above a deep valley and the mare was leading them to the mouth of it. There was no sign of habitation, no scent of a home fire, and no bell nor bleat of sheep. His chin fell to his chest and he struggled to open his eye, before realizing it was open and it was his vision that had clouded. Was it time already for him to join his kin and ancestors? He had thought he would have more seasons. Make children. Accomplish something worthy. Frustration and sorrow forced his chin up and his mare nickered softly, as though exhorting him to stay strong. The thought brought a smile to his lips and he looked back at Neugen to share the joke. Through the darkness, he saw his friend was likely to fall at any moment. He heard himself yell a warning, but wondered how he had done so? He had not opened his parched lips. Beneath him, his mare picked up her pace, leaving Neugen drifting behind them and Caros unable to move his hands to rein the horse in.

Hands reached from the dark and pulled Neugen from his horse and Caros groaned in anguish. Someone was clutching his mare's bridle and he reached for his falcata, but his traitorous arms would not move. He cursed and heaved thin bile down his chest while a voice spoke in his ear.

"Leave the blade, warrior! Leave it, I say!"

Caros rocked on his mount and stared. An old woman held his wrist fast. That was what was preventing him pulling the blade? By the gods, he was weak. The woman stared up at him with the blackest eyes he had ever seen. She turned her weathered face and called to someone out of sight. A giant approached through the fog invading his sight and he wondered for how long he had been wandering the land of the dead.

"This one has a hole in his head. Lift him off the horse; I cannot do a thing with him all the way up there." The giant reached up with thick arms attached to a barrel-like chest to lift him from the horse as though he were just a little child. A sharp slap sounded. "Do not lay him down here! Take him to the yard." The old woman chided the man who had been on the verge of laying him on the trail. "And take care not to spill his brains out that hole."

Caros' eyes closed as he felt himself drifting. Murmured words washed over him without meaning, but he was not in pain anymore and for that he was thankful. He began to fall and thought he could hear the joy of his ancestors celebrating their next life.

Caros' mare had led them to the valley of her birth. The old lady and her son, the giant man who had lifted Caros off his horse, lived in a sturdy, rock-walled home in the deep valley. They had retreated into their home at the first sight of the two horsemen riding on the slopes above. With wide eyes pressed to peepholes, they had watched the men and waited for others to appear and the attack to begin. None came. The lead rider swayed dangerously on his mount while the second rider looked asleep. Still, the family remained silent. The man's wife stifled her sobs of fear and clasped her suckling babe to her milk-engorged breasts while holding a hand over the mouth of the toddler on her knee. The old lady, whose sight was as sharp as the youngest of her clan, exhaled deeply.

"Could be hill warriors drunk on pillaged ale, but I think not."

"What do we do?" Her son was a hardworking, but unimaginative man.

The old matriarch pursed her wrinkled lips in thought. They had survived the last raid on the valley because their home was well hidden here. She was reluctant to test the patience of the gods again and bring attention to their home. As it was, the two riders appeared to be passing the homestead and heading to the village. The lead rider turned his mount into the valley and the second followed. The old woman, eye pressed to a crack in a heavy cedar shutter, saw the spear shaft. A hand's length long, it jutted from the second rider's chest. Her eye darted to the lead rider who sat slumped and she became certain his horse was picking its own course. She made her mind up.

"Those men are injured. They will not be long on their mounts. Open the door so I can see what tending I need to do." The man inclined his head and began removing the thick beams barring the door. His wife squeaked in protest but was silenced by one withering glance from her mother-in-law.

"Have water boiling and fresh linens ready. Hurry now!"

She jumped to obey, sending her toddler sprawling while the babe squawked in protest as her raw nipple pulled from its mouth.

Matriarch and son ascended the valley side nimbly and approached the riders. Both appeared oblivious to their presence although their horses nickered nervously at the approach of the strangers.

The big man reached the second rider just as he slumped from the mount and catching him, lowered him gently to the ground. The old matriarch approached the first rider and started when he reached for his blade. His eyes were sunken and dark, his head and face coated with a blackened crust of blood. She gripped his wrist tightly as he stared all about and yet did not notice her. After a brief tug to loosen his wrist, his strength seemed to die. This one was not long for this world.

Once both men had been set on cots, the old matriarch sent her son to retrieve the horses while she removed Neugen's armor and cut away the tunic from his body. The young mother brought linen and tore them into strips as ordered. The old lady glared at the broken spear shaft and prodded the purple flesh gaping around it.

Pus oozed out and she leaned close to sniff. "One good thing. The black stink has not started. Come!" The man lumbered over from where he had hobbled the two mares. "I am going to place a blade either side of the spear. When I say, pull the shaft out. Pull clean, do not twist!"

He grunted and his wife's eyes grew round as the old lady deftly slid a bronze blade into Neugen's chest alongside the shaft. Blood and yellow pus pulsed from the opened wound. Without pause, the old lady took up another blade and slid this into the wound on the other side of the shaft.

"Grab it tight. Ready?" He gripped the shaft with one large hand and nodded. She levered the wound open with the blades. "Now!"

He exhaled and tore the shaft free. With a wet smack, the head came unplugged from the black hole in Neugen's chest. More blood and pus flowed from the wound. Neugen's back arched and his feet kicked spasmodically on the cot, sending motes of golden dust dancing through the late afternoon sunshine. The young mother turned and hurried behind a tree while the man stared at the iron tipped javelin in his hand. The head was the elongated pyramid shape used to punch through armor. This was fortunate for Neugen as it meant it could be extracted with far less damage than caused by barbed heads. The old matriarch gave instructions to the young mother to clean the wound.

"Deeply! The poison must be removed or the black stink will claim him by this time tomorrow."

Fresh from throwing up, she nodded weakly and set to irrigating the awful injury with warm water. Calling two of the older children over, the old matriarch ordered them to fetch maggots from the donkey stall. "Off you go now! The smaller the better and do not harm them. I want them lively!"

The pair giggled and loped off to complete the strange quest. They knew better than to question their grandmother. She looked at her son, still examining the bloody javelin head and gave him a slap on his elbow.

"Put that thing away and help me with this other one. Here, get these clothes off him, my back is too sore to kneel any longer." Wordlessly, he unlaced Caros' armor and pulled his tunic off over his head. Caros groaned in agony, his eyelids twitching. The old matriarch shuffled closer and leaned stiffly over him. With a gnarled thumb she lifted first one eyelid and then the other.

"Hmm, not good. Whoever sliced him should have done him a favor and taken his head off." She straightened and kneaded her back. "You know, he looks familiar. Aside from the extra hole in his head, he is a good-looking lad."

"I know him."

"What?" The matriarch squawked in surprise.

The man nodded hastily. "I do. This is the son of Joaquim, the merchant of Orze."

"No! Truly? I thought he looked familiar did I not say!" The young mother turned hesitantly to stare. "What are you looking at? Is my son not man enough for you?" The old matriarch rounded on her and she squealed and flinched away. The old matriarch's cackles turned to coughs before she could speak again. "It is a jest, no need to squeal so." She clutched the younger woman's arm and gestured to the wound in Neugen's chest. "You have done good work. The poison is cleaned away nicely. It will return though. Now where are those children of yours?" As though summoned, they appeared, each with cupped hands and still giggling.

"Ah, you have found us some little maggots then." The old matriarch exclaimed. They thrust out their hands to display the dozen white maggots squirming in their palms. "Och, poor things. Look at your filthy hands, here give them to me." The children laughed and dropped their haul into their grandmother's creased palm. The young mother asked the obvious question and even her husband looked intrigued.

"Ah-ha. Watch." With a groan, the old matriarch bent her knees, clicking audibly, to crouch down beside Neugen. "Boy will be the death of me!" Carefully, she dropped the grubs into the bruised and swollen wound. The young mother gasped and even the children looked shocked. "Now no need to go off behind the tree again, girl. These little ones will do what your dainty fingers and my bent old stumps could never do. And they will do it all night." The old matriarch kept three of the fly maggots and turned to the younger woman. "They will eat away the flesh that becomes corrupt and with the will of the gods, keep away the black stink." She held out her hand shakily. "Here then, clean up young Caros' head there and pop these on before wrapping the wound with linen."

When the injured men's wounds were dressed, the young mother and two older children set up an awning over them. Neither man recovered consciousness that evening. Instead, both groaned feebly throughout the night as their wounds brought on the inevitable fever. She rose periodically to tend to them and dribble water through their lips.

By morning, Neugen was flushed red with a raging fever. He stared vacantly, speaking only to those not present in flesh and the woman and children ignored his delirious mumbling. More concerning was Caros' growing silence. He lay still; only occasionally muttering slurred words. The old lady feared the boy had the worst of the wounds. What damage may have been done to the lad's brain was not something a healer could mend.

One moment he was floating in a sea of disparate thoughts and voices and the next he was staring up at a makeshift canopy above him. He traced the patterns woven into the tired and dusty fabric until his eyes could shift no more and he blinked. The spell broken; his body came alive. Pain rushed to fill his mind and unravel the peace he had felt. He clenched his teeth as the monster reared in his skull. His right eye throbbed and shut, trapping the pain behind it. He wanted to scream but was too afraid to. Something fluttered against his skin. A hand, he thought. Something cold, something not attached to the pain. He opened his eyes and saw an old lady hovering beside him. Another face moved beside hers. Ilimic? He smiled, felt the pain tear his face, but ignored it. He tried to focus on her, but his right eye blurred and wavered. The old lady pushed linen between his lips and he swallowed the tepid broth she trickled onto his tongue. When the old lady extracted the linen, Caros was again senseless.

When next he awoke, he reached for Ilimic and discovered she was not by his side. A wrinkled, gray-haired woman hovered into view above him. He smiled at her, warmed by the kindness in her dark eyes. She fed him a thin dribble of watery soup and, when his jaws ached and his head throbbed, he closed his eyes and grunted his thanks while wondering where Ilimic was.

A new presence appeared alongside him and smiling, he opened his eyes to find Ilimic, only it was not her. It was a woman older than Ilimic, with a heart-shaped face and thin, black hair. She smiled at him and laid a hand on his brow and his heart froze. Memories of the ambush swamped his mind. The pale shape of Ilimic on the road, crying out in fear.

Furious with despair, he snarled at the woman who screamed, snatched away her hand and fell back from him.

"What has happened?"

The woman sobbed in fright. "Nothing Ma-ma, he just gave me a start. I think I frightened him."

Some part of Caros regretted venting his anger and anguish on the woman, but another did not care. He closed his eyes and tried to sweep his thoughts clear. The woman receded, but the pain did not. He fought it, but in the end, it was stronger and like a predator, it smelled his weakness. He rolled clumsily onto his side, wondering where he could go to leave the agony behind. The movement unleashed another attack by the monster and his stomach turned, forcing him to gag and retch.

In the cool pre-dawn, Neugen, sweating with fever, lay on a pallet beside him. His eyes were closed, and Caros wondered if the same nightmare was haunting Neugen's sleep.

He lay awake as night turned into day, trying to keep his mind clear of memories of the ambush and attack.

"Caros." Neugen's voice had a breathless quality and Caros slowly opened his bloodshot eyes. "Caros? We live!" Neugen smiled weakly. "You do not look too well, but I expect I look about the same?"

Caros said nothing, just closed his eyes and breathed deeply. Nothing Neugen could say would help. His friend tried again to speak to him, but Caros had no will to respond. He was a reminder of the pain, of the loss of his kin, the loss of Ilimic. He had accepted enough loss. Neugen talked, but Caros closed his eyes and shut his ears. There was nothing to say. Was he to be happy at being spared? The village dogs had it better than this; there was no more to say. Neugen lapsed into gasping silence.

Using all his will, Caros managed to clamber upright the following day. He was weak, but two days of lying helpless while Neugen tried to raise his spirits was more than he could endure. The old woman clucked at him in disapproval while the dark-haired woman cowered behind her and watched him with frightened eyes.

His naked body trembled at the effort, but he stood upright and gingerly tottered to a water trough. He wanted no help and glared at a barrel-chested man when he moved to aid him. The big man shrugged and went back to his chores.

After washing himself at length, he felt marginally better and sought out his tunic. It had been cleaned and mended. As he dressed, he stared at his hands shaking weakly while trying to tie the laces of his sandals. The right side of his head throbbed, and the pain had grown until his right eye streamed and he could only use his left. He felt Neugen's stare and willed himself to finish dressing. His friend tried to laugh about their condition. He then tried to talk about what had happened and Caros concentrated on tightening and adjusting the belt at his waist. Struggling into a sitting position, Neugen wore a wary expression.

"Thought I would be up singing and eating long before you rolled your sorry butt off your pallet. Looks like you beat me there, hey?"

Caros stared back flatly. "You will be up soon." The words felt thick with insincerity. Neugen had a life to go back to. He still had one of the horses Caros had traded him. Little wonder he could lie there and make light of their wounds.

Neugen sighed. "Caros, things did not work out, but we are alive and that is a gift."

The words brought Caros' blood boiling to his cheeks and anger swelled in his breast, even overwhelming the pain.

"Neugen, how stupid are you? Is it impossible for you to see I do not want to talk about those things?"

His voice was like a whip across Neugen's face and his friend smiled sadly.

"How about what I want? You hold pain to you like a shield, Caros. It is not a shield. It is a… it is not a shield." Neugen finished lamely.

Caros stared at him. "A shield? What is a shield for but to protect? Now you have these sudden deep insights, why not tell me what I have left to protect? Where is my mother, father, brother? Where is the woman I love? I have no shield because there is nothing left to protect."

"If you believe that, then you are a fool. You think you are the only one who has lost loved ones? Look around you, Caros. The living go on and get over it." Neugen doubled over, gasping and the young woman rushed to his side.

Caros, head swimming with pain and panting with anger, watched his friend spit blood into the dirt beside the pallet.

"Oh, leave him alone. Can you not see he is enjoying the breeze and living a life of gifts?"

Contrary to her usual subdued nature, she turned on him like a mother lynx.

"Enough! You speak with no thought. You are bitter with anger and self-pity! He is your friend. If you do not see this, then you do not deserve his friendship. Now leave us until you are calm!" Caros was startled. Before he could utter a word, she emphasized her meaning. "Go! Go! Go!"

He stepped back, away from her fury. The children were staring at him and the man was watching from a nearby orchard. Silence fell over them, interrupted by wheezes from Neugen. Caros tottered back a step more. His gaze fell on the old lady, standing still as a statue and staring at him with hooded eyes. Nobody moved. He felt as though the world had gone mad, or was it he? In the oppressive quiet, he turned and walked unsteadily toward the livestock corral

The man met him at the gate with a frank stare. "You want to ride away? You are too ill and what about your friend?"

"I am fine, besides you heard her." He snapped.

Unfazed, the big man responded. "She did not mean to leave… you know, just go."

Caros almost laughed at the man struggling to explain. "I know what she meant. Are you going to open this gate or not then?"

He said no more and pulled open the pole gate. Caros did not need to call her; the mare was already on her way, whinnying her greeting. "Good girl. Come on, let me see how you are." Caros patted the mare which shivered in response and leaned against him as he scratched her coat. He looked her over and was relieved to see she had come through their ordeal with nothing more than a shallow furrow across her rump. An arrow or javelin had come cursed close.

The man left to fetch Caros' pack and silently returned to help him mount the horse. When he was done, Caros nodded and burrowing in the pack, brought out a silver stater. He thrust it towards the man who ignored him and returned to the orchard. Caros felt a flush of shame, but quickly snuffed it with the more familiar anger. He clicked his tongue and the mare obediently set off.

One last glance showed the women removing newly bloodied linens from Neugen's chest. The warrior caught his eye and raised a hand to wave farewell. Caros turned his eyes forward and rode from the valley.

11

They were fortunate. A day after capturing the wagons they had been overtaken by the Lusitanian and his two companions. The man advised Berenger that a column of sixty odd horsemen were coming down on them from the north. He smiled at the news that this column was just a half-day behind them and riding hard. It was unlikely that the horsemen would attempt to retake the wagons when they encountered a force equal to theirs in size. They might pursue and harass Berenger's column, but more of his men were streaming back by the day and soon the enemy horsemen would be outnumbered two to one. If they had not fled by then, they would pay a steep price.

"Good work. Odd that they were so far behind the wagons, but no matter, take fifty men and guard our rear. Let me know when they come into sight."

The wiry Lusitanian tribesman blinked. "As you wish."

Berenger frowned as Rudax pulled his horse around to gather the rearguard. "Wait! There is something more on your mind?"

The Lusitanian's impassive expression faltered. "These riders are not Bastetani. They are unlike any I have seen before."

"How do you mean?" Berenger was curious.

"They are not of Iberia. They ride differently, dress strangely. Even their horses are different."

Berenger was bemused. "Ride and dress differently? Look around you. We are all mercenaries. The hills are full to bursting with men who ride and dress differently."

"You asked. I will take the fifty now." With that he urged his horse back to the column.

It was true that in the last ten years the hills and valleys of Iberia had rung to the clash of iron wielded by men from many lands. It was as though the land drew those who lusted after violence and power. Mercenaries were the order of the day. Between sunrise and sunset, a leading man could bolster his troops with mercenaries from ten different lands. Show them coin and they would follow. Show them loot and they would fight. Show them mercilessness and they would win.

By evening, the wagons and column had travelled a dozen leagues. True; it was mostly downhill, so they had made good time, but Berenger fretted about every day between them and Sagunt. Added to that, the strange horsemen Rudax had observed had not reappeared. That may not be a bad thing, but Berenger preferred to know where his enemy was. It was possible they had no connection with the wagon column. On the positive side, two bands of the raiders he had flung out like a net of death over the Bastetani lands, had now returned and his eighty men were bolstered by an additional forty. A warhorn sounded from the hills to his right, another incoming band. Return calls sounded and soon a string of riders materialized into view as they slipped down a forested hillside to join their fellows on the road. Berenger and his leading man watched as the riders joined their companions, counting off the number returning.

"That is Turro's lot and he is short by seven men."

"Eight. They now have a woman with them." Josa argued.

Berenger looked again and realized that Josa was right. Cold anger burned his insides as he watched the incoming band.

"Order camp set; the sun is almost gone."

Turro had made no move to seek out Berenger and report to him. This maddened him still more and he ground his teeth as Josa rode off yelling for the camp to be set. Men cheered happily and amongst them, Berenger could hear Turro's baying laugh. No doubt regaling his peers with his tales.

It was dark and flames snapped hungrily at the dry branches collected to build Berenger's fire beside the lead wagon. He sat on a cask taken from the wagon and swept a whetstone down the sword blade time and again. Across the fire, Josa quaffed a slug of potent ale liberated from the stores on the wagons. He hiccupped and leaned forward to turn the haunch of goat roasting over the fire. Berenger sighed and sheathed the wickedly sharp blade, taking care to wrap the whetstone and return it to his pack. Josa sat up and plugged the spout of his flask. Berenger smiled across the fire at him; a tight, icy grin to which Josa responded by displaying his axe.

The two men rose together and strode down the line of boxy wagons. Ahead more fires blazed and men sang and shouted. Laughter rose and fell in tides of boisterous abandonment. The men were recounting the past weeks' raids and skirmishes. Their tales encompassing everything they had accomplished from daring bravery to wanton horrors. Berenger, dressed in black, swept from the shadows to appear among the warriors.

The men stood in a wide circle around a large fire. Flames and sparks twisted into the velvet darkness above while yellow light reflected off their bared torsos and bronze and silver armbands. Many swigged from skins of ale. An entire goat looked to have been consumed already and bones and scraps lay scattered about. One man laughed and roared loudest among the thirty or so men. An arm, corded with iron-like muscle, lay draped across the shoulders of a fellow warrior as the two drank in fellowship. The flickering firelight played over the giant's chest where old scars, white with age, writhed and battled with more recent livid blue and purple scars. This was a warrior who accepted battle at every opportunity and laughed at death.

Men about the scarred warrior fell silent as Berenger appeared. The warrior slapped the man beside him on the shoulders and sent a boom of laughter into the night at some jest he made. Despite the hush that had fallen, the warrior lifted a skin of ale and poured a stream down his throat. He thumped his chest and issued a huge belch before smiling ingenuously over the fire at Berenger.

"Berenger! Drink with us!" Berenger cocked his head. Men muttered and the circle shifted as they stepped back. The warrior was unperturbed and laughed. "It is a fine ale. Brewed by some Bastetani in Baria. You must try some and I will tell you all about how we got our hands on it."

"You are eight men less and you brought a woman back."

"Ah, you know the way of it. Some things look like things they have no business looking like."

"She is not a woman then? One of your cousins dressed as a woman?" Berenger responded, knowing Turro's band of warriors was formed exclusively with men of his own kin. Brothers, uncles, cousins and nephews. Turro gave a roar of laughter.

"Excellent. I admit there are a couple of my kin that could clean up like a girl if they put a thought to it." He tossed the skin of ale to a nearby warrior who fumbled it. "If you will not have ale, perhaps you would like to hear how we came by it?"

Berenger stepped past the fire. A figure appeared behind him. It was Josa, clad in armor and hefting both axe and short sword.

Turro stared hard at Berenger. "What do you want, Berenger?" His voice had gone cold as iron. This was not a man who acknowledged fear.

"What do I want? For a start, perhaps you could remind me who pays you your silver?"

Turro was no fool and his jaw tightened. "You do." He spat.

"Do you know what that means?"

"Piss off, Berenger. I fight well and you know it. If you need men to lick your asshole, look elsewhere."

"See, now that is where I am confused. It seems I am too insignificant to merit even a brief report. Is that it?"

Turro glared at Berenger. "I fight for your silver. Neither I nor my kin owe you more for we are free men." Around the fire, men shouted in agreement.

Berenger was seething. These fools were quick to take silver in return for swinging a sword, but thought nothing of strategy or discipline. That was why the Barcas could crush the tribes.

"I am disappointed, Turro. You could have been a champion, a leader of men, but you cannot see past your own short sword, so will always just be fighting for somebody else. If you cannot bring yourself to do a thing as simple as reporting to me, then I suggest that you take your kin and leave." Berenger was ready to kill the warrior, but the bastard had a dozen kin here and who knew how many friends who would fight for him.

Turro stepped towards Berenger with a growl, but an arm snaked around his chest as an older man stepped into the firelight. Berenger could not name him but knew the man as one of Turro's kin.

"Berenger, our apologies for not reporting sooner. It is regrettable, but we lost good men; brothers and cousins in a skirmish just yesterday. We thought that we could relive their glory with our kin and report to you on the morrow."

Berenger's eyes narrowed as he listened to the diplomat of the family. "Who are you among this lot." He indicated the circle of warriors.

"My pardon. I am brother to the father of Turro here."

"His uncle. Here it is then; you want the coin I am paying you to fight, then you and your men obey my orders like good bitches."

The warrior recoiled before he caught himself and smiled. "Thank you…"

"That is not all. You have a captive, a woman. She is now forfeit and to be sent to my campfire immediately." Turro growled again and even the diplomat frowned. Berenger did not allow him to argue. "And finally, your nephew and I end this now." His meaning was clear as he patted his sheathed sword.

The uncle whispered furiously to the powerful warrior who shrugged him away with a laugh.

"If that is what you want, then I will be happy to obey." He swept up a war axe from the bundle that had been lying in the shadows at his feet. Berenger's eyes widened and he dragged his sword from its sheath. With a loud rasp, the blade flashed free and he sprang at the grinning Turro. Turro might have expected some surprised hesitation from Berenger when he lifted the axe, but it was he who was surprised at how fast the champion responded. He was hurriedly forced to defend as Berenger lunged. This was a death match and there would be no drawn out parrying. Each man knew his life could now be measured down to a few last frantic heartbeats. Their blood pounded and their breath raced. Outwardly they appeared to be reveling in the challenge and the warriors in the circle were quickly joined by more and more from other campfires until a throng of men stood crowded about the impromptu battlefield.

Sword and axe clashed and the men cheered as the two combatants came together at the chest, their weapons straining against one another over their heads. Berenger angled to bring his sword down through Turro's shoulder, while Turro used his great strength to try smash his blade through Berenger's skull. For the space of several heartbeats they strained like that and then, quick as a lynx, Berenger twisted his hip and reversed his effort to pull on Turro's axe. The warrior lost his balance and stumbled onto Berenger's knee which took him in the crotch. He groaned in agony and his face turned purple. Berenger had not intended to knee the warrior in the sack, but to throw him to the ground. He had mistimed the move, unprepared for how fast the big warrior had compensated. Now though, he had the momentum and tried to plunge his sword down behind Turro's collarbone and into his heart. The point of the blade pierced the man's skin, but only sank that far before Turro drove his axe shaft up into Berenger's solar plexus.

Berenger sprang back, dragging his sword free with blood pursuing an arc through the air, splattering like vivid tribal war paint across the bare-chested warriors encircling them. Turro launched himself after Berenger who gasped for air, his chest seized up from the blow. He swiveled around Turro as the man charged, axe hissing. With practiced dexterity, Turro swapped it to his left hand and as he passed Berenger, lashed out with a backhand blow that struck Berenger's hip. With an agonized grunt, Berenger whipped his blade at Turro and laid the warrior's left arm open from shoulder to elbow. Turro gave no sign that he felt the blow and snapped back, coming in low and fast.

Berenger found his mobility dangerously limited by the injury to his hip. Turro again had the advantage and Berenger knew he had to end this fast. Still breathing raggedly from the two blows he had taken; he vowed not to underestimate the big warrior's speed again. Instead, he would use his trusted countermove against a fast, powerful and above all, skillful warrior.

Every graybeard and champion has a favored trick. In Berenger's experience, powerful men like Turro were used to men shying away and fighting from a distance. Such warriors became used to it and timed their swings in expectation of their opponent gliding away, just as Berenger had done before being struck. Turro had probably killed many experienced warriors with just that move. Berenger made to back away; just a slight twist of his hips to give an indication of the direction he would move. He smiled inwardly as Turro adjusted his grip on the axe handle, preparing to lash out.

He swung the axe and blood sprayed from his flayed arm with which he still gripped the weapon. Berenger flicked his eyes in the direction his hips pointed and then moved the opposite way. Into the swing. His sword blade across his chest, Berenger drove sideways into Turro. To his credit, the warrior saw the feint the moment Berenger flicked his eyes. He tried adjusting the arc of the swinging axe, but it was not enough and was forced to dip his shoulder, hoping to deflect the sword point off a rib.

The noise in the camp rose to a crescendo. Warhorns blared and men roared. The guards on the perimeter had long since left their posts and clambered onto the shoulders of their brothers already in the circle. Others became so incensed by blood lust that they began to fight amongst themselves. The oxen bellowed in fear and strained against their traces. Under the rear wagon the dazed and hurt woman lay bound. Her fear grew and she sobbed uncontrollably even as she felt her bladder loosen. Unfamiliar birdcalls issued from the dark hills and eyes followed the movements of the warriors around the fire.

Berenger was disgusted that the warrior had struck him twice, winding and bruising him. His blade did its job well as he put the point neatly between the upper ribs of the man's chest, through lung and heart. Turro died with a bloody-toothed smile, still sawing his axe into Berenger's armpit where it peeled skin from muscle.

Berenger stood panting, hand firmly gripping his sword while he rested his forehead against Turro's own. The two warriors looked deep into each other's souls then, even as one panted air and the other sucked blood. Turro stilled and the spark in his eyes fled his corpse. His weight dragged the blood-slick sword from Berenger's hand.

In a heartbeat, Josa was beside Turro's uncle, his sword pressed into the man's gut. The warrior had grown pale at the death of his powerful nephew.

"She is beneath the wagon. I will send her to you."

"Report at sunrise or go your own way." Josa replied.

Berenger caught the warrior's eyes and held their stare until the man nodded curtly. He was satisfied. Turro's kin would remain. The death of a skilled warrior was a loss, but one Berenger was willing to pay to demonstrate who was in charge.

"Saur's dogs!" Berenger cursed between gritted teeth. Without pause, Josa worked the battered leather armor and under padding free from Berenger's torso. His hip was swollen, the skin split from the force of the blow delivered by Turro. "He almost had me with this blow."

"Ah, does that feel like it looks?" Josa squinted at the huge wound in the firelight and prodded a finger into the swollen flesh.

Berenger jerked. "I will have your head!" He sucked air through his teeth and began to laugh, as did Josa.

Swallowing his laugh, Josa leapt to his feet, axe held across his chest. Three figures approached. As they emerged into the firelight, Josa moved aside and stared hard into the dark from which they had emerged. He was a cautious man.

"We are alone." One of the young warriors assured him.

He grunted and continued to keep watch. The warrior shrugged and pushed the third figure further into the light of the fire.

Berenger, naked save the smallclothes about his loins, stared at the woman Turro had brought back with his band. She looked pitiful in just her torn and bloodied tunic; her chiton having been ripped from her body. Her bare legs were blood-stained, and her hands bound behind her. Her shoulders heaved, but he heard no sobs.

"Untie the gag."

The young warrior yanked her towards him, slid a knife under the linen and sawed. Her head jerked and the linen, more torn than sliced, came away with a thick clump of her hair. She spat the cloth free, gagging and panting. Berenger noted they had used her undergarment to gag her.

"You should keep a better edge on your blade." The warrior looked at him warily. "Tell your graybeard to report here before first light." The two warriors backed away and disappeared into the night while Berenger studied the woman. "Lift your chin." She froze and he was about to speak again when she raised her chin. It became obvious why Turro had decided to hold on to her. Although beaten, she still had an aura of vitality. "Josa, what do we do with this one?" He had only demanded the woman to anger Turro and goad him. Josa lifted the frayed hem of her tunic while glaring into her face. Although bruised and bloodied, she had a firm body with sensual curves.

Josa grimaced. "They have taken her a time or two. Still, I have a thought." He grinned at Berenger who cocked his head curiously.

Berenger had almost forgotten the fifty riders guarding their rear. Now, just a few days from Sagunt, a rider clattered to a stop beside him.

"I have news." The man gasped.

Berenger clicked his tongue as his black stallion sidled aggressively towards the messenger. His hip was inflamed and still stabbed him with bolts of pain when he jarred it.

"What?" He demanded curtly, sweat beading on his brow.

"The horsemen following us have attacked. We fought them off easily enough, but we think the main attack will be on the column center. And soon."

Berenger glanced at the rider. "Tell me their numbers, how they attacked, and what weapons they used?"

The rider was caught off guard. He had no doubt expected Berenger to sound the alert as soon as he heard the news.

"Er, they charged us."

"Silence! Now listen and answer." The rider paled and nodded, wide-eyed. "How many?"

"A dozen or more, maybe."

"In a single charge?"

"No. They rode at us a handful at a time."

"How many times?"

The man paled further, sweating profusely. "I do not know."

"What weapons did they use? You did notice those at least?"

Nodding vigorously, the man answered. "Javelins. They chucked javelins at us."

Berenger rolled his eyes. He briefly considered asking what kind of foe they were, but decided, based on the young warrior's observational skills, that the question would be pointless. "Very well. Return to your column and advise your leading man to listen for our warhorns. Two long blasts and he is to return at speed. Two long blasts."

"Two long blasts. Got it."

With palpable relief, the rider spun his lathered horse about and galloped back into the dust that hung over the wagons and near two hundred men now in the column. Berenger scanned the slopes rising gently on both sides of the valley road. He was ahead of the column by two lengths and entirely exposed if they did attack. He smiled and halted his horse in the middle of the road to wait for the column to reach him.

The attack occurred at sunset. Berenger almost yawned at the predictability of the timing. That was nearly his undoing. The column meandered out of a steep cutting and jolted its way into a wide valley. With the sun fast approaching the western hill line, this provided the perfect place to spend the night. Intuitively, Josa trotted up to Berenger to confirm if they would stop there. Making an overnight camp was a quick affair. The wagons simply stopped where they were on the track and the oxen were hobbled. Men tore branches from dead trees and made their campfires. The horses were hobbled together in the groups their riders rode and fought in. Game hunted through the day was spitted or else the stores on the wagons were used.

These things had all been done when a yell followed by a thrumming of hooves interrupted the usual camp sounds. At first nobody paid the sounds any heed. Another yell split the air and the quality of the shout brought the warriors at their tasks to a halt. Berenger sat massaging his hip and gloomily tried ignoring the sweat burning the shallow wound under his arm. He was watching the woman build the fire and prepare their meal. At the second yell, Josa appeared beside Berenger, his axe held at the ready.

"Under the wagon, woman!" Berenger rose and glanced about. The drumming hoofbeats rebounded off the bank of hills they had passed between. He turned to squint into the valley ahead of the column. It was a difficult task as the setting sun was blinding. It was a misfortune that while they were heading east towards Sagunt the track took a turn into this valley that placed the setting sun before them. This was the attack the rear-guard's leading man had predicted.

"Josa, form a line behind the last wagon. Tell the men to ready spears."

Josa glanced once more into the sun and then trotted off to carry out his orders. Berenger marveled that he had never noticed quite how bandy-legged his leading man was. No wonder he rarely dismounted. Stories told how Josa had even dragged women onto his horse during raids and used them as he rode about slicing their kin apart. He believed the first half of the tale. Berenger trailed after Josa on foot, leading his mount. He cursed as he remembered the woman under the lead wagon. He turned to call for her, but noticed a swarm of enemy riders, silhouetted by the sun, closing in on the wagons. "That is a shame." He truly hated Josa's cooking.

He reached the jostling shield wall as the attackers charged past the lead wagon. Unhurriedly, he passed through the shield wall Josa had formed. He had elected to form a wall one hundred men long with a second line of eighty men behind the first. Berenger turned behind the second line as a hail of javelins flew from the galloping attackers. Now he would see just what these horsemen were. If they were expecting to run over his men, they would be surprised.

Instead, it was he that was surprised. The first shower of javelins was devastating. Far more lethal than such weapons had a right to be. The men of the first line took the brunt of the deadly missiles. Although light, they flew at speed on low arcs and, to the horror of the men in the shield wall, many of the javelins punched clean through their wooden shields and pinned them. Josa roared the command to launch javelins in reply. Both lines of men flexed and hurled, sending their javelins soaring towards the attacking horsemen. They rose briefly before plummeting swiftly towards the enemy. Except the enemy was no longer where they had been. The horsemen had spun their mounts and raced beyond the range of the incoming missiles which punched uselessly into dry ground.

Berenger watched the first wave of attackers angle away down the valley in eerie silence, leaving only a thick veil of dust hanging over the shield wall. Men groaning in pain, were dragged to the rear trailing bloody smears in the dirt. One man shrieked hideously and Berenger, throwing an irritated glance in his direction, winced. Somehow the man had received no less than three strikes. Two javelins still wobbled in the man's lower chest while the third dragged between his legs having disemboweled the unfortunate warrior. Coils of purple gut slithered along the man's legs. Berenger paced over to the warrior who was taking another gurgling breath and forestalled further screams by opening his throat. The warrior who held the injured man's shoulders, released his grip and recoiled in shock.

"Back to the line and hold your shield further from your body."

The man sped back to the line. Hooves thundered and another wave of horsemen bore down on them. Berenger tugged at one of the javelins buried in the dead warrior. It pulled free with a wet smack and he examined the iron point morbidly. It was the elongated pyramid style designed to punch through armor. He had never seen one used with such deadly force. Through shield and armor. He heard Josa roar the order to throw and was pleased he issued the command before their enemy had retreated. Again, they surprised him. They had anticipated the order and swerved away without launching any of their spears. Once again, his warriors' javelins fell uselessly on empty ground.

"Can it be that these men are so well trained?" Berenger murmured to himself. He felt the first stirrings of concern as he paced back to the center of the rear line. His warriors muttered uneasily, not having even seen the enemy properly through the dust and sun. Berenger paced along the line and tapped the shoulder of every fourth man in the second line, signaling them to drop out and find their horses. These men ran with relief to their hobbled mounts.

Without warning, another wave of enemy riders appeared briefly to send more javelins thumping into shield and flesh. Josa went purple with rage and screamed at his withering force to answer with another flight of javelins. They had not heard the enemy approach and now three more men lay skewered while their own javelins thudded harmlessly for a third time into the ground. At this rate they would have no javelins left by nightfall.

Berenger whistled to Josa who stormed in frustration between the two lines of shields. He raised a hand and strode over. "The bastards will not stand and fight us!"

Berenger had seldom seen him so agitated. "I have pulled a score of men back to take to their horses. The goat turds may be able to avoid our javelins, but we will see what they make of horsemen charging them!"

Josa objected. "We do not know how many of them there are. You could find yourself surrounded."

Berenger smiled. "How many javelins do your men have left?"

"Ah, I see your point."

"I was not asking your opinion. I wanted to let you know so you do not put a javelin through my back."

Josa nodded grimly. "Did you want me to lead the charge? Your hip..."

Berenger gave him an icy stare. "I will lead the charge. Keep an eye on me and do not let a single javelin fly."

The enemy struck a fourth time and by now the warriors in the shield wall were separating into two types. Berenger watched as some became maddened and yelled insults at their invisible assailants, daring them to fight like men. The others muttered and tried to fold themselves tightly behind their shields, contorting themselves in some quite ingenious poses.

Twenty grim-faced warriors waited with Berenger, mounted on his stallion, at their head. Each armed with a quiver of javelins, they remained behind the rear rank of the dismounted warriors. Berenger drew his sword and lifted it slowly, squinting to see through the fog of dust, ears alert to the sound of hooves. He heard the rustle of javelins flung by the enemy as they made another silent charge.

His sword flashed down and his stallion leaped forward. The warriors rode past the right flank of the shield wall in a tight wedge. Berenger pledged to himself to gut any of the sheep-shaggers in the wall that sent a spear their way.

He broke through the heaviest of the dust moments later and was startled to find himself charging parallel to the enemy horsemen who were so close, he could almost reach out and touch them with his sword point. He looked into the widening eyes of an enemy rider, as surprised at his appearance as he was of theirs. Berenger and his mount acted with one mind. His steed neighed and swerved towards the enemy rider's horse and while his mount snapped at its neck, Berenger hacked at the copper-skinned face of its rider. A cry of jubilation and battle rage tore from Berenger's throat. Behind him, his warriors followed his lead and careened into an outnumbered group of enemy riders. Javelins were hurled at or rammed into the enemy. For their part, the enemy riders were empty-handed, having just hurled their javelins at the hapless shield wall.

The butchery was over in heartbeats and just two of the enemy raced unscathed into the sun. Berenger considered giving chase but decided against it. He reined in to scan the valley. Not a stade away, a mass of enemy horsemen sat unmoving. At the sight, an unfamiliar feeling stole over him. Dread. Around him, his men whooped and shouted their victory.

"Gather yourselves!" Berenger roared.

The warriors were startled into silence and following Berenger's gaze, their jaws fell slack and they glanced back to measure the distance to their shield wall.

"I will kill the first man to break." His voice was like a sword being dragged over a whetstone. The warriors sat their horses in silence. Berenger turned to the nearest. "Tell Josa to sound the warhorn. Two long blows. Go!"

Swallowing hard, he bolted while his fellows watched him ride away with envy. The enemy started forward on ponies smaller than the Iberian mounts, but which looked every bit as dogged. The horsemen all wore mustard-colored tunics, tied with sashes at their waists. Many also wore wrapping about their heads and faces, showing only their eyes. Berenger exhaled. In truth, he found himself a little envious of their uniformity. He understood now what the Lusitanian graybeard had tried to convey to him when he had said they were different. How had so many managed to be so silent? He shook the irrelevant question from his head and raised his bloodied sword. To his rear, two long wails issued from a warhorn. He hoped it was not too late.

As though the warhorn was their own signal, the enemy riders broke into a canter. Berenger's warriors shifted nervously, sliding imploring glances his way. He watched the enemy close the gap towards his small force and a wave of relief washed through him. It had dawned on him that while they appeared to be many, this was just because of their uniform dress. As they bore nearer, he estimated their numbers were double those of his men.

"What are we waiting for? Let us teach these donkey lovers some Edetani manners." Berenger spurred his stallion forward. The enemy were tenacious and fast. He had never fought an enemy like them. While his men had javelins and spears, he was armed only with a sword. He led the charge directly at the center of the enemy horsemen who simply flowed away to either side of his small column. Perplexed, Berenger frowned. Then in a sudden swoop, the enemy who had been flowing away changed direction and galloped down Berenger's flank. Their javelins whistled into his men. He heard solid impacts and a horse screamed, struck in the ribs. Its rider cried out in fear and sprang off the dying beast to avoid being maimed when it crashed to the ground.

His men quickly spread out and returned a volley of javelins. Berenger cursed. They had not scored a single hit and now somehow had the enemy between themselves and the shield wall. He pulled his stallion around savagely and raking its ribs, charged back at the elusive enemy. Again they melted away, now in two bands that streaked back down both sides of his riders. More thumps. Without looking, Berenger knew he had suffered still more losses. Where was Rudax? He was frustrated beyond anything he had ever experienced. This was pitiful. Selecting one of the enemy formations at random, he again led his men, now far less vocal, at the enemy. He ordered them to spread out and the maneuver partially succeeded, resulting in a short clash of blades. Berenger himself did not make contact, but at least some of his warriors had struck the foe. Buoyed by this small success, he led another charge at the enemy. Again, they managed to make limited contact and a brief melee ensued in which Berenger hacked another enemy rider off his mount and confronted another. The man was short and slender. Berenger expected to slice him in two, but the enemy rider seemed to be everywhere and nowhere all at once. Hip aching and armpit burning, Berenger cursed the rider loudly as he fruitlessly struck and sliced at the man. Without warning, the rider turned and galloped away, leaving Berenger panting.

Behind him, hooves thundered as Rudax's fifty horsemen burst from the valley. Berenger spat a mouthful of dust at the ground. His remaining riders walked their winded mounts back to the shield wall without a word to Berenger. He was too busy marveling at yet another surprise. He walked his stallion towards a mound in the trampled grass where one of the enemy's ponies lay dead. There was a greasy bloodstain on the ground where its rider had fallen, but no corpse. Berenger shook his head at the deep gash in the throat of the pony. In the midst of a life and death battle, the enemy had taken the time to put an end to an injured mount's pain. He looked over the entire field and saw not a single fallen enemy rider. A chill ran down his spine. What kind of enemy was this?

Berenger had returned to the wagons by the time Rudax returned from the field. He sat on a cask and leaned back against one of the wagon's giant wheels, trying to massage the pain out of his hip.

"We gave chase, but our mounts were winded and the enemy dispersed. Even so, two of our riders have disappeared. I fear the enemy has taken them."

"You searched for them?" Rudax did not deign to answer and for once Berenger did not mind. Once night falls, a warrior has no business hunting lost brothers with an enemy such as these about.

"They slew the oxen of course. Tomorrow we pack spare horses with the most valuable of the cargo and burn the rest. Your fifty remain now with the column."

"As you wish."

The man stalked into the new evening, leaving Berenger alone while Josa prowled the nearby rocks and brush cover. Berenger had forgotten all about the woman until he had returned to the shield wall. Upon inspection she was no longer under the wagon or anywhere else in sight. It was possible the enemy riders had come upon her and taken her.

The following dawn Berenger rose stiffly from the floor of the wagon. There were few men awake apart from those on watch. He clambered from the wagon bed and nearly went sprawling as he tramped on a soft object that rolled from under his foot. Regaining his balance, he saw that he had stood on the body of the woman. Josa must have found her hiding in the hills. Her tunic was wrapped tight about her and she shivered with cold. Josa had bound her to a wagon wheel to keep her from trying to escape again. On an impulse, Berenger nudged her in the back with his foot. "Roll over and show me your wrists."

She huddled tighter in on herself. Exasperated, he drew a short knife and straddled her. She whimpered and using Greek, begged him.

"Please release me. I have friends who will pay you well for my return."

Berenger frowned. It was unusual to have such an articulate woman as a prisoner.

"Oh yes? Who would these friends of yours be then?"

"My name is Ilimic. My friends are merchants from Baria. They will reward you for releasing me to them."

Berenger was intrigued. Ransoms such as she spoke of were not uncommon, especially when the hostage was an important person, but a mere girl with no ties to a clan leader? Berenger sucked his teeth.

"We will see. In the meantime, light the fire and prepare me a meal. Oh, and do not spit in my porridge today."

Berenger split the cords binding her and, blushing with guilt, she hurried to relight the fire.

Sagunt appeared in the distance below them just before midday. They had moved fast once the packhorses had been loaded and secured. The warriors had muttered angrily about burning the wagons and goods they could not carry. They were a subdued column as they moved out, their pride somewhat crushed by the skirmish of the previous evening. The only person still in a good mood was Josa. He had returned to the wagons with the recaptured girl long after Berenger had lain down to sleep, having given up on a cooked meal.

Berenger looked at Josa from the corner of his eye and out of pure mischievousness, decided to dent the man's happiness a little.

"I have been thinking about this woman." Josa snapped his head around in surprise. Berenger almost came unstuck immediately and fought to control the smirk tugging at his lips. Taking a breath to compose himself and not burst into laughter, he sighed dramatically. "I know we agreed to your suggestion, but as it turns out, she happens to come from a wealthy family."

Josa's face turned purple at the possibility of his plan coming to naught. Berenger sighed dramatically, enjoying himself immensely. He really should not toy with the man like this, but he was almost in civilization again while at his back, the lands of his enemy burned. "Thing is…" He went on. "You know what it costs me to run these missions and yes, I do get funds from the limp prawns that run the council, but we just saw a lot of plunder lost."

Josa glared back at the woman staggering behind his horse. He had used the wagon traces to fashion a collar about her throat and had her tethered to his belt.

"Her kin have no silver. She lies! I know this."

Berenger perked up still more. "You do? Tell me."

Josa's face turned a shade darker. "Turro's men told me they took her on the road to some sheep-shagging village. They killed the men with her, eight of them. Those were her kin. Poor farmers."

"Lies!" She yelled from behind them.

Berenger and Josa ignored her. "That is a pity. Of course, there were probably only one or two men with her, and they may have even survived and left her to fend for herself." Berenger said loudly.

Josa was jerked backward on his mount. The girl had turned crimson and was bracing herself against the tether. Angrily, he grabbed it and prepared to jerk her off her feet.

Berenger's hand closed over his in a vice-like grip. "Hold."

Josa was startled. "You believe she is from a wealthy family?"

Berenger laughed heartily. "No! What do you take me for? She is a woman and will say and do anything to get her way. She goes to the priest as an offering to your god, Catubodua, just as you suggested." Berenger called to the stricken woman. "Sorry, we have blood debts to pay."

A blood debt to priests. From her stricken look, she knew her fate. For a fleeting moment, Berenger's glee at tormenting her with possible freedom was overcome by a deep sadness, but with a grunt, he dispelled the feeling and grinned at Josa.

12

Caros stopped frequently to rest. The ride to his family home was just a half a day's journey, but the throbbing in his head at times threatened to make him pass out and topple from the horse. He chose a little-used track to bypass the village of Orze. He wondered if anybody had remained in the village after the Arvenci raid. It felt like something that had happened to someone else a long time ago. He reached the homestead in the late afternoon, having taken time to sleep through the hottest part of the day.

He paused within sight of the home and stared hard, willing his mother, brother or father to appear. He seemed to hear their voices in the breeze blowing through the burned tiles and recollections of family saturated the view before him. The sun was almost set when he tore himself from the visions of the past. Wearily he blew his nose and rubbed his tear-stained face clean with his tunic. He slid off the horse and tottering alongside her, made his way to the water trough. He was relieved to find that it held fresh water. His mare drank from one end while he rinsed his face and head at the other. Refreshed, he led her to the corral. It had been rebuilt; although there were no stock corralled in it at present. There were other signs too that rebuilding had or was taking place. By the time he had rubbed the mare down and collected an armful of fodder for her, he could barely walk. He stumbled into the dwelling and finding no furniture, ended up curling up under his cloak on the scorched floor of what had been his room.

Voices came from a long way away and Caros shied from them. They became louder and were punctuated with bangs and thuds. He muttered thickly with sleep and then flew awake with a gasp, reaching for his missing falcata. A man yelled in shock as Caros jerked awake. Gasping in pain, he clutched his head and through tear-filled eyes, stared about the unfamiliar room before focusing on the man standing in the doorway. Another figure pushed into the room while Caros slowly remembered where he was. The second figure approached him. Ugar, the stonemason.

"Caros! You frightened us half to death!" The man laughed loudly and the first man stepped closer to peer at him.

"Welcome back, Caros. It is good to see you returned although that wound looks raw." The man was a neighbouring farmer and it was his daughter who had been promised to Caros' brother. Caros stared at the men through a fog of pain. He recalled asking the village elders to find some men to start rebuilding the home before he had left with Alugra.

"I am well." He snapped. "Just a little pain still, but that will pass." He leaned away from the men and against the outer wall which shifted under his weight.

Ugar frowned in concern and backed away, a hand out to Caros. "Careful, the walls have a lot of hidden fire damage."

Caros straightened in alarm as pieces of plaster fell. Gathering his cloak close, he followed after Ugar. Village men crowded the central room and were already at work. Caros nodded greetings and they returned smiles, some giving him a tentative pat on the back. He followed Ugar outdoors, perplexed at the reception.

"Thank you for coming to rebuild the place. I know how busy this time of the year is." Caros smiled gratefully at the men. "I never expected so many men to help and so quickly."

The father of Julene laughed. "These men are proud of what you did; bringing back so many of the stolen livestock. They would be ruined if not for you."

Caros shook his head, ignoring the flare of pain the movement caused. "I was not the only one from the village who went. It is Alugra to whom we all owe thanks."

"Yes, we owe thanks to Alugra, but we heard of your bravery. No arguing, you did our village proud and your father would be pleased too."

Ugar had been studying Caros quietly and now he spoke. "You are badly hurt. You need a healer, Caros. That wound is recent. Were you attacked on the way back here?"

Caros briefly told the men what had happened; the words like ash in his mouth. He was reluctant to look them in the eyes while he spoke; afraid to see their judgement. Before he was finished speaking, they were growling in anger. Incensed that such a thing had happened to one of their own, they vowed to find the attackers.

"We will search for your woman, Caros. We will find her and kill these vermin. Such deeds will be punished."

Caros swayed on his feet as they vented their anger and turned to the corral. "I plan to go back to where it happened today."

Ugar gripped Caros by the arm. "You cannot do anything, Caros. Trust us. We will go."

Caros tried to pull his arm free and lost his balance, his head pounding and his vision clouded. "I must."

He came to in the dark to find himself lying on a cot. Hearing voices from the central room, he clenched his teeth against the pain and sat up. Setting his feet on the cracked dirt of the floor, he stood and shuffled the few steps to the doorway. A couple sat beside a fire burning in the hearth. At his appearance, the woman started with a yelp while the man jumped to his feet.

"Caros, you must remain in bed. You do not know how bad that wound is!"

Ugar looked upset while the woman with him, Julene, held a hand to her mouth, eyes wide.

"What news, Ugar? Have you found Ilimic?"

Julene came to his side and gently took his arm. "Sit at least. I will fetch you some water." She helped him to a bench while Ugar frowned and fidgeted. Caros' hopes died.

"Tell me." His words came out as a rasp of anguish.

"We found the horse and men searched the ford and hills all afternoon. They lost the tracks before nightfall."

"They have not found her body?" He had thought they would find her bloodied and dead, but this was worse. They must have taken her with them as a prize to be used as they wished. He cursed them and sent a prayer to Saur to feed their shades to his dogs. He would find them and they would not die easily.

Julene placed a cup in his hand and he lifted it to his lips. The water was bitter on his tongue and gagging, he hurled the cup into the fire.

"I should be searching! I vow I will always search for Ilimic and I will kill those dogs even as I vowed to avenge my kin." Panting with anger, he wiped at the blood trickling from under the dressing tied around his head. Julene backed away nervously, eyes wet with fear. Ugar's face showed only despair as he gripped Caros by the shoulders with powerful hands.

"That is as it should be. Now you must rest and recover, or you will not see another moon."

"I am leaving in the morning, Ugar. I will find them somehow. Saur's dogs await their shades and will feast on them."

"Yours is the only shade that will cross Saur's lands if you do not allow your wound to heal. How will you find your woman if you are dead? How? Think beyond your anger. Think as your father taught you to, Caros."

Caros shuddered, loathing his infirmity. If only he had strapped his helmet on tighter or avoided that blow. He could have cut every one of the attackers down. He heaved with fury and grief as he allowed the stonemason to help him to his cot.

It was some days before Caros left the cot again. Julene sat and spoke with him at times, but he said little and retreated into his own pain-wracked world. When he did rise, he did so before first light to avoid having to speak to her. He slipped out into the cool morning and visited his mare. The mount was well cared for which he was thankful for. His weakness frustrated his determination to find Ilimic, but the presence of the horse gave him comfort when his mood was darkest.

Ugar had broken the news some days earlier that no amount of searching had revealed where they had left her body or where they had gone. Caros had known this would be the outcome. This was something he would need to do, as though the gods themselves were testing him to see if he was fit to love and protect.

Julene smiled when Caros entered the central room where she was busy lighting the morning fire.

"You are up. That is good as long as it is just for a little while. How do you feel?"

Caros settled with a tight smile onto a bench. "I wish I was able to ride." The fire began to crackle and Julene set a cup of vinegar and water in front of Caros.

"I am sure you do." She sighed deeply. "Your brother was just like you. Remember when he popped his shoulder when that bull charged him? He was so mad, even with his arm hanging useless, I thought he was going to charge right back at the bull!"

Caros smiled reflexively, but he was in no mood for reminiscing. He drank the water slowly to avoid speaking. She was patient and kind and he felt bad that he was not more gracious, but his thoughts were too dark. Every thought seemed like a thread in a garment that unraveled unerringly back towards Ilimic.

Seeing she was going to get no more than that smile, she went back to work preparing a morning meal. Footsteps slapped on the beaten dirt outside and a moment later, Ugar arrived at the door. His face brightened on seeing Caros.

"Ah, Caros. Feeling a bit better?"

"A little. I could not lie still another day." He replied miserably. "Has there been any more news?"

Ugar ignored Caros and greeted Julene. "Hmm, smells good. This woman is too good to me, Caros. I have told her a dozen times that my wife feeds me before I come down here." The stonemason took a seat opposite Caros, avoiding his eye for a heartbeat longer. He glanced at Julene who was engrossed in stirring the porridge over the fire. Taking a breath, he fixed Caros with his gaze. "The men have done all they can. Even the old wolf hunter lost the tracks once they rejoined the road to the east."

Caros' mouth was as dry as dust. "So? Are you saying there is nothing more we can do? It is over? Ilimic taken and we are powerless to do anything?"

Ugar shook his head sadly. "No…" The stonemason faltered and tried again. "We have sent messages to villages and towns from here to the coast. North. South and West. Every trader knows of the attack. If there is news, it will reach us."

Caros felt a flutter of hope. "Yes, that is a good plan! This does not happen in our lands. The Bastetani will find these hill-warriors and Ilimic will be saved. I am sure of it. Whose idea was it to send messages? It was brilliant."

Ugar smiled uneasily. "It was Hunar's idea. If someone sees these men; we hope to hear of it." He sighed and cracked his knuckles.

"What is it, Ugar? What are you not telling me?"

"There have been other raids. On small villages and groups like yourselves. Travelers everywhere are being ambushed, murdered and worse. This was not an isolated act, Caros." Caros squeezed his eyes shut so he could think. If there were so many raids, news of Ilimic's abduction would have the impact of a gnat. He gritted his teeth. As soon as he was able, he would begin to scout the surrounding villages and towns himself for news. Ugar continued. "We sent a message to Baria and Marc has responded. He too is searching for Ilimic."

Caros dreaded seeing Marc, having taken Ilimic from where she was safe and in less than two days, losing her in such a way. He looked up. There was one other person he needed news of. He needed to know how complete his failure was.

"My friend, Neugen? Does he live?"

Ugar grinned. "He is recovering. He returned to Tagilit some days ago."

He gaped in surprise and then smiled crookedly at Ugar. "Neugen is pure Bastetani. Too dumb to die from a mere spear."

Julene set two bowls of porridge in front of the men and returned with her own. Caros ate slowly, grateful he did not have to chew the meal as that set off the pain in his head.

"That is good to hear. What of the repair work?"

"Better than I expected. Some parts of the walls needed rebuilding, but for the most part, they were still sound." Ugar wolfed down his meal despite his earlier protestations. Julene giggled when he licked the bowl and then belched. "Right, that will keep me young while I work. I have some stones I need to square." He bounced up and left the kitchen in a bustle.

Caros pushed his half-eaten meal aside. Julene paused and looked worriedly at him. This is what he hated. All the cursed concern for him and it was Ilimic who was missing.

"Caros, I must return home today. My mother needs me there and you are no longer unable to move. I hope that is alright?"

Caros shrugged and nodded. He needed time alone. "You have been very kind. I owe you a great debt for tending me." He found the words to thank her at least.

"I will visit and bring fresh bread and there is food for a few days in the root cellar."

He had not thought that anybody would be working on the burned homestead when he had returned. The men repairing it had been coming early and working until mid-morning before going off to their farms and crafts. Most of the damage had now been cleared and repaired, including the roof. When they finished their tasks and left that day, he was amazed to see the home looking almost as it had.

Caros picked through the debris the men had cleared from the house, recognizing burned and smashed items. A piece of pottery or item of clothing, trivial things, yet somehow seeing these items consigned to the heap made him melancholic. He stood a long time before the pile of rubble, not aware of time passing or much else beyond finding Ilimic. The heat of the sun at last returned him to the present.

With a chaste hug, Julene returned to her home after their morning meal. At last he could be by himself. He shifted and rolled his shoulders slowly, fearful of enraging the monster in his head. Slowly, he shuffled over to the water trough to drink. His stomach growled with hunger and he filled it with water. Sated, he then opened the corral gate and allowed the mare to roam the yard to feed on the fresh grass growing in a soggy ditch. Caros sat on the edge of the trough listlessly. Everyway his mind turned seemed to be blocked by a wall of hopelessness. All the times in his life he had ever felt angry, fearful or unhappy seemed to be times of sunny joy compared to what he felt now. Shaking his head, he stirred the monster. He both envied and despised his former self. How little he had known and how blithely had he lived without considering life.

He walked stiffly to the shade in which the mare grazed and stopped in surprise at the sight before him. A goose appeared from the undergrowth, trailing behind her a line of three bright yellow chicks. Honking, she led her goslings on what was clearly a first expedition into the world beyond their nest. Caros watched in amusement as the chicks bounced, rolled and stumbled their way along behind their mother. Every time she scratched the ground, a billow of dust and grass would blow at least a couple of them off their two little stick legs. The goose watched the mare, keeping a beady eye out for any insects flushed out as the horse cropped the long grass. Her experience was rewarded as grasshoppers and bugs scattered from before the mare.

"Life goes on." Caros muttered to himself. The words had a familiar ring.

He cursed when he opened the root cellar. It was days since Julene had left and the only food remaining were some shriveled roots. The flat bread had turned black and he had eaten the last of the cured meat the night before. He wondered if he had the energy to go into the village to purchase provisions. Looking around the root cellar, his mother's domain, he recalled her complaining that it was becoming too cramped. His father had argued that it was new and the same size as the old one. Caros wondered if his mother had also used the old one if this one was too small. If she had used it, the Arvenci may have missed it as it was unintentionally hidden beyond a mound of saved stone.

He crossed the yard and took the path around the pile of stone. He would mention them to Ugar who would have a use for them. Sure enough, the old larder door stood closed. It was no wonder the raiders had missed it. Weather-beaten and warped, it could have passed for a piece of scrap wood tossed onto a mound. Caros grinned and tried to pull the door open, but it was warped shut. He had to jerk and lift the thing before it would move. How had his mother coped? The difficulty in opening the door worried him. Perhaps the larder had been empty for a long time after all? He squeezed into the dark cellar and missed the first step, his foot thumped into the second, jarring his back and head. Tears rolled from beneath his tightly shut eyelids until the pain slowly ebbed.

The morning light shining through the door was enough to allow Caros to see a row of sealed clay jugs on the floor along one wall. Above those hung all manner of dried herbs, onions and beets. There were also three large amphorae partially buried in the dirt floor and Caros knew they would contain milled grain. In smaller vats on the shelves above these, he found the meat. Pickled and smoked. There was enough ham to feed a family for weeks. Caros rejoiced at not having to go to the village. This was a real boon and he would start with a good meal and then get some more sleep.

Curious, he reached out and felt one of the clay jugs which was cold to the touch. He broke the clay seal and tore at the stopper until he could get a good grip and then yanked it out of the spout. The scent of ale rose to greet him. Without thought, he lifted the jug to his lips and drank down a long swallow. He had to use both hands to lift the large vessel. The ale poured down his throat like a mighty cleanser and Caros felt his empty stomach glow warm. Wiping a hand across his mouth, he belched and grinned. With a jug in one hand and a smoked ham in the other, he kicked the door to the larder shut behind him and strolled back to the house.

13

Berenger led his column of raiders through the city gates, his relief turning sour as he recalled the strange enemy riders. The way they fought was unnatural. Warriors should scream and hurl abuse as well as javelins at their foe. They should blow warhorns and drum shields with spears. He had long ago learned that a battle was joined before adversaries clashed and blood was drawn. The horsemen had done none of those things. He gritted his teeth as the cold fingers of dread touched his neck; wondering at what other wild fighters the Barca would unleash.

Guards teemed at the gate and Berenger noted their increased numbers. The outer walls too were carrying more warriors than usual. Overcoming his sullen mood, Josa eyed the warriors.

"The city has doubled the guards."

"I see this. Maybe we have poked the hornet's nest harder than they thought we would."

The riders clattered through the gate in the outer of the two walls encircling the city. Within the outer walls were the homes of the lowliest of the city's inhabitants. It was also where the butchers bought and slaughtered livestock, tanners cured hides and slaves were held in corrals like other livestock. The stench was as thick as fog and had so many levels that it made the eyes stream. It was also where his riders would be billeted and their injured would receive treatment. As his men peeled their mounts away from the column Berenger gestured to Rudax who came to his side.

"Remain here with the men and tell them to be at the Red Bull at sunset for their share of the takings." Rudax inclined his head and trotted off.

After seeing their horses stabled, Berenger and Josa led Ilimic through the gates of the second wall into a more urban environment. He noticed men from his column carrying an injured warrior into the inner city. He could not blame them; the care and attention for whatever the fellow's injury was would be far superior in the inner city. Here there were homes doubling as places of trade. Families lived above or behind inns, shops or workshops that they owned and traded from. Vendors also filled side streets and alleys with baskets of produce, trinkets and other wares. The growl of a thousand voices rumbled constantly in the confines of the narrow streets. Animals were not permitted within the second wall, not that Berenger would have been able to force his stallion through the crowds of people surging up and down the main roads.

Battling through the throng, Berenger felt claustrophobia settling over him. A young man stormed past, using his shoulder to barge Berenger aside. Unable to retaliate, Berenger snarled in exasperation.

"Where did all these goat turds drop from?"

Josa stayed alongside him, dragging Ilimic behind. "I have never seen so many people. Look at all the sods."

"There can only be one reason there are so many more people here." Berenger paused as another man hurried straight towards him. He had caught the man's eye, so he knew the bastard had seen him, but still he brushed his shoulder. Berenger turn swiftly and kicked his ankle, tripping him up. Josa sniggered as the man sprawled in the dirt and Berenger, who had not stopped to watch, smiled coldly at the sound of the man's surprised yelp.

"I am beginning to think that a lot of these people have fled here from outside the walls."

Josa grunted and Berenger knew the burly man was taking pleasure in shoving people aside. Berenger, adapted to the press of the crowds, batted men and women from his path rather than sidestep them. Angry curses were all any of the goat turds dared to throw after him.

He rounded a familiar corner and strode through slightly thinner crowds to a large black doorway set in a large mud-brick building. No sign decorated the front. The proprietor needed none, their location was known to their customers and what they sold could not be taken away. It was known as the House of the Crow. Berenger thumped once on the door which opened quickly. He pushed through the doorway into the gloom beyond. Josa, dragging a mute Ilimic, followed. The sallow-faced man who had opened the door mumbled a greeting as he shut it behind them. Berenger ignored him and walked purposefully into the depths of the building. Inner walls and flooring of heavy timber muffled noise from the street and the gloom was pervasive. He knew where to go and made his way to the cooking area which was sheltered in the rear courtyard.

A hulking woman named Rose ruled the house and she could most often be found cursing and beating the kitchen slaves. Standing taller than Berenger and twice as wide, she was like a boulder. Nobody other than the high priestess of Catubodua, knew if she was free or enslaved, but all agreed that she had never left the house since she had arrived there countless seasons past.

Berenger stood just inside the courtyard and studied the huge woman who at that moment, was kneading a bucket of dough. Her thick arms twisted and punched at the mixture as though it had angered her. Her stout legs were set like sturdy pillars holding up her weight and he shuddered at the sight of the purple flesh bulging over her ankles. With no definition of hip or shoulder, her body rose like a column on top of which perched her dome-shaped head. Thin hair hung in greasy ropes down her back and a balding patch shone with an oily gleam.

Berenger inhaled through his mouth. "Greetings."

The mountainous woman turned and glared Berenger's way. She ran her eyes over him and Josa before fixing on Ilimic. He watched her dark eyes glinting malevolently and, for a heartbeat, pitied the girl. Rose thumped the stiff dough one last time before lumbering across the courtyard.

"Berenger. I heard you were hunting in the lands of our ancient enemies. Back for your rewards?" Her voice whipped and snapped like a pyre guttering in the wind. As she approached, her eyes moved from Ilimic to Berenger.

"As the gods permit."

She stopped in front of Berenger who sensed Ilimic flinching behind him.

"The gods permit what they see fit upon the most dutiful. Are you dutiful?"

"I trust you already know the answer." He would have said more, but the odor leeching from the woman, lodged at the back of his throat and he closed his mouth with a snap. If he were a better man, he would put his great sword through the beast in front of him and the world would be less odious for sure. Instead, he smiled thinly, suppressing the urge to gag. Her eyes swiveled back to their captive, impatient to get to the meat of the visit.

"What is this?"

"The gods blessed us with keen eyes and sharp swords. Our enemies have bled greatly and even their women and children lie dead. It is fitting that we give thanks with the finest they have to offer."

Josa shoved a sobbing Ilimic towards the big woman. Like a snake, she grabbed Ilimic's hair and with a merciless wrench, pulled her head about to inspect her face. Ilimic cried out in fear, eyes wide and tears coursing down her cheeks. Berenger watched in morbid fascination as Rose squeezed the Ilimic's mouth open to inspect her teeth. There were still ribbons of dough caught in crusty scabs on the woman's knuckles and Berenger shook his head. She grunted and flared her nostrils, taking in the Ilimic's scent and testing for evil shades. He stepped back superstitiously and glanced at a pale-faced Josa. A sudden ripping jerked Berenger's attention back to the two women. Ilimic stifled her scream while Rose ripped her tunic off, uncaring of the burns this caused. Seeing the Ilimic's nakedness again, Berenger suddenly wished he had not consented to this. She was a beautiful woman and Rose thought so too;

for the first time, her bulging lips parted in what Berenger assumed was a smile. A wet tongue darted across them as she took in the terrified woman's form. Rose pawed Ilimic's breasts, kneading them like she had the dough earlier and leaving white trails of the stuff where her bulbous fingers dug into the soft flesh. Ilimic sobbed quietly and screwed her eyes tighter when she felt the woman reach lower.

With a snarl, she raised her fingers. "You took her!"

Berenger scowled. "She was taken by the men who captured her. Their leading man died on my blade."

"Still. How do you expect to make an offering of this?" She hissed, spittle flying at Berenger. He stood his ground despite the wet projectiles.

"Clean her. Purify her. It is what you do, is it not?" He glared angrily at the woman, having had enough of her presence.

"It will cost you, Berenger. The priestess expects only the best."

"How much?" He wished more than ever that he had not agreed to Josa's request.

Rose pursed her lips and her eyelids drooped in folds. "Ten staters."

"Ten! Gods, give her back. I would rather just open her throat like I should have." He stepped forward angrily, playing the game expertly. Rose muttered and pulled Ilimic towards her possessively.

"Oh, not so hasty Berenger. That would be a waste. Perhaps not ten then, maybe just five?"

"Two and make sure your priestess knows where she came from."

Josa stepped forward and flicked two staters at the woman. She caught one greedily in a meaty fist, but the other tumbled off her body onto the cobbles.

"Pick that up!" She threw Ilimic heavily to her hands and knees after the coin.

"Sure, that will clean her up and heal the bruising."

Berenger shook his head at the grotesque woman. Spinning on his heel, he elbowed Josa out of his way and stormed through the building and onto the street.

In the eastern corner of Sagunt, stood the heart of the city, the hill fort, forum and basilica. Leaving Josa at the House of the Crow, Berenger approached the hill fort in a sour mood after his encounter with the high priestess' hag. Someday he would cut her open just to hear her beg for mercy. Something she had never offered the unfortunates that were taken to her for sacrifice to Catubodua.

He reached the forum and turned to the gate of the hill fort. There he was greeted by guards who nodded him through. He knew his way and was soon climbing stone stairs to a short passage and oak door. He pounded on the door and heard a scrape as the door chock was pulled free. Without a glance at the servant who had opened the door, he entered a large, well-furnished room.

"Berenger, excellent timing. I expected you would show up soon."

The speaker stood beside a narrow window set in the thick stonewalls. Tall with silver hair and gaunt features, when he turned to Berenger, he showed a face of angled planes as though hewn from a stubborn cliff.

"Come sit. You have much to report?" The man limped to a high-backed stool and sat with a grimace. To the servant. "Bring us wine."

Berenger approached and took up a seat opposite the city's Strategos. He looked drawn and on edge and did well to disguise it. Berenger's esteem for the Strategos grew with each turn of the road for Abarca walked a dangerous path in this Greco-Iberian city. The city was allied to Rome, yet the Barcas of Carthage were growing in power in the lands all around the enclave of the Edetani people. The Barcas were far from satisfied with what they had. Daily, their armies forged deeper into the Iberian heartland. The rich silver mines were now almost all controlled by the Barcas or tribes allied to them. The oligarchy of Sagunt saw their coffers dwindling and watched in fury as trade went south to ports at Baria, Abdera, Malaka and Gades. Unable to stand this state of affairs and fearing the outcome they had decided upon a course of action that would lead to certain war. To guide them through the war was the Strategos sitting before him.

Once the wine had been served, Berenger began his report. Abarca listened quietly and without interruption throughout. He did purse his lips when hearing of the lost wagons and bounty of iron they carried. Berenger ended his report by pulling from under his tunic a belt with leather pouches attached. He let it fall heavily onto the table beside the flagon of wine.

"That is the city's share of the takings."

Abarca nodded his thanks disinterestedly. Unlike the rest of the ruling elite in the city, Abarca was not avaricious. Instead, he placed his untouched wine on the table and leaned forwards.

"I have had other reports of these horsemen you describe. They have appeared these last weeks to the west and north."

"The Barca sets his noose about our necks."

"So it seems. They will be tasked with depriving us of reinforcements and supplies."

"You want me to strike directly?" Berenger presumed the Strategos would want to keep his supply route from the north open.

Abarca turned his flinty gaze on Berenger and shook his head. "Let them come. I have a bigger role for you."

14

Caros staggered, a flagon of ale in hand, to the house and slumped onto a bench. He had found an easy rhythm in these long days since he had returned home. The village men would come midmorning and work till the sun grew too hot then they would return to Orze leaving Caros to his preferred solitude. He would open a flagon of ale and drink through the afternoon until he passed out on the bench at the front door.

This was where Julene found him late in the afternoon. He cracked open one eye when she wiped his forehead with a damp cloth. The ale still ran thick in his veins and seeing her bosom shift beneath her chiton, he felt himself stir. The concern in her face and her large, shining eyes beckoned him and without thought, he reached up and gently cupped her breast. Her lips parted and she closed her eyes. Caressing her, he savored the form of her breast. Her nipple grew under his thumb and his body's response echoed hers. He pulled her closer, seeking her mouth with his while his hands loosened the pins of her chiton. She parted her lips to his probing and met him urgently. Her chiton fell free and his hands found her flesh, stroking and caressing.

Standing to remove his tunic, he noticed a rider at the entrance to the yard. Julene's youngest brother. Staring at the youngster, Caros felt shame course through him and he cursed. What was he doing? Julene was in the act of removing her chiton, her body plump and bountiful. His dead brother's woman. What had he been thinking?

"Stop. Your brother is here." Stepping forward to shield her from her brother's sight, Caros waved at the youth. How much had he seen? The boy looked afraid. Behind him, Julene scurried to pull her chiton back into place and broke into quiet sobs. The youth walked his horse slowly forward. These were deep country people who lived by honor and virtue. Clearly Julene had some experience of acts of love, it was only a matter of a season or so before she would have wed Ximo, so this was perhaps no surprise. Under those circumstances, while not permitted, intimate acts were at least understandable. Caros spared a quick glance over his shoulder and saw her still struggling with the pins.

"Quickly, he is almost here."

The heavy wooden table on the front portico helped block her from view, or so Caros hoped. He uncovered the basket of foods she had brought with her. With feigned nonchalance, he removed a fresh baked loaf from within and broke it. He made to smile at the boy, but the smile died on his lips. The boy no longer looked afraid. Instead, he sat glaring at Caros, his arm extended, pointing directly at him. The words the boy shouted nearly made him choke.

"Put the bread back! I saw what you were doing. Is it not enough that you abuse my sister?"

Stunned, Caros stared open-mouthed at the boy not yet sprouting hairs. He allowed the bread to fall from his hands and gritted his teeth. Finally dressed, Julene scampered past him and down the stairs. She fled through the yard into the trees taking the shortest route home. He watched her run, chiton held off the ground, pink soles kicking up behind her. The boy was talking again, his voice rising and breaking as was usual in lads of his age.

"When my father hears, he will dash in your head properly this time!"

"Enough!" Caros snapped. In a single motion, he snatched up the basket and hurled it at the youth. The basket flew straight and to his consternation, struck the boy in the face. Caros shook his head in disgust.

A shrill screech came from the yard and Julene was back; screaming at the top of her lungs as her brother clasped his face, blood running in twin streams from his nose.

"Do not dare hurt my brother! Look what you have done!"

Her screeches went on and on driving all feeling from Caros. His earlier embarrassment drained from him and he turned and lifted an upright flagon. Outstanding, it was at least half full. Sitting, he stretched his legs and plonked his sandaled feet up on the table. Taking a long swig, he felt a rush of comfort. The screeching from the yard blurred.

"…tried to kill me… monster… deserves to be punished."

He stared at the brother and sister who yelled intermittently his way and sobbed into each other's shoulder. Her brother's bloody nose had stained Julene's tunic and her tears had made a dark stain on his. Carlos took another long swallow and shut his eyes.

No men arrived the following morning. Caros knew why. He spent the day brooding about what had happened with Julene. It was possible her father would look to restore his family honor, although in the end the fumbling had not gone that far. Caros briefly considered going over to his neighbor and apologizing, but felt that would attribute more to the sorry episode than it merited. In the end, he did what he had done almost every day since returning. He fetched another flagon of ale and drowned his guilt.

Ugar arrived in the late afternoon. Caros was bleary eyed from sleep and struggled to his feet to greet the stonemason. Ugar's face betrayed his anger and Caros thought for a moment the aged man would strike him.

"From the look on your face I would say you have heard about…"

"Hold your tongue, Caros!" Ugar's vehemence startled him into silence. He had never heard such a deadly tone from the kindly man. "What, by gods did you do?" The question stumped him. From the way Ugar asked it and the set of his shoulders, Caros gathered the man had heard something horrific. He stared, thinking hard and trying to make some connection that made sense. "I thought I knew you. What I heard yesterday sickened me!"

The stout old man was right in Caros' face. This was enough to start him getting angry and on top of that his bloody head was throbbing like a shaman on mushrooms.

"I…" He willed himself calmer. "It just happened. She was leaning over me when I woke." The stonemason looked on angrily while Caros struggled to put into words how he had felt. "I needed someone, Ugar." He finished lamely, an acute loneliness welling up within him. He sat on the bench and leaned on his knees, trying to harden his heart.

"You needed someone!" The stonemason exploded. Caros looked up at Ugar with a sense that something was unbalanced. There was more afoot here than what he had expected.

"I have never seen you so spitting mad. What in the name of Endovex are you on about? We never got beyond tits and tongues!" He thought how a couple of moments more and her stout little brother would have had a lot more to screech home about. In truth, he felt like he had dodged an arrow. "See, her brother arrived to see us kissing." He regretted using the 'tits and tongues' bit; cursed foul-mouthed Greek sailors.

Ugar lowered himself slowly on the opposite end of the bench, his face grey in the wan afternoon light. "Is that the truth?"

Caros explained what had happened and when he finished, the stonemason bowed his head and sat silent for long heartbeats. With a deep sigh, he looked up at Caros.

"Your story has the ring of truth but differs from what is being spread." Ugar told how he had heard that Julene and her brother had arrived home bloodied and crying. "Their story is that you forced yourself on Julene and turned on her brother when he tried to drag you off her."

Caros was stunned at the turn the true tale had taken. The elders could demand that he be executed for such a crime. He leaned low over his knees, his thoughts a whirlwind of confusion. Finally, he sat up straighter, resolve in his face.

"I have told you how it happened, the what and why, as best I could. I am not saying I am an innocent and I am not accusing anybody of anything. Know this though. I will not apologize to Julene or her father. Nor will I sit here meekly if any of their kin decides to act on the false tale told. In return for leaving me be; I will resolve to stay away from the villagers. I do not know what my future holds. Maybe in time I will leave, or this wound will poison me entirely. I do not know." He looked away to the north, to the blue mountains of the Vascone clans, the Celt and others. Was there any place he could find peace? Ugar's fists were tightly clenched and his eyes dark as he listened. He grunted and flexed his shoulders.

"I will speak on your behalf, Caros. There are already more than a few disbelievers of the untrue version, so do not despair. I agree that you should stay away and I am afraid no more work parties will be coming. Fortunately, most of the work is done. Stay here, rest, lay off the ale and get your strength back. There is a future for you, a good future, even though it appears dark before you right now. Visit the tomb of your kin, you may find some solace closer to your ancestors."

Caros blinked slowly, his gaze on the far mountains. He did not hear the old man leave.

Caros rolled slowly onto his back, dreading the resurgence of the beast in his head. A buzzing began in his ears and the dark presence arrived just as he began to heave. He threw up; the remnants of another day of drinking ale. When the heaving subsided, he found himself on his knees, eyes squeezed tight against the pressure behind them. Blinking away tears of pain, he fought to focus, not even wrinkling his nose at the sour-smelling spew pooled a hand's breadth from his face.

This was the norm these days. He would have liked to say he knew how many days he had been home, but that was something he had forgotten in a blur of drinking ale in solitude. He peered about through blurry eyes to see where he was and was mildly surprised to find himself on a hill road, his mare cropping grass nearby. Choking back a stream of bile, he pushed himself upright on his elbow. He remembered waking that morning and then drinking. At some point, he decided to visit the tomb in which his kin's ashes were sealed. He did not recall reaching the tomb and guessed he had passed out and fallen from his mare.

Rolling away from the pool of vomit and flies it attracted, he closed his eyes. When next he awoke, he coughed through a lungful of dust. Dust hung thick in the still afternoon air and men's voices were raised. Through the ground he felt the drum of hoofbeats. He sat up to see the hill road teeming with riders. Some stared at him disinterestedly while others milled around, conversing in a familiar tongue. They were Masulians. Two riders converged on the others, one coaxing a horse along. Realization dawned on Caros. They were taking his mare.

Outrage drove him to his feet, and he paid with a hammer blow of pain from the head injury. Gasping, he staggered towards the men with his horse.

"The horse belongs to me!" He shouted angrily.

The Masulians fell silent, turning their glittering eyes on him. After a heartbeat, one spoke rapidly in his native dialect, earning laughter from the rest. Caros reckoned there were upwards of three hundred horsemen on the road. He closed on the men with his horse and one rider drove his mount between Caros and the man who had the mare's reins. Caros tried circling the mount, but the rider easily twisted his horse to block him. Furious, he grabbed the man's leg and heaved. Caught by surprise, the rider yelped, lost his balance and fell off the other side of the horse. The man's companion snarled and rode his horse at Caros who barely avoided being knocked to the ground by the animal. He snatched at his mare's reins and as his hand closed on the leather, he was struck from the back. The downed rider tackled him to the ground. Caros roared and struck at the man with his fists, but his blows lacked strength and the rider easily rolled on top of Caros to strike back. The first blow was delivered with an open handed and this infuriated Caros even more. To be struck by an open hand was a grievous insult amongst the Bastetani. With renewed strength, Caros batted away the next blow and grabbed the man's tunic at the chest to jerk him close. As he did so, he rammed his forehead into the man's face. The blow stunned the rider and his nose bubbled bright red blood. He fell back, his tunic ripping while Caros' saw white bolts of agony behind his eyes. He made to lunge at the Masulian, but the rider jumped to his feet with a cry of surprise. With one hand pinching his nose closed, he began shouting. The effect was like a bird twittering and many of the riders began laughing at him, not hearing his words. Those who did, fell silent and drew closer to inspect Caros. At that moment, a single rider galloped down the length of the column to pull in his horse abruptly, lifting a plume of dust.

"What are you men up to? Who is the camel turd and why is he rolling about in the dirt?"

The milling horsemen fell silent and dipped their chins to the rider who carried himself with the confidence of a leading man. The man with the bloodied nose judged it a good time to remove his hand from his nose and speak.

"This man is a drunkard who left his poor beast to wander thirsty, far from water or grazing."

The leading man frowned and looked Caros' mare over while clicking his tongue.

"So, take the mount. It is a beautiful beast."

"He gave me this bloody nose when I tried, but that is not the problem. He wears an amulet."

The leading man's gaze jumped between the rider and Caros, who had recovered enough to draw himself to his feet.

"Explain."

"He wears the white lion around his neck." His spoke the words with reverence.

The leading man's eyes widened and he looked hard at Caros whose amulet dangled at his throat. He addressed Caros in a dialect of Greek.

"You wear a powerful amulet; one that is not of your people. Where did you come by it?"

Caros straightened slowly and stared at the man before him. While shorter than Caros, he held himself with calm strength. Caros drew the amulet from where it hung on his greasy tunic. "This? This was gifted to me by one of your own." He paused to remember the name of the Masulian who had given him the amulet. It seemed like lifetimes ago. "Massibaka. The man who gave me this was a Masulian named Massibaka." Caros was confident he had the name right, but the leading man frowned skeptically. Inspiration struck and he recalled that the man had also given him a war-name. "Massibaka rode from Malaka with Gualam, a Turdetani leading man. He also gave me a war-name."

There was a subtle shift of expression in the man's eyes. "The war-name you were given, what is it?"

"Claw-of-the-Lion."

The riders congregated all around began to murmur amongst themselves. The Masulian stared hard at Caros for long moments before inclining his head briefly in acceptance of Caros' tale. While taking in Caros' disheveled state; vomit-stained tunic, stringy hair, and still raw head wound, he smiled and thrust out his hand. Uncertainly, Caros reached out and the leading man clasped Caros' arm below the elbow.

"My name is Aksel. It is an honor to meet a brother with such a powerful war-name. You must tell me how this came to be? It is customary among our people to give such names to those who offer daring feats. It appears we have come along at a good time; not wishing to be rude to a newly met brother, I have to tell you that you are a mess!"

Caros blinked a moment before an embarrassed smile grew across his face. Then he laughed aloud. Aksel grinned and around them, the watching horsemen nodded to one another. The rider with the bloody nose led Caros' mare to him with a sheepish grin.

Taking the reins, Caros thanked him. "Sorry about the nose."

"It is nothing, had I only known I grappled with a Claw warrior. Humble apologies for striking you with my palm." Caros smiled again.

Aksel interrupted, "Can you ride? I am told you were lying drunk beside the road."

Caros' face burned with shame and he ducked his head. "I can ride."

"Good. You should take yourself home and clean up. You need a healer to look at your head. Wounds like that need care."

Caros nodded dumbly for a moment. Bizarrely, he found he did not want to part from these men. "If I may ask, to where do you travel?"

Aksel regarded him evenly. "We hunt those who prey on travelers."

Caros was baffled. These foreign riders were enforcing law in Bastetani lands? His curiosity was piqued. What had he missed in the time he spent on the farm? An idea came to him. "I have land nearby with good grazing lands. Why not camp there this evening? It is almost dark already."

The Masulian paused and then smiled. "That is a generous offer. Thank you. Some of my men are carrying hard wounds and two of them cannot sit their mounts. May we stay for a few days until they have recovered?"

Caros was delighted, not that men were injured obviously, but that Aksel had assented. "Of course, my family bred horses there. There is plenty of grazing for all your mounts for as long as you wish. Regrettably, I do not have enough provisions to feed your men."

"No matter; they have rations and will hunt as necessary. This is fortuitous. Perhaps you will be able to tell me about your war-name and how you met Massibaka?"

15

Caros led Aksel and his column of Masulians across the hill and through a valley to his land. Neighbors were still caring for those horses he had recovered from the Arvenci with Alugra's help. Aksel nodded approvingly as they rode through the empty horse pastures.

"Good lands. This is a fertile valley. I am surprised there are not more farmers?"

"The village is new and men and women to settle the land prefer farms closer to Tagilit." Caros shook his head. "There was also a recent raid by Arvenci warriors and many good people were killed while others have fled to safer places.

"Ah, that is the hard way of life sometimes."

Caros glanced at Aksel, unused to the strange turns of phrase the man used. The sentiment was clear though. "A stream of sweet water runs along that tree line. Your men should think to camp on the land below the bend over there."

Despite the growing darkness, Aksel was able to discern the features Caros pointed out. He called instructions to his riders and Caros was struck by how quiet the Masulians were. Even when issuing orders, Aksel never raised his voice more than necessary. The riders dispersed towards the fields, leaving Aksel and Caros to ride on to the house.

Once they had rubbed down their mounts and put them out to graze, Caros led Aksel inside. On the portico, his second step kicked an overturned flagon, sending it clattering across the stone. Aksel jumped at the sudden crash and, embarrassed by the discarded flagons and stink of sour ale, Caros quickly pushed open the front door. At the hearth he lit a fire using the flint and oil kept there. Next, he lit two oil lamps and set them in high up to throw light into the dark corners.

Aksel looked about uncertainly. "You have no one else here? No wife?

No servants?"

"No, my kin were killed in the raid."

"Even so, I thought there would be others here."

"I live alone." Caros frowned in irritation at the Masulian's forwardness. "I will fetch food and ale. I will be back in a moment." Aksel dipped his chin and sat.

In the root cellar, Caros found a remaining flagon of ale and a haunch of cured ham that had begun to turn, the flesh mottling. He drew his short knife and cut away the worst of the bad meat. Looking at the meagre fare, he shrugged unhappily. His mother would have been able to lay a spread that would have included fruits, cheese and sweets before her guests.

They talked about trivial matters. Aksel had as many questions as did Caros, but the poor meal and eerie quiet of the empty home lay heavily on both men. Caros appreciated Aksel dismissive laugh when he apologized for the quality of the meal. He noticed that Aksel took mere sips of ale from his cup and did not seem fond of the drink. After the meal, Aksel smiled at Caros, his teeth white in his nut-brown face.

"Thank you, Caros. If you will excuse me, I need to tend to my men. I am worried about those with injuries."

Caros had forgotten. "Yes, of course. Why not let them stay here? They will be welcome. Your healer too."

Aksel smiled again, his eyes bright. "Unnecessary, but your offer is appreciated." He paused for a moment, one eyebrow raised. "Will you come to my tent for your first meal after sunrise? One of my men is a fine cook and we have plenty of provisions. How does that sound?"

"Thank you. I would like that."

He slept fitfully that night, but he went to sleep sober and with a lighter heart than he had felt for a long time. The following morning, he washed and dressed in a fresh tunic. His stomach rumbled as the sun rose and the night mists began to fade over the fields alongside the stream. Taking pleasure in seeing the stocky Masulian horses grazing the unused pastures, he strolled leisurely through the mist, the scent of horses a perfume in the morning air. Ahead of him, campfires were already lit and thin columns of smoke rose languidly above the field in which the Masulians had camped the night.

A young warrior met him at the edge of the field with wide eyes. The man smiled widely and waved. Caros greeted him in the pidgin Greek used among traders and travelers, but he laughed good-naturedly and spoke in his native tongue. The warrior gestured for Caros to follow and they threaded their way through the campfires. The Masulians were all awake and preparing and eating their morning meal. Many called greetings to the pair as they passed. It seemed to Caros that the Masulians were much more animated and boisterous than when he had ridden back with them the previous evening and put it down to them being rested. Aksel spotted them from where he was tending a horse tethered to a tree and waved.

"Greetings, Caros. You look well this morning."

"Thank you. You were not jesting when you said sunrise for breakfast!"

The Bastetani, like other Iberian people, ate later in the morning. Aksel grinned at him. "Best time of the day, my friend. Where we come from, it is best to rise early and do as much as possible before the sun becomes too warm." He spoke quickly to the young warrior in their native dialect and then bade Caros to follow him to the fireside. A thick carpet of woven wool had been laid on the ground and a choice of foods was arranged on wooden trays. A short man with a swarthy complexion was fussing over something at the fire.

"Our guest has arrived. Can we eat?"

The cook looked over his shoulder and flashed a wide smile. "All is ready. I am just doing the last of the eggs."

"Good." Aksel motioned towards the carpet. "We will sit here. Burney will bring the eggs, hot from the fire. They are a delicacy for us."

Caros sat and Aksel poured two cups of wine and handed one to Caros. "Burney mixes the wine with spices. They are more difficult to come by in your land, but he is a great explorer. What do you think?"

The wine was cut with fresh water and the spice left a lingering aftertaste. Caros smacked his lips. "It is good. What spice is used?"

"Burney! Caros wants to know what you put in the wine!"

The cook rose and came from the fire carrying a pot of boiled eggs in a hand wrapped in coarse toweling. "Ah, it is called cinnamon. Good for the spirit and keeps old men like me vigorous!"

Aksel snorted. "You are only a couple of years older than either of us."

Burney laughed. "Exactly! Here we go." He carefully tipped a handful of boiled doves' eggs into a bowl and crouched alongside Caros to shove a wooden platter into his hands. "Help yourself or we will starve while Aksel grows fat."

The men piled into the spread of dried dates, figs, olives, eggs, cheese and warm flatbread. Licking his lips, Caros finished off his meal.

"Aksel said you were an excellent cook. He was right! Thank you, it is been a long time since I ate so well."

Burney looked delighted and threw a hard look at Aksel. "So, you think I am excellent at preparing meals, do you? The silver that is my due has just increased."

Aksel snorted. "I do not give you silver, Burney. You just appear!" The men chuckled together as Aksel rose. "Come, I want to visit the men and see those that are wounded."

Caros spent the day with Aksel as the Masulian leading man ensured his men and their horses were in good shape. He knelt at the sides of the men who had been injured in a skirmish two days earlier. Both lay stricken in their bedrolls and while Caros could not understand the conversations Aksel had with them, he came away feeling that Aksel had lifted their spirits. The Masulian leading man seemed to have an easy confidence with his warriors. They instantly brightened when they saw him, but not with familiarity, rather with respect and pride. Caros tried to reconcile Aksel's way of leadership with Gualam's. They were worlds apart. Alugra on the other hand, had the same ability to lead his men without hard words.

Aksel also met with his leading men. They were veterans if their scars were anything to go by. One, a man named Manat, had a rippling silver scar down his right forearm and his hand boasted just three fingers and a thumb. Caros watched the five men squat in a close circle. They simply bent their knees and sat resting on their haunches. It was not a style common among his countrymen, but he recalled seeing Gyptos and North Africans sit in the same fashion. He emulated the men and crouched. It was an oddly comfortable way to sit, if you could call it that. It seemed to him like his rear end was hanging on a spring. He shuffled a little to get more comfortable and then paid attention to the gathering. Aksel introduced Caros to the four. Manat, with the silver scar; Kouf with jet black hair hung in ringlets hinting at Phoenician blood; Hahdha with sharp, green eyes and Jinkata; a leathery veteran with a hooked nose more akin to a beak. The men nodded solemnly in greeting. Caros listened to Aksel confer with them in their native African language and they spoke freely. Caros could detect no clashes or personal enmity between the five men. These Masulians would be formidable allies or foes depending on whose side they were on. The meeting ended after a short while and the men went their separate ways.

"They are happy to be here, Caros. They need the rest and time to take stock. Thank you again for granting us your hospitality."

"You and your warriors are most welcome here. They certainly look like seasoned warriors."

"Ah, many of them are. Others were just breaking into manhood when we arrived. They have shaped up nicely since then though. It has been a good experience for them."

"You mentioned you were scouting the land and hunting hill-warriors?"

Aksel raised an eyebrow. "Hill warriors?"

"Outcasts from their tribes who prey on travelers."

"Ah, bandits. Yes, but I sense the real question is whose coin are we taking?" Caros blushed, but Aksel just laughed good-naturedly. "It is no secret. The Barca has bolstered his forces with many Masulians. I believe he has mighty ambitions."

Caros nodded, his thoughts confirmed. "The Bastetani have been friends of the Barcas since the days of Hamilcar, Hannibal's father. It has been a good alliance for both sides and the Bastetani have grown wealthy in that time."

"Nevertheless, the young Barca wishes to expand his alliances north and west. There has been much resistance from those tribes he has encountered."

"The tribes prefer war to peace. It has always been the custom. It is fortuitous that we Bastetani saw a better way."

Aksel grinned and fingered the amulet hanging at his throat. "Yes, peace is a blessing, but every man has the urge to go to war. It is how men are, I think. We are content with one woman, but we always seem to find a way to want another. Peace is like that. It makes us content, but in time, we begin to look for reasons to start a war."

Changing the subject, Caros offered to show Aksel around the farm. He took the leading man around the rebuilt home and outbuilding.

"What is the land of your people called?"

Surprised, Aksel thought for a moment. "We do not have a name for our land for it is many lands and many people. We have names for the mountains, deserts and rivers, but no name for our land. I think this is similar to yours, am I right?"

"That is right, although the Greeks call all this land Iberia for the river Ebro and so others call it."

"Ah, yes, then you will have heard of Numidia. This is what the Greeks call our territories."

"Numidia! I have heard this name mentioned when dealing with merchants."

They had circled the farmstead and now arrived at the corral where Caros kept his mare. Aksel leaned up against a post to admire the horse. "That is a fine animal. Just the one?"

Caros shook his head. "I have ten more with neighbors who care for them."

Aksel cocked his head questioningly. In response, Caros described the efforts to recover the stolen livestock after the Arvenci raid. He found himself opening up and telling Aksel what had happened afterwards and how he had been wounded. Aksel was a good listener and if he had questions, he kept them to himself as Caros spoke. When he finished his tale, the Masulian was silent, his eyes far away. Caros leaned on the topmost corral pole, his chin on his hands, staring at the mare as she chewed through her feed. He felt better for having spoken of the events and about the loss of Ilimic.

Aksel cleared his throat. "Your head wound looks bad. I do not think you have been looking after it, but that is understandable. Our healers have a lot of experience with wounds. One of them even studied the lore in the land of the Gyptos." He turned his deep eyes on Caros. "Would you permit him to look at it?"

Caros was touched by the offer. He knew the injury was growing worse rather than better. Never before had he taken so long to heal. True, he had never been this badly injured, but the skin should have closed by now. Instead, the gash still leaked blood and pus.

"You are right. I have not tended it as I should have." He touched the swollen wound gingerly. "I would be most grateful if your healer would look. Thank you."

The afternoon found Caros seated before a short, sinewy Masulian. This was the healer Aksel had referred to. Caros had expected him to be older, his mind conjuring the image of a studious character complete with long grey beard. Instead, Aksel had introduced him to a warrior who spoke Greek fluently.

The healer cleaned away thin, weepy scabbing and probed the puffy flesh around the injury while Caros clenched his teeth against the pain. The man next looked deep into his eyes and with a strong hand clasped around his neck, turned Caros' face from side to side. "There are two injuries we must deal with. The first is this gash which is foul with evil shades. The other is beneath the bone of your skull." He rinsed his hands in a pail of water as he spoke. "You have much pain behind your eye, yes?" Without waiting for him to answer he went on. "The blow that split the flesh has also caused blood to pool under the bone. This is allowing evil shades to torment you and cause you pain. I can drain the blood and free the shades, after which the discomfit will be much lessened."

He knew the answer would terrify him, but he had to know. "How do you drain blood from beneath my skull?"

The healer grinned and proudly flipped open a leather bag to display a selection of shining instruments tucked into pouches sewn within the larger leather cover. These instruments were of brass and finely made. The merchant in Caros guessed that they were worth a small fortune.

The healer pointed to the instruments. "These are as good as any you will find among the Greeks or Gyptos. I learned to use them in Alexandria from skilled healers in that city."

Caros tore his eyes from the dazzling display of sharp blades and bits. "Tell me how you do it and have you done it yourself?" He smiled mirthlessly. "After all, I have just one skull."

"Yes, I have done this before. This happens when men have been injured when falling from their horses or in battle. The how is usually enough to make most men walk away. Or crawl if unable to walk." The healer grinned and paused expectantly. When Caros just stared at him, he glanced at Aksel who dipped his chin. The healer shrugged and drew out a drill bit from its pouch. "I use this to drill a hole through the bone to where the blood pools. This blood then pours out and washes the demon from your head."

Caros paled at the images that leapt to his mind. Surely none could live with a hole drilled into their head! The idea was absurd. He looked at the drill bit in the healer's hand and pointed at it. "With that one?" The healer nodded. Caros looked at Aksel who studied him silently. He felt he could trust the Masulian leading man and Aksel had faith in the healer. He looked at the calmly confident warrior and nodded slowly. "I trust you. If you think this is what needs to be done, then do it." Caros had always enjoyed his health. This constant throbbing terror in his head was robbing him of it and if he ever hoped to regain some measure of happiness in life, healing was a first step. He nodded more resolutely. "Yes. I have never heard of such healing, but I want you to do it." He swallowed and sent a prayer to Endovex, god of health. "Plus, those things look like they have a life of their own. It would be a shame not to use them."

The healer smiled and Aksel clapped his hands. "I am glad you have agreed, Caros. You will see this is a good decision!"

"When can you do this?"

The healer shrugged. "Right now."

Caros' heart leaped like a lynx against his ribs and his throat tightened, but there was no backing out of this. He grinned weakly. "That is good."

The healer went to work preparing a broth over a fire and in a short time, thrust a cup into Caros' sweaty palms. "Drink this. It will make you sleep so you will not feel the bite of the blade."

"I do not need to sleep like a babe, I can manage pain."

"No doubt. I can see that, but if you move; flinch even by the merest margin, it could kill you. I cannot do this thing if you are awake and when you do wake up, the spirits that torment you will be gone from your body."

Unable to speak, Caros nodded dumbly. Moments passed in a blur as the healer prepared the instruments and Caros sipped the broth. It was bitter. Salty. Not unpleasant. In a short while, Caros noticed the effects. His hearing became more acute, then faded as though his ears were plugged with wool. While he was wondering at this strange phenomenon, his sight began to darken. He found his eyes had drifted closed and blinked. He was surprised to find himself lying on his back and as he stared about, he smiled at the distorted figures about him, imbued with glowing colors he had never imagined were there. These were his last thoughts before the medicine dragged him under.

When he came to, he was lying on a cot with his head resting on a fleece. Above him, billowing in a breeze, was a tent top. The world melted and flowed around him, soothing him as he drifted among the shades of those who had passed. He woke again in the depth of the night with firelight playing softly on the fabric above him. His mouth was woolly and for a moment, he wondered where he had passed out. Then the memory of that afternoon returned and his eyes widened. He had lived! As if summoned, pain burned afresh through his head. It was of a different quality though. More burning and less throbbing. He lifted a hand to the injury. The movement attracted the healer's attention.

"No, you must not disturb the wound. It needs to sleep to heal. You are thirsty?" Caros cracked apart his dry lips and blinked, unable to form words. "Do not move your head. Here, I will place this reed in your mouth. Draw on it and you can drink without rising." He placed a thin reed between Caros' lips. The other end was submerged in a cup of fresh water and vinegar. Caros sucked on the reed dubiously, unfamiliar with the method of drinking. Cool water dribbled across his parched tongue and it seemed he had barely drunk a sip before the reed was pulled from his mouth. "Not too much at once. You can have more later, but too much now may cause you to vomit." Caros blinked in understanding. He woke up next the following morning. The healer was again at his side.

"You have slept deeply. How do you feel?"

Caros gave a tentative smile. "Fine. May I have some water?"

"As long as you move slowly, you may sit up to drink."

Caros edged himself into a sitting position on the cot. As he drank, he felt the same burning heat in his wound. It was infinitely preferable to the roaring, throbbing pain that he usually experienced when he moved his head. He finished the cup of water greedily.

"Thank you. The pain has gone." He grinned optimistically at the healer.

"I thought it might have. It was as I explained; blood had accumulated below the skull and as soon as I pierced the bone it was released. I drained it into a cup and placed the cup in the flames. The spirits that tore at you have now been banished from this land. How about your eye? Can you see any better?"

Caros blinked in surprise. His sight was clearer and looking out the tent door at the bright daylight did not hurt as it had. "Yes! You have done a fine job! Thank you."

16

With the draining of the blood and spirits from his head, the pain that had haunted Caros became a thing of the past. While he still felt the loss of his kin and Ilimic keenly, this pain was assuaged by the presence of the lively Masulians. The daylight hours saw him in the company of the Masulian leading man and his horsemen. Caros learned much about the Masulian's land across the Inland Sea in North Africa. Aksel's father was a prominent leading man from the region of Zama and their king was Gala. This king had pledged his warriors to Carthage in return for silver and trading rights. Warriors from across the eastern lands of the Masulians now flocked to fight for Carthage, their hopes set on plunder and adventure.

When Caros could once again ride, he asked Aksel to accompany him to the village. He had been meaning to go as soon as he could to advise the elders of the Masulian's presence. He worried that the villagers would think these foreign horsemen had come to prey on them. Until then, the Masulians had not ventured off the pastures along the stream. They had instead, spent their time resting their mounts and making necessary repairs to their equipment. Aksel brought two of his leading men with him, Jinkata and Hahdha, and the four men left mid-morning for the village. They encountered few people in the fields and those that spied them coming, quickly fled.

On approaching the village, Caros asked Aksel to hold back while he rode ahead. A pair of thin hounds growled and barked as he rode up to the gates that stood shut. A scuffle sounded and a man's face appeared over the top of the flimsy palisade surrounding the village. Caros waved and called a greeting. The man glared at him and then beyond him to the Masulians who waited patiently some distance back.

"You know me. I am Caros, son of Joaquim. These riders are my guests. We wish to visit with the elders." Without responding, the man disappeared from the wall. Caros sat his horse calmly and waited. The villagers were being cautious and he did not blame them after the appalling losses they had experienced in the last raid.

At last, he heard a commotion and more heads appeared above the wall. Caros squinted up at them. "Hunar, it is just me and some guests I wish to introduce." He gestured at the Masulians.

"Caros! You should have come sooner! Half the villagers have fled to the hill fort and have been there for the past four days!"

"What! Why?"

"Brent came with his family to warn us that a troop of strangers were encamped on your land. We did not know who they were, only that there were many hundreds of armed riders."

Caros grimaced up at Hunar in apology. "I am sorry. As I am here now though, are you going to let us in?"

Hunar shook his head in exasperation at Caros and gestured to an unseen person inside the walls. Moments later the gate was heaved open. Caros signaled to Aksel who rode up, flanked by his men.

Once the gates were opened and the riders had entered, Hunar sent a messenger to the nearby hill fort to let the villagers know that the riders were not to be feared. Caros introduced Aksel, Jinkata and Hahdha to the elder who greeted them with a poorly disguised air of disdain that embarrassed Caros. He would have preferred it if Luan had been present.

The village elder invited the men to the village's central hearth. This was the focal point of Bastetani villages and where the leading men, elders and warriors discussed matters of importance. Once there, he gestured to two youths hovering nearby to water the mounts. They came forward eagerly but paused in bewilderment. Of the four horses, only one had a bridle and reins with which to lead it. The Masulian mounts had no reins and wore only a saddle blanket. Aksel smiled widely at the youths who eyed the Masulian ponies suspiciously.

"Never mind, they will follow Caros' mare."

Those villagers who had remained after the raid were gathering and a fire was built over which a freshly slaughtered goat was spitted. Flagons of ale were brought out and soon enough the nervous village men were transformed into the warriors. The Masulians accepted the ale but drank modestly. Someone thrust a cup into Caros' hand and he nodded his thanks. Blowing the froth aside, he savored the strong smell of fermented grains. Licking his lips, he lifted the cup and drew a tentative sip. Swallowing the thick brew, he felt his palms grow slick with the desire to lose himself to the magic of it. He spat the taste into the dirt and emptied the cup onto the ground. He was not healed yet, and he had had enough of ale for a while.

Aksel was being questioned by men as they stepped forward and gave their names and deeds, as was custom. He did his best to answer the multitude of questions thrown at him and Caros thought that he did well. He was the kind of man that other men instantly marked as a leader and trustworthy. The men of the village nodded approval at every answer Aksel provided, even to the simplest of questions.

While Aksel was engaged with the crowd, the elder cornered Caros. "There is a matter you have to answer for. This is not the time, of course, but the people expect it, are due it."

Caros winced inwardly while remaining expressionless. He looked at the elder wordlessly until the man blinked rapidly, understanding dawning on him that Caros was not going to be baited.

"You know of the matter, Caros. Do not take me for a fool."

"I know of no matter. I have heard an untruth and I am unconcerned by it."

"She was to be your brother's..." The elder stammered as Caros' glare hardened. The older man had known Caros since he was an infant, but he did not recognize the scarred man that glared back at him. That cold stare rattled the elder and he swallowed nervously. "As I said, this is not the time to discuss it. I simply wanted to remind you that the matter is not resolved."

Caros stared a moment longer at the elder. He was aware that there were many eyes on him and whispers circling through the villagers. His nostrils flared as he smelled the fermented ale that flowed and thought how good a flagon would make him feel. He shrugged and rolled his neck, putting the craving from his mind along with the villagers' speculations.

"What news of Alugra?" He had grown fond of the veteran warrior in the few days he had known him.

The elder shook his head. "He is said to be dying; speared in the liver during a battle with Olcades warriors."

Caros was equally both distressed and alarmed. Other men heard and Aksel got some respite as their attention turned to talk of battle. The subject was obviously a heated one and men cursed the Olcades in a hundred ways. To Caros, this was bleak news. While Alugra was no longer young, he still had good years ahead. His loss would be a loss to the whole tribe. To compound this, the Olcades were a powerful tribe on the northern borders of Bastetani lands. If their leading men united to march in force on the Bastetani, the war would make a thousand widows. All the gains made by the Bastetani in the last twenty years would be diminished.

The elder had to raise his voice to make himself heard. "Much has been happening among the tribes. It is almost impossible to travel between our own villages without risk of attack by hill warriors. The raid on us was just the beginning and we were fortunate. Bastetani villages in the west and north have been raised. The people all killed and even the livestock butchered. The Barca is said to be moving tens of thousands of warriors north. Overland and by ship."

Caros watched Aksel. The Masulian was listening intently and his expression gave nothing away.

"I thought the Olcades had sworn a peace with the Barca last autumn?"

The elder grunted and spat. "Not the men and women who matter. Those, their keener champions and graybeards took refuge among the Carpetani and stirred them up so that they and their neighbors, the Oretani, are now intent on war again."

"Who leads the Bastetani of Tagilit now that Alugra is injured?" Caros had a good idea who did, but he asked to be certain.

"Alfren. You would have met him with Alugra's warriors. He was Alugra's leading man."

"Yes, a dangerous man. Not of the same cast as Alugra, but as good a leader as we are likely to have." He remembered the dour Lusitanian and knew he would be more than capable of leading a Bastetani army.

"We are expecting a column of his warriors here any day now." The elder shot a poisonous glare Caros' way. "We sent word of the horsemen to him."

"They will be disappointed to find no enemy." Caros grinned at Aksel.

The elder showed a cold smile. "It will be good to have trustworthy warriors in the area to clear out these infernal hill warriors."

"That is the reason the Masulians are here. They were sent to find the hill warriors and wipe them from our lands. That is why they are camped at my farm. Some were injured in clashes with them."

The elder sharpened his gaze suddenly as realization dawned. "The Barca. They answer to the Carthaginian!" He looked at Aksel who stared back. "No need to say a thing. I see the pattern. It is obvious you are taking Barca silver."

Two days later, while Caros accompanied Aksel and a party of the Masulians on a hunt in the hilly country north of the village, they spied a dust cloud in the southwest. The men halted and sat watching the dust moving west to east. Aksel and Jinkata conferred in their tongue before Aksel turned to Caros.

"Those are riders heading to your village."

Caros watched the cloud and concluded the Masulians were right. "Could be Alfren's warriors? They are expected." He felt nervous for the village though. They may just as easily be Olcades or Carpetani warriors.

Aksel thought the same thing as he revealed in his next comment. "We can hunt again another day. I think it best we go and have a look. It appears there are many hundreds of riders judging by the size of that dust cloud."

Caros nodded his agreement and Jinkata quickly blew his warhorn twice to reassemble the hunters. In moments, the scouts appeared and before long the column was streaming down the hills into the valley. Aksel sent a pair of men to gather the Masulians who had remained at the farm. While the pair rode off westwards, the main party flew down the valley towards the village.

The village came into sight as the men whipped their mounts through the fields north of the walls. Aksel cursed and pointed at a column of mounted warriors to their right. These had entered the valley passing the old hill fort and the trails of the two columns of warriors were converging. They became aware of one another at the same time and in heartbeats, both columns reined in and turned to facing one another across a distance of just two stadia. The warriors with Caros and Aksel numbered less than twenty. Across the fields were five hundred horsemen. Caros could tell they were Iberians, but at this distance he could not be sure of which tribe.

He felt a nervous sweat on his brow. Even with the Masulians coming from the farm, they were badly outnumbered if the opposing column was hostile. Caros noticed two things at once; the drum of hoofbeats from their rear and the unknown Iberian horsemen jostling into a loose formation. The bulk of his warriors were ranging up behind them in the distance. Aksel glanced over his shoulder and waved.

"Now we have the numbers for a fight."

A warhorn sounded and Caros swiveled back to see the unknown horsemen starting forward at a walk. Aksel shouted an order to his tiny column to fall back to meet with the rest of his men. They turned but halted in consternation when they saw their leading man had remained with Caros. Aksel gestured to them to go, spitting curses at them in frustration. The advancing column was picking up speed. In just moments they would cover the distance between them and their first volley of arrows and javelins would decimate the small Masulian hunting party.

He needed to act fast. "Go Aksel. Your men will not leave without you." He did not wait for Aksel's response, instead, he urged his mare towards the advancing warriors. As he did so, he cast a hurried prayer to Runeovex, god of war, that these were Alfren's men and not the enemy. The mare broke into a trot with Caros aiming her at the center of the advancing lines. He threw aside his hunting spear and raised his hand.

"Warriors! I am Caros of the Bastetani!" He continued to shout while urging his mare onwards still faster, his weaponless hand above his head like a banner. By Runeovex, they were going to ride him down! He dared not spare a glance over his shoulder to see what the Masulians were doing. Instead, he fixed his eyes on the rider at the head of the mass of warriors. He shouted again, but his voice was drowned out by the hoofbeats of so many mounts. Warriors drew back their throwing arms, iron-tipped javelins balanced on thumb and forefinger. Sweat dripped from his brow and he wiped his arm along the raw scar on his head.

As though tiring of the game, the gods interceded and the leading man gestured to a wild warrior beside him. The man raised a warhorn to his lips. Two trumpeting calls pealed through the valley. The signal to gather. The oncoming warriors began drawing on their reins. The charge slowed and Caros reined in his mare, his heart was beating through his ribs. Just a heartbeat more would have seen him pierced through. He waved weakly at the men before him. The rider in the center walked his horse forward and Caros grunted in surprise.

"By the gods! Is that you, Caros?"

Caros smiled shakily. "Neugen! You scared the shit out of me."

"Ha! It is you; same lousy jokes!"

Both riders threw themselves from their horses and ran to embrace. Laughing hard, they slapped one another's backs as though making sure they were not the shade of the other, but living, breathing flesh. They danced a wild jig there in the valley surrounded by two lines of bewildered warriors. Panting hard, they stopped and stared at one another, hands locked on shoulders. Caros saw the flickering memories in his friend's eyes and knew Neugen saw the same as sadness darkened his joy for a moment.

Then his face brightened. "Caros, I scarcely recognized you with that scar across half your head. You must have frightened away every woman and child in the village by now!"

Caros laughed. "Last time I saw you, you had a hole in your chest that looked like a hill warrior's asshole." Insults traded, both men laughed happily.

Aksel led his Masulians back to the farm as Caros accompanied Neugen's force to the village. Neugen explained how they had received the plea for assistance from the village and Alfren had cursed to hear of enemies at his back. They had been harassing enemy Oretani and Carpetani war bands for the past several days. He had been committed to a battle and could not spare any warriors to return to the village. It had been hard fought three days earlier and the enemy warriors had broken and fled. Only then did Alfren send Neugen, who had volunteered to lead the column.

"So, the Oretani and Carpetani are truly at war with us?"

The pair arrived at the village and Neugen sent his warriors off to feed and rest where they could.

"Oh yes, the Olcades stirred them all up. They are massing a host of warriors. Alfren has been hitting them where he can, but he has less than four thousand troops, most on foot."

Even so, Caros was amazed at the numbers. Four thousand warriors! "You say four thousand as though that is not enough?"

Neugen grimaced. "Together, the Oretani and Carpetani have upward of thirty thousand and still more are gathering every day."

Caros blanched. "Such numbers. They will overrun us then! We must draw forces from the south. Has Alfren sent for them?"

"Of course, but this has happened so quickly. We suspect that they have been preparing for this for a long while now."

"This must be in order to strike back at the Carthaginians. They will tear Hannibal's army apart along with every tribe loyal to the Barcas."

Neugen frowned. "Well, nothing like a little optimism." His frown turned to a grin. "We will sort them out. Even if we have to fall back until we are at the coast."

"Baria?"

"Not likely, probably to Qart Hadasht. Combine with Barca's army and then we will be able to match their numbers."

"This must be Alfren's dream come true. Matter of fact, you look like you are bloody enjoying yourself." Caros accused Neugen, who smirked.

"I am as a matter of fact. I lead five hundred mounted warriors. Come a long way since we met my friend, and it is thanks to you."

Caros swallowed uncomfortably, his guilt at abandoning Neugen casting a shadow over his mood. "I did nothing."

"You have had a bad time of it. Those things you said when you left Tarren's farm; we knew it was the wound and grief. Do not apologize. If I had not been so badly injured, I would have been able to remain with you." His voiced trailed away uncertainly.

"I am recovered, Neugen. Nearly killed myself with drink and self-pity, but Endovex interceded and sent the Masulians my way. They have a healer who trained in Alexander."

"I do not know where Alexander is my friend, but if you say so."

Caros laughed and then the two men were laughing chatting together again like old times.

Caros rose before dawn and shuffled beyond the camp, loosening his smallclothes as he went. He reached a tall pine and directed his stream against the trunk while bracing himself upright with his free hand. He swore and moved his footing to avoid the steady stream of piss flowing towards his toes. In the distance, a lynx screamed and the sound woke him completely. He felt the hair on his neck rise at the cry and smiled. Behind him came movement from his companions. Neugen, Aksel, and several of the Masulian warriors still lay about the campfire.

They had returned to the hunt after Neugen sent word to Alfren that all was well. Neugen had been only too happy to join them. Four days of racing down deer at sunrise as the animals warmed themselves. Whole mornings spent stalking wary mouflon in the high passes and once, seeing the flash of a lynx in its mountain fortress, all made for a high time. Today they would make for the best boar hunting lands in the region and with fortune, one of them would face and kill one of those ferocious beasts. Now though, he needed some food.

"Hoi! Whose turn was it to light the fire?" He laughed as he returned to the camp.

Aksel sat up yawning, stretched and then bounded upright. "Ah, today we hunt the mighty boar! I have heard tales of these beasts and have longed for a chance to try my hand at killing one."

Neugen groaned and rolled over to face him, opening one eye. "Well, any chance we had is gone now."

Aksel's face fell. "Why? Have I offended the gods of the land?"

Caros dropped his chin to hide his grin. Neugen had kept the Masulian spinning with his jests for four days.

"Oh, it is not complicated." He rose so he could better deliver the punch line. Probably also to see how big an audience he had. He was pleased to see the rest of the Masulians were awake and listening. "It is just that your shouting just scared every one of the big, hairy bastards all the way to Albion!"

Aksel's mouth formed a perfect circle of surprise and then spread into a mischievous smile.

"So, it is the noise is it?" He glanced at Caros. "All the way to Albion? Hmm, seems to me that any noise made was made by you."

"What? I was asleep till just now when you started on about 'the mighty boar'!"

"You were asleep yes, but between your snores and your ass-belching, I hardly slept the entire night. Seems to me that and the stench of your guts, I know a good healer by the way, is what has scared away the boar."

Neugen and the Masulian shared the same vein of humor and it had made for a lively hunt. Caros grinned at Neugen, wishing he had one or two come back lines as good as Aksel's. He cracked a handful of twigs and together with dry grass, shoved them into the ash-covered embers of the night's campfire. He leaned closer and blew, shutting his eyes against the inevitable billow of old ash. Soon enough, he had a merry fire crackling and leaned back on his heals. "Right, we warm up some meat and then find a boar. The bigger the better."

Neugen grumbled, but rolled to his feet, discarding his cloak. Caros heated meat left from their evening meal and soon they were all washing it down with cut wine.

"Time to go hunting fellows. The valley we should sweep is the next one over. It is thickly wooded and not great for goat or cattle. In the past my father speared two good sized boars there, so I expect that with a few beaters to flush them out, we should meet a boar."

The men split up at the head of the valley. The Masulians headed west on the upper slopes. Caros, Neugen and Aksel remained at the head of the valley until they judged the others had reached a suitable distance. At Caros' nod, they clicked their tongues and began forward on their mounts.

No ordinary spear was used for a boar hunt. Instead, they carried spears as thick as two javelins. The sun scarcely made its way through the canopy above to where the hunters stalked the valley floor. Caros inhaled the deep odor of the moldy vegetation and focused his eyes ahead of him, trying to accustom them to the deep shade of the valley. This was the perfect place for boar. Untended, deep forest, with plenty of water, nuts and roots to feed on. It was no wonder this valley was a good hunting ground. Who knew what other denizens they might unearth? Aksel appeared momentarily on his right and a few strides later, Neugen appeared in a shaft of light to his left. He tried to focus on the trail, but it was difficult. He was happy again, he had not believed he could be, but being among men like Aksel and Neugen, he was. He felt raw inside at the fate of Ilimic, but that pain had somehow shifted. He thought of her as she had been and avoided dwelling on her fate.

A long flat pebble appeared on the ground ahead and Caros cocked an eye at it. At this point in the valley, sunlight barely ever penetrated as far as the ground below and moss or lichen covered the rocks and even fallen branches. He scanned the ground and his heart began to beat with excitement. This was not virgin dead leaf, but instead, a mulch of treaded ground. It was surely a regular trail of one of the great boars. He had thought about hunting one in the way someone dreams about a beautiful, yet unattainable woman. Yet now he was straddling the path of one of these monsters. To either side of him were reliable friends and beneath him, a loyal horse. Caros hefted the heavy boar spear, experimenting with its weight. From the tales told over fires and through ale, boar were extraordinarily tough creatures. These characteristics, together with a devious and vengeful mind, made them formidable adversaries. He felt a tingle of apprehension spiral through him and grinned stupidly to himself. He felt good. He owed a great debt to the Masulian leading man and his cheerful warriors. He had found in their absolute joy of life, an antidote to the depression and guilt that had darkened his spirit.

He passed the pebble he had seen and stared at it; noting that a thin cover of dry lichen had been folded back on one side of it. This was what he had expected to see. Something was amiss though. He stared at the rock and the pattern formed when the lichen had come away. The imprint looked at first glance like a random pattern, but on closer inspection, Caros discerned a sandal print. Whoever had stepped on the rock, had slipped a moment before stepping off it, which had distorted the footprint. What was clear was this had happened after sunrise that very morning. The lichen, still partially flattened, was lifting back into shape before his eyes. Caros glanced at the rest of the valley floor about him. The torn-up leaves and general size of the disturbance which he had taken to be a well-used boar trail could in effect be the trail of a band of warriors. He whistled for Neugen and Aksel. Both men immediately paused and gave him questioning looks. Impatiently he beckoned them to him. He did not want to raise his voice, wary now that there were others in this valley.

"What? Have you picked up a trail?" Neugen asked in a low voice before his horse stepped through a screen of low-hanging branches.

Caros did not bother to reply as Neugen's face immediately register the fresh tracks on the valley floor. Aksel, approaching from the left, also immediately saw the tracks for what they were.

"How long have you been on this trail?"

"A fair while." Caros smiled sheepishly. "Thought it was a boar trail. Until I noticed a sandal print in the moss on that rock."

"This is probably a boar trail. Thing is, I do not think boars wear sandals." He flashed a grin at Caros.

Aksel stared at the rock for a moment. "They are heading towards the others. These tracks have been made recently. Maybe seven men with horses."

Neugen's eyebrows rose and he gave the Masulian a nod of respect. "That is what I was thinking. We should keep following them. If they are enemy warriors, they will be trapped between us and your men."

"My men will not know they are coming. They may be taken by surprise..." He pursed his lips before smiling. "They will be fine. It is these travelers who will be worse off if they prove to be hostile."

"Aksel, take the lead. Neugen and I will stay right behind you." Caros pointed at the deep layer of rotted leaves. "This stuff is great for muffling sound. We keep silent until we see them."

The three men nodded and immediately set off down the valley. They not ridden half a stadion when they heard a yell ahead of them. Then a barrage of voices calling and shouting in the Masulian tongue followed. The three men froze for a heartbeat and then kicked their mounts forwards to catch the enemy in the rear. The shouting died down and apparently the alarm subsided. They could hear lots of voices talking and even the neighing of horses, but the sounds of battle were absent. Confused, they slowed their horses to a trot as they rounded a natural bend in the valley floor. There before them, sat their own riders, smiling and talking with a group of seven Masulians who were not part of the hunting party.

Jinkata broke away from the group to greet them and introduce the new arrivals who looked weary enough and injured. That they had been in some skirmish was not in doubt. Aksel listened intently as one of the newcomers spoke. From his gesticulations and tone, whatever he was describing was something important. Aksel listened silently until the man finished speaking then questioned him. Apparently satisfied with the answers, he looked over the other six riders, noting their condition.

"Looks like we will not be eating boar tonight." Neugen mused. "What is happening?"

"The war everyone expected has begun."

"These men have seen battle. Who are they?" Caros rode closer, eyeing the bloody dressings worn by the newcomers.

"They are scouts and messengers on their way to Qart Hadasht with news for the Barcas. It seems a large army of the tribes has gathered inland and is making its way to the city of Sagunt."

"Why does that city keep cropping up whenever there is trouble?" Neugen grumbled.

Caros agreed wholeheartedly. "Did the messengers say which tribe this army was from?"

"Not one tribe, but many; including Oretani and Carpetani."

"I knew it!" Neugen exclaimed and then looked puzzled. "Why Sagunt though? I would have thought they would tear straight through Bastetani lands to Baria and Qart Hadasht?"

"Hannibal has marched. He is no longer at Qart Hadasht, but on his way to Sagunt. In fact, he may be there already." Caros' eyes widened in surprise. There was a lot of enmity between Sagunt and the Barcas, but he had not expected the Carthaginians to attack the city. Had the murder of Sagunt's Carthaginian sympathizers forced Hannibal's hand? Aksel went on. "The Oretani and Carpetani will fall on Hannibal's rear while he besieges Sagunt."

Neugen looked at Caros in alarm. "I told you how many of them there were and there are probably even more now! This is going to be one bloody battle." Through the alarm, Caros could sense excitement in his friend's voice.

"I am no Greek strategos, but being caught from the rear like that is a bad thing, right? I assume messengers are on the way to Hannibal's army?"

"Yes, and their leading man thought it prudent to warn the garrison at Qart Hadasht. I will be taking my men to join the rest of the Masulians with Hannibal's army." He looked at Caros. "One day we will finish one of these hunts, you and I."

Neugen looked at Caros. "I will need to return to my column and see what Alfren is planning. If I know him, he will be shadowing the bastards every step of the way while he draws more warriors from the south." Caros was suddenly at a loss. Both men knew exactly what they had to do. He, on the other hand, seemed to have no purpose. As if sensing his thoughts, Neugen asked, "Why not join me, Caros? We will need every warrior we can field, and you are worth at least two."

Caros smiled widely. He did not have to consider his answer for even a moment.

"Just two, eh? Well Runeovex knows I am not going to sit around on an empty farm while you fellows have all the fun!"

The three men burst into spontaneous laughter, eyes alight with excitement at the prospect of battle.

17

Abarca crossed the courtyard amid a bellowing of warhorns and the sound of thousands upon thousands of voices raised in alarm and excitement. This was the endgame. The day of impact had arrived. Even with his limping gait, caused by a javelin wound long years past, he speedily made his way to the hill fort's wall and climbed the stairs to the battlement overlooking Sagunt and the plains surrounding the city. He reached the ledge below the highest parapet, sweating from exertion, but with fire in his eyes. To the south and west, were long columns of warriors. The heat of summer together with the clouds of dust, obscured much of the converging columns, but that they were numerous was not in doubt. He swiveled to look to the east and saw yet another column. Easily many, many thousands strong, Hannibal's army had arrived. Abarca's heart beat wildly and he breathed deeply to calm himself. This was the culmination of over a year of planning by the oligarchy ruling Sagunt.

Abarca motioned to his aide. "Are all the warriors within? The gates closed?"

"Yes, Strategos. We have some seventy thousand warriors within the walls and all gates are sealed. The outer walls are now fully manned, and we have forty thousand warriors in reserve."

Abarca smiled. Seventy thousand warriors, most of them of the Edetani tribe. It was no mean feat to bring together so many spears, even of the same clans. The tribes of the Iberian peoples were based on a loose confederation. Within any one tribe were numerous leading men who each ruled a large settlement and smaller outlying villages. He had known that to regain their wealth they would need to bring together all these leading men and their warriors. Promises of plunder were made, but the rulers of Sagunt had still needed to front precious silver to bring all the clans together.

The anvil was now ready and Hannibal had placed himself upon it. Abarca hoped desperately that the second crucial factor in his plan paid off. This part relied on Berenger and Abarca was confident that the dangerous warrior would be able to fulfil his part.

The Strategos paced along the walk, staring towards the western hills. On the plains beyond the outer walls, the columns resolved from distant specters into the forms of individual warriors. Abarca studied the columns and tried to estimate the numbers. All his intelligence indicated Hannibal had upward of one hundred thousand warriors on the field. The figure was a mind-boggling amount considering that the largest settlements in Iberia numbered a fraction of that. His spies had told of how energetically Hannibal had been recruiting warriors from amongst the tribes he had subjugated. His gaze lowered to take in the preparations for defense. In truth, Abarca had expected Hannibal to launch this assault much sooner in the season. The unexpected delay had given the city still more time to bring in reticent leading men and lay on more provisions to see them through a protracted siege.

His aide cleared his throat. Abarca turned away from studying the city walls and looked along the walkway. Two members of the oligarchy were climbing the stairs to him on shaky legs. Their tunics drowned under the finest robes of the richest colors. Abarca detested both, but knew without their influence and wealth he would have no chance to succeed. The men stepped gingerly from the steep stone stairs onto the walkway. Both were of mixed Iberian and Greek blood, but they looked more like swaddled toads than either powerful Iberian or statuesque Greek. Abarca found himself enjoying the men's obvious fear of heights.

"Aniceteus, a pleasant surprise? Glauketas you are up early. It is particularly noisy today is it not?" Abarca maintained a look of innocence while inwardly, he rejoiced at their discomfit.

Catching his breath, Aniceteus, the wealthiest of Sagunt's merchants, replied with a glare.

"I expected you to warn us of Hannibal's arrival." He turned and stared over the wall at the massing army. Beside him, Glauketas was forced to stand on his toes to see over the parapet to the plain below the city. He was as evil a person as Abarca had ever associated with, but he held sway as high priest in the temple of Cariociecus, god of war. His equally maniacal sister, Carmesina, was the high priestess in the temple of Catubodua. Abarca revered Runeovex as god of war, but kept that to himself. Both Cariociecus and Catubodua were bloodthirsty gods of times past, but with cunning and guile, Carmesina had thrown down the newer, more benevolent gods and reinstated the old deities. The oligarchy had gone along with this, happy at the tighter rein on their citizens it afforded them.

"You were informed just yesterday that Hannibal was a day's march from the city walls." Abarca responded mildly.

Aniceteus harrumphed and peered at the approaching army. "Looks like an awful lot of warriors. Are those horsemen?" He stuck a flabby arm over the parapet and pointed to the west. A mass of men on horseback thundered through the low foothills onto the plain. It was like watching some strange river of flesh that streamed out of the mountains and swallowed the ground.

"I see them!!" The priest squealed. The short creature bounced excitedly and brayed with laughter. "Ride to me you fools!"

Abarca could not keep the contempt from his face and saw even Anicetus flinch away from the unhinged priest.

The merchant looked at Abarca, one eyebrow hitched high. "Horsemen against a walled city? That seems odd?"

Abarca sighed. "They are men, not centaurs. They can dismount and scale ladders.They will also be able to run down our messengers."

"My sister, the High Priest Carmesina, has high hopes for the rituals and I am eager to honor our warriors in the same vein tomorrow. You will be there as Strategos will you not?"

Abarca suppressed a shudder. In a moment this creature could turn from an excited lunatic to a calculating viper. Through their whorehouse, the House of the Crow, Carmesina and her brother had bought numerous virgins for these rituals. Knowing the depraved minds of these siblings, Abarca could only begin to imagine the fate awaiting these girls. Nevertheless, as Strategos it was incumbent to show his leading men that he never shirked his responsibilities. Now was not the time to let his sensibilities alienate him from a large portion of his fighting forces. He smiled thinly at the high priest and nodded. "Of course. It is most important everything be done to raise the blood our more barbaric warriors."

Glauketas smiled happily for a moment before a glimmer of confusion crossed his face. The merchant covered his grin at Abarca's barbed words and their effect on the priest who threw a wrathful look at Abarca before storming off.

Abarca grunted. "I should not do that. There is no honor in it."

Anicetus nodded. "But the look on his face. Ah, such moments are to be relished.More importantly, you now have Barca and his army here against our walls." He made a show of turning in a circle to gesture at the encircling forces. "I believe you described our city as the anvil. Where is your hammer?"

Abarca, eyes fixed on the sea of warriors surrounding Sagunt, wondered the same thing.

18

Dawn raised a silver mist along the deep river valley while the crests of the hills burned bright. From the shadows of the trees above the mist, she screamed, proclaiming her kill. Tearing into the belly of the young mouflon, she reached the sweet liver. Pink flesh gave way to white fangs and she ate down a mouthful. Her young would be able to drink deep after this meal.

Black-tufted ears twitched, and she growled deeply as a familiar and hated scent reached her. Unsettled, the hunter bit and ripped away more flesh, swallowing whole chunks as she gorged. All the while, her eyes darted from shadow to shadow and her ears remained in motion.

In the valley below her, the mist swelled and birthed dark forms. She growled again from deep in her chest and rose; her kill forgotten. Pacing lithely to an outcrop of guano-stained granite, the lynx leaped to the tallest point. Through golden eyes, she watched the valley fill with the forms of men.

Berenger had accomplished the impossible. So many obstacles had stood in his path, but he had overcome them all to gather a great army. The combined warriors of four of the most warlike Iberian tribes flowed through the hills towards Sagunt in the east. Warriors of the Olcades and Vaccaei from the north, hard men with good blades. Warriors of the Oretani, men who had fought the Carthaginians before and boasted still that it was they who had slain Hamilcar Barca, Hannibal's father. And the numerous warriors of the Carpetani; through whose land the massed army now moved.

His greatest obstacle was arranging this alliance. In his experience, uniting two leading men of the same tribe was difficult enough. When Abarca had first asked him if he would do this, he had openly laughed at the Strategos. Abarca had persisted with the idea; arguing that unless it was done, the city of Sagunt would be isolated and fall to the Barcas, if not in war, then through a decline in trade. There were few as wily as the Carthaginians when it came to trade. Berenger had realized that wisdom in the Strategos vision and resolved to plan and deliver it.

Little did Hannibal realize it, but he had inadvertently made Berenger's job easier. In the previous two years Hannibal had subjugated first the Olcades and then the Vaccaei. Those of their warriors who refused to accept this subjugation had fled to Carpetani and Oretani lands. It was these warriors more than anything that had raised the battle fever in the Oretani and Carpetani tribes. By the time Berenger arrived with Sagunt silver, the warriors of the tribes were all but frothing at the mouth for war.

He rode his black stallion through the snaking river valley in a southeasterly direction. The mighty Tagus still flowed strongly from the past winter rains. He was leading the newly forged army upriver and there at the river's source they would wait on the signal to strike at Hannibal's rear. Abarca would be awed at the number of warriors that would arrive to crush the Barcid army against the walls of Sagunt. Berenger estimated the strength of the army at anything between fifty and sixty thousand. He received reports daily of more warriors joining and of more leading men coming over to his side. It was possible that by the time they reached Sagunt, he would have a hundred thousand warriors. He marveled at the numbers and the thought of what he could do with such an army bubbled in his mind.

The river mist was burning off and Berenger felt the heat of the new day begin to rise. They were making good time and would reach the final rendezvous point at the river's source within three days. Josa cantered back down the road with two riders trailing him and Berenger reined in beneath a shady tree to wait for him. He guessed the two riders were messengers. One was certainly from Abarca. He was curious as to who the second was.

"Berenger. These two have messages for you."

"Which of you is from Sagunt?" Berenger asked the two men as they came to a halt in the sun beside Josa.

A thin man, grey with dust, spoke.

"I am." He produced a cylinder from within his tunic and passed it to Josa who handed it to Berenger.

"I will give you a reply momentarily. In the meantime, go take some water."

"Very well." The man turned his horse about and plunged it skillfully down the bank to the riverbank below.

Berenger turned his gaze on the second rider. The man's one good eye flicked away from Berenger's hard stare. His other was a puckered red hole. Berenger thought it looked amazingly like an asshole and wondered why the man did not wear a patch over it. Perhaps he liked to tempt men to insult him and then battle them. In that case, maybe he was one of those warriors who loved killing for the sake of killing. He could always do with men like that under his command.

"What message do you bring me?"

The man glanced to where the first messenger had gone down to the river. Josa's face remained impassive even as his hand tighten on his sword grip.

The man grunted, picking at scabs on his neck. "I got nothing fancy with lines on it like that one. Was just told to let you know Barca scouts have discovered your army."

"Why not tell me who sent the message?"

"Oh? Did I not say?" The warrior smiled, revealing a mouth full of black stumps. Berenger thought he glimpsed maybe one white tooth left whole. He had seen that before. The end of a sword or spear breaks off the teeth top and bottom. Good way to disable a warrior for a moment while you dealt with a more immediate threat.

"Spit out the name or you will be spitting out the rest of your shitty teeth."

The warrior smiled even wider. " Cortocus. He got after them and we cut them up. Still, some got away on their little daemon ponies." The man shrugged and spat a wad of phlegm at his mount's feet.

Cortocus was a Carpetani champion who led two thousand warriors, a quarter of whom were mounted. From Berenger's recent experience with the strange horsemen that rode for Hannibal, it was unlikely that Cortocus' men had 'cut them up' as the messenger had put it. There was little he could do about word of their presence reaching the Barca now. In any event, it was already too late for Hannibal to react. He could of course run back south. Then the army holed up in Sagunt together with these warriors could take the battle to him. He gave the messenger another look.

"What else?" The man cocked his head as though thinking and then shook it. "Nothing? Then tell Cortocus to be more vigilant. Go!"

Josa lifted his hand a fraction, showing a finger's width of bright blade. The messenger grinned, turned his mount about and with a wild cry galloped away, leaving Josa spitting dust.

Berenger laughed at the spirit of the man. Still chuckling, he broke the wax seal on the cylinder and unrolled the parchment within. The message was short and to the point. Abarca wanted him at the city walls in no less than five days. The army was to remain out of sight in the hills to the west of Sagunt and attack upon a signal from the city. The signal would be a column of black and then white smoke. Three times this column of smoke would rise and Berenger was to fall on Hannibal's rear on the third. He crumbled the parchment in a calloused hand and threw it to the wind. Josa yelled for the first messenger to return and within moments the man leaped his horse through the brush and onto the road.

"Let the Strategos know I have received his message and it will be as he requests." The man nodded. "Hannibal is at the city walls?" Berenger asked.

"Yes, he arrived days ago, but nothing has happened. His horsemen tear across the plains, and his warriors eat what little food we left them in the surrounding countryside."

"Siege engines? Any of those?"

"Nothing we have seen so far."

"How do you get back to the city? Surely no one will be able to get in?"

"I lived there all my life and know every fold of the countryside. They will not see me till I am at the north postern gate showing them my hairy, white ass."

"What about your horse? Can you get it in?"

"Of course!" He patted the mare's neck affectionately. "Those bastards would probably eat her if I left her outside the city."

On an impulse, Berenger asked the messenger to draw him a map of his secret route into the city. The man frowned, but one look at Berenger's expression persuaded him. Using valuable parchment unneeded for Berenger's response to Abarca's instructions, the messenger sketched a crude map and talked him through the route. Burying the map in his tunic, Berenger was confident that if necessary, he would find his way into the city through the besieging forces.

The following day the army encamped on a plain to the south of the Tagus near the little settlement of Peñalén. Berenger was chewing vainly on boiled goat when a party of mounted warriors, shouting to one another in excitement, galloped up. Josa walked over to Berenger's side as they reined in, shouting to Berenger who waited impatiently for them to make sense. A grizzled warrior, older than the rest of the party, snarled at the rest to shut their mouths and nodded to Berenger.

"We were scouting to the south, near the headwaters of the river. Their tracks crossed a ford there and we thought they might be Carpetani warriors coming to join us. We followed them downriver. That is where we spotted them; thirty thousand warriors. All mounted."

"How far from here?" Berenger snapped.

The warrior answered immediately. "Not half a day's ride."

"They are on the other side of the river?"

"Yes, the north bank."

Berenger looked at Josa. "They will be here early tomorrow. We want the warriors on the north bank at sunrise. This is our chance to crush them."

Josa grunted and spat. "Thirty thousand mounted warriors. We defeat that and the Barca army will lose heart."

Berenger looked at the warrior before him. "Send your riders out to summon the leading men here for a war council."

The man dipped his chin and led the scouting party into the encamped army. Behind them, Berenger hoped desperately that Hannibal led the enemy horsemen himself. Victory over the Barca general would forever mark Berenger as more than a skilled warrior, but as a great leader as well.

19

Arriving back at his farm outside Orze, Caros discovered that Alfren had brought his men down to the valley, recruiting more warriors from every settlement as he rode. Bastetani from the south had also come north to join the growing column. Alfren numbered his forces at over six thousand, with two thousand of those warriors being mounted. He had also received word of the siege of Sagunt. Apparently, the news had spread throughout the land. Warriors were appearing from everywhere to take sides. The southern tribes were aligned with Hannibal. The tribes to the west and north were primarily aligned with Sagunt, purely because they wished to throw off the Carthaginian alliances they had been forced to accept.

Aksel's men had left ahead of Alfren's column and ridden north to Sagunt to join forces with the main body of Masulian horsemen. Caros had been sorry to see the ever-smiling Masulian leave but promised to meet outside Sagunt. Alfren forced his column at a brutal pace and the warriors had not complained. Within four days they had spied the coastal plain ahead of them.

The city of Sagunt sat defiant on a rocky outcrop in the midst of the plain. The hill on which the city had been built was elongated and dipped slightly in elevation at the center. A hill fort commanded the eastern end of the hill. Even from a distance, it was obvious the defenses of the city, both natural and man-made, were formidable. The plains about Sagunt were already invested by tens of thousands of warriors.

"We have not missed the fun then." Neugen gazed about, eyes bright with excitement.

Alfren shook his head at the sight. "Orko, god of mountains, will need to be on our side for us to cross over those cliffs and walls. I hope Hannibal has a bloody good plan or this is all folly."

The comment surprised Caros, who thought that if anybody was up for the challenge, it was Alfren. Studying the city walls overlooking the steep-sided hill, he could easily understand the man's sentiment.

The following day they made their way onto the plains. Caros had never seen such a mass of humanity. There were countless thousands of warriors, many from peoples he had never encountered before. The more striking warriors bore swarthy complexions and Caros guessed they were Libyans.

"By all the javelins of Runeovex, who are all these warriors?" Unlike Caros, Neugen had never been beyond the shores of Iberia and rarely saw people from other lands. Now, witnessing an army that consisted of men and women from all the peoples that populated the shores of the Inland Sea, he was astounded. Caros had to admit that the many different tribes arrayed around them were an impressive sight.

Alfren may have been impressed, but his face did not show it. Instead, he shook his head. "Looks like a grand cock-up. There is no order to any of their positions. They are camped around outside the city like they are waiting for an invitation inside."

They were walking their mounts ahead of their column that streamed out behind them. The men had moved far and fast and they wanted to get them camped up and rested as soon as possible. Caros had to agree with Alfren. For all the show of iron and leather, a closer look revealed that there was no hint of military organization. This did not bode well for a battle against a city with defenses as tough as those of the city before them.

"Seems we should have let the men rest in the hills. This place is quickly becoming a cesspool." Neugen gagged. Caros felt his eyes stinging as the wind veered and blew the scent of unburied shit to him.

Alfren reined in his mount. "This place is filthy; they are shitting everywhere. I am not having our men sleeping amongst this lot."

"Want me to take them back?" asked Neugen hopefully.

"No! I want you two with me. Get one of the other leading men to take them back to last night's campsite. Since we may be here awhile, designate an area for latrines. Preferably downwind."

Neugen was back moments later and the entire column was shuffling around in surprise. "All done! Now what do we do?"

Alfren hawked and spat as though trying to rid his mouth of the stench filling his nostrils. "We find the headquarters of this Barca fellow and see what's going on is what."

The trio established from a Turdetani whom they waved down as he galloped by, that the headquarters of the Carthaginians was to the northeast of the city. They were directed to cross the shallow river that flowed east and then turn towards the coast. The headquarters of the Carthaginians was midway between Sagunt and the coast.

"That helps. Good thing we asked him, it would have taken all day to ride around looking for the place." Neugen commented dryly. The trio trotted their horses around the besieged hilltop, through camp after camp of infantry and horsemen. The further they rode, the more disorganized things looked. It became apparent that while the Carthaginians had brought a great army, they held only loose command over the varied contingents within the force.

Passing an encampment of foot soldiers, Alfren shook his head in wonder. "How does this Barca win any battles with this rabble?"

Caros ventured a guess. "I think they rely on speed and shock. One day you are sitting pretty on your hilltop, admiring your harvest and the next morning you are surrounded by tens of thousands of warriors."

"That would work on a place like Baria or Althaea, but the Saguntines do not appear overly worried." Neugen said as he eyed the steep and rocky hilltop with its high walls encircling the city like a crown.

"Hannibal can throw all these warriors at those walls as often as he likes, but unless he starves them out, he is not getting inside that city." Caros responded.

Alfren growled. "He can throw his warriors at those walls, but he is not throwing the Bastetani at them unless he has a decent plan."

Neugen smiled and winked at Caros. They did not doubt Alfren's bravery, but they were relieved that he was not going to sacrifice the Bastetani warriors needlessly.

They found and forded the shallow river and then progressed east along its northern bank. The river was fetid with the waste from the thousands of warriors and horses that used it for both drinking and washing. All along the bank, gangs of men were filling water skins or washing and some were even swimming in the shallow water. Caros squinted through the dust raised by countless marching feet and the drifting smoke from a thousand fires. In the distance, the sun reflected off polished armor around a blister that shimmered on the horizon.

"That looks like a tent fit for a king." He said, pointing in that direction.

The men rode on and before long, they reached a perimeter guard of two score formidable looking warriors. Caros eyed them, noting their dark complexions, shining cuirasses, helmets and heavy spears. Each man carried a sheathed sword at their waist in addition to the spears they brandished. These men were veterans and there was no mistaking it. The trio were halted with a curt command from a muscular Libyan who blocked their path with confidence.

"State your business." He ordered brusquely in Greek.

Caros, the only one of the three who spoke that language, responded. "We wish to report to the general, Hannibal Barca."

The warrior eyed them in silence for a moment. "You have the watchword? The general does not receive reports from the ranks."

Caros turned to Alfren with a curse. "We need a watchword or we do not pass. What do we do? Tell this chap and expect him to pass the news on?"

Alfren glared at the warrior. "Tell him the watchword is ten thousand Carpetani spears up his ass if he does not let us pass." Neugen laughed and Caros chuckled briefly until Alfren's glower sobered him.

The warrior had become restless and his men were gravitating towards them. "Look, make your report to me and if necessary, the general will hear it. Start with telling me who you are."

It did not sound like a request to Caros and he chafed at man's dismissive tone. "Very well. We have brought a Bastetani army as allies of the Carthaginian people." The warrior cocked his head, unimpressed. "Six thousand warriors to contribute to Hannibal's army." Caros shook his head, surprised that such numbers made no impression on the man. "We also have news of a large Carpetani and Oretani army approaching Sagunt. We believe they are allied with the Saguntines. This is a serious threat which is why we would prefer to speak directly to the general." Caros stared hard at the warrior and then looked beyond him to the pavilion that formed the headquarters. The warrior was silent and Caros knew he was in a predicament. If he sent them away and their information was correct, he could lose his position or worse.

"What is the size of this Carpetani army?"

"Carpetani and Oretani." Caros stressed. "The last figures are upwards of fifty thousand warriors and as many as a third of them are mounted. They are no more than a few days away."

The Libyan was quicker now. "You have seen them or is this just rumor?"

Caros clenched his jaw in anger at the insinuation. "We have fought them!" It dawned on him that Aksel had probably already reported the enemy army to the Masulian leading man, Massibaka. "The report can be corroborated by Aksel of the Masulians."

At this last the Libyan relaxed a little. "I know Aksel. He arrived two days ago. Look, I believe you. You understand we cannot just let anybody through to see the general. I will pass him the report. Why not wait here and I will see if the general will admit you?"

Caros translated for Alfren who nodded. To the Libyan he said, "Thank you. We will wait."

The Libyan grinned. "Make yourselves comfortable. I do not have the general's ear. I will be as quick as I can, but it could be some time. Have some food and drink. We get plenty of rations, one of the perks of being the honor guard." He winked at Caros as though he was his greatest friend and then shouted to one of his men to show the trio the food and drink before mounting and riding off to the headquarters.

The three Bastetani dismounted and strolled over to where a Libyan gestured to them. They had a thick carpet unfurled amidst some rocks that the men used as seats. Several baked clay pots held the Libyan's rations. Dried dates, figs, goat cheese, raisins and boiled grain. Neugen chuckled at seeing all the foods and sighed contentedly.

"Does not take much to keep you happy, does it?" Caros ribbed his friend.

"I am what I am. What would be great would be to see what type of womenfolk these fellows have. Have you ever seen skin that color? Like a new copper coin!" He shoveled a fig loaded with couscous into his mouth and continued. "Hmm, not too bad. What do you reckon? Are their women shiny as a coin too? Imagine that, eh!"

"You are talking with a mouth full of food about women you have never seen, probably will never see, and spraying food everywhere." Alfren sighed. "With this we must win a war." Neugen assumed a vaguely hurt look and dropped his jaw open. Yet more couscous spilled down his tunic. Caros burst out laughing and Alfren glared at him. "You are only encouraging him." They all laughed. A pair of the Libyans watching them, smiled and shook their heads. Alfren glared darkly at them, causing them to chuckle. "See, he is contagious. Even they are laughing at him and they do not even know why."

"I could explain to them how he would like to lift their mothers' chitons and admire their 'shiny' thighs." Caros smirked.

Neugen swallowed. "Hold on there! They are big bastards and I am not in the mood for a fight. I am still eating." He smiled. "How about asking if any of them brought their sisters along though?"

Alfren grabbed a skin of drink from where it was hung in a pail of water to keep the contents cool. He uncorked it and sniffed cautiously. "Smells like piss." He promptly chugged down a goodly swallow before wiping his chin and smacking his lips. "Bit light, but I guess if we do see the Barca fellow it would not do to be all squint-eyed." He offered the skin to Caros, who also sniffed it. It smelled of a light ale. Caros hesitated for a moment and then took a sip. It washed the food down nicely.

Neugen grabbed the skin from him and took a long swallow. "Ah, good. Now unless you have any plans, I am going to get some rest. We could be here awhile."

"Not so."

"What do you mean 'not so'?"

Caros pointed. "Not so. Here comes our friendly Libyan and he is coming fast." It was true the Libyan returned a lot faster than he had left.

"Come along! The general wants to see you right away. All of you."

They left their mounts with a servant who led them away from the pavilion entrance. Caros stared at the lime-washed walls of the pavilion; sewn from the hides of some animals. The Libyan hurried them on and through the entrance. For a moment they stood shuffling within the doorway, blind in the dim light. As his sight adjusted, Caros noticed more details. There was a large rectangular floor area covered with thick, richly colored woolen mats and deep cushions. Five men stood around a large table at the far side.

The Libyan spoke. "General. These are the Bastetani. Should I remain?"

A young man with an open, clean-shaven face looked up at them. "Yes, stay please." He walked over, staring at them with quick, intelligent eyes. It occurred to Caros that this man, barely older than he, was Hannibal Barca of the Barca clan of Carthage. He stepped forward only to feel a heavy hand on his shoulder. He looked over his shoulder into the hard eyes of a bearded warrior. It made sense of course that Hannibal Barca would have bodyguards to protect him. Hamilcar Barca, Hannibal's father, had been slain in Iberia through the actions of a cunning Oretani champion and Hannibal himself had come to be general after an Iberian slave had assassinated the previous general, Hasdrubal.

"It is all right. Remove your weapons and leave them with the guards." Hannibal smiled reassuringly.

Caros quickly translated for Alfren and Neugen as Hannibal had spoken in old Greek. The three removed their sheaths and left them at the door.

"I apologize for that, but as you can expect, every precaution must be taken. The rulers of Sagunt have mastered the art of deviousness and dishonor."

Alfren grunted, his face dark as he gestured to Caros to speak for them. Caros responded in kind. "No need to apologize. We have heard of the killings in Sagunt. These are not the actions of an honorable people." Caros touched the fingers of his right hand to his brow and dipped his upper body forward in the traditional Carthaginian greeting of respect. Hannibal's eyebrows rose fractionally in surprise and Caros smiled to himself. No doubt the Carthaginian expected the Bastetani to be unaware of Carthaginian etiquette. Caros had learned well in his father's merchant business the importance of displaying knowledge of others' customs. It often stood you in good stead when the bartering became sharp.

He nodded to Alfren. "Alfren is leading man of the Bastetani warriors and wishes to apologize for not being fluent in Greek. He is able to speak the Greek patois if that is acceptable?"

Hannibal looked at Alfren and Neugen and greeted them in fluent Bastetani. Caros cringed inwardly at having presumed the general was ignorant of their language. Hannibal led the trio to the other men in the pavilion. Here were the men of Hannibal's Command, the leaders of his army and governors of Carthaginian territory on the Iberian Peninsula. These were Hannibal's brothers, Hasdrubal and Mago, both of whom commanded forces within the army. Others present were Bomilcar, who commanded the Carthaginian navy and Prince Massinissa of the Massylii, son of King Gala.

Caros was awed to be in the presence of such powerful men and greeted each with the respect due their station. He was grateful of the opportunity to step back with Neugen once the greetings were done and allow Alfren to convey the report to the generals. Caros studied each man while their attention was turned to Alfren who showed no sign of being intimidated. Hannibal, as Caros had noticed before, had eyes that spoke of a quick understanding of people and situations. Hasdrubal was the tallest man present and wore his dark hair plaited and had cultivated a beard, colored a deep red and cut square. Beside him was the youngest Barca brother, Mago. Unlike his eldest brother, Mago had nondescript features. His height and frame were also of an average size. Somebody it would be easy to underestimate, until you noticed his penetrating, blue eyes, which at that moment were locked on Alfren. Caros expected the younger brother too, had a quick mind. It was little wonder Caros thought, that the sons of Hamilcar held such power as they did in Carthage and Iberia. Bomilcar, the Naval Commander stood beside Hannibal. Here was an older, more weathered man and given his maritime occupation this was no surprise. His heavy chest and thick waist were sure signs of excess fondness for rich foods and drinks and he carried an air of lethargy about him.

Standing on the furthest side of the table was the final figure present, the Massylii Prince, Massinissa. Caros inched surreptitiously forward to get a better look at the man. He was tall and athletic looking with ropey muscles visible on his forearms. His black hair was long and tied at the back of his head with a knotted scarf. He was dressed simply in a flowing, white tunic tied at the waist with a belt of plaited leather from which was hung a curved dagger in an ornate sheath. The prince was young, Caros guessed younger than twenty years. His coppery skin glowed in the subdued light of the pavilion and he stood proudly as Alfren deliver the report. Caros thought of Aksel and decided they were nothing alike, these two Masulians. The prince sensed Caros' eyes upon him and returned the stare before lowering his gaze to the amulet hanging at Caros' throat.

Alfren finished his report and Caros turned to Hannibal who was nodding his head slowly while rubbing his clean-shaven chin, deep in thought.

Hasdrubal was speaking. "We are not yet invested here. We could move back to Qart Hadasht."

Silence fell, the only sound in the pavilion, the rasping breath of Bomilcar.

Alfren ended the silence. "We attack them. Give me a large force of horsemen and I will take the battle to them." The warrior seemed more surprised at his brashness than anyone else. The leading men turned impassive stares on Alfren who stood unflinching before them, his eyes bright.

Hannibal spoke first. "What do you say, Massinissa? The Bastetani want to take only horsemen to the hills. Is this possible?"

The Masulian Prince studied Alfren for a heartbeat. "It can be done. One would need only choose the right moment and the horsemen of my people can destroy an army ten times their size."

The words were delivered in a mater-of-fact tone. Caros thought the prince was either a sycophant or remarkably confident.

Hannibal smiled broadly at Alfren. "You said you had what, two thousand mounted warriors, yes?"

"Two thousand and all experienced horsemen. Good mounts, five hundred spares and the men all with good leather and iron armor."

Hannibal looked animated. "We received the news of this army some days ago. Twice. The last report was from the leading man of a minor Masulian clan. We have sent out scouts to locate it, but it has disappeared. I had begun to doubt the reliability of the original reports."

Caros froze as Alfren interrupted the general. "Because have not found them you cannot decide what to do." He opened his hand before him, calloused palm up. "This explains why there is no siege out there. It looks like your army is ignoring Sagunt. I will find them and finish them, but I will need more than my two thousand horsemen."

Mago coughed into his hand in a poor attempt to disguise his laugh while Hasdrubal rubbed a hand over his face and shook his head. He looked at Hannibal who was glaring at Alfren dangerously.

"Do not get angry brother. You know better than anybody what our Iberian allies are like. They tell it as they see it. That is what makes them such cursed fun to command."

Bomilcar snorted in disgust. "I do not know how you manage. Honestly, give me Tanit's children any day of the year to command." He lumbered on bowed legs to a hill of cushions, snatching a flagon of wine from a servant as he went.

Hannibal flashed a look at Hasdrubal and then turned to Massinissa. "Have ten thousand of your best to be ready by midday tomorrow."

The prince inclined his head. "As you wish. I will send them under the command of Massibaka."

Hannibal grunted and rubbed his chin. "Mago, is Muttines returned yet?"

"Yes, he arrived last night. He will be able to field five thousand more."

Hannibal thought for a moment before addressing Alfren. "With your men that is seventeen thousand horsemen. I will lead. Muttines will be in command of the heavy horsemen; your warriors and the Libyans. If you can raise more Bastetani and other Iberian horsemen between now and noon tomorrow, they will be yours to command under Muttines."

Alfren smiled; a rare thing to see. "Just one other thing. Remember my Bastetani when we take Sagunt. We are not throwaway warriors."

Hannibal cast his eyes to the roof of the pavilion. "Thank you for your report. I will have my treasurer reward you your due. Until tomorrow."

The Libyan that has escorted them in, appeared behind them as they exited the pavilion. Wincing at the bright afternoon sunshine, the trio walked over to their horses while the Libyan eyed them reflectively. They reached their horses and Caros swung up onto his mare, as did Alfren. The two men looked on as Neugen stopped in front of the Libyan who looked down at him curiously. Neugen cocked his head, smiled and held out his hand. A heartbeat later, the Libyan sighed and with a sheepish smile, withdrew four leather pouches. They were dyed white and bore the red crescent of Tanit. He slapped them into Neugen's palm where they made a muffled, but satisfyingly metallic sound. Alfren grinned at Caros through his thick black beard.

Caros laughed. "I believe Neugen is the true merchant here."

Neugen bounded astride his mount and tossed two bags over to Alfren and a bag to Caros before pocketing the remaining bag. "I figured you two would be too busy thinking about tomorrow and would forget all about the 'reward you your due' bit."

They laughed aloud as they rode off to their camp, Neugen bringing up their rear. As they reached the perimeter, he turned in his mount and threw the Libyan an obscene gesture.

20

The fire danced and streamed sparks into the bowels of the night as fat dripped from the goat that hung suspended over it. The smell of roasting flesh made Caros' gut rumble and Neugen laughed at the sound. They sat with the other leading man of the Bastetani. Around them flickered countless other fires as the army rested. The enemy was somewhere under the same stars and the following day they would clash.

Caros wondered how things had happened so fast. Five days earlier he had been sitting at a campfire, looking forward to spearing a boar. Now he sat among men hoping to spear warriors on the morrow. Near as he could tell, Hannibal had peeled away twenty thousand of the horsemen from the walls at Sagunt to meet this Carpetani-Oretani army. They had ridden hard into the western highlands. After raising an additional three thousand well-equipped horsemen from the steady stream arriving at Sagunt, Alfren had approached Hannibal again the afternoon they rode out. He laid before Hannibal his reasoning of where they should concentrate their search. Hannibal had listened, considered and agreed. When Alfren told them that Hannibal had agreed to ride towards the headwaters of the Tagus, Caros had looked in surprise at Neugen. They were not surprised that Hannibal followed Alfren's advice, which was sound, but at the newfound respect in his voice when he spoke of Hannibal. Alfren's gruff explanation for this respect was that a general who listened to reason would go a long way.

Neugen hopped up from where he sat and with a deft slice, removed a piece of roasted goat meat. He threw his head back and dropped the succulent flesh into his mouth. Caros growled and pushed him aside. Pink flesh showed where Neugen had sliced away the cooked meat.

"Bastard! I was eyeing that piece!" He found another promising bit and took that instead.

Mouth full, Neugen smirked. "Hmm and now I know why. Tasty."

The other men about the fire laughed. They were tense with battle nerves and laughter was welcomed to release the tension. Of course, Neugen loved the audience and played to it every moment he got. Caros hoped when it came to battle, his friend would not try slaughtering the enemy with his jokes. Come to think of it…

Men approached the campfire and Caros was the first to notice the bronze muscle-cuirass worn by Hannibal. Swallowing, he elbowed Neugen and pointed with his chin at the approaching men. He rose with the others as Hannibal stepped into the firelight, accompanied by Muttines and Alfren. Caros had never had an occasion to see such armor before. Metalworkers had molded it to look like a muscular male chest and stomach. It was striking and gave the wearer a heroic quality.

"No need to rise. Just making sure you are all fed and ready for battle?" Hannibal did not require an answer. The men felt honored to have their general ask after their welfare. Caros eyed Muttines. This was the first time he had met the Libyan Commander of the Horse. He was swarthy complexioned and had tight black hair plastered to his scalp. Despite his hawkish nose and narrow-set eyes, he had a surprisingly genial face. The men nodded happily and sank back to their meals or weapon sharpening. Caros remained standing alongside Neugen.

Hannibal looked at the pair and smiled. "Ah, I remember you fellows. You ride with Alfren here. Be sure to eat your fill of bread and meat before you sleep for tomorrow you will need your strength."

The men murmured their agreement and bade Hannibal and Muttines good night as they left to visit other campfires.

"Alfren has really got his ear. Our Alfren." Neugen did not try concealing the pride in his voice.

It was true, Caros thought. "Right, makes sense. None of them were doing a bloody thing before Alfren woke them up."

Neugen looked at Caros, his eyes bright. "Hey, remember when we were after the Arvenci along with Alugra? I told you about how I longed to be on a real campaign?"

"Sure, why?"

"Pinch me because I am dreaming that I am on a campaign and a bloody Barca just said goodnight to me!"

Caros elbowed Neugen. "Shut it. Curses man, he probably heard you."

Neugen yelped. "Gods! I said pinch me not break a bloody rib."

Caros gave up and slumped onto his cloak. "It is pretty unreal though, you are right."

There were nods from the men around the fire as their minds drifted to what would occur the following day. Their mortality, their prowess, the fickle gods of fortune and war that could see them rich, dead, captured or mutilated. Sleep was elusive for many that night.

In the false dawn, that time of night when outlines begin to take form, men came through their camp to wake them. They were not concerned about noise and the first warhorn was blown long and loud just paces away from where Caros lay. Like all the warriors, he had slept in his tunic, discarding his iron cuirass and helmet. Curses and groans erupted about him as men started from their troubled slumber. He grunted and threw his cloak aside. The air was cold despite it being summer. With a silent prayer to Endovex for sending him the Masulian healer, he rubbed the rippled scar on his head and stood. Buckling on his cuirass, Caros made for a nearby bush to empty his bladder. Neugen shuffled up beside him and proceeded to direct a stream into the bush.

"Good day for a victory." He remarked groggily.

Caros shook himself and tucked up. He looked at Neugen who was humming away, eyes closed. "Looks like you slept well last night."

Neugen half opened his eyes. "I did. Dreams of spoils."

"Oh, I was just thinking I might ask Hannibal to come say goodnight to you every night." He sprang back with a laugh as Neugen directed a stream of piss at his toes.

Night grew into dawn and the army of Hannibal Barca took to their mounts. This was a day for war and Hannibal was determined to end this threat at their back and return to mete out justice to Sagunt. Scouts began to return from the positions they had held through the night. Everywhere Caros looked, mounted warriors sat tall on horses which breathed streams of smoke from their nostrils like mythical beasts in the morning cold.

A barelegged youth with a threadbare tunic rode by and Alfren beckoned to him. The lad showed him the lozenge that proved he was a messenger and recited the first orders of the morning.

Alfren shifted in his seat. "The enemy have crossed the river and are already marching towards us."

"Gods, they got up earlier than us. They were on the other side last night!" Neugen cursed.

"Cannot kill men that are on the wrong side of the river. Let them come."

Caros considered their options. Recent reports put enemy numbers at eighty thousand. Pitted against such numbers, victory would depend on their mobility. On an impulse he walked his horse up an incline and looked over the Masulian camp. They formed the bulk of the column but were the lightest armed.

Their fires were dead and no smoke issued from the grey ash. Of the ten thousand warriors, there was not a sign. Caros urged his horse to the top of the incline and looked to the distant hills. Nowhere could he see a sign of the Masulians. Alfren arrived, followed by Neugen.

Caros gestured. "They left long before dawn. We cannot hope to defeat the enemy in open battle without them. They are too many."

"What is the plan then?" Neugen asked quietly.

Alfren turned to him. "We bait the enemy and force him to fight on our terms."

He pointed south, to where the Tagus flowed. "We trap him at the river and break him there. Nothing less than total defeat will do."

Caros was not sure how they would do it. "How will the river help?"

"The Masulians should already be in position on the south bank. They will remain hidden. We feign retreat and lead the enemy to the river. The hope is they will cross the river to pursue us. The Masulians will then strike."

Caros saw the opportunity. The river would slow the enemy warriors and allow the Masulians to strike them down with their javelins. If it worked, they could break the enemy at the river. If it worked.

A warhorn sounded. One trumpeting call followed by another and another. Advance! Alfren turned his mount, the early sun's rays reflecting a deep raven blue in his thick beard. "Come on! They have seen us. Time for battle."

Neugen flashed a wide grin at Caros. "And a good day for it!" He laughed and followed after Alfren.

Caros looked to the northwest and caught his first sight of the enemy. They streamed like ants through the valleys and over the hills towards the position of the Bastetani and Libyan heavy horsemen. As he watched, he saw Hannibal, his armor like burnished gold, at the front of a column of Libyan horsemen. Hannibal commanded the right wing, the most northern of the Carthaginian forces and those furthest from the Tagus. The most dangerous position if he were to be cut off by the enemy. Caros felt his heart beat faster and his mouth dried at the sight of the hills filled with the enemy. Their numbers seemed to grow with every heartbeat. Caros heard Alfren shout his name and pointed his mare down the incline. The Bastetani horsemen were moving forward. Caros broke his mare into a canter and rejoined the column beside Neugen and Alfren.

Neugen gave him a glance. "Like old times!"

Caros smiled. "We will make the crows fat with their bodies."

Alfren gave a signal and a warrior blew the advance. The Bastetani horsemen formed the middle of Hannibal's lines. Muttines commanded the left wing of Libyans. Warhorns began to sound from all three formations and the Barcid forces walked their horses forward. There would be no wild charge. The ground was too broken for antics like that.

A wedge of Carpetani warriors broke from a copse of trees at the mouth of a shallow valley ahead of them. The warriors streamed towards them, armed with swords and javelins and defended by their stout shields. Their numbers grew as they surged forward towards the Bastetani ranks. Alfren shouted a command and the signaler drew a deep breath and blew. Caros found himself holding two javelins in his left hand and another in his right. The warhorn sounded deafeningly and the horsemen reacted with battle cries, raking heels across their mounts' flanks and leaping towards the enemy. They had no intention of charging into the lethal spears that the warriors were already bracing, butt-first into the ground at their feet. Instead, they swept past the front ranks of Carpetani warriors, hurling their javelins at their contorted faces. Caros hurled two javelins and turning the mare so he would slide past the front of the enemy, he let fly the final javelin. Enemy warriors succumbed to battle frenzy and broke ranks to attack the horsemen thundering by. Caros heard a horse squeal in agony, the sound reaching above the cries of injured Carpetani and the drumming of hooves. Then they were past the wedge of Carpetani and the warhorn was sounding the call to fallback. The Bastetani streamed back to their position, leaving behind those warriors unlucky enough to have been struck by arrow, javelin or slingshot.

Neugen was grinning maniacally as he rode uphill beside Caros. "That was a charge! Did you see their eyes? Ha, they tasted our iron!"

Caros grinned weakly. In truth, he did not even know if he had scored a hit. Looking over his shoulder, he saw the Carpetani surging forward as though untouched. More were now coming over the near slopes of the hills behind. Their numbers were endless. Alfren gathered the horsemen at the top of a gradual slope. It was a hard slope for a charge, littered with loose rock, making their mounts' footing unsure. Caros wondered what he had in mind. He glanced towards Hannibal's flank, but could see little through the dust that had been raised on the battlefield.

Alfren bellowed and cursed at the Bastetani horsemen, readying them for the next attack. Men dragged javelins from their quivers and readied themselves for another charge. Caros cursed inwardly, feeling this was madness on the treacherous slope. He need not have worried for Alfren was no fool and led the horsemen at a slow walk towards the Carpetani who had now hit the incline and were laboring up it. Caros saw their faces and it dawned on him how much experience Alfren had. The Carpetani had sprinted into the valley after crossing the river in the cold before dawn. They had then taken the impact of thousands of hurled javelins and then charged on. Their impetus was broken and they were exhausted. As Caros watched, the Carpetani urged one another up the slope, winded and drained. Only the proximity of the Bastetani horsemen gave them any incentive to push upwards. They saw the Bastetani bearing down and screamed insults and shook their spears at their enemy. The more experienced Carpetani tried to order the warriors into ranks and ready their shields. They were partially successful only because many of the warriors were panting and grateful to stop to catch their breaths.

Alfren chose his moment and gave the order to let loose the first volley of javelins. The Bastetani had the advantage of targeting a stationary enemy below them. The javelins arced upwards like a curtain edged with iron. These missiles were still airborne when the second volley followed. The first struck home, burying iron into shields, knocking helmets askew and in some cases finding flesh and knocking men to the ground. The second volley struck, finding many more targets as the Carpetani reeled from the first. Then Alfren ordered the third and final volley. They were now so close to the front ranks of the enemy that Caros hurled his javelin in an almost flat trajectory. He watched as the warrior he had targeted, yelled at the man beside him, encouraging him to hold. The javelin struck the Carpetani in the chest, punching through his armor. The warrior lurched back a half step and stared down at the quivering shaft. The Carpetani warrior looked up and it seemed their eyes locked. The man's face was ashen, but he glared ahead and then dropped his spear, drew the falcata at his side and with his eyes still fixed on Caros, hacked the javelin's shaft off, raised his blade above his head and cursed the Bastetani foe.

On the hilltop, the horsemen turned to watch the Carpetani reform. Alfren grunted his admiration for such a valiant foe. Despite taking heavy losses, they were not yet beaten and began to advance once again.

Neugen looked at Caros. "Bastards will not lie down and quit, will they?" Caros saw the warrior he had pierced leading the Carpetani on. No, they would not.

Alfren watched for a moment. "Right fellows. Looks like it is time to cross the river." He gave the sign to his signaler who duly blew the retreat. The Carpetani roared when they heard the signal and surged forward with renewed vigor. Caros looked around, despite the signal, many of the Bastetani sat spellbound, watching their foe strive to close on them. He saw pride and admiration in these men's faces and looking at the struggling Carpetani, he felt a strange sense of hope. Such strength and honor was what made great warriors. The warhorn called again and the Bastetani began to stream away to the south. Caros wondered where Hannibal and his Libyans were. It was impossible to see through the dust of battle to their last location.

Alfren cantered up beside Caros and diverted his thoughts. "If you want to live to see the river again, then get your blade out!"

Startled, Caros realized the warriors around him had all drawn their swords or held javelins at the ready. The column was streaming across a hillside towards the river, but they could barely see more than ten riders back or to the side. The enemy could be anywhere at this point. Just because they had bested one charge of Carpetani did not mean others had not penetrated this far. He dragged his blade free. It was a new blade he had purchased to replace the one lost in the ambush that had claimed Ilimic. They walked their horses forward calling to the right and left, ensuring they were amongst their own. A mass of movement ahead gave them pause until a troop of Libyans appeared. The Libyans started at the sight of the Bastetani, unable to identify them until Caros raised his voice and bellowed.

"Barca! For Carthage!"

At that, their leading man raised a hand in salute and they turned to stream back into the cloaking dust.

"Good thinking." Alfren called, a half-smile curled under his beard. Caros squinted; something was caught in Alfren's beard. It had not been there a moment ago. Alfren's eyes grew large, protruding from his face and his face lost all color.

"Alfren!" Caros cried.

Neugen spun around to look. An arrow was lodged in Alfren's shoulder. Another missile zipped past Caros. They were being targeted from downhill; the enemy, knowing that horsemen were the cause of the roiling clouds, were firing blind into the dust. Caros raced his mare to Alfren's side.

"Alfren, where has it struck?" Caros expected the worst. The arrow had plunged from on high and must have hit him in the throat above the neckline of his cuirass. Alfren looked down and pulled his beard aside. The arrow had indeed struck above the neckline of the armor, but had lodged in his left shoulder rather than his throat.

"Would you look at that? Luckiest shot I ever got hit with."

He reached up and gave an experimental tug and grunted. Caros expected him to snap the shaft, but with a sudden wrench, Alfren tore the arrow from his shoulder. Caros saw skin still attached to the barbed head and blood pool at his neck. He quickly tore a strip off his tunic and thrust it at Alfren who grabbed it, balled it up and pressed it into the wound.

Alfren tottered on his horse unsteadily, fighting blood lose and shock. Then he opened his eyes. "Order the column to head east and then come back sharp to the north and hit the river. We must reach the other side and the sooner the better."

Caros looked around for the signaler with the warhorn. The fellow was slumped over his mount's neck. Cursing foully, Caros spurred his mare up to the warrior. He had taken an arrow in the thigh and his boot was black with blood that dripped steadily to ground. The man was pale and breathed with rapid gasps. Caros grabbed the warhorn off him and blew the signal to move east and away from the arrows still arcing down amongst them. He blew it again to be sure and then draped it over his shoulder. "You plan to bleed out and die here?" An unreasonable anger at the warrior's apathy had flared in his chest. He tore a strip from his already ripped tunic and split it in two. One piece he wrapped tight around the arrow shaft where it stood proud in the man's thigh. The second strip he used to tie the first piece tightly to the man's leg. That would hold back the blood. Looking at the man, Caros thought it was touch and go.

Neugen trotted up. "Leave him, Caros! You need to remain with Alfren!"

Caros unwrapped the reins from the wrist of the injured warrior. "Hang on!" He spurred the mare after Neugen.

Arrows fell amongst the Bastetani, but they were moving out of range of the missiles now. They descended the reverse side of the hill. The lower flank was too steep for anything other than goats to clamber down, so the Bastetani were forced south, across the hill. Caros saw a glint of water in the morning light. The Tagus lay ahead, its course marked by dense stands of ash, elm and poplar trees. With luck, they would find a ford across it. He wondered where the Libyans with Hannibal and Muttines were and trusted that they had managed to extricate themselves from the battlefield. A roar drew his head around. The crest of the hill above teemed with the enemy. Thousands upon thousands of raging enemy warriors had sighted the Bastetani column. Caros quickly put the warhorn to his lips and blew. Break! The Bastetani needed no urging. They were on the back foot now. The enemy held the high ground and every javelin and arrow they loosed would plummet into the horsemen below.

As though reading their minds, the lead warriors threw their missiles and a wave of speeding javelins arced into the blue Iberian sky. Warriors, beating their horses in their panic to outrun the oncoming wave of angry missiles, overtook Caros. A horse went down on its rump ahead of him. Slowed by the mount of the injured signaler, he easily avoided colliding with the fallen horse. Others were not so lucky and either fell or were felled. The Bastetani reached a scree slope that led down to the banks of the Tagus and sped down it in a flood. Neugen rode alongside Alfren who rode hunched over, his left arm held up against his cuirass while Caros kept them to a slow trot to avoid any sudden mishap. Near half the Bastetani force was now off the hillside and Caros saw the first figures emerge from the river on the opposite bank. They had managed to ford the river! He experienced a rush of relief, having imagined being trapped on this side of the river with enraged Carpetani warriors breathing down his neck. Alfren turned stiffly on his mount and surveyed the hillside behind. Sadly, it was littered with downed horses and fallen Bastetani warriors. The Carpetani were swarming downhill and their lead elements were harassing the Bastetani stragglers.

Warriors who had lost their mounts were struggling across the hillside after their mounted companions. Caros watched in awe as riders braved the oncoming swarm to double back to save these men. A single horseman could support a warrior on each side as long as that warrior was prepared to grip the rider's waist and leap along beside the horse. It was an ancient way to use their horses to move many more man speedily across country, and they used it here to good effect. Time and again though, these brave riders were trapped and then a mob of Carpetani would pull horse and rider to the ground.

Neugen prompted Alfren to continue. "We must go. There is nothing to be done!"

"Go then! I am their leading man and will be the last off the hill."

Caros looked back at the injured signaler. "Can you ride alone?" The man licked his lips and reached for the reins Caros held out to him. "The goddess of the river will guide you across the water. Go!" Caros slapped the rump of the man's horse with the flat of his blade, sending it whinnying down the scree slope.

Carpetani warriors were steadily overwhelming the tail end of the Bastetani column. One bare-chested brute with red hair and beard, launched himself off a boulder and onto the shoulders of a man too old to be riding to war. The first the Bastetani rider knew of the attack was when the warrior crashed into him. Caros winced as both men slammed into the ground beyond the mount. Enemy warriors ran parallel to the fleeing riders, sending arrows hissing into them at will. The Bastetani horsemen were trapped between the wall of warriors above them and the steep drop into the wooded valley on their left. Each time a horse went down, those following would be tripped up or slowed down.

Caros silently urged the last of the riders on, watching the fight closing on him, his face grey under a layer of dust and grime. He lifted his shield from where it hung at his knee and turned the mare to face back the way they had come. A grin widened beneath his beard and he nodded to Neugen. "Shall we?" Without waiting for his friend, he raised his blade and bellowed into the dust-laden air. "We are Bastetani!"

Neugen cursed Caros and then laughed and echoed the call. As one, the pair galloped their mounts across the hill. White-faced Bastetani stared as the pair charged past them. Caros led the way with Neugen a pace behind and on his flank. The enemy were so intent on the fleeing warriors that they did not see the pair until the last moment. Wide-eyed, they turned to see Caros' falcata. They saw nothing after it bit. Swing, slam, slice. Timing his blows so his blade did not bite into bone and stick fast, he hacked down one than another and another of the enemy. Those who remained upright after being struck were run down by Neugen. Even his mare shared the blood fervor and struck men down with her hooves or bit deep into their faces and shoulders.

Their impetus could not last. The Carpetani were pouring down the hillside in numbers too numerous. A last Bastetani warrior came into sight. The man knew he would not make it to the scree slopes despite the two warriors hacking and slashing to keep the path open. Caros looked on as the warrior reined in his horse, encircled on three sides. The man caught his eye and grinned. Blood frothed from between his teeth, driven from his lungs by a spear plunged into his side. The warrior's horse whinnied and neighed as it pranced wild-eyed, daring any to charge. The horseman lifted his bloody blade to his lips as he invoked Runeovex's strength and then he growled at the Carpetani. Howling their war cries, they fell upon him. The Bastetani's blade rose and fell for a heartbeat and then he and his mount disappeared beneath the enemy. On the verge of charging the mass of warriors as they cut down the brave rider, Neugen's hand fastened on his shoulder.

"Our duty is to live and fight on the river. We must get Alfren back across the Tagus."

His senses returned as the bloodlust cleared. Caros screamed his defiance at the Carpetani again and again as his mare rose on her hind legs and joined him. The enemy warriors stood within close range of him, both down the trail and on the slopes above. None hurled their missiles, instead, they raised their blades in salute and gave a ragged cheer.

Neugen eyes popped at the spectacle. "How did you do that? They had us! No, do not answer, ride!"

The pair doubled back to where Alfren was waiting on the slope for them while the Carpetani cheered. Lips pressed tight, he stared hard at Caros for a long moment before grunting and starting down the slope. Within moments the three hit the valley floor and threaded their way through the riverine growth. Even here, some unfortunates had dropped from their mounts, giving way to wounds dealt to them on the slopes above. The men picked their way past the bodies, eyeing them for any signs of life. Those that still breathed, they helped pass on, making sure their shades parted swiftly from their bodies.

They reached the bank of the river and plunged down it to the muddied waters below. The river here rose just high enough to make their horses falter and then swim, but the riverbed rose quickly and they could walk the horses most of the way across. The Bastetani forces had rallied across the river as planned and Caros was relieved to see that their numbers had barely been depleted. The trio were the last of the Bastetani to reach the southern bank of the Tagus. As they exited the waters and rode up onto the churned riverbank, a mighty cheer rose up from the Bastetani warriors. "Runeovex! Runeovex! Runeovex!" The god of war would hear their adoration and bless them.

Caros sheathed his falcata. It was time to find the Masulians for without their numbers, they would not be able to hold the southern bank. Two of Alfren's leading men trotted up. Caros never even considered that he was not in charge; he just immediately fired the question at them. "Have you located the Masulians or the Libyans?"

"No, but we have sent scouts to range up and down the river. We will hear their warhorns the moment they encounter either."

"Good, then we should not tempt the enemy. Have the column shelter away out of sight of the far bank."

The leading men looked bewildered. Caros was not in charge; he was virtually militia, yet in front of their leading man, he was giving orders. They looked to Alfren who lifted his chin and glared at them from under his thunderous brows.

"You heard him!"

The men spun their mounts, riding off to move the column out of sight of the enemy on the north bank.

Berenger rode at the fore of a band of eleven of the more powerful leading men and petty kings of the Carpetani and Oretani. They had splashed through the Tagus long before sunrise to reach the north bank. Behind them, tens of thousands of warriors had risen and followed. They knew the Barcid enemy were on the north bank and hopelessly outnumbered. However, Berenger knew something that the common warriors did not. A rider had arrived late in the night when campfires glowed only weakly beneath layers of ash. He had delivered a short message. "Hannibal leads." At those words, Berenger's hopes had soared.

If the Barca general was leading this small force, Berenger had the opportunity to rise beyond his wildest dreams as the champion that had bested Hannibal, son of Hamilcar and leader of the great Carthaginian Barcas! The early morning sun had not yet risen high enough to illuminate the deep, narrow valleys on this bank of the Tagus. As yet, their warriors had not closed on the enemy, although scouts reported they were encamped nearby.

He paused on the eastern slope of the hill and watched as the warriors of the Carpetani ran tirelessly upriver. The majority were content to take the easier flatter routes close to the riverbank, but many had fanned out to proceed over the higher hills. He had encouraged this, as he wanted to hit the enemy horsemen with as broad a wave of warriors as he could. In this terrain, men on foot held the upper hand. For the same reason, he had ordered the Oretani to march five stadia beyond the river before turning east. The Oretani would force the horsemen against the river while the wild Carpetani drove into them like a broad-bladed spear.

Cractas, a burly Carpetani champion, rode up beside him. "My warriors are hungry for this victory. We have fought this enemy for many years. It is our time to kill one of Hamilcar's own blood."

Berenger smiled grimly at Cractas while eyeing his muscular chest and arms. Cractas' massive build, together with his ability to plan ahead, had seen him become a legend among the Carpetani. Neighbouring tribes had learned from brutal reprisals, to avoid raiding settlements under the protection of Cractas. "I pray to Runeovex the message was accurate. I too would like to see the Barcas finally defeated."

Cractas grunted and flexed his shoulders while watching proudly as the Carpetani warriors poured unendingly upriver. The evening before, Cractas and Berenger had argued heatedly about the placement of their ten thousand horsemen. Cractas had wanted to send them with the Oretani to complete the encirclement of Hannibal's column. Berenger had argued that the Carpetani horsemen remain on the south of the Tagus. The argument had almost come to a clash of arms as Berenger's patience slowly wore away. He had sensed that Cractas was testing his strength as a leader. The others had wisely remained silent in the standoff.

"They will reach the enemy in a short while. Will you lead them with me?" Cractas asked with a shrewd smile.

Berenger knew the Carpetani had seen the irritation flicker through his face, but his constant push to be the leader was trying. "I will be leading where the battle is thickest, my friend. In other words, wherever Hannibal fights."

It was now Cractas' turn to be irritated, but Berenger knew better than to gloat. As trying as Cractas was, Berenger recognized qualities in the Carpetani that would serve him well in the future.

A man whooped nearby and both men turned to see what had elicited the wild yell. "They have flushed the game!" A leading man of the Olcades shouted, pointing to the river.

Berenger made out a line of enemy horsemen on the crest of a low hill. Carpetani warriors were streaming towards them over the rough terrain, like dogs on the hunt. He wisely kept the analogy to himself. Cractas growled and hefted his sword. He used a falcata of an impressive size. Berenger guessed it was double the size of any falcata he had ever blocked. It would take a horse's head off cleanly, or so Cractas had boasted, and Berenger believed him. "Hold! Hannibal will not be there. Have patience and he will reveal his position soon enough."

Cractas spat and rolled his head on his shoulders. The other leading men shifted in anticipation of a charge and the coming, bloody fray. They or their fathers had all in the past been bested by a Barca; subjugated and forced to provide levies. Tribe had turned on tribe, blood on blood, through forced loyalties sworn to the Carthaginians. In the south, tribes had become weak shadows of their former selves and had grown meek. These leading men and kings of the Carpetani, Oretani and Olcades would never allow that to happen to them. Those few Olcades and Vaccaei among them had watched their strongest settlements defeated and burned. They had fled to the Carpetani and Oretani and spread their hate of the Barcas.

Further movement in the east brought Berenger's attention around. The Carpetani were advancing on another hillside. He thought the horsemen could be Iberian judging from their more colorful and varied outfits. He swiveled his gaze back to the first of the enemy they had seen alongside the river. Yes, they wore a more uniform colored outfit than their companions. He pointed out his observation to Cractas. "Those will be the Libyans. So, the others must be the Bastetani or Turdetani horsemen."

Cractas narrowed his eyes and glanced from left to right. "Hannibal will not lead Iberian horsemen. So, if he is not with the Libyans alongside the river..."

Berenger nodded knowingly while the leading men who had been half-listening paused, wondering what they were missing. Cractas twisted to look deeper into the hills away from the river's course. "Then, if Hannibal is indeed on the field, he has their right flank. Of course, he chooses the flank that has the most options for retreat!"

Berenger winced. That was one view. "Or he may be concealed deeper in the hills to strike our flank when we commit our forces to attacking the Libyans and Bastetani."

Cractas looked disgusted. "It is time we flushed him out then! He is not going anywhere with the Oretani coming down on him from the hills." The Carpetani king blew long on his decorated warhorn. From their backs rose the roar of the greater part of their forces. These warriors now surged forward, following Cractas who led the charge.

Unmoving, Berenger watched the leaders flow after the burly champion. He closed his eyes and enjoyed the comfortable early morning warmth on his face. The clip-clop of hooves behind him signaled the approach of Josa.

"It is done."

Berenger grunted his approval.

Caros established a line of mounted warriors away from the riverfront, hidden behind the denser, riverine growth. Under strict orders, no horsemen were to be seen on the open slopes above the river.

Caros wanted to establish where the Masulians were as soon as possible. This was of overriding importance, as only with their added numbers would they still be able to spring the trap. Neugen held a skin up for Alfren to drink from. He sat bare-chested on his horse while a warrior applied a dressing to his wound.

"There are others who have lost their mounts or are injured, some seriously. It may be prudent to have these men start back to Sagunt now."

"Yes, yes. Glad somebody is thinking. The lightly injured can escort them back."

"I will arrange it." Caros turned his mount on the narrow game path threading through the growth. He began passing the word around to have the injured men gather. The settlement of Peñalén was not ten stadia from their location, and he had word spread that the injured gather there. Once there, he walked his horse between the men. Many were carrying wounds caused by arrows and javelins. In some instances, he wondered how the bearer had come this far. Others sported broken limbs from falls taken during the skirmishes and in the desperate flight off the hillside.

The last of the wounded trickled in and Caros informed them their battle was over and that they should now leave for their camp outside Sagunt. Voices were raised in relief and many men shouted their thanks to the gods. Just then, men began to look beyond him and following their stare, he saw a column of riders racing towards the settlement. Men murmured angrily, supposing the band was either an enemy raid or deserters from their own force. They were neither. Caros recognized the distinctive ponies and turbans of the riders. He spurred his horse towards the band and waved. The Masulians galloped almost right up to him before bringing their mounts to a halt.

Caros waved away dust to see a familiar, smiling face. "Aksel! By the gods, I did not know you were here!"

Aksel laughed. "I wondered where you were. Imagine my astonishment when I saw a lion roaring and charging his enemy!"

"You saw that. I was not thinking when I did it. Expect I will have a few nightmares about how that could have turned out."

"Your war-name is well given Caros, Claw of the Lion!"

Aksel raised his voice and addressed the Bastetani warriors watching from the shade thrown by the flimsy town walls. "Mark this man, warriors of the Bastetani. He, whom we Masulians call Claw of the Lion, is a warrior to weave legends about and we are glad to know him as a brother!"

The Bastetani stared wide-eyed at Aksel, many not knowing what he was talking about. Some though, had seen Caros' charge on the hillside for they had been injured in that last flight. Now in relative safety, they recognized Caros as the blood-mad warrior who had torn past them and waded into the Carpetani, giving them time to escape. The word spread, rippling through the men, and they began to cheer him. Caros reeled and not knowing how to respond; turned to Aksel and shrugged.

It is expected that warriors boast when filled with ale or wine. Some few boast at the wrong times and are judged arrogant. It is when a warrior performs brave deeds and remains humble that others begin to boast for him. The warriors saw Caros' humility and, because there is no one more heroic than a humble warrior, they cheered all the louder. Someone began to chant 'Caros the Claw'. Others took it up and in a heartbeat, all were chanting. Curious faces peered over the settlement walls. The frightened inhabitants stared; drawn out by the sounds of cheering, which were deemed more favorable than the screams of battle.

Seeing them, Caros realized the din would carry over the river to the enemy. He held up his hands and waved the warriors quiet. "It is time to leave. Those with lighter injuries or without mounts are to assist the others. Do not abandon anyone unless their shade has left their body. We will meet again before we storm Sagunt." He grinned, showing his teeth. "And I will expect each here to buy me a jug of ale!"

Laughing, the men rose to begin their journey back to the Bastetani camp outside Sagunt.

Caros hurried back to the riverbank with Aksel who explained where the Masulians were. They found Alfren and Neugen by a giant willow tree. Alfren sat resting against the tree in the deep shade, while Neugen had climbed high into its limbs to see what the Carpetani were up to on the other bank. There had been no pursuit which was not surprising. The Carpetani had been strung out and exhausted after their race to cut the Bastetani horsemen off. They would soon regroup though. The problem was the Masulians were downriver, hidden beyond a natural ford. They had been told the Bastetani and Libyans would cross there, drawing the pursuing enemy after them.

When Alfren heard that, he cursed. "I asked where we would cross, but Muttines just said to follow the Libyans."

"Did you see where they crossed or even if they did?" Aksel asked.

"Neugen saw them, or at least some of them, they seemed to have been driven back inland, away from the river."

Neugen called down from the treetop. "Lots of dust downriver!" The men held their breath. "I saw them! Just for a moment and it looks like they are making for the ford just like Aksel said!" Twigs and willow leaves rained onto them and Neugen swung down out of the tree to land lightly on his feet.

"What in the name of Runeovex did you see?" Alfren blurted.

Neugen's eyes were bright. "I saw the Libyans riding like daemons were after them. They are going to reach the river downstream."

Aksel spun his horse around without a word and galloped away through the growth. His men joined him in the distance as they made their way back to Massibaka's position downriver.

Caros looked at Alfren. "Do we go?"

"No, we wait here. If they had planned this better, we would know where to be, curse them."

"If Hannibal's Libyans cross the river at the ford, that is where these Carpetani will follow. Should we not at least help Aksel's fellows?"

Alfren grinned. "They will be fine. There are times too many spears is a weakness."

Berenger, accompanied by Josa and his column of two hundred, followed in the wake of the skirmishes. They came upon the hillside the Bastetani had first held. At its foot, just where it started its gentle incline, they passed the first of the Carpetani casualties. Berenger estimated near five hundred men lay dead or injured here. Bloodied groups huddled together, tending their injuries. Fathers bound the bloody puncture wounds of their sons, brothers stripped dead siblings, preparing them for the pyres and sons gave water to their fathers. It was ever the case that the tribes of Iberia fought as clans and kin against their enemies.

Only once they were on the hillside did they encounter any Bastetani dead. These were few and any injured had been dispatched when the mass of Carpetani had surged up the hill. At the top of the slope, Berenger halted the column to take in the lie of the land. To his left, a steep-sided ridge ran parallel to the river valley. To the right, the land fell away to the banks of the Tagus.

"The Bastetani have crossed the river. We have only the Libyans before us." Josa remarked.

Berenger eyed the Libyan lines. They had withdrawn after their first contact with the Carpetani, long before the Bastetani had broken away. He was amazed they too had not fled across the river, unless they planned to join with Hannibal's column. Berenger looked to his left and watched the dust of battle where Hannibal skirmished with the Carpetani right flank.

"Cractas is driving them back. He struck too soon." Berenger would have fumed at the premature attack led by Cractas, but he knew the ways of Iberian warriors. Even the best of them lost their heads when they scented battle. Unfortunately, in this instance, all his attack had accomplished was to drive the Barca columns out of range of the flank attack by the Oretani. He was already contemplating how they should proceed to Sagunt when Josa exclaimed and pointed.

"They are doubling back! See, they have skirted the ridge!"

Berenger stared and saw the dust rising from beyond the ridge. The Carpetani warriors would never be able to climb the steep ridge in time to cut them off. The Libyans to their front were also moving now. They were trotting forward while before them the Carpetani warriors were strung out over the rough terrain. While they numbered in the thousands, they were too widespread to halt the oncoming Libyans. The bulk of the Carpetani force had followed Cractas, smelling victory and not realizing that the Libyans holding the left flank were still on the field. Berenger looked at Josa and the two reached an unvoiced agreement. They turned and led their column downriver. He had anticipated Hannibal's plan and had just the remedy.

Caros rode his mare up a ravine until he found a goat track that curled up the steep hill on his left. He could not sit at the river's edge and just wait for something to happen. He hoped the track would take him high enough to get a look at what was happening across the river. It had not been long since Neugen had spotted the Libyans heading for the ford downriver, but it had seemed like a day ago. His doughty mare stumbled a little on the rocky path, but quickly found her footing again and kept going. Near the crest, Caros reined in and springing to the ground, ran to the summit where he flung himself to his stomach.

Finding it impossible to see through the dust and rising heat of the day, Caros watched the thickest dust clouds, presuming the Libyan horsemen were the cause. They lay over the hills adjacent to the ford. A breeze shifted the early summer grass before him. Strengthening, it thinned the haze, allowing Caros to catch the glint of armor and weaponry. His eyes focused hard on the distant melee and he heard the muffled thunder of hooves. Had he been hearing that all the time? It was getting louder. There came the distant whinny of horses and a warhorn blew from across the river. The first of the riders rode into sight and watching, Caros realized there were two columns flying down from the hill.

Both the Libyan columns were racing to the river and Caros jumped up and cheered. Feeling somewhat foolish, he crouched again to watch. The white pennant decorated with the symbol of Tanit, mother goddess of Carthage, streamed above the horsemen. The two columns wormed out of the clouds of dust and into the valley through which the Tagus flowed. To their rear, the Carpetani began regrouping, having failed to trap Hannibal's Libyans. With Hannibal and his Libyan horsemen now back on this side of the river, the odds were excellent that the Carpetani would try to ford. He smiled in anticipation.

Berenger led his men across the Tagus far downriver. Emerging on the other side, dripping muddy water from their boots, they rode up between two hills and onto a wide shelf. Waiting for them there were the Carpetani and Oretani horsemen. The same horsemen Cractas thought he had persuaded Berenger to send with the Oretani. The column reined in to wait while Berenger rode on to where the leading men sat their mounts in the shade of leafy trees.

"Berenger! What news? Have Barca's horsemen stood to fight?" A graybeard asked. Another laughed and shouted there had better be some left for his men to hunt down.

Berenger brought his black stallion to a halt. "Their horsemen have run from skirmish to skirmish. They are baiting the Carpetani warriors, but not closing with them."

One of the leading men swore. "What are we doing here then? They cannot run from us!"

Berenger glared at the man and silence quickly fell. "Hannibal is outnumbered by our warriors, but he hopes to spring a trap and even now is doing so. We will be the iron-spear of the tribes and we will break his trap. That is why I requested that you remain here with all your horsemen."

Those present glanced at one another. "What trap is he planning?"

"If you shove a spear into a wasp's nest the wasps fly about angrily. This is what he has done and our foot soldiers are the angry wasps. Even now his horsemen have crossed to this side of the river with these angry wasps buzzing behind. They will rush the river and that is when cunning Barca will spring his trap. The warriors will be struck down as they cross the river."

"I say I would rather be an angry wasp than sit around here like a lazy fly! We must ride at once to their aid!" A scarred champion shouted angrily, receiving calls of support from others.

"We will and we will strike Hannibal from the rear while our warriors hold his attention on the river. This way; he will be trapped and we will smash his horsemen and send him weeping into the land of Saur to join his father in the bellies of the god's hounds!"

"Hannibal and the Libyans have crossed the ford to where the Masulians are in waiting. Should we not aid them, Alfren?"

Alfren lay under the willow tree and Neugen looked to be asleep in the crook of two branches above them. "Look, this is not a race, it is a battle. Each unit has a role and a place. Hannibal gave us our role which we did the best we could."

"But…"

"But nothing. What was the role assigned to the Masulians?"

"They were to keep out of sight and then ambush the warriors who gave chase when they tried to cross the river."

"That is right. That is their function. Let them do this, if we try to assist, we may hamper them."

Caros spun and kicked a piece of driftwood into the river. He understood Alfren's reasoning and it made sense, but he could not help himself. He wanted to be there to see the outcome. He could not just sit here; he would only end up irritating Alfren who was doing his best to master the pain of his wound. Caros had never expected that Alfren could be so relaxed while a few stadia away, his comrades were in a pitched battle. He hopped onto his mare's back.

"Where in hades are you off to now?"

"Up to the settlement. I want to make sure all the wounded have left." He walked the mare back up the ravine; conscious she had had a hard morning of it. He looked at the sun, but it was not even midday yet. Time had seemed to slow since this day began. The distant clamor of the Carpetani warhorns came almost constantly now from across the river. This was the final battle and it seemed the Bastetani were not to be part of it. War, he had to concede, was something that did not come naturally to him.

He reached Peñalén to find the gates open and the homes deserted. The inhabitants must have decided to leave with the Bastetani injured. Considering how many angry Carpetani and Oretani were roaming these hills, this made sense. A bitch with swollen teats growled at Caros over its shoulder while slinking away. The deserted settlement carried a sense of foreboding. He turned the mare and headed for the gates, eager to leave the place. Eager to be doing something. It was not in him to sit around and wait for the battle to end. Turning the mare downriver, he heard in the near distance, warhorns and under their strident song, the roar of many warriors. Across the river, the hillside swarmed with the enemy who were now advancing.

Caros urge his horse forward, tracing the easiest line to bring him out above the ford where the Masulians would be meeting the attackers. The hillside before him was laced with goat tracks and he opted to take a route near the top. It would offer a better view of the bend in the river where the ford lay. As he followed the trail, his eyes were fixed on the river and there he finally saw the ford. The sight of the massed Carpetani warriors, now joined by their allies the Oretani, caused his heart to pound. There were too many! They were plunging into the river in waves. Warriors held their shields and weapons above their heads to wade all the faster through water which reached to their armpits. Overeager warriors jumped into the river only to knock their fellows off their feet. The river flowed strongly and made regaining footing difficult, especially encumbered as they were with armor and weapons. In desperation, many made the fatal mistake of discarding their shields so they could push all the quicker across the river.

Further up the trail, Caros got his first view of this side of the river. The Libyan columns with Hannibal were milling around in apparent confusion. The attackers had not yet reached this side of the river. Caros reined in to watch. By now the river was a mass of warriors boiling towards the Libyans. The water had been turned foul and muddy by so many feet stirring up the riverbed. A shrill note sounded from the thick vegetation below Caros, followed by loud ululations that caused the hair on his arms to lift. The near riverbank erupted with movement and thousands of Masulians appeared from the dense foliage. They galloped swiftly over the wide shingle beach and suddenly the air filled with their javelins. The first ranks of Carpetani were stumbling out of the river when the Masulians struck. Almost to a man the Carpetani were felled and already more javelins, thousands more, were flying at the next rank. In the river and on the furthest bank the Carpetani and Oretani roared in anger. The sight of the Masulians drove them wild and they plunged into the river with no regard for those in their way. Caros felt a cold breath trace a path down his neck and his urge to join the battle shriveled and died. He saw clearly the fate of the enemy now. Hannibal had their measure and had planned this battle based not on his strengths, but on his enemy's nature. It was a lesson Caros would never forget.

He was about to turn away and return to the Bastetani position upriver when a glint caught his attention. It came from the next ridge downriver from the ford. He drew in a sharp breath; the entire ridgeline was filled with horsemen. Alfren had remarked on the absence of enemy riders earlier in the morning. Now Caros knew where they had been. The Carpetani and Oretani horsemen had hidden themselves away on this side of the river! Had they foreseen Hannibal's plan? Either way, if the Masulians and Libyans were trapped between the enemy horsemen and the warriors across the river, they would die there.

Caros hastily pulled the warhorn to his lips and blew! It was already too late. The enemy were pouring over the hill towards the ford, their warhorns sounding wildly amid their yells and battle cries. Across the river the warriors raised their warhorns and roars in greeting to their mounted comrades. Caros spun the mare around roughly and risking their lives, raced her back past the settlement. He could have wept at the thought of how close their victory had been. He leaped the mare into the ravine at speed, drawing cries of alarm from the Bastetani lounging along its sides. "The enemy is at our backs! Mount up!" He screamed as he tore at breakneck speed towards the willow tree.

Neugen had already dropped to the ground and mounted his horse. Alfren was on his feet, his face black with anger. "Caros! What are you doing? Was that you signaling?"

"Yes, the enemy horsemen have just attacked Hannibal's rear. They have been waiting this side of the river all along."

Hard lessons learned in countless skirmishes and battles had prepared Alfren for moments where instinct and action blended into something seamless and deadly. Without a moment's hesitation, he leaped onto his mount.

"Now is the day of the Bastetani. We ride!"

The Bastetani, already with a sense of something amiss, were leaping to their mounts in moments. Caros barreled his way up the ravine with Neugen and Alfren close behind. Their horsemen were spread out in the hills above where they had crossed the river and would need to regroup in order to be effective. The cleared land about Peñalén would be ideal. His mare leaped from the ravine and immediately the sounds of the battle raging downriver grew distinct. He chafed as the Bastetani extricated themselves from the thick growth they had taken cover in. Eager to see firsthand what was happening, Alfren and Neugen raced their horses to the summit of the hill overlooking the ford. Caros waited at the settlement, grinding his teeth as the Bastetani numbers slowly swelled to two thousand. Judging the numbers great enough and no longer able to wait, Caros raised his voice.

"Bastetani warriors! The battle hangs in the balance and it is up to us to turn it as only Bastetani warriors can. Are you ready to slaughter Carpetani?"

The Bastetani horsemen were ready and as one roared back. "To battle!" They sped down the steep incline toward the ford. There was no time to pick their way downhill over rocks and goat tracks. The superb Bastetani horsemen on their redoubtable mounts flew down the hill, the sounds of battle growing ever louder. Neugen leaped his horse down the near hillside to meet Caros, taking his place beside his friend with a wild yell.

The enemy horsemen saw and heard them coming and their rear ranks turned to face the onslaught. Caros led the Bastetani charge with Neugen beside him and together, they plunged their mounts into the enemy ranks. A javelin whipped past Caros' cheek and then his mare struck a horse in its flank as its rider tried to pull aside. His mare bit and Caros yelled and hacked. The Carpetani took the blow in his shoulder where a great sliver of flesh opened up, spraying blood high into the air. With an anguished scream, the man fell from his mount to be crushed under an avalanche of hooves. Time froze as Caros fought deep into the enemy ranks until finally, he and the mare were so slick with blood, he began to slide from her back. He cursed and jumped into the maelstrom of flesh and iron. Beneath his feet, the ground was slick with gore and trampled bodies. A riderless horse kicked at him and a spear hissed by his face. Cursing, he dodged and ducked while backing up against a tree where Neugen joined him panting. The two men hacked at any enemy that came within an arm's length of them. Most of the riders had abandoned their mounts and it was a press of men fighting between confused and frightened horses. A giant Carpetani's eyes fell on Caros and with a roar, he charged at him, roaring and swinging his falcata. The warrior never even saw the horse that kicked out and caved in half his head.

The battle was thinning and for the first time Caros could spare a glance to assess their situation. The enemy horsemen had struck the Libyans who formed a shield of heavy horse around their lighter Masulian comrades. The quick thinking of Hannibal and Muttines when they saw the charging Carpetani horsemen had enabled the Masulians to concentrate on the warriors in the river. They never stopped launching their lightweight javelins, loosing shower upon shower and turning the water between the drifting corpses the color of ox blood.

In the early afternoon, the warhorns across the river sounded time and again and the roaring of the attacking warriors changed. Their voices fell away to be replaced by the ringing clash of iron as the enemy horsemen also began to retreat, fighting their way back into the hills.

Caros collapsed to the blood-drenched ground at the base of the tree. He looked at his hand clutching his blade and it seemed there was no force on earth that could unclench his fist from the hilt. His eyes were distant, as were those of many of the warriors left alive on the shores of the Tagus that day. Men stumbled about, calling for their kin and sobbing in shock. Others dropped to their knees and pressed their faces to the ground to give thanks to Runeovex, god of war, for their lives.

The Masulians were quiet; no further targets presented themselves to be pierced. They turned away from the river and many were stunned at the charnel house behind them. They had been so focused on keeping the endless waves of warriors crossing the river at bay that they had not noticed the battle to their rear. Massibaka led his men in respectful silence through the dead and dying and away into the hills. They did not remain to help with the wounded or collect the dead. Taking the bodies of their kin, they left to perform the rites of burial according to their customs.

The battle had been hard won, but the Bastetani's earlier lucky escape on the opposite bank was the edge that gave Hannibal victory. As for the enemy, the brave warriors of the Carpetani and Oretani had suffered grievous losses.

They took away twenty thousand dead. Many more again were injured and watching the enemy carrying their dead and wounded, Caros was certain neither great tribe would offer war again for long years to come.

21

The army besieging Sagunt had been left under the command of Maharbal. The young general was a horseman at heart and excelled in open battle. His birth was the accident of a liaison between a Carthaginian merchant and a Libyan woman of noble blood. In Carthage, such offspring were rarely allowed any positions of power. His father had therefore decided his son would instead excel at war. From the earliest age, Maharbal trained with both Libyan horsemen and the Masulians. He was just fifteen years old when he was involved in his first skirmish against an outlawed Masaesyli champion. In subsequent years he had risen in the hierarchy of the Libyan military, which was to say he fought for Carthage.

When Hannibal's victorious horsemen returned to the plains around Sagunt they found that the besiegers had undergone a transformation. Maharbal had whipped order into the rank and file and where there was once chaos there was now determination. Reserve camps were designated to support forces. Valuable Balearic slingers were now placed behind the heavy Libyan infantry who formed the three lines around the besieged city. Horsemen were assigned their proper role on the outskirts of the great army where they patrolled continuously to prevent spies, messengers and mercenaries from entering the camp or penetrating to the city. To the north of the city, beyond the shallow river, carpenters and builders worked to construct rough-hewn battering rams, covered with stout timber roofs. These camps were guarded by a maniple of Greek mercenaries.

The siege had now lasted more than thirty days and as yet not a single engagement had been fought, not a single stone disturbed from the city's walls. This would end with the threat to Hannibal's rear now neutralized. Hannibal was ecstatic at the preparations that had been made. He had besieged large Iberian settlements before, but these paled to insignificance against the vault that was Sagunt. Now with preparations already underway and the tribes inland pacified, Hannibal needed to lay Sagunt low as quickly as possible. He was keenly conscious that Sagunt had close ties with Rome. While his spies in that far-off city reported a confusing malaise amongst the senators of Rome regarding his siege of Sagunt, he was aware that at any moment, they could vote to send their iron-hard legionaries to break the siege.

His first order of business upon returning to the besieging army with his horsemen, was a victory celebration. His orders were that for two days the army would feast, drink and give thanks to their respective gods for the great victory. To the tens of thousands of warriors encircling the city, this was a welcome diversion from the tedious camp tasks and drills that had been their lot throughout the siege. Sparing no expense, Hannibal ordered vast quantities of wine and ale shipped north from as far away as Malaka in the south. The horsemen became herders and brought in herds of cattle, goat and sheep; all paid for with good Carthaginian staters. An air of anticipation permeated the entire besieging force.

From behind the parapet of Sagunt's inner fort, Abarca watched the transformation of the besiegers from disorganized and disparate to cohesive and energetic. From this same spot he had watched Hannibal lead out his horsemen to challenge the massed warriors that Berenger had brought together. On that day he had thought that soon the siege would be broken for the numbers that Hannibal took could surely not prevail against the tens upon tens of thousands of warriors Berenger had gathered. Somehow though, Hannibal had prevailed and returned. Abarca needed no messenger to give him news of Berenger's defeat. Hannibal's return was testimony enough.

He slammed his fist down on the parapet. He had urged the oligarchy to allow him to sally out and attack the besiegers the day Hannibal had left. There had never been a better time, with their camp in complete disarray and their general away with a third of the army, they had been ripe for the picking. He had been denied the opportunity. "The Romans will come to our aid." he had been told. "We are safe on the rock of our ancestors, behind the walls built for this purpose." The rebuffs had been dismissive. He should have argued more vehemently! Now he looked at what lay ahead with a feeling of dread uncertainty. Bring on the Romans, those hard, haughty descendants of Romulus and Remus.

Caros raced Neugen through the wide valleys in the hills west of Sagunt. The heat of the day was mercifully gone and the two men needed a break from the tedious days in the Bastetani camp where the only diversions were dueling, drinking and gambling. Caros reached the shallow bed of the river, his mare ahead of Neugen's. He reined in, laughing as Neugen slowed and trotted up beside him. Edging their horses into the water, still cold from the mountains, they allowed them to drink.

"It is good to be away from the sight of that cursed city! It is always there; at the edge of my vision." Caros complained.

"Hmm, I know what you mean. Two summer moons gone and we are no closer to breaching the walls. Not that we have tried!"

"Those Greek rams are ready to be put to work. They look as solid as the walls of Sagunt themselves!"

"I tell you I am going to spend some time in one of them. I want to be the first to strike the walls. It is going to make the bark of Saur's dogs sound sweet."

Caros laughed at the image of Neugen swinging the huge battering ram. "I bet you do! I am not so sure though. I expect the Saguntines will have a thing or two to answer them with."

"It is going to make Tagus look like a skirmish. The battle for those walls?"

Caros hated to think about it too deeply. For some reason, he had a deep dread of the battle ahead. He could not imagine such defenses falling to men. He knew it could be done. There were enough tales of Greek and Phoenician cities being vanquished despite their high walls of rock. "Before the battle though, we have tonight and tomorrow to look forward to, eh?" He was referring to the victory celebration Hannibal had arranged. Every warrior in the army anticipated the games, the roasted meats and the ale. Everywhere a man went, it was all the talk.

"Cannot wait to sink my teeth into a piece of beef. I have no idea when I last did. I like fowl, goat and game well enough, but after a while…"

"If these foreign generals are anything like the Carthaginian merchants, they will want to make sure everybody knows who has paid for the party, so there will be a lot of ceremony before we can get stuck into the fun part."

The focus of the victory celebration was held on the north bank of the river, in easy view of the walls of Sagunt. A parade of Libyan horsemen, followed by a phalanx of Greek mercenaries, Libyan warriors and lastly, Masulian horsemen was planned. These troops had been issued new tunics and their armor and weapons were polished until it hurt to look at them. Ten thousand troops were to march in the parade that was to begin in the late afternoon behind a low hillock in the west and then meander south around the city of Sagunt, cross the shallow river over a wooden bridge, and end in front of the generals' pavilion.

Aksel joined Caros and Neugen and they, like many others in the army, sat on the rocky bank of the river near the wooden bridge. The beating of war drums thrumming in the distance was the first indication of the approaching parade, and before long, men could be heard cheering in great pulsating roars. Caros felt the hair on his arms rise at the sounds and he looked at his two friends who grinned back. They all felt the martial power in those sounds of victory. Caros glanced up at the walls of Sagunt and for the briefest moment, felt pity for the inhabitants who had been imprisoned there for almost the entire summer. They must by now know of the destruction of the army raised to break the siege. Hannibal was rubbing salt into their wounds by staging this ostentatious celebration in full view of the city.

"Aksel, why are you not in the parade?"

The Masulian glanced briefly at Neugen before shrugging. "Many of us from the Tagus are not in the parade."

Caros eyed his two friends, wondering for a moment if they held a secret from him. Dismissing the feeling, he clapped Aksel on the shoulder in commiseration. It festered that no contingent of Bastetani was included either. He had commented on it when he heard who would be parading and instead of the expected curses from Alfren or Neugen, they had made excuses. He sighed, every time he felt and thought he was becoming part of this great beast of war, something else occurred to remind him that he was not brought up to be a warrior or leading man. He told himself he did not mind and once this campaign was over, he would return to Orze, make amends with Julene and her kin, and begin raising horses in earnest.

Neugen nudged him. The sun was low on the horizon and he was lying on his back half asleep, listening to the drum rolls and roaring of the warriors. He sat up and Aksel clicked his tongue and dusted the back of his tunic off. Caros grunted his thanks, eyeing Aksel uncertainly.

"Look there, fellows. The mighty Libyan horsemen appear!" Neugen exclaimed.

Aksel chuckled while Caros stood to get a better view. The prancing horsemen had appeared around the eastern edge of the rock upon which Sagunt was fastened. They looked like champions as the rays of the lowering sun shattered against and bounced from their gleaming cuirasses and spearheads. Their mounts shone with vitality as they slowly trotted forward. Men tasked with dampening the path ahead of the marchers, sprinkled water over the dusty ground. Warriors from all the diverse peoples in the Barca army lined the way and roared, cheered, whistled and yelled.

Behind the Libyan horsemen came four men walking in pairs, beating massive drums of wood and hide. Caros and Neugen exchanged glances. They had never seen such men before. Tall, regal and the color of blue grapes on the vine. Across their shoulders were draped the pelts of a golden-hued beast with spotted black markings. They wore headbands of the same pelts and mythically large plumes of black and white bobbed high above their heads. Perspiration glistened on their skin as they walked with an easy gait and above all, swung their muscled arms in a continuous, beating rhythm.

Caros felt tears burn his eyes at the magnificence of the spectacle. His chest grew larger as though he was expanding to be part of this army. Beside him, Neugen clapped his hands above his head and roared with the crowd. Aksel, grinning broadly, grabbed Caros around the shoulders, lifted his chin and gave vent to a warbling cry. Caros gripped the Masulian and drew Neugen to him with his free arm and the three men roared along with the army of Hannibal. They roared of their coming victory. They roared their unmitigated defiance of faraway Rome. They roared because they were warriors and the drum's beat was the beat of their hearts. Never had such sound engulfed Caros before and tears ran freely down his face and the cheeks of his friends. All around, men were cheering and weeping. The Libyans reached the bridge and their mounts' hoofbeats hammered in unison with the drum roll, driving the cheers of the warriors to new heights.

The Greek phalanx came next and from their forms one could only wonder how they did not rule the world. They thumped their heavy spears against their round shields as they marched. The sound rolled like thunder over the spectators, surged against the walls of Sagunt and climbed into the heavens as though honoring Zeus. Neugen wiped his face with his tunic and laughed, embarrassed and ecstatic at once. Aksel stood leaning against Caros, his arm still draped over his shoulder. Caros knew what his friend was waiting for and he felt for him. The Libyan infantry came next and a giant of a man preceded them. He was taller than the tallest stallion and towered over the Libyan infantry behind him. His armor was white enameled plate, worn over a red tunic. His helmet bore hinged cheek plates and was topped with a silver horsehair tassel that hung down his back when not whipping in the evening breeze. On his left arm, he bore an oval shield with the signature red emblem of the ancient Phoenician and Carthaginian mother goddess, Tanit. In that hand, he held a staff from which flew the pennant of the Barca family. At intervals this giant would lift a great warhorn to his mouth and give a mighty blast. The sound crashed over the warriors, drowning all other sounds. Caros could not hear his voice, neither could he hear Aksel's ululation beside him when the giant Libyan let forth these mighty blasts. The Libyan infantry marched over the bridge and across the face of the white pavilion where Hannibal and his generals watched the procession.

The cheering faded and the bubble of excitement began to wane. Aksel stood dead still, waiting. Beside him, both Caros and Neugen watched expectantly for the Masulian contingent to appear. They heard the massed warriors roar in the distance and above that came a strange bellowing. Each bellow sounded closer and the anticipation of the warriors grew greater. The sun was so low now that the city of Sagunt threw a long shadow across the parade route. Caros discerned movement in that shadow, as though a boulder had broken free from the hill and come to life. He stood taller and strained his eyes to see. Something vast moved there and for a moment stories of mythical mountain monsters were remembered. The warriors closer to the moving shadows gasped in awe.

Neugen beside him, cursed. "What am I seeing?"

Aksel stood silent, a faint smile held on his face. Caros gasped as a monstrous form stepped from the shadows. Magnificent and terrifying in one breath; it strode forward with the Iberian sun striking and lighting it from the west, throwing a giant shadow across the awed warriors on the east side of the beast. It lifted a long appendage on its head into the sky and the source of the bellow became apparent as the beast blew a long triumphant call across the Iberian landscape. Tens of thousands of warriors who had lost their voices suddenly roared in wonder at the majesty of the beast. Effortlessly, it strode towards the bridge and Caros noticed for the first time that there was a contraption attached to the back of the huge beast in which two men stood. A third man sat right behind the domed head of the beast, wielding a short rod with which he controlled the creature.

"What, for the love of the gods, is that beast?" Neugen pointed.

Aksel tore his gaze from it, his face shone alight with pride. "We call this an elu. The Greek call it an oliphant."

Behind the oliphant, the Masulians rode their horses with pride, mustard-colored tunics glowing gold in the late afternoon sun and beaded scarves wrapped high on their heads. Their round shields were newly painted with all manner of animal symbols and they each held three ceremonial javelins with feather plumes tied behind the iron tips. The oliphant stepped with one foot onto the bridge and the warriors nearest held their breaths as the structure groaned, the figure sitting on the beast's neck shouted a command and the oliphant resumed its steady pace. The bridge continued to creak and groan alarmingly. The Masulian horsemen crossed next and as the last of them also crossed the bridge, they gave their distinctive ululating cry.

Across the plains, Hannibal's army celebrated the victory at the Tagus. The herds of livestock brought here for the occasion were already slaughtered and turning over fires to feed the thousands. Free wine and ale sated long thirsts and men celebrated.

Caros and Neugen turned on Aksel and demanded to know all about the oliphant and what other strange beasts they could expect to see.

Aksel laughed heartily. "How much time have you fellows got then?"

Neugen elbowed Caros in the ribs. "Say, should we ask to take it for a ride? It cannot be that difficult; did you see the little stick that fellow was using to drive it? I swear, when it sees the size of…"

Aksel interrupted. "Since its own is large enough to be mistaken for a tree, it will only pity you."

Caros snorted. "You walked into that, Neugen."

Neugen had a contemplative look. "Yes, that is a good point. A beast that big has got to have one big cock!"

"All that yelling has made me thirsty and downing a flagon of ale will be a whole lot better than standing around talking about oliphant cocks." Caros laughed and stood on his toes to see where the closest ale wagon was pitched.

"Hang on, I forgot to mention that Alfren wants us up at the pavilion right after the parade." Neugen slapped a palm to his thigh.

"What! Now? When did he tell you this?"

Neugen did not answer but grabbed Caros by the elbow. "I will bet there is some good stuff to eat and drink there. Maybe we will get lucky."

"You still talking about food and drink or something else?" Caros quipped.

Pushing their way through the throng of warriors, the three men emerged into the clearing in front of the pavilion, ringed by Libyan guards.

Neugen did not hesitate. "Mind letting us through, fellows? We need to see someone called Hannibal."

The Libyan glared at him until he heard a call from one of his comrades. "Let them through, they are expected!" The Libyan they had met when they first arrived at Sagunt approached. "Greetings. You have made a habit of visiting the general." He grinned. "Come on." He moved off without explanation.

"What exactly is going on, Neugen? I have a feeling you know something." Without answering, Neugen followed the Libyan. Caros turned to Aksel who was looking out to the coast. "You also know something! What is it? What have you buggers cooked up?"

"I do not know a thing, my friend. I am just keeping you company and looking out for some good wine and a tale to tell my sons one day."

Caros glared at him. "Right then, play dumb. I will see for myself." He took off after Neugen, who was approaching the front of the pavilion. Caros' heart dropped. He did not want to have to bow to Hannibal or his leading men on this day of all days. He took a breath and approached the pavilion, unaware that Aksel had dropped back. At about the same time, Caros recognized Hannibal Barca at the front of the group of generals, he also heard a warhorn and a steady drumming that seemed to reach up to his belly through his heels. He looked around as he walked forward, noting Aksel some distance away, talking to a Masulian urgently. Caros licked his lips nervously. Had he committed some crime? He had done nothing punishable that he was aware of. He suddenly remembered Alfren castigating him at the Tagus for not following the plan and cursed silently, wondering if that was what this was about. He braced himself for some sort of humiliating rebuke; after all, what did he know of Carthaginian military etiquette? Squaring his shoulders and lifting his chin, he strode purposefully towards Hannibal.

The Barca general stepped forward, a grim set to his square jaw. The men in his presence quieted and turned to watch Caros approach the pavilion.

Around the perimeter, the guard collapsed inwards until they were side-by-side, just ten paces from the front of the pavilion. Caros slowed and stopped a polite distance before Hannibal.

"General. Congratulations on a fine parade." He kept his voice steady despite the churning apprehension in his gut. A quick glance around confirmed that every leading commander was there apart from Muttines. He failed to notice Alfren and Neugen some paces behind the generals, both smiling broadly.

Hannibal stepped forward and placed his left hand firmly on Caros' shoulder while staring him in the eye.

"Caros, son of Joaquim of the Bastetani, three times now we have met. You brought me reports of our enemies, then you berated your companion for his comments about my wishing you all a goodnight and now on this day."

Caros blinked wildly and did not resist when Hannibal used the hand on his shoulder to spin him about to face the assembled warriors. Effortlessly, Hannibal's voice lifted over the crowd whose every eye was fastened on Caros.

"Warriors! Friends of Carthage! Today I have shown you the heroes of our victory over an enemy many times more numerous than us. You have seen these brave warriors and been lifted by the very sight of them." Men and women cheered his words and as the sound died away Hannibal continued. "You know Carthage to be kind and forgiving of her enemies, despite their duplicity, despite their hubris and despite their lack of fides!" It was clear Hannibal was talking of the people of Sagunt, and Caros thought his use of the Latin word for faith was a good touch. "You also know that Carthage, under the care of our mother Tanit, is a generous friend and a trustworthy partner who rewards those of her citizens and allied citizens who serve her well!" The mercenary army and the levied warriors cheered, clapped and whistled. They were clinging to every word Hannibal spoke and Caros was beginning to regain his shaken composure. "Today I offer you a champion. A hero who, single-handed, slew a hundred warriors to save his companions and risked his life in one mad, glorious charge!"

The warriors roared and whistled. "Who is this warrior! Who is this hero! Show us! Yes, show us!" They called. Caros was speechless. All this for a single reckless act?

"I will, I swear. There is more though! Surrounded by the enemy, sure to be cut to pieces, this warrior raised his bloody sword to the god of war he knows as Runeovex and challenged the enemy. Three times he challenged and three times the enemy cheered him so great was his valor!"

As Hannibal spoke, the warriors bayed with admiration, basking in the heroism described. The Libyan guard were hard put to hold back the press of cheering warriors.

"Our hero then returned to the battle, united his Bastetani warriors and led yet another valiant charge into the heart of the enemy!" Hannibal grabbed Caros' right hand and lifted it high. The roar rose into the darkening skies above and reverberated off the walls of Sagunt. "I give you Caros! Claw of the Lion! I give you our champion!" Hannibal turned to Caros who was shaking his head, wide-eyed while the warriors cheered.

"How did you know my war name? Who told you?" Hannibal grinned at him and Caros shook his head and looked about at the warriors shouting their praise and cheering. A rhythm emerged in the crowd and a chant gathered momentum.

Caros the Claw! Caros the Claw! Caros the Claw!

The steady beat of thousands of hooves drowned out the warriors and out of nowhere a great body of Bastetani horsemen appeared. The massed column thundered past the pavilion with their warhorns blasting. Caros could barely see through his tears. Hannibal had honored the Bastetani, not forgotten them. He grinned at Hannibal, noticing that his eyes too, were swimming with tears.

The general, reading his mind, laughed. "Bloody dust!"

Caros sputtered and laughed shakily. The rest of Hannibal's leading men approached and congratulated Caros, touching their brows and inclining their heads in respect.

22

Men cursed and strained to keep the battering ram level as they pushed and heaved it up the rock slope to the foot of the outer walls. Moving the battering rams to the walls was taking a supreme effort. Already one battering ram had been lost when it had lurched off a rock shelf, causing the great beam suspended within to swing to the side, crushing several men and overbalancing the structure. Men had shouted in alarm and dived out of the way as it plunged into a cleft in the side of the hill. On the walls, Saguntine defenders had jeered and hooted their derision. Hannibal, surrounded by his generals on the plain below, had cursed mightily. He was determined to take Sagunt quickly and could ill afford any setbacks.

Maharbal had organized a workforce of slaves and soldiers to construct the battering rams so that when the victory celebration was over, they had sprung immediately into action. On the morning after the two days of games and celebration, the army had been roused before daybreak. Reeking of all they had drunk and eaten, the men had been ordered to their positions. Skirmishers were sent forward to take up posts among the rocks on the slopes; the first of these being the famed Balearic slingers. These men made up for their lack of numbers, being only two hundred in all, with their deadly accuracy. Supporting the slingers, were hundreds of archers. Together these skirmish troops were tasked with keeping the defenders engaged in order to allow the teams hauling the battering rams some respite.

Despite the arrows and slingshot that thudded and slammed against the stone parapet, the defenders still inflicted heavy casualties on the men sweating to move the rams into position. By the third day, Caros estimated that four hundred men had been killed or wounded getting the rams to the outer wall. The moment they were in position, teams of men began to pound the rock face with the great iron-nosed beams suspended within. They worked under the protection of a lattice of boughs covered in several layers of green animal hides saved for this purpose. The hides smelled rank, but were vital in deflecting the arrows, javelins and rocks the defenders on the walls directed at them. Heaving, the men hauled back the huge cedar tree trunks, hung by thick rope from cross beams that formed part of the protective canopy above them. Once it had reached the apex, they cheered and released it to swing in a giant arc towards the wall of stone. A crude fist of iron had been fixed to the thick end of the trunk and this fist smashed at force into the stone. With every strike, sparks and splinters of rock flew outwards from the face of the wall and a surge of dust billowed upwards towards the defenders. From a distance, the rams looked and sounded like mythical beasts devouring the walls amidst clouds of dust.

For days the relentless, rhythmic din of grinding, splintering rock surged in waves across the plains. The men working the rams were rotated at every watch so that the constant pounding never faltered. This also meant a constant stream of warriors were moving up and down the slopes, which inevitably resulted in mounting casualties.

During the last watch of the eleventh day, a ram, swinging through its arc, collided with the battered rock and plunged deep into the wall. The man in charge of the crew was ecstatic when the dust cleared and he saw that the ram had battered right through the wall. His thoughts flashed to the rewards Hannibal had promised to the first squad to break through. He turned with a broad smile and his crew cheered and danced, clapping one another across the shoulders as they cavorted under the cover of the rotten leather above them. Still smiling, the leading man paused to cock his head and exhorted his fellows to hold still. One after the other they paused and quieted, and in the pre-dawn silence, the ominous groaning of stressed rock was accentuated. They looked at one another, eyebrows raised until the dust-covered leading man set his hand against the wall and felt it moving. His eyes snapped wide and he screamed a warning to his crew. Yells and panic followed as they fought to flee from the rear of the ram. Behind them, an entire section of wall began to slump tiredly, its base smashed through by the incessant ramming. It leaned, stilled, and then began to tumble outwards. The sound was that of a titan roaring above the men as they sprinted and leaped down the hillside. Men tripped and fell headlong as rocks crashed and rolled above, over and through them. The echoes carried on across the plains into the western foothills.

Then came a second, more subtle sound. The gates of Sagunt creaked and then slowly inched open. Warriors slipped silently from out of the city into the pre-dawn gloom and raced towards the nearby rams.

In his tent, Caros jerked awake. He could just make out the gloom of a new day through the open flaps. With a curse, he bolted from the rough wooden cot that was his bed and tripped through the tent opening. Standing silent for a heartbeat, he allowed his hearing to attune to the morning sounds. There! In the distance, a sound like thunder was dying away, allowing another to replace it. Sharper, more defined. Iron and voice, the songs of blades and cries of death.

"Up arms! To your horse Bastetani!" He knew the sounds of battle too well by now to mistake them. Flinging himself into the tent with a curse, he grabbed for his armor and weapons.

"What is all the racket about?"

"The Saguntines have led a sortie beyond the walls!"

"The bastards! I hear it!" Neugen exclaimed as he tumbled from his cot.

The ringing of metal on metal and cries of battle echoed faintly, but unmistakably from the walls of the city. Neugen bounced to his feet and began pulling on his armor.

Caros cinched his belt and sheath onto his waist. "Hurry! We need to get up there!" He cursed their fumbling. They should not have been caught so unprepared. Complacency had taken root and he vowed that would change. Around him, the Bastetani camp was slowly coming awake. Caros had brought his father's warhorn and now lifted it to his lips and blew. Its trumpeting alarm tore through the camp like a winter wind. Warriors took up the cry and at last, the Bastetani were moving. Caros blew again and again. He turned towards Sagunt and sounded the call to charge, before sprinting to the horse enclosure. At the gate, he whistled for his mare. Within moments he heard her nickering back and then she appeared from amongst the herd.

"Good girl. The only one here who is awake!" He let her out, gave her a pat and mounted up. More Bastetani warriors were running towards the horse enclosure, led by Neugen. "Neugen, have the men mounted but hold them here. We are not charging that hill in groups; we are doing this as an army."

"That cannot be good. Look! Look at that!" Neugen pointed frantically at the hill and Sagunt.

Caros whipped about on his horse. Along the base of the city wall, flames were flaring wildly into life. He knew then that they were too late and cursed viciously.

23

Berenger watched the oligarchs through narrowed eyes as they reeled at the news he delivered. He had escaped the carnage at the Tagus together with Josa and a handful of his original two hundred men. These had melted away that first night on their journey back to Sagunt. None had wanted to be trapped in the city and endure a siege; especially after living through the battle they had only just survived. Berenger had merely listened as they slipped away in the dark. Josa had given him a questioning look in the wan moonlight, but Berenger was glad they were going. With fewer men, he was more likely to slip undetected through the enemy lines into the besieged city, using the hidden trail the messenger had described to him. In the end, the two men had been able to gain entry to the city easily as the besiegers lay intoxicated after their celebrations.

"The Romans must come. What news from them?" Anicetus' voice trembled.

Berenger sneered and wondered if returning had been a wise choice. He grunted in frustration. He had had no choice. All of his wealth was secreted within the city and he was not about to start again without a stater to his name. Besides, if he could gain access to the city, there was every chance he would be able to escape it should the need arise.

"They will come! We pledged allegiance to them." The sniveling whine came from Glauketas who sat peeling grapes and slurping them through stained lips. The high priest looked at the priestess of Catubodua, his sister, seeking validation for his faith. She stood at the window that opened out to the east and the Inland Sea. An afternoon breeze rustled her raven black tresses and flattened her sheer flax tunic against her firm body. Berenger could see the shadows of the areola around her nipples and the prominent mound between her thighs through the thin, white garment. His blood only flowed colder at the sight. As though reading his thoughts, she walked to the center of the room and smiled at him. The hair at the back of his neck rose every time she looked at him. This woman fed off the fear she sowed among the devotees of the ancient goddess, Catubodua. A bead of perspiration at his brow edged toward his eye and he cursed it, fighting the urge to wipe it away like some weak merchant.

"These are distressing tidings you have brought to us. You are certain the tribes have left us to fend off the foreigner and his lackeys on our own?" Her voice had the rasping quality of locusts' wings.

Of the oligarchs, Abarca alone had no fear of the priestess. "Berenger has told us so you may as well believe it."

The Strategos looked strained, but there was a new fire in his eye. The priestess spun on him, scowling. Berenger cringed at the depths of hate in her green eyes.

"You sound pleased, Abarca! This was your plan and for it you have used silver from the temples. Now what have you to show for it?"

"Nothing! The Strategos has nothing!" The man-child clapped his hands in delight at his sister's fury for Abarca. Juice sprayed from the grape crushed between his sticky palms.

Abarca stood his ground. "This is war, priestess, and in war, the victor knows he is just one step from defeat and a leap from victory."

"Clever words, but words will not stop Hannibal!"

"The walls will." Abarca responded. The priestess glared at him, caught off guard. He went on. "Look at his army. Thousands upon thousands and what does he have that can knock down our walls? A few battering rams? It will take him months to crack the outer walls alone. The man can buy warriors, but he cannot take Sagunt."

"Yes! This is true. The Olcades with their mud walls and ditches held him at bay for a season." Anicetus reasoned. The merchant's confidence drained away and he lowered his eyes from Carmesina's sneer.

"So, this is the great plan? Hide behind the walls like children behind their mother's chiton?" She hissed.

Berenger winced for Abarca, in another place and time the Strategos would have struck her down for the insult.

Now he smiled coolly. "They buy us time. Anicetus is right; Rome will come to our aid.In the meantime, I propose we offer Hannibal a truce."

The priestess considered this and then smiled. "While you offer him terms, I will offer the goddess the blood of maidens to ensure our warriors are victorious."

"Blood. We will offer blood Strategos." Glauketas' voice had now taken on a deep baritone and Berenger suppressed a shudder. The creature was possessed. They were both possessed, and he wondered if now was the time to flee the city. First though, he would see to some business and retrieve his wealth before slipping away. As he pondered how best to do this, he only half-heard the priestess describe the ceremonies she had in mind to bring Hannibal to ruin.

Once the doors closed behind the departing oligarchs, Abarca fell into his seat and Berenger stepped forward. He noticed the fire in Abarca's eyes had dimmed somewhat.

"It is like trying to do battle against an enemy before you and a foe within. That pair are barking mad. What do they know of battle, eh?" The Strategos poured a cup of wine and gestured to Berenger to do the same.

"You are in command of the garrison and all the allied auxiliaries. Surely you have the power to sweep her and her mad brother aside?"

"Oh, I have thought about it. How do you think a creature like Glauketas ever became a high priest? His family is powerful and have so many eyes and ears about that I reckon half my leading men are in their pay."

Berenger pondered this as he drank. This was an ominous portent for a besieged city. Any hope of survival lay in a unified defense. Abarca was fighting the battle with one hand tied at his back.

The Strategos sighed. "This is what I meant when I said a foe within. Also, it diverts my attention from the real battle. From planning an effective defense."

"You are still in a powerful position here and it is true that Hannibal does not enjoy much success in siege."

"That can change with one good victory." The Strategos smiled at his own grim joke. "It is true, but I will not rely on Hannibal being poor at conducting siege warfare. I need to be able to take the battle to him on more levels."

Berenger's eyes creased in thought. This was the Strategos he knew. One who could take any small opportunity and turn it into a victory. He smiled coldly.

"How about we burn those cursed rams then? They make sleeping a chore."

The sounds of battering reverberated through the city as though the hill itself had a beating heart. In the still hours before dawn, while the citizens and the refugees slept, Berenger led several hundred battle-scarred warriors to the west walls. All were armed with swords and wore leather armor and helmets. They reached the western gate after threading their way through the reeking gutters and shacks that made up this section of the city. Berenger brought them to a halt and sent Josa up the wall. He would command the archers and javelin throwers who had congregated silently on the battlements. Their role was to harass any counterattack by the warriors guarding the rams.

Josa whistled softly when he reached the parapet in the darkness above. Berenger just made out the whistled signal above the thud and crunch of the rams just the other side of the wall. He hawked and spat a gob of phlegm into the filth around his sandals. The air here was thick with dust raised by the constant battering against the walls. Drawing his sword, he smiled grimly as he flicked it, feeling the tension leave his shoulders and wrist. From the dark of the night he heard a crack and rumble of rock. Moments later came distant yells and shouts. His first thought was that Hannibal had attacked the walls. His warriors began muttering and milling about. The sound of sandals flapping wetly through the muck echoed from the walls. A youth rounded the corner of a nearby stable and skidded to a stop in front of the warriors, his spear raised before him. The hard-bitten warriors scoffed at him and Berenger cut his sword through the air, silencing them.

"You! What was that noise?"

The youth approached hesitantly in his homemade leather armor, padded with hay, over a threadbare tunic. Voice cracking, he answered. "A ram has broken through the wall. I was sent to alert the Strategos."

"The wall still stands? The enemy have not entered the city?"

"It stands, but not for long. It started crumbling as I was leaving."

Berenger dismissed the youth and considered if he should continue with the attack. He was planning on tedium and the time of night to be his ally, but the enemy would be awake and excited at this breach. He made his decision and forsaking the quiet he had insisted upon, called to the warriors. "Now! You know what to do. Do it fast and do not linger to loot or you will find yourselves locked out!"

A line of guards threw off the locking bars and shoved hard at the gate, pushing the heavily reinforced structure outwards, slowly and quietly. Berenger charged through the moment he could fit between the gates. Behind him, the warriors streamed out in single file, then in pairs and then a broad front, which broke left and right along the walls. Berenger hurled himself into the gloom beyond the gate, towards the closest ram. It appeared as a bulky, shadowy mound before him and he charged towards its open rear.

The glow of embers warned him of a campfire just paces ahead and he leaped it just as a startled guard sat up. A pale oval of a face, mouth open wide in surprise, looked up at him. Berenger thrust his sword down, feeling the resistance of flesh. Then he was past, leaving behind the sounds of a brief scuffle as his warriors silenced the rest of the guards around the fire. The thick leather walls of the ram were in front of him and he charged to the rear access, sword before him, ready to receive any attack.

He had expected it to be darker than the underworld inside, but the team working the ram had hung several lanterns along the walls. In their oily glow, he made out the huge ram being heaved forward towards the wall. As he watched, men jumped away from the speeding trunk and flattened themselves against the leather walls of the ram. The sound of the impact against the wall was physical in the confines. Berenger used the crunching boom to mask his attack and in moments, killed three men with slashes to their unprotected throats. A cry of alarm rose when he was seen, but for the crew of this ram, it was too late; Saguntine's warriors blocked their only path to escape. They fled to the front-end of the ram, where it butted up tight against the city wall, shouting in panic as Berenger approached, bloody sword ready. His warriors charged past him and with howls of rage, fell on the men as they pressed against the wall they had been trying to smash through.

Berenger backed away, shouting to still more warriors crowding in. "Come, these are done. To the next one. Come."

There were two more rams to dispatch and they raced to these. The hillside was coming alive as the guards realized that Saguntine warriors were amongst them and wreaking havoc. Those guards close by were overrun, still reaching for weapons or armor. Others fled, giving the alarm. Now his men began to bellow on their warhorns. The loud braying rattled over the hillside, sowing fear and confusion through the warriors Hannibal had set to guard his rams. They encountered the next team as they were fleeing the siege engine. He hacked at one man as he sped past and the sword sliced through his arm at the elbow. Screaming, he sped even faster downhill. A javelin suddenly planted in his back, threw him tumbling into the rocky hill in a billowing pile of cloth, blood and dust.

Berenger did not even enter that ram, but just kept going to the most distant ram on the south west of the wall. Here the team had already fled, but a wall of guards was approaching from the south. He led his warriors hard at the few guards. They had obviously come hurrying to their comrades' aid, expecting to bolster the numbers already here. Instead, they realized they were the only cohesive force left guarding the rams. Berenger could almost read their minds from the posture of their bodies. Shoulders tensed in readiness, then drooping at the realization they would not see dawn and then squaring as they determined to make their last fight a good one. He smiled in appreciation. Good men! He hoped whoever commanded them would know of their bravery. He roared and charged at their center, picking a swarthy looking warrior with a plaited beard. The warrior hitched his shield and lowered his left shoulder behind it. Berenger kicked the shield and swiped away a thrust of the warrior's falcata. His larger, heavier sword hacked at the man who nimbly bounced back. Berenger had foreseen the move and threw himself at the shield, blocking another slash aimed at him. He crashed into the shield and the force knocked the man to the ground. Without missing a step, Berenger kicked the downed warrior between the legs and drove his sword through his throat. Around him, the Saguntine warriors were in amongst Hannibal's men and their numerical superiority ensured the fight was brief. Berenger grinned and ripped his blade free of bloody flesh. His men were already dousing the ram with oil. A torch was flung onto the structure and in moments, it was crawling with flames.

They had accomplished their goal and it was time to retreat behind the city gates. The warriors were boisterous and shouted abuse down the hill to where the remnants of the guards had fled.

The Saguntines fought an easy withdrawal against the warriors who had come too late to save the rams. Caros and a few hundred of the Bastetani reached the hillside, just in time to watch the last of the Saguntine warriors retreat into their city, dragging the gates closed behind them. They had left every ram burning fiercely in their wake. The stink of scorched flesh hung thick as the slaughtered teams burned to cinders inside the battering rams. The hillside was strewn with the bodies of guards.

"Whose were they?" Neugen asked, pointing at a group of five men lying dead where they had slept.

"Not sure. They are Turdetani so maybe Gualam's men."

Neugen winced. "This will wake everyone up."

Caros looked morosely at the burning rams. It would take days to get more up here, they had plenty, but the effort and cost in lives just to place them was a high price for letting down their guard. In the flickering firelight he caught sight of an oddity alongside the wall as it curved to the north. Peering through the murk and smoke, he began to smile. Now he knew what had woken him.

Within the walls, the gate drawn fast behind them, the Saguntine warriors crowed with victory. Berenger walked amongst them, handing each man his reward, courtesy of the city's war chest. They would soon be drunk and bedding the city's whores. He was curious to see the damage that had been wrought on the outer wall before they had set out and made his way to the scene. He found the breach in the wall made by a ram. The wall had collapsed on itself and out down the hill leaving a dangerous pile of jagged rocks heaped in the breach to the height of a man. Still defensible, although a sure promise of what was in store for the future.

A thousand warriors had been drafted to guard the breach against a possible attack. Berenger could have told them none was coming. It would take nimble warriors to cross the loose, sharp rock and then they would be sitting targets as they crested it. With only four of five men being able to pass through the narrow gap at a time, they would be funneled into a killing field.

He climbed the nearest stairs to the parapet to survey the ground beyond the breach. Mounted warriors were approaching the walls from the east. They milled about in the half-light and as he watched, the group split up with riders making off in different directions. A pair of riders remained, slowly circling the walls and making for the breach. He guessed these were scouts or even leading men come to view the damage. They edged closer still. Were they idiots? They were getting close to the maximum range of a skilled archer and did not show any sign of backing off. Eyes suddenly bright, he jerked about to see who else was watching from the walls. A good many warriors stood on the parapets on either side of the breach, celebrating the successful sortie. He assessed the route the riders were taking and made up his mind.

"You! Get those men out of sight and tell them to shut their mouths or I will have their tongues." He directed the command at the nearest warrior whose eyes widened at the ferocity of the command. The man quickly made his way along the wall relaying the order. Berenger hastily scrambled down the wall and bounded past the breach to find his way up to the parapet on the other side where again, he silenced the warriors and had them keep out of sight. Keeping low, he peered over the parapet and found the pair of riders. They were indeed entering the range of a good javelin thrower and coming closer yet. He could throw a javelin, but had never become proficient with it. Unless the target was within spitting distance, he knew he would miss. He whispered to the warrior nearest him. "Who is best with a javelin amongst you fellows?"

The man glanced along the wall, taking the time to weigh his choice from among those present. Reaching a decision, he thumbed his chest. "I am." Berenger's eyes became slits in his face. He glared at the warrior, not wanting to hear boasting. The man read his expression and stuck out his chest. "I can strike a racing hare from twenty paces as Runeovex is my witness."

Berenger thrust his chin at the riders beyond the wall. "Could you hit them?"

The warrior looked and squinted while seeming to gauge the distance and breeze. "They are too far to be sure, but if anyone can, it is me." He spat between his feet to ward off evil luck.

Berenger realized the man was confident and not just boasting. "Do it then. Either of them." Berenger watched as the warrior limbered up his shoulders and bounced lightly on his heels while crouching below the parapet. The warriors along the wall had seen what was happening and their tension had not gone unnoticed by the warriors set below to guard the breach. All present held their breath and watched. Berenger grimaced and hoped the man could handle the pressure of an audience. The warrior eyed the riders and slowly rose with his left foot braced forward. He leaned his upper body back, the javelin's shaft resting along the inside of his outstretched right arm and its iron tip pointed steeply into the sky beyond the wall. Taking two deep breaths, he blinked rapidly while mouthing a silent prayer. So fast, Berenger almost missed it, he snapped forward and swept the javelin into the air beyond the wall, his right arm stretched far forward. He remained as still as a statue while his eyes tracked the missile. With howls of excitement, warriors along the parapets surged to their feet, unable to resist the temptation to follow the javelin's flight. Berenger was right up there with them. He tried to spot the javelin, but quickly gave that up as hopeless and instead concentrated on the riders. He saw the closest brace and thought for a moment he had been struck. In the next heartbeat, a shadow passed the man and the second rider jolted while his horse whinnied and pranced sideways.

The warriors on the walls were hurling their javelins, inspired by their comrade's success. The horseman did not fall, but he had been struck. Berenger imagined he could see the shaft of the javelin protruding from the man's leg. With javelins flying thickly at them from the walls, the riders backed off. Coolly, the uninjured rider grabbed the reins of the other's mount and together they bolted away down the hill. Berenger slammed a fist into the wall with a snarl.

Hannibal was far calmer than Caros had thought he would be as the general surveyed the devastation when he arrived. Maharbal, on the other hand, looked livid, his mouth set in a grim line. Caros greeted Hannibal respectfully and the general smiled briefly at him.

"You got here quickly, Caros."

"I fear it was not quick enough, general." Caros gestured at the burning rams and scattered dead.

Hannibal grunted. "Which contingent was on guard?"

"Turdetani from Malaka." Maharbal answered.

Hannibal's calm demeanor frayed. "This means another bloody delay, Maharbal. It is taking too cursed long. We have not even breached the outer wall."

Caros realized the long siege was starting to tell on even the usually calm Carthaginian.

"We have more rams, but yes, there will be a delay."

Caros ventured to interrupt. "General, the outer wall has been breached."

Hannibal turned to him. "The wall is breached? Show me!"

Caros rode forward past the two men who followed him until he stopped and pointed. They could clearly see the tumbled rock of the wall forming a mound at its base. The breach was not big, perhaps as wide as five men abreast. They would not be storming the city through a breach that narrow.

Hannibal smiled widely. "Now that is a good sign! Why did you not say so sooner?"

With a wide grin, Maharbal quickly added. "If one has succeeded, the others must also be near to breaking through. I will get the rams up here within the day."

Caros was surprised at how optimistic Maharbal had become. An insubstantial victory was worth a lot to morale he noted.

"Yes, send teams to bring them up. And men ready to storm the breaches."

Maharbal turned swiftly to set about readying the next rams. Caros thought Hannibal would leave for the pavilion, so was surprised when instead, the general rode forward, an eager expression on his face. Caros urged his mare up alongside the general. The fallen wall allowed a narrow glimpse into the city, but it was too early to see much. He became anxious as Hannibal walked his horse along the wall, staring at the cut rock, probably imagining the whole structure tumbling down, Caros thought. He glimpsed a shadowy movement on the walls above them. They were too close.

Making to voice his concern, he felt the air move and an instant later a heavy impact sounded beside him. Hannibal gasped and cursed. Caros dragged on the reins and rode right up beside Hannibal, lifting his shield to cover him. Another javelin whipped past his mount's nose and struck sparks off a rock. Shouts sounded from the wall; the enemy were revealing themselves, hurling javelins and insults at them. Hannibal tottered on his mount; a javelin impaled in his upper thigh. Caros grabbed the reins from Hannibal.

"Hold on. Tight." He urged his mare down the hill; away from the city with jeers and insults following them from the now bristling walls. Their mounts scrambled and plunged down the hill in a shower of loose dirt and scree. Caros ground his teeth, expecting at any moment to be flung from his mare as they careened ever faster downhill. Men had noticed their wild ride and heard the catcalls from the walls for they were charging their mounts up the hill, Neugen at their front. His face paled when he saw the javelin protruding alarmingly from Hannibal's thigh.

"Ride ahead, Neugen. Alert the healers." Caros urged his friend who clenched his jaws and raked his heels down his mount's sides.

Doubled over his mount's neck, knuckles white as he gripped the mane, Hannibal panted and cursed all the way to the pavilion. When Caros arrived with the general and his mount in tow, a throng of men were waiting. He leaped off the mare and turned to Hannibal who was breathing tightly through his teeth. Grabbing his arm, he lowered him carefully from the horse. Neugen helped, and between them, they carried Hannibal Barca into his pavilion and laid him on his cot. Hannibal's leading men clustered close, shouting for Asklepius, Hannibal's physician. Hasdrubal pulled Caros aside the moment the Greek healer appeared.

"What happened? What is going on up there?" The smell of wine was strong on his breath and he looked as though he had not slept all night.

"We were studying a breach made by a ram. The Saguntines waited until we were within range and the first javelin found its mark."

Hasdrubal grimaced. "Bastards! The bloody bastards. If he..."

Mago appeared at Hasdrubal's side. "Do not say it, brother. Tanit will shield him." Mago turned to Caros. "Thank you. Seems you manage to crop up wherever you are needed." He smiled grimly at Caros. "Tell me, did I hear you say the wall has been breached?"

"Yes, that is where we were. I should not have let the general get so close, but it appeared so quiet." He shook his head at the suddenness of the attack. "Maharbal is bringing more rams forward; Hannibal wanted the men ready to storm the walls."

Hasdrubal pacing agitatedly in circles, spun about and growled. "I will put the entire city to the sword. I want my Libyan column to be the first in."

Mago eyed his brother who looked pale and ill. "We will discuss it later. Let us see how Hannibal fares first."

Hasdrubal groaned. "Cursed wine has turned my guts. Fine, we discuss it, but I am leading the Libyans through that wall the moment we attack." With that, he staggered into the gloom at the rear of the pavilion.

Mago turned to Caros. "He handles his sword better than his wine. He did not sleep last night for playing dice and drinking with his leading men." He thought a moment. "The rams will need protection as they are brought up. Have your men ready to keep any more of those bastard Saguntines away from them. You have our thanks and trust Caros."

24

Days passed as the new set of rams were placed and began again to pound the walls of Sagunt. Caros found himself more and more at the pavilion. His previous status as a champion now reinforced by being the man at hand to save the general in command of Carthage's forces in Iberia. Warriors from all the diverse contingents of the Carthaginian army knew him by sight. Wherever he went, he was greeted with respect by grizzly old warriors and with awe by young bloods whose eyes grew wide when he smiled back at them. Neugen could not get enough of his friend's new status and teased him mercilessly, knowing he hated the attention and did not consider himself due the respect. Neugen never mentioned that the livid welt above his ear leant itself to Caros' reputation, marking him as a fierce warrior that had cheated a killing blow. It was the one thing Neugen never mentioned. The night they had nearly died was a dark thing in their past. A thing best unremembered.

Even Alfren, that somber warrior, afforded Caros a greater measure of respect. Under his tutelage, Caros found himself learning the trade of war. He learned of the contingents that could be relied on, those that were best in a fight to the death and those best to use when all odds favored victory. Alfren's depth of knowledge of war constantly surprised Caros. One day, he ventured to ask him how he knew so much about the contingents in Hannibal's forces.

He furrowed his brow and looked irritably at Caros. "Tell me, as a merchant, would you venture into an unknown harbor without first discovering something of the nature of the people there?"

It was not the first time Caros had seen the similarities between trade and war and he quickly saw Alfren's point. Knowledge was vital to success. The difference being that in war, the commodity was power; the currency used to buy it was men.

He also learned through his visits to the pavilion of the precariousness of the balance of power at play behind this vast army. Many of the oligarch in Carthage viewed Iberia a temporary source of wealth and had no heart in supporting a mercenary army to occupy the territory. Hannibal Barca only maintained his position as general in command through a slim majority of the oligarchs in the mother city.

Hannibal's wound improved rapidly under the ministrations of his Greek physician. His temper though, was becoming frayed by the delays in making any further breakthrough in cracking Sagunt's defenses. As second in command, Maharbal bore the brunt of Hannibal's frustration despite working tirelessly at deploying reserve battering rams, guard contingents and drilling the troops. Maharbal voiced his concerns over the morale of the warriors. They were becoming bored and agitated; fights between different contingents was constant and deaths alarmingly frequent. There was little to occupy them when they were not drilling or on duty.

Food shortages occurred too often and illness flared like wildfires among the camps on the plain. Against this backdrop, Hannibal and his leading men reached a conclusion. They needed a victory regardless of the cost. The siege, now into its seventh month, was about to become a lot bloodier.

The breaches opened by the rams were too few and too narrow to be useful. Almost as soon as part of the wall collapsed, the defenders would raise improvised defenses. Hannibal had not ordered a single attack, knowing the cost would be too high and the chances of holding ground would be next to nothing.

It was now late summer and the afternoon lay turgid over the plain. Three days earlier, Alfren had ridden into the Bastetani camp with their orders. The leading man's eyes were like twin embers in a face flushed with excitement. Hannibal was moving the siege forward and his army was readying for an assault on the weakened walls. Three columns of Hannibal's warriors now filled the plains to the west of Sagunt. Forty thousand men, armor fastened on, shields at the ready and blades honed. Caros listened in awe as warhorns bellowed in unison, driving a wall of sound rushing towards the defenders crowded along the battlements. Drums of wood and hide were beating a deep bass below the strident calls of warhorns and the sound resonated through the columns of warriors as they marched.

Mounted on his mare, Caros watched the Bastetani warriors move forward. They shouted to make themselves heard over the warhorns and drums, teasing one another and making promises of what they would do once in the city. Many beat their swords and spears against their shields as the column inched towards the hill. Eyes were stretched wide and untested warriors wore beads of perspiration that had nothing to do with the day's heat. Men drank frequently, their mouths suddenly and inexplicably dry. Caros recognized the signs since he was experiencing them all himself. He knew that under the ribald suggestions and brash boasts, their warrior hearts were drumming as urgently as his.

He licked his lips and looked at Neugen. His friend was staring at the city as it loomed over them. With lips drawn tight, he clenched and unclenched the pommel of his falcata.

"Want a drink?" Caros uncorked his waterskin.

"Good idea. Yes, give us a belt." He drew a mouthful and swallowed, grimacing. "It is water!" He choked in shock.

Caros laughed. "What did you expect?"

Ahead of them, Alfren turned on his mount and smiled tightly. "Water, Caros? Really? There are forty thousand warriors on this field and I wager my sword and mount that not more than a handful have water on their belts." He let out a belly laugh, receiving looks of surprise from nearby warriors.

Caros shook his head, looking at the waterskin Neugen had thrust back into his hand. He plugged and tossed it aside. "Never occurred to me. Now what have you got to drink?"

Alfren and Neugen grinned at one another and Neugen tossed him a skin. "The good stuff, my friend. No worthy Bastetani should raze a city before downing it."

Caros sniffed and drank. A bolt of white heat slid down his throat and wrapped around his gut. Eyes watering, he wordlessly passed the skin to Alfren. Feeling as though he was breathing fire, he coughed and fought to catch his breath. Alfren grinned and upended the skin over his wide-open mouth, taking a long draught of the honey-colored liquid.

Neugen rode closer and slapped Caros on the back. "Now we can go do battle!"

Archers swarmed the hillside in their thousands. Across their backs were slung quivers packed with the arrows they would loose at the defenders. The Saguntines on the walls jeered and cursed, their arrows and javelins ready to repel the attackers. The first flight of arrows rose and the killing began. Behind the archers, the three columns climbed the hillside. On their shoulders, they carried long ladders made from felled saplings tied together with hemp rope. Libyan, Iberian and Numidian warriors pushed forward at the heads of their respective columns.

Hannibal was gambling on overwhelming the defenders on the walls weakened by the months of savage battering. He wanted to enter the city before nightfall. Once his warriors had gained a foothold within the walls, they would have the additional cover of night to consolidate their forces.

Wave after wave of arrows flew at the defenders, taking them in the throats and heads, thinning their ranks. Men fell wounded or dead by the score to be pushed aside as fresh defenders climbed to fill the spaces. Their own javelins and arrows rose, killing archers in droves. Screams of dying men punctuated the bellow of warhorns as each side let fly volley after volley of missiles. The columns broke into a jog as they entered the killing ground beneath the wall. Warriors braced their shields against multiple impacts of javelins and arrows. They grunted in frustration as razor sharp iron found their flesh. Some fought forward to the walls despite the wounds, others fell dead or writhing in agony. The columns reached the foot of the walls and the ladders rose and lodged against the battlements. Screaming their hate, men raced up the ladders into a storm of arrows, javelins and slingshot. The Bastetani column surged against the foot of the wall and simultaneously, a dozen ladders grew out of the mass of warriors and slammed into place.

Warriors climbed as fast as their armored arms and legs could take them. Caros, Alfren and Neugen dismounted to move through the packed warriors. Above them, the defenders dropped rocks and sent arrows hissing as fast as they could into the milling men. Caros watched as a ladder, laden with screaming warriors, was roughly levered away from the walls by the defenders. The packed ladder toppled and slid sideways down the face of the wall until it crashed into a second ladder and stuck there. Those warriors who had not already fallen, jumped clear. The foremost warrior on a third ladder reached the parapet and slapping aside a spear thrust, clambered onto the wall. The defenders swarmed over him and hauled the man, screaming curses, into their midst. His fellows climbed up to take his place and were cut down, but more followed, until slipping on the blood of their comrades, two warriors gained the parapet and held the defenders back. More warriors surged up and joined them. Twelve men had died going over that lip of stone to gain their precarious perch on the wall. Steadily, more men followed, replacing their fallen comrades.

Alfren lifted a restraining arm to Caros' chest. "Not yet, Caros. They must take the walkway and they volunteered to be amongst the first wave."

Caros ground his teeth and clenched his falcata. It was against his nature to hang back while good men died so futilely. His eyes were stretched wide, his breath coming in bursts and he had not yet struck a blow. The Bastetani were gaining the top of the wall now in greater numbers. He sensed a movement in the press of warriors. The attacking men had stormed their way up a pile of broken rock in one of the many partial breaches and were hacking and tearing at the crude, wooden palisade placed there by the enemy.

Caros pointed. "Alfren, the breach. We can force that!"

Alfren grimaced, looked back at the ladders choked with climbing warriors and then grunted in agreement. Caros bulled his way towards the breach and clambered up the loose rock. The defenders above had been thinned, but arrows still thudded with gut-loosening regularity into shields and bodies all around him. A javelin hurtled over the wooden palisade. The defenders had tied an oil-soaked strip of cord to the weapon and lit it. Burning furiously, the javelin struck a warrior's shield. The man grunted at the impact and hacked at the javelin to dislodge it. The burning cord ignited his braccae and, screaming, he flung aside the shield to tear off his clothing. More burning javelins flew over the palisade creating pandemonium amongst the Bastetani. Men wailed in agony as they became human torches. The courage of the warriors around Caros faltered as kin and friends died in agony at their sides. Men began to back up fearfully and all the while, archers within the city were whittling away the Bastetani who had gained the top of the wall. He stumbled up to the palisade and a spearhead suddenly thrust through the upright beams at him. The warriors hacking at the crude wooden wall had made no headway and were being cut down as they tried to pull down the barrier.

Caros grabbed a sweating, bloodied warrior and shouted into his ear. "Get ladders up here now! I want as many as you can get. Go!" He hunkered down next to Neugen and Alfren who both held their shields above them and tried to keep their bodies as small as possible. Suddenly warriors were passing ladders over their heads towards the breach. Four ladders came swiftly over the throng of men and in short order were lodged up against the rim of the wooden palisade. The lip of the palisade was much lower than the city walls the ladders had been built to scale, so they lay at a gentle angle. Caros deftly swung himself onto the first ladder and realized he would not need to use his hands to climb due to the gentle incline. He hefted his shield and shouted to the warriors behind him. "Bastetani! Let us take these sheep-shagging bastards!"

A roar sounded from the warriors as they surged across the ladders. Caros ran, praying to Runeovex that he would not miss his footing on the bouncing structure. Warriors fell from the ladders as they ran, but more were sweeping forward. He reached the palisade's rim and prayed it was not far to the ground beyond. With a wild, desperate war cry, he launched himself over the rim.

The enemy packed along the wall, raised their shields as he flew into them feet first. With his ankles locked together, he slammed into a shield and knocked the owner into the ground. Lashing back-handed with his falcata at the packed warriors who had little room to maneuver, he swung in a circle, knocking away spear thrusts. He could not hope to keep them all at bay and in moments a warrior slammed into his back and tried to ram a spear into his neck. Caros staggered forward, blocking hungry blades with his shield as he furiously elbowed the man behind him. Suddenly the weight bearing down on him was gone and he heard a voice bellowing at him.

"Are you insane! Saur's dogs, that drink has splintered your senses!" Neugen looked genuinely peeved as he hacked the enemy warrior's throat open, ending his life. More Bastetani were hurtling from above into the Saguntine defenders, giving Caros a moment to regain his footing and breath. Alfren appeared, battering two warriors to the ground and killing them with quick, savage thrusts. Eyes alight, he grinned widely at Caros. A spearhead slammed against his chest and gouged a shining trail across the armor. In a flash, Alfren roared and drove first shield then sword into the hapless attacker. Caros grinned back at him; the defenders were falling away and the Bastetani had formed a wall of shields and were already driving forward. Enraged by the number of their comrades that had been slain and the fear that made their limbs heavy, they plunged into the defenders like a living blade. Their wild attack had forced the city's archers to retreat. In their place; Bastetani archers were brought forward and took a strong position on the walls from where they could fire down on the defenders as they fell back.

Caros found himself in the shield wall with Neugen beside him. Behind them, Alfren was shouting to the men, urging them into the line. They needed to exploit their hard-won foothold and drive the enemy back quickly. A mass of some hundreds of Bastetani now surged into the city, filling the streets and lumbering over any defense the Saguntines attempted. Ahead of them, the afternoon sun lit up the city's inner wall. They pushed relentlessly towards it. Caros staggered and slipped over a pair of dying warriors who lay choking in an open sewer. He gagged as entrails looped around his ankle and was forced to kick his foot free of the slippery mess. As he did so, a Saguntine charged from a dark doorway, thrusting a broad-bladed spear at him. Caros deflected the blade with his shield and stepped in close to the crazed Saguntine. The man spat at him even as Caros drove his falcata into the warrior's midriff. Caros then batted him away with a vicious headbutt, his iron helmet knocking the dying man back through the doorway. Around him, the Bastetani struggled to fend off similar suicidal attacks from doors and rooftops. Unnoticed, the enemy rolled a log off the edge of a roof to drop with a sickening crash onto the warriors in the street. At the same time Alfren staggered under the impact of a rock hurled from above and dropped dazed to his knees.

Caros turned to the rear ranks. "Send the archers up here and onto these roofs. Clean the bastards off them!" He then helped Neugen drag the man off the street into what had been a bakery.

"Bastards do not know when to give up. Here, help me get him up here."

Heaving, they lifted the heavy man onto a sturdy table. Alfren tried sitting up, but fell back with a groan. Caros looked at Neugen and shook his head worriedly.

"We need to send him back. As soon as our archers are in place on the roofs, we should be able to risk it."

"It is not long to nightfall. It may be better to wait till it is dark." Neugen cautioned.

"I do not think so." Caros wiped his bloodied falcata off with a bundle of linen lying beside an oven while exploring the room. "When night falls, the Saguntines will counter-attack using the dark as cover."

Neugen slammed a fist into a mud-brick wall with a curse. "I hope the other columns had better luck than us. Those flaming javelins are nasty bloody things. Trust these turds to come up with that idea."

Caros walked to the doorway and glanced out. The Bastetani warriors were holed up in every doorway along the street. The splintering of furniture, shouts, and ringing of blades sounded from within many of the buildings. He needed to take control of things and come up with a plan. They had been so intent on breaching the wall and getting into the city that they had not stopped to consider the possibility of fighting the Saguntines for every cursed building between the outer and inner walls.

He looked back speculatively at Neugen, considering his friend's last remark. An idea flared in his mind; one he did not like. The more he considered it, the more he knew it would need to be done to avoid losing all they had gained. He made his mind up and called across the street to a pair of warriors who sheltered just inside a doorway. "You two fellows, come over."

One man spat and then with nervous glances at the roofline, the two darted across the street.

"Neugen, get Alfren back over the wall with these two fellows. I am going to be bringing the rest of the men back. Tell any warriors coming forward to return to the breach and have everybody handy tear that palisade down. We may need to get out of here in a hurry and that thing will be in our way."

Neugen frowned, not liking the urgency in Caros' tone, but he held his tongue and gestured to the two men to grab Alfren who lay, ashen faced, on the table. They got him up between them and made their way out and down the street as fast as they could go. Neugen paused beside Caros with a questioning look to which he responded. "Trust me; if I am right, we are going to need to move fast."

Caros darted from doorway to doorway, ascertaining where the Bastetani warriors were and ordering them to fall back. Their archers were struggling to make their way forward and the men were still dodging missiles from the roofs. A handful of enraged Bastetani warriors took the fight to the Saguntines above the streets, but the defenders, who knew the layout of the city intimately, quickly outmaneuvered them. In a short while the Bastetani warriors' headless corpses were thrown to the street below with jeers while their bloody heads were fixed to spears and mounted on the rooftops. As galling as it was to see brave men killed and dishonored so, Caros shouted his men down when they clamored and bayed to go after the killers. He formed the men into tight squares and hunched below their shields, they shuffled back down the streets. Warhorns called the retreat and as the Bastetani fell back the emboldened Saguntine warriors materialized at their rear. Slingshots, javelins and arrows rained down on the Bastetani. A man beside Caros shrieked in pain when a javelin smashed his knee. The man could not stand and would be killed by the advancing Saguntines in a moment. Caros roared in anger and physically dragged the injured man to his feet. "Get up! Here take him, we leave no injured!"

The mood among the beleaguered Bastetani solidified into grim determination. Men grabbed the injured man and hauled him back with them after tearing the javelin from what was left of his knee. Others fell injured along the way and were likewise lifted and carried back with the retreating band. Caros was becoming more and more incensed by the Saguntine mob baying and heckling them between every throw of a javelin. They were building their courage and on the verge of charging his ranks.

A sudden strumming of taut bowstrings sounded from above them and the Bastetani cringed, but the arrows sped over them to pierce the Saguntines. Caros cheered and the sweating, bleeding men around him joined him in praising their archers. They were nearing the outer wall where Neugen had managed to secure a row of buildings and had placed archers to cover the retreat. They were in the shadow of the west wall and thousands of Bastetani were hemmed in here. Caros ordered shield walls in place on all streets and alleys in a rough semi-circle about the area of the wooden palisade on the breach. He met Neugen returning from supervising the demolition of the wooden palisade.

"Alfren?"

"He does not look good, poor bastard. The men are pulling up that palisade like you said." He looked across the city. "Did you see how many were still in there? It was a bloody good thing you pulled us back when you did. Sorry I questioned you."

Caros grinned and slapped him on the ear. "You get a knock on the head or something? When do you ever not question me, eh?"

Neugen shook his head to clear the ringing. "Ouch!" He laughed. "Well, here is a question. What now?"

"Fire."

"Yup. Go on."

"What is happening with the other columns?" Caros asked.

"Same story. Masulians made the wall, held it and then pulled back. The Libyans are holding the wall, but a couple hundred of them are trapped beyond the first streets and cannot fall back. Sounds like they will be meeting their ancestors before this day is done. Hope that fool Libyan is not amongst them. Kind of liked the fellow."

"Bullshit. You kind of liked the dream of the sister you do not even know he has."

"He has a sister?"

Caros felt better for the banter, but the position of the Libyans worried him. What he was contemplating was bad enough without their comrades being trapped in the city. At that moment warhorns signal a full retreat. The entire army was withdrawing from the city!

Neugen looked grim. "Guess that means the Libyans are finished."

Caros glared about. "Archers! I want every archer to fire flames into the city. Douse everything and set it alight."

Neugen spun around, eyes wide. "Burn it? Burn the whole city? What about the people?"

Caros stared at Neugen with red eyes. "What people? I did not see a cursed shade apart from their warriors. Their people are long gone." Or will be soon, he thought. In his heart he knew there would be innocent people within that part of the city, but none of the warriors had seen a single woman or child, even within those homes or buildings they had taken shelter in. "We will be back in days and when we come back everything will be burned clear. As it is, every bloody hovel in here is a hill fort and I am sick of seeing our fellows with their heads stove in." He clenched his fist and swiped his falcata across the cityscape. "Fire the whole cursed place."

From the plains, the mauled army watched in fascination as the buildings within the outer walls burned. The army had pulled out from the city, bloodied and hurt. Estimates at this point put losses amongst Hannibal's forces at some four thousand of their warriors. The Libyans had lost a disproportionate amount of men despite their better armor. They had struggled more slowly up the ladders and through the narrow breaches and then many had been trapped too far into the warren of alleyways and cobbled lanes.

Now the army slunk back to the plains to watch the enemy city burn, spared at least the jeers and catcalls of the defenders. Caros quickly ascertained that Alfren was still alive. He had been removed from the field to the pavilion where Asklepius could work his talents as a physician.

Caros gathered the Bastetani warriors at the foot of the hill. It was still light enough to see the figures of stragglers, from every contingent of Hannibal's army, making their way down the many goat tracks to the plain. Libyans, Masulians and others limped and staggered in a daze past the massed Bastetani. Caros walked his mare part way up the hill before turning to address the assembled warriors.

Filling his lungs, he shouted. "Who are we?" The milling warriors looked up at Caros, exhaustion carved into soot-blackened faces. He gazed across the sea of battered warriors. "I asked who are we?" He encouraged the closest warriors. "You men. Who are you?" They looked about uncomfortably and even Neugen sat with a frown. "You know who you are! Tell me!"

An aged warrior stepped forward on shaky legs and leaned on his spear shaft to spit a wad of sooty phlegm into the dirt. Squaring his shoulders, he spoke.

"I am Bastetani!"

Caros smiled, his doubt falling away. In days and years to come, when men spoke of Hannibal, of Maharbal, and other champions; Caros would remember that old warrior and he would acknowledge him as a true hero. From behind the old warrior, his kin stepped forward. "We are Bastetani!"

Caros nodded and looked again across the battered warriors. "Who are we?" Now men murmured and stood taller. They began calling hesitantly. Caros raised his falcata, silencing the discordant voices. "I asked who we are?"

"Bastetani!" The ragged call came back. Caros lifted both arms. Warriors rose. "Bastetani! Bastetani! Bastetani!" They growled and then roared.

Caros danced his mount in a circle to look up at Sagunt and added his voice to the cry. As he shouted, stragglers from other contingents paused to watch. Their eyes widened at the sight of warriors with all manner of wounds, raising themselves on their spears to chant the name of their people. Men and women too injured to stand unaided were helped up by their kin. A Libyan, burned and bloodied, sank to his knees, tears marring the soot and blood on his cheeks. Masulians, carrying the body of a comrade, slowed to gaze in awe at the spirited warriors. More and more men gathered, marveling at the spirit of the roaring Bastetani. They stood on the plain and watched, as in the face of defeat, these warriors declared their name. They were not broken, nor were they defeated. They were stronger.

A rapidly approaching dust cloud signaled riders. As the Bastetani's cheers gathered Hannibal's bruised army, that general sped towards them with Maharbal at his side. Caros watched as Hannibal was forced to slow and pick his way through the crowd of Libyan, Masulian and Turdetani warriors viewing the Bastetani. The general came to a stop beside Caros and surveyed the gathered thousands. He looked appraisingly at Caros, one eyebrow cocked before smiling and lifting Caros' arm above his head. The Bastetani howled with pride and then began the chant that brought a flush to Caros' cheeks. It quickly spread through the massed warriors.

Caros the Claw! Caros the Claw! Caros the Claw!

"You fired the city." Hannibal's voice was grim.

"I did. The second wall is now wide open for the taking." Caros replied, the burning city reflected from the blade clutched in his fist.

25

Hannibal had ordered Maharbal to retake the outer walls at first light. In other circumstances, the army may have required days or weeks to recover their morale after having been forced to relinquish the tenuous grip on the city they had gained so bloodily. Hannibal however, recognized that through Caros' actions, in both burning the buildings between the outer and inner walls and, more importantly, in so deftly turning their rout into a victory of sorts, their army was now more ready than ever to crush Saguntine resistance.

Throughout the summer night, bloodied warriors were moved to the reserve lines and fresh contingents brought forward to bolster the depleted front ranks. Runners flowed in a continuous train between the pavilion and the front lines. Rams were brought forward from the lumber camp where they had been hastily built. Hannibal ordered drummers to beat the great leather and wood drums throughout the night and for a phalanx of men to circle the city, blowing huge warhorns. He wanted the Saguntines to know they were coming; he wanted them to sit through the night wide-eyed and in terror. To remember the flames that had destroyed more than a third of their city and to know their fate was sealed.

Caros sat beside Alfren and told the grim warrior of what had happened. How much Alfren heard, he was not certain for the injured champion slipped between consciousness and sleep with no rhythm.

Neugen stepped into the tent. "Here you go. Specially brewed just for nights like this." He passed a cup to Caros who took it gratefully, inhaled the bitter aroma and wrinkled his nose. "It is good. Something Alugra used to have us brew up after a battle. Wine and herbs. You wake up feeling strong, provided you do not drink more than a cupful." He laughed at Caros' expression and then his smiled faded and he frowned at Alfren who lay senseless. "Looks like you are in command, Caros."

"At least until Alfren here decides to quit taking it easy." Caros shook his head and then downed the warm drink. Outside, starlight sparkled like a thousand spear points in the night-black sky above the pair and Caros sighed up at them. "I am in command, yes. Hannibal has confirmed it, but I would prefer that Alfren recovered quickly."

A man wailed nearby, overcome by his agony. A constant, low exhalation of fear and pain seeped into the night from the many scattered huddles of warriors. Healers and helpers scurried from campfire to tent to aid the injured. They would be busy all night.

"Have the men turned out early tomorrow to build funeral pyres. Then I want three thousand of our best warriors ready to leave for Sagunt."

The following morning the Bastetani began building the funeral pyres required to cremate their dead. By midday, they had built eleven pyres, each large enough to receive the bodies of two hundred slain warriors. Once the bodies had been lain on the log platforms, the Bastetani shuffled past in double lines to throw objects into the banked tinder and wood. Brooches, statuettes, articles of clothing and even food were offered along with invocations to the god Saur, who ruled the land of dead and to Endovex, who ruled all.

Caros sat his mare and watched grimly until the army had passed the pyres and formed into rough ranks upwind. He wore a new outfit he had purchased from the camp merchants that morning; a red and yellow tunic of double-spun flax and over it, his iron cuirass which still smelled of scorched building and charred flesh. Placing his helmet on his head, he eyed the sun.

"It is time, Neugen. Hand me the torch."

Neugen beckoned to one of the mounted warriors that accompanied them and the man passed a burning torch to Caros. Sliding from his mare, he strode to the first pyre and lit the oil drenched fuse at its base. The fire took and ate its way into the heart of the pyre where it reached the tinder which ignited with a roar of heat and flame. Caros threw a silver stater into the midst of the conflagration. He repeated the rite at each pyre until at the last, he lit the fuse and threw both torch and silver stater into the flames.

Remounting, he addressed the Bastetani, reminding them that of all the people in Hannibal's great army, it was they who had held the wall the longest, had plunged deepest into the city and had bested the Saguntines and burned their outer city. When others had sunk in defeat, it was they who roared defiance. For this, Hannibal had taken the greatest pride in them, for they had re-ignited the courage of the entire army. The Bastetani warriors growled and roared, their mood grim as they ached to crush the Saguntines once and for all.

Caros had allowed for a meal before his contingent set off for the walls. While the warriors tore at roasted meat and drank the ale that he had purchased, he walked among them. Calling on the leading men to offer his thanks for their spears, he also greeted many of the regular warriors by name, commending them on their bravery or enquiring after injured kin. The men greeted him with a mixture of admiration and respect. He had become their talisman. Wherever he went, the enemy fell and the Bastetani were victorious.

After the funeral rites, Caros led them to the besieged city. Here, he dismounted at the outer walls along with Neugen and the warriors that formed his guard. The devastation caused by the fire was appalling and what had been a thriving town was now a smoking ruin. Carrion crows screamed from the air above them as they eyed the meals they had been forced to abandon amongst the wreckage. Across the ruins, a thin cloud of oily smoke hung in the still air, throwing a sickly light over the ruins. A rider approached through the wisps of smoke. Caros recognized Aksel, who waved.

"My friends! I am glad to see you both uninjured." The Masulian swung off his mount and embraced Caros and Neugen in turn.

"Good to see you well, Aksel." Caros smiled at the Masulian. "What are you doing up here?"

"I have come to see if you have left anything for the rest of the army!"

"Oh, even better; I left you a whole new wall just over there." Caros pointed.

Neugen groaned. "Do not get him started, Aksel. You know how lousy his jokes are!"

Aksel cocked his head. "Actually, I was sent by Hannibal to fetch you."

"They are up here or at the pavilion?"

"Right around the corner. Follow me."

"Neugen, sort the men out with guard duty. However unlikely an attack is, I want them prepared."

"Right, will do. I will get some men up on the walls so that we do not have to rely on the Turdetani."

Mago and Hasdrubal sat on stone stairs, while above them Hannibal and Maharbal walked alongside the parapet of the outer wall, studying Sagunt's second line of defense. Massinissa stood nearby and waved a greeting. Caros greeted Hannibal's brothers before ascending to the parapet. Blood had soaked into the stonework, leaving dark stains that drew scores of incandescent flies.

Hannibal limped to the head of the stairs, wearing a wide smile. "Caros, it is just as you said; the way is now open for us to storm the inner wall."

"It has been a long siege. It will be good to conclude it, but the Saguntines will defend their inner wall to the death I think."

"I expect they will, but time is not on our side. We must act quickly to bring this bloody business to an end."

Alerted by Hannibal's tone, Caros asked, "Has there been some development?"

Hannibal looked strained. After a moment, the general pursed his lips and spoke. "There has. The Romans have stirred themselves and even as we speak, a deputation from Rome has sailed on to Carthage."

Caros knew of Sagunt's alliance with Rome and had heard the recent rumors that it was at the recommendation of arbitrators from Rome that the pro-Carthaginian faction in Sagunt be expelled or executed.

"Let me guess, they are not happy with us laying siege to Sagunt?"

Hannibal flashed a wide grin. "They are definitely not happy. Bomilcar alerted us the moment his ships spotted a Roman vessel approaching the coast. We detained the Roman tribunes on the shore, but they will have verified from their spies that we are besieging Sagunt. They left some weeks ago to stir up the issue in Carthage."

Caros had a sudden sense of foreboding. This was not going to end with the fall of Sagunt. The Romans were a hard and martial people who considered their fides a fundamental part of their way of life. From the expressions on both Hannibal and Maharbal's faces, they too knew the Romans would not let the attack on Sagunt go unanswered.

"So, we fight the Romans?"

Hannibal laughed aloud and clapped Caros on the shoulder. He thought the general had perhaps misunderstood him and that he wished for war with Rome. He had absolutely no desire to do so. Once Sagunt had fallen, he would return to his farm and raise horses, trade in the summer months and stay away from other's battles. He said nothing though and smiled as Hannibal's laugh died. "Eh, Caros, you are a bright young man and will always have a place in my army, but today we put aside thoughts of war with Rome and look to finish the battle we have before us. How would you propose to end this siege quickly?"

Caros took a deep breath. He had been pondering on this question all morning. The rams had done a fair job under poor conditions but taken too long. They were best suited for pounding down wooden gates and palisades rather than walls of rock. Ladders were easy to make, but the cost in lives scaling the walls was immense. He had thought perhaps building towering platforms as high as the walls, might enable warriors to attack in strength. While thinking of this he had remembered a trick his father had taught him. The principle was that whenever you had a solution to a challenge, you would examine the opposite solution. It was not an easy exercise, but in this instance, he thought the resulting idea might be the perfect answer to defeating the wall. With a gleam in his eye he told Hannibal of his idea.

Rams had been brought forward to batter the two heavy wooden gates in the second wall. This was more for their distraction value though. Under the cover of heavy lattices of woven branches and hides, men were digging trenches into the rocky ground at the foot of the second wall. Night and day, the clinking of pickaxes rang across the hill. Two hundred men toiled continuously in the trench, prizing their way into the rock and foundations of the second wall. Caros had turned the obvious solution on its head; instead of going over the wall, they were going under it.

On standby to protect the miners were thousands of armed warriors. The burned buildings had been cleared away to leave an open space on which Hannibal's army waited for the fruits of the digging. Caros paced beside Aksel, watching the defenders throwing their infamous burning javelins at any target that presented itself. The lattices protecting the miners were often set alight by these javelins and needed constant mending.

In addition, the Saguntines had taken to launching lightning raids on the rams and the diggers. In the darkest hours, they would send rope ladders over the walls and their men would hastily descend on the workers in the trench. After the devastating sortie on the battering rams, Hannibal's men had expected a similar surprise attack and were better prepared to defend the rams and the diggers.

That night, two score of the Saguntine warriors, smeared black with ash and carrying spears, had dropped onto the men working below the walls. The battle had been wild and bloody. The miners fought like cornered beasts, swinging their pickaxes at the Saguntine warriors. The sounds of battle and cries of alarm had brought Hannibal's warriors racing to the wall and the enemy were quickly dispatched. Less than twenty miners had been killed or injured, but the others were badly shaken. More warriors had been injured as they closed within range of the javelins, arrows and slingshots loosed at them by the defenders on the wall. These had clearly been waiting there in silence for exactly that opportunity.

By the time Caros arrived, their archers and slingers had begun to fire back at the defenders on the wall and the skirmish was over. From the darkness came a shout of alarm followed by pounding feet. Spinning, he saw a shadowy figure sprinting away from the wall. It seemed that one of the attackers had escaped the slaughter and decided to flee the city rather than die in the siege. A bowstring twanged and the deserter stumbled. Desperately, he righted himself and tried to run on, dragging one leg. He had no chance and when he tripped, he was engulfed by furious warriors and miners. They would slaughter him where he lay. While the man's death was of no consequence, Caros realized the man may have valuable information on circumstances in the city. He broke into a run.

"Hold! Do not kill him, by Runeovex, or I will take your bloody hands off at the wrists!" He might have been whispering for all the effect his words had. He reached the vengeful warriors and laid into them with the flat of his blade, beating his way through. Behind him, his guards manhandled the warriors back. Caros reached the prone form and was relieved to see the man, curled in a ball, slowly lower his hands to peer up at him, the whites of his eyes huge in his soot-blackened face. The last words he expected to hear came from the warrior's lips.

"You! You live!" The man gasped.

"What do you mean? How do you know me?" Caros shouted, his falcata held menacingly at the man's throat.

"I know you! I swear it. Please, for my life, I beg you for my life."

Piercing the soot and skin of the man's cheek with the tip of his blade, Caros asked again. "Speak now. What do you know of me? I have never seen your miserable hide in my life."

His guards formed a grim-faced circle about the pair, eyes glowering.

"You do not know me, but I know you. Please, what I say will enrage you, but it is useful. Something you will want to know. Give me your word you will not kill me when I speak?"

Caros was baffled and found himself shaking with emotion. His intuition told him that whatever words this man spoke, they would change his life in some unalterable way. He lowered his blade from the man's face.

"Very well. Upon my word, you will have your life. Now speak before I change my mind."

The man rose unsteadily to his knees, his hands held imploringly before him. He looked around at the circle of hostile faces and with breath whistling through a bloodied and broken nose, he began. "My kin and comrades were paid to plunder the countryside of the Bastetani. It was spring. We came across you in a village near Baria. You were with a man." He hesitated, terrified to shaking. "A woman also." Caros' blood froze in his veins and his hand clenched the falcata in a white-knuckled grip. The man began to weep silently, tears tracing pale lines through the soot on his cheeks. "We attacked you on the road. I saw a fellow warrior land a blow to your head. Never gave you a chance, that blow would have killed almost anybody. You and your friend fought bravely, killed one of my brothers and injured four more men. You escaped into the dark, but we took the woman."

Caros wanted to tear the man's head off his shoulders. He wanted to open his gut and feed it to the pigs. He grunted, sweat pouring from his brow, body taut as a bowstring. He recalled the two men he had passed in the little village while walking from the well.

"Where is she? Where is Ilimic?" His voice came from far away and sounded like a stone on a blade.

"She lives! I swear she still lives. I have seen her with my own eyes right here in the city! Please, you swore."

Caros' vision clouded. His chest was on fire and he felt as though the world had crashed away from him. He raised his blade in fury and for long heartbeats, it quivered with a life of its own above the deserter. Out of nowhere, Neugen appeared. He must have heard part of the man's testimony because when he stepped before him, his eyes were filled with rage and his hard-jawed face was waxy.

"I have not sworn to let you live." His words were like arrows from his mouth and he would have killed the wide-eyed warrior right then except a firm hand stayed his arm. A powerfully built guard looked apologetically at Neugen.

"Not yet. He needs to explain about the woman. If she is held in the city, it may be that we can free her."

Neugen glared at the guard who stood his ground. "You are right, of course. Bind him and remove him to the outer wall. We will be there shortly."

Caros let out a long breath and lowered his blade. Neugen took him by the arm and silently led him to where his tent was pitched.

Caros alternated between fits of rage and depression. He worried and gnawed at the idea that Ilimic was alive and captive. Thoughts of what she was enduring burned through his mind, reducing cool reasoning to unrecognizable indecision.

"I cannot believe it! I do not know if I want to. That she might be alive and captive in the very city we are attacking. What she must be enduring!"

Caros had put deaths of his family and then Ilimic from his mind. Now, just as they were on the verge of defeating the city of Sagunt, this news. To him, this was either the worst of tricks played by the gods or a favor. Neugen and Aksel sat in the shade beside his tent, knuckles tight and eyes hard. Neugen breathed deeply and spat into the dirt between his boots.

"Caros, I cannot answer these questions. I do not even want to think along those lines and implore you to think of her as still being the same woman you loved. Request Hannibal's aid. He can arrange to buy her freedom. The Saguntines will surely do anything to lessen the severity of their fate."

"No! Not that! No one must know other than us three. Imagine her being bought like some slave and walked from the gates like a cow released from a slaughter pen with every eye in the army watching. I could not endure that." Caros stopped and stared hard at the city, a look of pure venom twisting his features.

The deserter was bound with chains to a stout pole and kept under guard. He had told them that the woman had been held by their leading man and on returning to the city, he had sold her to a notorious house. Caros made the man draw map after map of the location, but each one seemed more confusing than the last.

"I will just take the bastard with us when we storm the place." Caros had finally raged.

The following day, he rose near noon, eyes crusted and breath like a barrel of sour wine. Staggering into the blinding light and heat of a summer afternoon, he dipped his head into a leather bucket hung in the shade. His stomach roiled and his head hurt, but these things mattered little to him on this day. Late in the night and after much wine, he had resolved his thoughts and now planned to hasten this siege to destroy the city and save Ilimic. Calling for food, he ducked back into the tent and dressed for battle. A short while later, a boy arrived with a bowl of cheese, olives and figs. A large pitcher of fresh milk accompanied the meal and Caros ate and drank it all while standing before his tent, staring at the last hurdle to his love.

26

Once again, the army was in position before the walls of Sagunt. The men digging the trench below the walls reported large cracks opening as they undermined its foundations. When they could do no more without risk of being crushed beneath it, they dropped their tools and ran, leaving only the two rams to batter the inner gates. The Saguntines had worked furiously to throw up palisades directly in the mouths of the two gates, so that when these did finally give way, Hannibal would be confronted by yet more defenses.

Caros strode forward and glared at the wall, willing it to collapse. Like a dying beast, it shuddered and a cloud of dust rose from beneath it, yet the defenders remained in their places. The dust subsided and the defenders hooted at the Barca army. One ambitious warrior shot an arrow that struck the dirt paces short of where Caros stood.

"Why in the gods' names will it not fall?" He cursed, stopped and picked up the arrow to snap it between his hands and cast it back at the defenders.

Behind him, Hannibal's army stood ready to sweep through the breach the moment the wall fell. They had stood to the moment the diggers had reported the cracks opening. Now the wall had seemed to heal itself.

Neugen approached, concern clouding his eyes. "Caros, if you need more scars to prove your honor, this is the place to stand. Come away, it will fall soon enough."

Caros swore under his breath, but seeing there was nothing more he could do, turned back to their lines with Neugen. His thoughts were a jumble of ideas on how to knock down the obstacle. Perhaps the rams could help, he pondered. Before him, his guards stood taller, squaring their shoulders. About to remind them it was not necessary to do so, he sensed Neugen falter. He turned just as the ground trembled. A growing thunder of falling rock, brick and timber followed by a billowing cloud of dust, swept across the no-man's-land. The dust rolled over Caros and Neugen and over the ranks of

Bastetani, Libyans and Africans. The wall was breached and judging by the amount of dust, the breach was no small one. Coughing, he caught Neugen's eye and the two warriors stared for a moment at one another. They each knew their roles in the coming battle. Neugen would lead the Bastetani and Caros would search for Ilimic.

From the walls of the inner fort, Abarca watched the gathered army beyond the inner wall. Reports had reached him advising that it had been undermined and would soon fall. Berenger stood beside him and stared at the teeming defenders risking their lives on the structure. They had been told to fall back, but many had refused to leave.

"Berenger, will you lead our warriors in the coming battle?"

He dragged his eyes from the scene. "When it falls, Hannibal's men will be all over the city by nightfall. What exactly do you expect me to do?"

Abarca smiled tightly. "They burned the outer city because we made them pay for every doorway and alley. We can do so again. The walls of the buildings down there are stronger; we can fight them from the roofs again. I agree, they will gain the city, but then they will face the stone fort. We can sue for terms and they will agree if we make them pay a high enough price down there."

Berenger looked down upon the city. There was some truth in Abarca's words, but if he led that fight, it would only be until he found the opportunity to escape the city. He had no intention of dying here for the Greek merchants and the twisted priest or his lunatic sister. He had seen their rites performed every night for the past month, each more gruesome than the last. A woman, usually just a girl, was taken from the slave pit below the shrine to Catubodua. The mob of warriors and town's people bayed for the blood sacrifice to receive the aid of the goddess. It was there that the priestess performed the sacrifice, while her deviant brother pranced in the blood that pooled on the altar's stairs.

He thought of the woman he had sold to the temple and wondered if she had met her fate there on the bloody altar. For a moment, he saw his sister's face and felt weak with horror at what he had done. It had seemed a small thing to sell her at the time. He shook his head and cleared his throat. Perhaps there was time for atonement?

"I will lead the fight." He cleared his throat again. "I will do this thing but know this Strategos. This is my last act in defense of Sagunt. I shall not return here." Berenger turned away even as in the distance, the wall lurched and begun to topple.

The warriors defending the wall cried out in terror as they felt it lurch under their feet. Many ran to escape down the stairs and others, seeing they had no time, flung themselves as far as they could from the fast crumbling structure. The wall folded, shattering and falling to pieces in a roiling storm of dust and screams. Hundreds of men perished in moments, crushed under falling rock, while hundreds more were horribly injured with broken limbs or trapped under the rubble. In moments, the stalemate ended and the final phase of the siege descended on Sagunt. Already the warhorns of Hannibal's army were sounding; the long keening of hungry wolves preparing to hunt. Then came the roar of an army that spies the enemy. Saguntine men, women and children paled and trembled. They had done all they could to forestall this day, even to following the high priestess' invocations as she offered the goddess the blood of maids.

Their warriors converged in the streets and on the roofs to fight this last battle. They would sell their lives dearly and die with honor while their women would make sacrifices of their children and themselves rather than be taken by the enemy.

Caros spun on his heel and issued the command to advance. Turning to Neugen, he allowed a brief smile.

"Well my friend, this is it." The two men clasped their right arms firmly and shook.

"To battle then! Let the swine pay for every woman and child murdered and for Ilimic. Do me a favor Caros, try not getting yourself speared." Behind them, the great Barca army advanced towards the inner city.

"I do not intend dying my friend, but should Endovex call for my shade this day, I expect you will still tell jokes at my expense." The friends grinned at one another.

"I hope Aksel keeps himself safe." Neugen muttered.

Caros nodded in agreement as the advance ranks arrived at his shoulders. Raising his burnished falcata, he turned to face the inner city and swept the blade down. With a single voice, the thousands of Bastetani warriors roared.

"Caros the Claw!"

The Bastetani plunged towards the dust, rubble and defenders. They swept through the choking cloud and raced over the shattered rock and brick. Resistance from the outnumbered Saguntine warriors who had survived the collapse of the wall was brushed aside.

From his vantage point, Hannibal watched his army surge forward. To his left the Bastetani surged towards the collapsed wall. Beside them were the dismounted Masulians led by Aksel. His center column consisted of Liby-Phonecians who would scale that part of the wall not yet fallen. Likewise, the column to the right, the African contingent, carried ladders and was racing to scale the wall at their front.

Defenders would have surged towards the breach, reducing their numbers on those parts of the wall still standing. They would soon realize their blunder. Between his columns, he had positioned archers and slingers who now let fly their missiles in waves at any defender rash enough to peer over the remaining parapets.

Beside him, Maharbal hissed in anticipation as the ranks of Bastetani disappeared into the dust cloud, following Caros. He turned to Hannibal.

"I believe the Bastetani warriors will need all their strength today to remain at his side."

"He refused to ask me for aid, thinking I would not learn of the woman. It makes me respect him even more, but I fear for him. The battlefield is no place to be distracted by personal agendas."

"His men will fight to the death beside him if necessary and it was wise of you to place the Masulians beside the Bastetani. The two forces work well together."

"The warriors follow the example of their leaders and everyone can see Caros and Aksel are close friends."

The two men watched as the army struck the walls, throwing ladders up and scaling them. The cloud of dust was settling and a breach of about a single stadion in width could now be seen; wider even than Hannibal had dared to hope. It was only fitting that Caros lead his Bastetani through the breach brought about by his plan.

Over the rubble and onto the street, the Bastetani poured. Their war cries augmented by the clamor of their warhorns. Before them appeared the first signs of cohesive resistance. Saguntine warriors had formed a shield wall and were steadily advancing towards the breach and onrushing Bastetani.

Behind Caros, his warriors adopted the plan that he insisted they use when they next found themselves attacking a breach. Archers immediately swarmed to high points along walls and roofs, their ranks bolstered by warriors assigned to protect them from counter attacks.

In the streets below, they cleared every building from top to bottom as they drove forward. While this slowed their advance, they were secure from surprise attacks in their rear. The archers sent a hail of arrows at the oncoming shield wall while the warriors hurled their javelins. Under this cover, Caros led his front rank into the fight. He drove his shield hard against a wide-eyed, screeching warrior, forcing the man to stagger back. Deftly, he hooked the man's shield rim with his own and pulled it aside while thrusting his sword into the warrior's exposed armpit. The falcata sliced through the muscle and severed the artery there with a spray of blood. Spitting bloody curses, the warrior sank defeated to the ground where he was torn apart as the Bastetani broke apart the shield wall and overran the defenders.

Caros spied more of the enemy gathering down every street. He checked the rooftops and was heartened to see Bastetani warriors and archers occupying those positions. Somewhere to his left, shrill ululations and a clash of blades and shields signaled that the Masulians were into the fight now.

"Right fellows, stay close and keep your shields before you. We have men on the roofs so the bastards will not be raining rocks on us this time!"

"They are coming at us from three sides though, Caros." Neugen observed dryly.

Caros did not want his men held up defending their small gain into the inner city. His instincts screamed to attack them relentlessly and by doing so, keep them from staging any counterattack. Privately, he wanted to cut his way through to where the deserter told him Ilimic had been taken. His face contorted into a mask of fury at the thought, but first he had a duty to his men.

"Neugen, I want the breach held at all costs, so get a dependable graybeard to hold it with five hundred men including archers. If the enemy counterattack, it will be from the right."

"No problem. Which way are we going?"

"Take a thousand men to the left and keep in contact with Aksel's Masulians."

"They wear little armor while the Saguntines have everything down to greaves." Neugen shuddered visibly. "They will make slow progress."

It was an observation Caros had also made. The Saguntine warriors were well equipped, the city having had time to prepare for war.

"That is why I want you to keep an eye on them. We cannot afford becoming encircled like the Libyans did."

"You are going to go straight through the center?" Neugen stared at Caros, knowledge of his friend's thoughts showing in his eyes.

Caros smiled thinly. "Straight through the center."

The shield wall shuffled forward up the winding street, allowing their archers to keep pace on the roofs above. At a crossroad, another hastily constructed barricade of furniture, gates and loose timber had been thrown together. Yells and jeers issued from above as the archers shot a volley at the unseen defenders. Pounding footfalls echoed from the roofs followed by a clash of arms. Moments later, an injured warrior toppled from the roof and struck the cobblestones hard, his legs twisted unnaturally beneath his body. He was a Saguntine archer, emaciated and toothless. Abruptly the fight above ended and a voice called the all clear to them in Bastetani.

Caros ordered his shield wall forward. "Faster now. Charge!"

Leading from the front, he leaped at the waist-high barricade, braced a boot on it and launched into the grim defenders behind. Spears thrust at him and he batted these away with his shield while hacking with his blade. He feinted for the defender to his left and swung his sword instead at the warrior to his right. The feint worked and he scored a slash across the man's knee. A spearhead clanged off his cuirass and another blade embedded in his shield.

He kicked furiously at his attackers and jabbed his sword at a warrior's face. He was surrounded by the enemy for long heartbeats and could do little more than keep them at bay. Then a Bastetani warrior was beside him and another and Caros quickly seized the chance to drive forward.

A hairy-knuckled hand gripped the rim of his shield and pulled it down with brute force, exposing Caros to a plunging sword. He twisted violently to avoid being skewered and found himself spinning his attacker into a press of the enemy. The collision knocked them off balance and Caros used the momentum to slash and hack two of them before turning his attention to the heavyset warrior still gripping his shield. He struck at the man's fingers, slicing off two. The Saguntine warrior cursed and released the shield to dance back. Caros followed, lunging at speed to plunge his blade into the man's groin where he sawed it deep into his gut. The barricade was taken.

"Hold! Hold!" Caros shouted breathlessly as his men started after the fleeing Saguntines. "Wait for the archers, curse you! Hold!"

His men paused and fell back, chastened. Wiping his hand on the tunic of a Saguntine warrior, he gripped the hilt of his blade tight to pull it free of the man's body. It jammed in the man's hip bone and in frustration, he braced a foot on the man's gut and wrenched. As the blade tore free, the Saguntine lifted a hand and squealed. Caros stared in repulsion as the man's breath rattled one last time from his throat and his hand dropped lifeless to the ground.

He wiped drool and blood from his face, his chest heaving. Darkness threatened the edges of his vision and he bent forward, elbows locked on his knees, to catch his breath and suppress the urge to throw up.

The Bastetani began tearing down the barricade and throwing the pieces aside to clear the street. An arrow struck a length of timber as a warrior lifted it and his comrades laughed when he cursed and dropped it. Shamefaced, he too laughed. So easily men become inured to war and death, Caros thought, even as another arrow rattled off the stones at his feet, almost unnoticed by the laboring warriors. Regaining his senses and breath, Caros hollered. "Archers, sort those bastards out!"

A Bastetani youth, bow in hand, peered over the side of the nearest building. "We are out of arrows! More are being fetched to us."

"Make it quick and do not let that happen again."

"Sorry, Caros." Flushing with embarrassment, the archer disappeared.

"Leave the barricade and bring water. We are not going anywhere until the arrows arrive."

Gratefully, his men sank against the cover of the adobe and stone buildings. Caros sent a runner to the rear. He could no longer hold off. They had fought their way, street by street, into the heart of the city and from the latest messages, Aksel's men were at their limit. Neugen had sent a runner to Caros just before the assault on the barricade, advising him to consolidate or he would risk being isolated. His men would hold here. Libyans were now also coming through the breach. They could come forward and relieve the Bastetani who had broken more shield walls today than most warriors did in a lifetime.

A Bastetani warrior, arms bulging with muscles, came up the street leading the captured Saguntine. Throwing the trembling man to the street before Caros, the man grinned.

"He could not wait, pissed himself with excitement and all."

Caros stared at the Saguntine. It was time to learn where this place was that Ilimic had been taken to.

"Do you know where we are?" He asked brusquely. The captive glanced about, blinked sweat out of his eyes and nodded.

"He is a deserter, a coward Caros. He will lead you into an ambush. He would sell his mother for another day of his miserable life." The muscular Bastetani warrior muttered grimly.

Caros smiled for a heartbeat. "Not so. If that were to happen, then his death would be a long painful one."

The captive licked his lips. "There is no ambush, I swear."

"Very well, show me." He gestured for the man to stand and lead. Caros followed with a score of men selected to accompany him. The band of Bastetani moved down the street warily. At every corner, they peered about cautiously, not wanting to stumble into a shield wall of Saguntine warriors. Arrows flew at them occasionally, but for the most part the skirmishes were to their rear. Those groups of Saguntine warriors that did chance upon them, either fled at the sight of the hardened warriors, or attacked wildly and died quickly.

The deserter came to a corner and peered around it. Looking back, he smiled hesitantly at Caros.

"It is down here. The large place in the center of the row on the right. It has the big black doors."

Caros peered around the corner. A single dog loped down the middle of the street. The sight surprised him as dog meat had been on the Saguntines' menu since their food supplies had dwindled to nothing. Other than the dog, there was no movement. He scanned the rooftops and saw nothing out of the ordinary.

"Hang on to him. If he is lying, make sure he dies slowly." He ordered the big Bastetani.

The warrior grunted in annoyance. "I want to come along. I am not staying out here while you have all the fun."

"Shut it and do what I say!" Caros' nerves surfaced. He gripped his falcata tightly and hefted his shield. This was it. What would he find? Sweat prickled his brow and dripped down his spine. He spat and started around the corner, picking up speed, he charged at the black doors. Bastetani warriors followed close behind, sandals and boots smacking like whip cracks on the cobbles, armor clanking loudly. He made to barge the door, only to be brushed aside by the big Bastetani who took the step in one stride and effortlessly kicked the door in with a crash. He grinned back at Caros.

"Do not worry. I gave him a little pat on the head and he will sleep awhile."

Shaking his head, Caros darted into the building, heart in throat.

Berenger surveyed the shield wall critically. Three ranks deep and stretched across the square, cutting off access to the hill fort. Warriors bloodied and starving. Months of deprivations had caused cheeks to shrink and teeth to loosen. Despite their hunger, or perhaps because of it, their eyes glittered dangerously. They were a mixture of local Edetani, and men of Greek descent and they were fighting for their lives. Advancing towards them came a contingent of Hannibal's well-armed Libyans. Armor shining even in the shadows and shields with the symbol of Tanit emblazoned in red on white. They outnumbered his warriors, but he reckoned the Saguntines had the edge, fighting as cornered beasts.

The Libyan leading man led his men forward purposefully. Berenger's estimation of the Libyans was increasing with each skirmish. At the last moment, the Libyan hollered his war cry and charged, his warriors at his shoulders. The Saguntines locked their shields and braced themselves in silence. With a crash, the Libyans struck the shields and Berenger watched as the two sides flexed and swayed. A curse here as a warrior slipped followed by a war cry as a Libyan drove a spear under a shield and scored a deep furrow through a bare thigh. The men in the front ranks slashed weakly, more as a deterrent, their main strength focused on holding their shields braced against their opponent's. Berenger signaled to Josa who lifted a warhorn to his lips to sound the charge. He had secreted twenty men in a building behind the Libyans. He focused on the doorway, eager to see them hurl themselves into the Libyan's unguarded rear. For a moment he feared they had been discovered because none showed. Then he realized Josa had not blown the warhorn, instead he stood with his head down, peering at the shaft of an arrow buried in the base of his throat, just above his cuirass. Warhorn and sword fell from nerveless fingers to clatter across the bloodied street. More arrows whistled from the roofs, followed by javelins.

Berenger knew immediately that the Saguntines would be cut apart and routed. As though led by his thoughts, the Saguntine lines tore apart, warriors felled by arrow and javelin. In moments, the Libyans were among the ranks, spears thrusting and blades slashing. Berenger gritted his teeth and sheathing his sword, turned and slipped away down a narrow alley.

He had gone from one skirmish to another all day, rallying warriors to fight together rather than in under-manned groups. That was the last. He had done what he could. He traced a well-used route to where he would perform one more deed before making his escape from the city. A deed not for the city, but to alleviate some of the guilt he carried. Stepping over a mound of foul refuse in a lichen-encrusted alley, he came to a sturdy door in a wall of stone. He tried the circular iron latch, but as expected, it was fastened on the inside. Cursing, he sheathed his sword and wiped his palms along his tunic. Eyeing the top of the wall, almost the height of two men above him, he planted a foot on a likely looking rock in the opposite wall and pushed himself upwards, fixing his body there by pressing his hands against the walls to either side. He inhaled and climbed higher between the walls until nearing the top, he nimbly propelled himself onto the wall and hauled himself over.

In the enclosure behind, a door barred his way, but this one was not built to keep a determined man out. He drove it in with a single kick. A shrill cry of fear sounded from beyond the splintered door and he glimpsed a fleeting shape dive behind a sack of rotten food. A pair of filthy feet scuttled out of sight. No doubt one of the slaves that Rose persecuted here. He drew his blade and flexed his shoulders with growing anticipation before striding across the deserted yard.

No fire burned in the cooking pit although the place still reeked of smoke and gruel. Smiling to himself and despite the sounds of violence that were rising now across the inner city, he let loose a bellow.

"Rose! Come out here!"

He would see how combative she was now that her champion was about to be toppled. Looking into the dark mouth of the passage leading into the building, he spied movement that belied a presence there. Could she be coming to challenge him? No. Instead, a figure more akin to a corpse, staggered out. It was a woman, partially clothed with fleshless bones moving below skin aflame with weeping sores. She reached toward him and opened her mouth to emit a groan thick with stench, forcing him back a step. This was surely a shade from the tombs? A sliver of sharpened bronze clutched in a bony fist, she lurched at him. He drew his sword and swung once, cutting her head from her shoulders in a single effortless stroke. Stepping past the corpse and into the passage, he spat on the body to avert its evil.

Another figure sprawled at the bottom of a set of precarious looking wooden stairs. A man this time, his tunic rumpled up around his thighs, revealing his flaccid member. The man watched impassively as Berenger drove his blade into his chest. Flies grew thick in the fetid air, alighting on him even as his blood pooled between his legs. The smell of old decay permeated the building and Berenger wanted the task done. He thought to call again, but the air was so loathsome and full of winged insects that he kept his lips sealed.

Climbing the stairs two at a time, he dived through the trap at the top. An axe splintered the powdery wooden floor a hand's breadth from his nose, and he scrambled to his feet. Rose flew at him with a speed hard to imagine. Recovering his anticipation, he smiled and punched with the pommel of his sword which sank deep into the guts of the woman. Easily avoiding the axe, he drove a fist into her neck. The two blows combined to drop her to the floor. The room shook at the impact of her body on the timber floor and dust motes danced in the dim light. Not yet done, she hacked at Berenger's ankles with the axe. Laughing, he stepped on her wrist and was rewarded with a pop; as though he had stepped on a juicy scorpion.

"Rose, you are being unfriendly today." Berenger chuckled while she hawked and spat. He grinned, unperturbed, as yellow drool slid down his grieves. "I hear tales of a snake that can spit its venom right into your eyes. The lynx also hisses and spits. You are no lynx, Rose. No, you are definitely the serpent."

She twisted her arm free from under his foot, enduring the cracking of more bones in the limb. Not bothering to cradle her swollen arm, she rolled into a corner of the room, her feet raised before her. Berenger kicked the axe through the trap so that it thudded down the stairs.

"Where is your all-powerful high priestess and that little toad spawn that calls itself a priest? Spread those fat thighs. Perhaps he is too scared to come out, eh?"

"Berenger, what are you looking for here? Are you so dull witted to think they would seek to hide away with the likes of us?"

He studied her intently in the gloom, not bothering to hide the revulsion on his face.

"Where is the woman I sold to you?" His blood boiled when he saw the beginning of a grin on her face. Would this creature tell him of the woman's death; dying writhing and screaming at the end of the priestess' blade or under the thrusts of her insane brother.

"For a price..."

She got no further before his blade snatched her ear from her head. Her mouth opened wide in shock.

"Should have done that first time I saw you. It suits you. You are a large woman and fairly bright after a fashion, so work it out. There is a lot of you to whittle away before we get to vitals."

Rose's eyes shrank to dark pits in her face. "She is gone. Days ago. She was the last."

"That so? What of that sack of festering bones that came at me with a knife downstairs?"

"One of the others. Not fit for the Priestess."

Neatly, he punched his sword into the sole of her outstretched foot. For the first time she showed pain, eyes growing frantic with agony.

"Berenger! I will not die here. I give you the woman and you will grant me my life?"

He said nothing, just cocked his head and let his eyes drift to her remaining ear. She moved faster than he would have imagined. As he bounced backward to avoid the presumed attack, she dived towards the trap in the floor instead. When the dust settled, Berenger stood stunned. Below his feet, heavy thuds gave way to hoarse wheezing. Curiously, he stepped to the edge of the trap. A fitting way to die, he thought, seeing her neck twisted and face buried in the bloody groin of the dead man. A final gurgle accompanied by a mist of red saw her bulky form stop heaving and settle. Obscenely, the dead man's head slumped forward just then.

Berenger started at a splintering crash from the front of the building followed by daylight falling over the macabre tableau at the foot of the stairs.

Maharbal stayed alongside Hannibal as the two men walked their horses to where the street spilled into a square before the gates to the inner fort. Guards in chain armor, wielding heavy spears and large oval shields bearing the signature Tanit symbol of Carthage, flanked them protectively. Hasdrubal waited in the square, looking both grim and victorious.

"Welcome to Sagunt, brother!" His voice rang with emotion.

Hannibal glanced around, looking for Mago. "Where is our brother?"

"He is fine. He will be along any moment. Let me introduce you to the Strategos of Sagunt."

Standing stiffly before the gates was Abarca. Hannibal eyed the undefended walls of the fort before pressing forward. Halting a spear's length from Abarca, he stared at the Strategos who looked back at him, defeated yet unbroken.

"Your walls are destroyed, Strategos. You spurned all terms and resisted our rightful war against Sagunt for breaking the peace we fostered in the name of Carthage. What can you possibly offer us now?"

"We give you Sagunt, Hannibal of the Barca clan of Carthage. You have taken the outer walls, but the inner fort will withstand your ladders and rams. I come to you out of pity for our people rather than in weakness. I come to offer terms."

Hannibal cocked an eyebrow at Maharbal while Hasdrubal snorted derisively behind him.

"Let your terms be heard. My scribe will note them and I will grant them as I see fit."

"We offer a treaty of trade and arms. We offer to ally with Carthage as our benefactor. These are the principle points, the finer details we can pursue once a broad agreement is reached, yes?"

Hannibal turned to his scribe who nodded that he had the points marked in the wax tablet.

"Good. Now break the tablet and burn the wax." He stepped close to Abarca. "Those are your terms? You are but a messenger for fools who have no idea how the business of war is done. I pity you." He eased up and took control of his anger. "Sagunt is no more, Strategos. I know you have but one cistern for water. You will all be dead of thirst inside a handful of days." He turned his mount and walked it along the base of the wall of the inner fort before returning. "These are the terms Carthage require. Every free man, woman and child remains free. Slaves become the property of Carthage, as does all your gold, silver and other items of value. The people of Sagunt will take two changes of clothing each and depart the city before nightfall. Where they go is of no concern to me." Hannibal paused to stare Abarca in the eyes. "Those, Strategos, are the terms as you would have known they should be. Go tell your Greeks and witch priestess. I expect the gates to remain open behind you."

Abarca ground his teeth at the humiliation. The Oligarchy had expected so much, even after losing the city, and as one they had made him their spokesman. There was nothing he could do; his power was broken and within the fort he commanded a scant three hundred warriors. All the wealthy had fled to this last refuge days ago and as Hannibal predicted, they would all be dried husks in just days.

"Very well, general." Without another word, he unfastened his belt and let it fall with his sword to the street. The gates were opened and he disappeared into the inner fort to deliver the terms.

"They will accept them, of course. Where will they go do you think?" Maharbal asked.

"North of the Ebro for the warriors and their kin. The merchants will take ship to Massalia or Rome." Hasdrubal shrugged.

Hannibal looked thoughtful for a moment. "How many of their warriors are still holding out in the city?"

Maharbal shook his head. "Given the thousands killed and taken captive so far, I cannot see more than five thousand still resisting. I have ordered our warriors to hold fast as long as we are not attacked."

"You suspect some trickery, brother?" Hasdrubal asked.

"Just say I am not overly optimistic these snakes will make the correct decision."

The smell struck him like a lash. The interior beyond the black doors was alive with iridescent flies and Caros had to fight back a compulsion to gag. He started at the sight of two bodies, recently dead, at the foot of a set of narrow wooden stairs. Cautiously, he entered the downstairs rooms with his guards close behind. The big Bastetani hawked and spat at the bodies as did the others.

"These are newly killed. They did not take their lives either. Argh, this smells worse than a tanner's ass."

Caros ignored the comments and curses from his men. "Split up and search the place. I want answers, so do not kill anyone unless you must."

The first room he entered held tables and benches. Two men lay prostrate and from their breathing and inability to wake, it appeared that they had drunk themselves to the brink of death.

"Bind them and drag them out to the street."

A yell and curse echoed down the stairs and two men tumbled down in a knot of flailing arms and legs. Judging from the deep head wound and sightless eyes of one man, he had been struck as he rose through the trap at the top of the stairs. The other groaned and dragged himself off his dead fellow. Another warrior hauled him to his feet and out the smashed door into the fresh air.

"Somebody up there is not being very hospitable. May I have a word with them?" The big Bastetani asked sweetly.

Caros squinted into the darkness at the top of the stairs. "Stay right behind me." He hefted his shield despite the narrowness of the stairs and with falcata readied, climbed the stairs one by one. Halfway up, he stopped when his name was called from below.

"Caros! Caros! Sagunt is fallen! The bastards have accepted terms. It is over!"

"Neugen! That is good news, but I am a little busy here!"

Neugen appeared at the bottom of the stairs, straining to see past the big Bastetani's muscular form.

"The whole cursed city and you pick the most evil-smelling building to storm." Catching sight of the dead man and woman, he gagged. "Oh, dear gods, what a lovely pair of dead people. I think I am going to be sick. What is up there? Is this the…"

"Yes! The captive said Ilimic was brought here where one of my men's heads has just been hacked off. Any more questions or can I finish this?" Caros barked. His nerves were frayed and the heat nearer the upper story was intense. He took the next step and heard a woman's voice call. Withdrawing his arm from the shield straps, he tossed it through the trap, diving after it into the gloom above the stairs.

With his upper body through the trap and sword useless under it, he was an easy target. Squirming to his knees, he began to clamber to his feet when he sensed a shadow rushing him. A mighty shove from the Bastetani warrior on the stairs catapulted him into the room where he crashed against the far wall. The gloom in the room was lifted as an unseen door swung open and light flooded in. His attacker hesitated between turning to where he lay, the trapdoor the Bastetani warrior was clambering through and the suddenly opened door. In the light, Caros saw a muscular warrior dressed in a red tunic and black armor with a small circular shield strapped to his back. The man pivoted nimbly on his feet to cover all three points. Beyond him stood a silhouetted figure, a shade, a dream.

"Ilimic! Shut the door!"

The warrior chose his target and struck swiftly, kicking the Bastetani on the stairs in the head. The giant warrior's head cracked against a timber beam and he dropped from sight. Caros darted forward, but the warrior was already across the room and even as the door was being swung shut, he kicked it open.

A cry of pain stabbed ice through Caros' heart. Not again! Not now! He roared in fury, leaping at the attacker. The warrior was fast, too fast. He spun and drove his sword at Caros. The overlarge blade punched into his cuirass, knocking him back. Regaining his feet, he made to charge again, only to see the warrior drag the crying woman to her feet and with his left arm wrapped about her neck, spin to face him. He stopped cold, heart beating in anguish and fright for Ilimic.

"Stop! Do not kill her! The siege is over. It is finished, you can walk away!"

The warrior laughed gratingly. "Over? You think? Has the inner fort fallen? Has Hannibal got his treasure? I think the war may be over, but the killing is not." The warrior wrenched the woman's head up into his shoulder so that her feet kicked for purchase as her slender hands scratched at his muscular arms. Caros growled in frustration until a calm voice spoke from behind him.

"Warrior, know this, if that woman is hurt you will answer to the hero of Tagus, the man who saved the life of Hannibal on the walls of Sagunt, warrior hero of the Bastetani, and the one the Masulians call 'Claw of the Lion'. If you let her go, that same man, who stands before you, will honor his word and allow you your freedom."

The warrior's mouth opened and his shoulders shook. Caros glanced at Neugen who stood braced, ready to kill.

"What is this whore to you?" The warrior asked while the face of the woman hanging by her throat in the crook of his elbow turned purple under the cascade of hair that covered it.

"Tread carefully. Her name is Ilimic and she is the one I intend to make my wife." Caros' voice strained as her hands fell to her sides and her body went limp. The warrior loosened his grip, allowing her feet to touch the ground and a ragged breath to fill her lungs.

"How does such a champion come to let his woman be brought to this place?"

"I was not always a warrior. I used to be the son of a merchant. She was taken from me in that life and that is the reason I am here." Caros lowered the point of his sword. "The choice is yours. Leave her and walk free. Why do you hesitate?" A horrible suspicion crept through Caros' chest.

The warrior dipped his chin and lowered his sword point. "You search for Ilimic? The gods must be close for that is the reason I am here. That and to kill that sow you saw downstairs."

Caros edged closer, staring at the hands of the woman. He tried to see her face, but her hair was too thick. "Let her down, she cannot breathe."

"No fear, champion. This one is not Ilimic." The warrior let the woman fall to the floor.

Caros blanched and stared as her lips quivered and she gulped painfully for air. Neugen's hand closed on his shoulder.

"It is not her, Caros."

His friend's voice held the same disappointment he felt. He did not need to be told and despair spread through his chest. If she was not here, then was he too late?

"You said you were looking for Ilimic? Was that the truth and if so, why?" Caros strained to understand.

"The woman you saw downstairs gathered maidens for the temple of Catubodua. My leading man brought your Ilimic here after she was taken from you."

"That does not explain why you were looking for her. If you think to fool us to save your life, you have made your last mistake." Caros stood ready to kill.

"I am Berenger. I protected Ilimic after she was taken. Ever since I let her be sent here, I have been plagued by guilt. Especially once I learned what the high priestess used these maidens for. That is why I returned instead of escaping the city. To kill the creature downstairs and release Ilimic if she was still held here."

Caros choked the words out. "What are they used for?"

"Carmesina, the high priestess, sacrifices them to Catubodua. She has done this since the siege began. I have lost count of the number of times I have heard their death cries."

"Neugen, search the other rooms, she must be here!" Caros cried in desperation while Berenger stood astride the senseless woman, unmoving.

"Beware, Caros. I do not trust him." Neugen stepped towards Berenger. "If not here, then where could she be? Where do they go from here?"

"The inner fort. That is where they are sacrificed."

"Stop saying that!" Caros spun back to Berenger. "She is still alive, I feel it."

Berenger just shrugged. "You are wasting time here. We are wasting time. If she is alive, that is where we will find her."

Neugen called warriors up from where they stood listening on the stairs. They surged through the remaining unsearched rooms. Finding nothing, they encircled the doorway to the room in which Berenger stood his ground. One look at the warrior told them he would be a formidable foe and they would pay dearly if it came to combat.

"Now what? I came to rescue your Ilimic. If the city is fallen, let me go my way." He prodded the woman at his feet. "I fought honorably and I tried to do the honorable thing for Ilimic. I will take you to the temple to search for her if you give me your word that I am a free man."

Caros glanced at Neugen and then he nodded to Berenger, his expression showing a sliver of hope. "Why should we trust you?"

Berenger sighed deeply. "I know where the temple is, and I know the nature of the high priestess and her insane brother. They will slaughter all the captives before surrendering, including Ilimic. As I said, I will help and not only for my freedom but also to assuage this guilt I spoke of. You need to decide quickly though, champion."

Hannibal smiled happily when Mago appeared on horseback on the wide street leading to the inner fort.

"Just in time, Mago. It appears the fort is ours." He jutted his chin at where the remaining defenders were trudging through the gates and tossing their weapons onto a growing pile.

"Not many of them left, were there? I want to see the merchants though. They are the ones with the wealth." Mago commented dryly, causing Hannibal to glance back at him questioningly. The younger Barca continued. "I have had trusted men searching all the public buildings, houses of the rich, everywhere. There is not a grain of gold or silver to be found. They must have bolted themselves in there with everything of value."

A feeling of disquiet grew within Hannibal. He needed the plunder desperately. His mercenary army would want payment and expected a share of the plunder. He would not put it past the snakes that ruled the city to attempt to cheat him of the spoils that should be his by right of conquest. Behind him warriors of every race and nation waited to be set loose in the fort to lay hands on the plunder and they were becoming restless.

Maharbal spoke up. "Why wait, Hannibal? The gates are open and the defenders all captive? Let us see what they are up to."

Hannibal wavered, not wanting to appear hasty. He was a Barca and a general. Not some bloodthirsty pirate.

A cry went up from nearby. "Smoke! The fort is on fire!"

No! They had terms. They had been granted freedom. Hannibal roared in anger and whipped his mount forward, scattering captives and warriors alike as he charged through the open gates.

Berenger led Caros and his warriors through a maze of lanes and alleys to the inner fort wall.

"Here it is. The tunnel runs under the wall and comes out beside the kitchens." He approached an unassuming building amongst many more opulent structures. The door was fastened closed from the inside. He gave it a kick that barely shook it. Grimacing, he looked around. "It is pretty sturdy. We will need to ram it open."

Caros ordered his men to find a ram and they quickly dragged a heavy post from one of the barricades the defenders had thrown up. Two warriors wielded it and with four good swings, caved the door in. They surged inside and screams of fear issued out the doorway. Caros bolted into the building to discover a group of a dozen men, women and children. Although well dressed, their expensive garments were filthy and they looked ill with hunger and fear.

"Please! Do not harm us, we have coin. Take it and let us live in the name of Endovex who is good."

Caros took in the pitiful group at a glance. "Give the coins to the warriors outside. Go!" He pointed at the open door to the street. The group scurried out with fearful glances all around, expecting trickery.

One of the warriors already inside called. "Here! This looks like the passage." He was on his knees, peering into a narrow, roughly hewn hole in the floor.

Berenger approached. "Yes, that is it. Those people have fled the fort, hoping to escape with their coin."

Without a word, Caros sheathed his falcata and dropped into the dark opening. Within, the darkness was complete and he shouted for a torch. One of those left by the escapees was relit and passed to him. With the flame lighting his way, he moved forward while the others followed him into the narrow confines.

Hurrying on, his cuirass scraped the sides where rocks had not been cut evenly. The passage was less than a stadion long and in no time, he made out the end of it in the torchlight. Holding the torch back, he saw daylight framing a dark rectangle. A doorway. He eased up to it and noted it was of wooden planking. There was no latch visible and when he pushed at it, it did not move. He shifted the pressure to the opposite side and was rewarded when the door swung open. Drawing his falcata, he shoved past the door into the room beyond.

It was a low-ceilinged room, filled with moldy grain and rotten produce. Flies buzzed at his face as he skirted carefully past split sacks and smashed amphorae. Neugen came up alongside him with Berenger who gestured.

"The kitchens are next. We go through them and a hall beyond before ascending steps to the level the shrine is on. It is not far."

"Wait! Do you hear that?" Neugen made his way to the outer entrance of the kitchens. Echoing from somewhere within the fort came unearthly wails. The men spat to ward off the evil the cries augured.

"I do not like this. I thought they had surrendered." Neugen muttered.

Unbidden thoughts of sacrifice and torture engulfed Caros' imagination, causing his breath to come in short gasps while sweat beaded his brow along the rim of his helmet. Impatiently, he charged forward, taking everyone by surprise. The kitchens were deserted and he bolted on through a hall. Behind him, the distinctive slap of warriors' sandals echoed as his men raced to keep pace with him.

The wails resolved into hideous shrieks the deeper Caros ran. Berenger was at his shoulder and pointed the way. They turned a corner and Caros sprawled up the stone stairs hidden there.

Berenger hauled him upright. "Nearly there, hero, just up these stairs and a little way further. Remember my help when this is done."

Caros shrugged him off and cursing at the pain in his knees, set off up the stairs. He reached the head of the stairs and ran into a wall of smoke.

"Shit, what is this? The place is burning!"

A hollow scream from his left lifted the hair at his neck. Berenger appeared with Neugen who immediately choked on the smoke.

"This is bad! Who set the place afire?"

Another drawn out scream rent the air, making him grit his teeth.

"This way!" Caros plunged into clouds of black smoke, heading in the direction of the last scream. Footfalls behind him reassured him of the presence of his friend and his warriors. Without warning, he slammed into a body and bounced into a wall with a loud clang as his cuirass met the stonework. He peered into the acrid clouds and made out a figure crawling on all fours. Diving on the figure, he planted his knee in the small of their back and pinned them to the floor. Caros grabbed him by the hair and jerked his head back, jabbing the point of his blade under his chin.

"Who are you?" As he spoke, he noticed the burns and lacerations covering the person's neck and arms. The smell of seared flesh was sickening. The figure wheezed once more and fell into a faint. He rolled it over and saw this was no warrior, but a matronly woman. Her bosom, arms and throat were burned black and she had deep lacerations in her left arm.

"Take her downstairs. She will die here otherwise." Caros ordered a warrior.

Neugen pointed in the direction of another anguished scream. Again, he forced aside visions of Ilimic being abused and murdered by some blood hungry priestess and ran.

Screams filtered through a pair of heavy doors on his left. Caros drove into them with his shoulder in a futile effort to break them open. Neugen and the other warriors threw their weight into the doors beside him a half-heartbeat later. Something splintered and the doors fell partially open. For a moment, Caros saw an apparition of a tall woman and beyond her a huge, hideous shape rearing high in the room. Smoke blocked out the terrifying sight although not the screams. On hearing the agony-warped cries, the warriors hurled themselves, cursing and yelling, at the doors with greater energy, until with a resounding crack, they crashed open fully.

Caros stumbled to his knees inside the hall, his sword slipping from his hand and skittering across the stonework. The temple flickered with the orange glow of a fire that burned fiercely at the far end. In that flickering light he saw a knot of people moving towards him, their drawn blades glinting with ominous intent. He grabbed his fallen falcata and sprang to his feet.

Neugen tapped Caros on the shoulder to let him know he was with him as were the rest of the Bastetani warriors.

"Looks like we found the temple. Do you see Ilimic?"

Caros thought he saw bound figures in the shadows beyond the fire. "No, but we will need to sort this lot out first." He stepped forward, feeling naked without his shield. "Sagunt is fallen! Lay down your weapons and submit!"

His words only seemed to enrage the approaching warriors who snarled and charged his men and him while from the shadows beyond the fire a shrill voice screamed for them to be killed.

"Kill the defilers! Kill them all!"

"By the gods, they are insane! Hold!" Caros yelled to his men who, he noted enviously, all still had their shields. The attacking warriors reached them and a burly man swung his shield at Caros, using the rim as a weapon. With no room to avoid the blow, he opted to take it on his cuirass and was staggered by the force. He next parried a sword that swept at his head before a second blow of the warrior's shield knocked him to his haunches. The warrior thrust his falcata at Caros, roaring through his full beard. Caros rolled and aside and slashed the man's ankle and as he did, a massive blow struck his back. His cuirass held, but for a heartbeat he thought his ribs had shattered. Struggling to draw a breath, he saw Neugen plunge his falcata into the warrior's kidneys, withdraw the blade and slice it viciously across the man's throat.

His breath returned and he rolled to avoid spear thrusts and sword cuts, expecting the bite of a blade at any moment. Rolling clear of the main brawl, he rose swiftly to his feet only to receive another ringing blow, this time to his chest. His attacker wielded an axe and was already preparing to deliver the killing blow. Blood rushed to his head and the panic and anxiety he had felt since learning of Ilimic's fate turned to battle rage. With a roar, he leaped at the warrior, grabbing the axe shaft with his left hand and thrusting his falcata deep into the axeman's neck. The blade scraped bone and he jerked it to the side as he pulled it free, opening the man's throat. The warrior staggered backwards, hands grasping at the mortal wound before tumbling across a bench.

The Bastetani were holding their own and he was beyond the surging mass of warriors and combat. Seizing the opportunity, he ran towards the fire and the bound figures he had glimpsed. In the next instant, he skidded to a halt as the enormous figure he had seen earlier, reared before him. The cold fear that had clutched his heart at the sight, thawed as he realized it was a mere shadow. Standing before the fire was a figure, arms held high, and a blade gripped in one hand. He started forward and the figure resolved into that of a short, plump man. Caros spat out a dry laugh at the incongruous little figure whose shadow was his most fearsome aspect. Looking beyond the chanting dwarf, bile burned up his throat at the sight of a woman bound before the priest.

Spread-eagled and naked on a stone block, she lay secured at both ankles and wrists. Caros gagged at the wounds on her body. This was where the maids were sacrificed and here lay one of the unfortunate victims. He glared at the tiny man, noticing that he was naked and worse, aroused. What kind of vile beast could do this? He hurled himself between overturned benches, making for the creature. Twisting past a fallen amphora, he hissed as something bit deep into his shoulder, knocking him halfway around. A long, slender shaft was buried in his flesh. With a growl of rage and pain, he looked up to find the archer.

A figure materialized beside the little man. Tall, slender and dressed in the sheerest linen he had ever seen, the firelight silhouetted her body so he could see the curve of breast and hip. Her face appeared out of the shadows and Caros spat to ward off the taint of the evil shades she possessed. It was she who had loosed the arrow and while smiling at him, she nocked another. He took his blade in his left hand and snarled at her, knowing he could never reach her before she loosed the second arrow. Calling on his gods to give him strength, he balanced the falcata in his hand and started towards her.Her smile remained as she lifted the bow and stared at him down the arrow shaft. He guessed the man beside her must be the high priest, the insane brother Berenger had mentioned. The brother, his member in one hand and his knife in the other, smiled malevolently at Caros.

The sacrificed woman groaned and Caros was horrified that she lived despite her injuries. Her groan drew the attention of the high priest who leaned over her. With a high-pitched growl, he clamped his teeth into her throat and worried her like a starved dog.

She cried out weakly. "Papa, where are you?"

Just a young girl and these monsters had torn her from her kin for this. Caros gritted his teeth, his rage burying the pain of his wounds. Mouth bloodied, the high priest plunged his blade into the girl's torn throat and a heartbeat later, the priestess loosed her arrow at Caros. As she did, blood pumped from the gash in the girl's throat, spraying the face of the priestess. Caros felt the arrow slide past his cheek and then he sprang.

Already the priestess was darting away into the shadows, dropping the bow and leaving the priest who belatedly realized his danger. He shrieked and jumped a foot into the air, arms flailing madly, but going nowhere. With disgust, Caros swung his falcata and the wicked edge took the man just above his crotch. Caros dragged the blade up as he ran past the shrieking monster until he felt it strike the bone of his chest wall. He did not look back but drove into the deeper shadows beyond the firelight. His foot went out from beneath him and he skidded in a pool of partly congealed blood. Flies buzzed hideously about his face, disturbed from their feeding. Waving them away, he heard movement and saw bodies lying contorted in death rigors. The corpses rested where they had been unceremoniously dumped after serving their purpose on the sacrificial altar to the ancient war goddess, Catubodua.

He steadied himself and wiped sweat from his eyes. The air was tainted with smoke, insects and the stink of corruption. A whimper came from the dark and Caros froze, listening. He heard it again, coming from the nearby corpses. He heard other sounds of life and realized that there were living people among the corpses.

"Ilimic!" He shouted. "It is Caros, answer me Ilimic! Are you here?" He went to the nearest body and reached to roll it over, but one touch of the icy cold shoulder told him the woman was dead. Wary of another attack, he moved from body to body, calling Ilimic's name.

A voice spoke from the dark. "Óc! I know this one. I know this Ilimic. Please here, help."

Galvanized by the foreign voice, Caros sprang upright. "Where are you? Is Ilimic with you?"

"Here! Here quickly please to save us. They killing us all. Please!"

Compelled by the urgency and fear in the woman's voice, he pressed forward into the deeper shadows. A knot of women lay huddled together, bound and naked. He could see the whites of their eyes as they stared up at him with fear and hope. There were at least a dozen living and he wondered where they came from, as many were fair-haired. He began cutting away the rope binding their wrists and ankles and as he did, they rolled their joints, whimpering as the blood flowed into them.

"Where is Ilimic? I have come to help her and take you all from this evil. Where is she?"

A girl nearby tried to sit up. "Ilimic. She fight too hard. They beat her."

Fear turned Caros cold. "Where is she?"

"She here. They hit her the head. She not speaking now. Look."

Caros scrambled past cringing women, past caring where he put his feet and knees as he scrambled through them. Ilimic! She lay beside a broad-cheeked girl whose call had first alerted him. Bound and breathing with difficulty, Ilimic lay with her eyes closed. Blood had dried in crusts across her brow and down one cheek. He grasped her bare shoulders and gently lifted her, ignoring the pain from his wound. Blowing on her eyelids in the gloom, he called her name over and over.

Caros sat with Ilimic cradled in his arms. Tears ran down his cheeks as he murmured to her. Footsteps sounded and Neugen hissed.

"Caros! What is wrong with her? Is she breathing?"

He looked up at his friend. "They have beaten her, and the gods knows what else. She does not open her eyes." His voice was hoarse.

"She is alive at least. Rejoice that you have found her! We should move from this foul place." He jumped up and tore down a curtain draped behind the altar.

Caros took it gratefully and wrapped her in it. All around him, men were seeking the living amongst the dead and cutting away their bonds.

A warrior with his arm bleeding through a makeshift binding, called from the smashed doors at the end of the temple hall. "The flames are getting closer. We do not have much longer."

"Take her, Caros." Neugen patted Caros on the shoulder. "We will bring the rest."

Caros rose with difficulty and only then did Neugen see the broken arrow shaft jutting from his shoulder.

"You have been wounded! Here, let me carry her."

"No! No, I will be fine. I will see you outside."

Reluctantly, Neugen acquiesced. The smoke was even thicker outside the temple hall and Caros could hear the crackle of flames as some part of the fort burned fiercely. He staggered back the way they had come, coughing as smoke burned his lungs and eyes. He could not tell where he was and knew he had missed the stairs leading to kitchens when he stumbled into an unfamiliar passage with large open slits in the outer walls. He was grateful that the smoke here was much thinner and took the opportunity to catch his breath. Lowering Ilimic gently to the floor, he winced as the arrowhead grated against bone.

Warriors emerged at a run from the far end of the passage, buckets of water slopping at their knees. He stopped the first and demanded one of the buckets. The man veered past him, no doubt thinking the soot-covered warrior crouched beside the shrouded body was one of the defenders.

Caros rose to his feet. "It is I, Caros of the Bastetani. I need that water, man!"

The warrior paused and shook his head before placing a pail beside Caros.

"I am Turdetani, but I have heard your name spoken. If I were you, I would leave the body and get out of this pyre." He grinned. "Unless, there is treasure wrapped in that cloth and not a body?"

"Thank you for the water, now go before you say something I am forced to gut you for." Caros gripped the hilt of his sheathed blade and squared up to the Turdetani. The warrior recoiled from his glare and dipped his chin before joining his fellows.

Caros soaked a corner of the curtain in the water and wiped Ilimic's blood-encrusted face clean. Next, he dribbled water onto her lips and to his joy, they parted and she swallowed. His heart leaped.

"Ilimic! Can you hear me?"

Her eyes opened and she gazed at him for a long heartbeat. Drawing her hand from under the cloth, she lifted it to his face and traced her fingers across the livid scar he now bore.

"Caros. They have hurt you too. Why?" Tears spilled from her eyes and coursed down her cheeks. "Why did you come here? This is a place of evil."

He smiled at her voice while tears dripped from his cheeks to run with hers.

"I thought you killed and my life without you was so barren. When I learned that you were alive, no walls nor army could stop me coming for you."

Still weeping silently, she shook her head sadly. "I am not the same, Caros. You should have let them kill me. Leave me here so that I can join my ancestors."

Caros' heart tore with grief. "We are together again. This place burns to the ground today and with it the evil and the memories. You will see. We will be happy once more."

She smiled and hooked her hand in his cuirass to pull him to her. Her lips brushed his and they kissed gently, deeply. He broke away and rose unsteadily, a wide smile shining on his soot-darkened face. "I will be back in a heartbeat. Neugen is near and I need his help to carry you further." She closed her eyes and laid her head back.

Men dashed past and he stumbled out of their way and back into the smoky passage. The fire seemed to be everywhere now.

"Neugen!" He shouted for his friend.

A warrior appeared; one of his Bastetani guards. "Caros! Neugen is in the kitchens. He sent me to look for you."

"Good, come give me a hand." Caros led the man to where Ilimic lay. The folds of curtain still lay there beside the pail, but she was gone. He dashed forward, kicking aside the pail and the cloth.

"Ilimic!"

Without being told, the Bastetani warrior ran up the passage, peering into doorways while Caros staggered in the other direction. Smoke poured from a doorway that had been closed when he had left Ilimic. Surely she would not have sought shelter in there? With a hand over his nose, he stepped through it.

Fire ran along the wooden beams of the ceiling and curled around legs of heavy wooden furniture. Mats smoked and wall hangings blackened and burst into flames. Caros froze. Ilimic stood in the center of the room, her face lifted to the ceiling and arms wide.

"Ilimic! What are you doing?" He held his good arm up to ward off the heat and pressed into the room. On hearing his voice, her gaze lowered and settled on his face. A sad smile teased the corners of her lips even as tears dripped from her soulful eyes.

"Goodbye, my champion." She pressed her fingers to her lips before holding her hand out towards him. Above her, the ceiling groaned and crashed down in a deluge of fire.

In a heartbeat, she was gone, engulfed by the blaze. Caros fell to his knee as the stone floor cracked, his cuirass scorching his neck and the fabric of his tunic smoldering. He cried out in anguish and pushed forward, but a firm hand pulled him back. Wrestling him out of the room, the Bastetani warrior pulled him into the corridor and out of the intense heat. Unable to breathe and heartbroken, Caros stopped flailing and slumped against an outer wall. The warrior looked back into the room and shook his head, his cheeks damp.

Epilogue

Fires blazed through the inner fortress all that night. The merchants who had staged the war, thinking that their alliance with Rome would save them, could never accept the terms Hannibal had offered. Abarca had known this when he walked back through the gates. Instead, the city oligarchy burned their wealth rather than surrender it to Hannibal. Knowing the outcome for their spite would be a painful death at the hands of Hannibal's army, the wealthy citizens took their lives. Men fell on their swords and women cut their children's throats before throwing themselves onto the flames they had ignited.

Reacting with speed, Hannibal ordered his warriors to clear the inner fort of all valuables ahead of the fire. Many died, suffocated by smoke, bags of silver across their shoulders. Despite their best efforts and sacrifices, much of the wealth was lost to the fire.

Hannibal's rage, shared by his leading men and mercenary army, was manifest the following day. The surviving populace of the city was assembled on the plains, heavy ropes about their necks. Surrounding them, the vast army that had prevailed. Hannibal ordered his men to separate out all the wealthiest survivors. Men, women and children were dragged to the banks of the dry river where they huddled in a tight group of fewer than a hundred. Not content, he then ordered every male over the age of fourteen, regardless of station in life, to join their wealthy neighbors.

Caros found Neugen at the head of the Bastetani contingent, his eyes fixed on the survivors being separated and herded to the dry river course. Neugen regarded him with a disapproving frown which Caros ignored. His friend had tried to persuade Caros to withdraw from his tasks to mourn his loss, but he had no intention of doing that.

"Greetings, Neugen." He tugged on the reins and halted his mount beside

Neugen who nodded his greeting. "You think we should be there? Doing that?"

Neugen turned from Caros to eye those being dragged apart. "I thought so. We lost four good men in the fire." He swallowed and pointed. "Look. In the center of the doomed ones."

"What is it?"

"The family that we found fleeing from the tunnel. They were among the first dragged to the riverbank."

Caros did not respond. He had received the message with Hannibal's seal, requesting that his warriors assist today. He had nodded politely and dismissed the messenger. When Neugen had asked what their orders were, he had smiled and told him to sleep with a clear conscience. Now, watching Hannibal's revenge unfold, he knew his decision had been the right one.

They said no more through the afternoon but remained with the Bastetani warriors to watch as thousands of Saguntines were executed. The river was a bloody sewer when the last captive was stabbed through the heart to topple to the ground.

Neugen wiped his brow and cleared his throat. Caros thought his friend would fall from his mount, his face was so pale.

"Thank you." Caros frowned questioningly. "Thank you for refusing the Barca and not sullying our hands." He grunted and nodded, his mind reeling at the slaughter that Hannibal had ordered. "They have not found the priestess or the warrior?" Neugen asked.

He gritted his teeth. "No. The warrior, Berenger, used the smoke and flames to hide his escape. As for the priestess." He spat to ward off her evil. "She disappeared into the tunnels and has not been found. I will hunt her. I will find her and kill her with my own hands."

Caros looked back at the river of execution, his face dark. He breathed deeply for long heartbeats before smiling wearily at Neugen.

"If Rome comes, will you fight with Hannibal?"

After a long consideration, Neugen dragged his gaze from the slaughter and turned to Caros, lips thin. "I was once eager to capture a city and make myself rich. I dreamed of poets weaving great tales of my bravery and daring. After what I have witnessed here, I have little appetite for war, Caros." Neugen squeezed his eyes shut for a moment. "If they come, I will ride as a Bastetani warrior to defend our people. It is my duty."

Caros took Neugen's arm and embraced him. "My friend. Take our warriors home to their kin and may that day never come."

The stink of blood and hum of flies' wings had faded when the drum of hoofbeats reached Caros. He drew on his reins and turned to watch as Aksel galloped his way.

"Greetings, Aksel. Your warriors have gone north."

Aksel nodded, eyes somber. He turned his mount to face north, where the mountains were topped by clouds. "I will join them soon. We will race our mounts in far lands, fill valleys with our voices and strange cities with our laughter." With eyes brimming, he thrust a small object into Caros' hand. "I will see you again my friend, I know it in my heart. Until then, ride safe." Without waiting for Caros to respond, he clicked his tongue and sent his mount racing away to the distant mountains.

Caros watched Aksel until the Masulian merged into the horizon. Unfolding his fingers, he looked upon the figurine Aksel had gifted him, newly carved from the tooth of an oliphant. A shade of a smile played across Caros' face as he traced the lines of a charging boar.

The end

GLOSSARY

Arroyo: A steep sided gully
Barcid: Of the Barca family
Cabar: Goddess of love
Cariociecus: god of war (ancient)
Catubodua: Gallic goddess of victory
Elu: Elephant
Endovex: Iron Age god of health (Endovelicus)
Falcata: Slashing sword with distinctive blade
Fides: (Latin) trust, reliability, faith
Javelin: Light throwing spear
Mouflon: Wild sheep
Numidia: Berber-Libyan kingdom in North Africa
Oligarchy: Ruling structure of a small minority and usually tyrannical
Orko: God of the mountains and rocks
Runeovex: God of the javelin (Runesocesius)
Sagunt (Saguntum): The modern-day city of Sagunto in Valencia, Spain.
Saur: God of the underworld or land of the dead
Stadion *pl.* stadia: Greek measure of distance equal to 180 meters or 600 feet
Stater: Ancient Greek coin widely used in the near east and dispersed through Western Europe by Celtic mercenaries
Strategos: Greek rank of general or military governor
Tanit: Phoenician and Carthaginian Mother goddess
The Tagus: The longest river on the Iberian Peninsula at 1,038 km (645 miles)

Places

Abdera	Bastetani coastal town
Athanagia	Ilerget city
Baria	Bastetani trading port
Ebusos	coastal village in the Balearic Islands (near Ibiza)
Helike	Greco-Iberian village (modern day Elche)
Malaka	Turdetani coastal city
Mauritania	home of the Masulians
Orze	Bastetani village where Caros grew up
Peñalén	village on the Tagus river
Qart Hadasht	Carthaginian city in Iberia (Cartagena)
Sagunt	Greco-Iberian city in Iberia

Sucro	Greco-Iberian town
Tagilit	Bastetani city
Zakarra River	enters the sea at Baria

Characters

Caros	Bastetani champion
Neugen	Bastetani warrior
Aksel	Masulian champion
Ilimic	Bastetani woman
Hannibal Barca	Carthaginian general
Berenger	Edetani champion
Abarca	Strategos of Sagunt
Adicran	Libyan warrior
Aniceteus	Merchant of Sagunt
Asklepius	Hannibal's physician
Bomilcar	Carthaginian admiral
Carmesina	High priestess of Catubodua
Cortocus	Carpetani champion
Glauketas	High priest in Sagunt
Gualam and Drasal	Turdetani leading men
Hahdha	Masulian leading man
Hasdrubal Barca	Carthaginian general
Jinkata	Masulian leading man
Julene	Bastetani maid
Kouf	Masulian leading man
Mago Barca	Carthaginian general
Maharbal	Carthaginian general
Manat	Masulian leading man
Marc	Bastetani merchant
Massibaka	Masulian leading man
Massinissa	Masulian prince, son of king Gala
Muttines	Libyan cavalry commander
Nerea	Neugen's lover
Rose	Edetani overseer
Rudax	Lusitanian warrior
Turro	Edetani warrior
Ugar	Bastetani stonemason

HISTORICAL NOTE

The Iberian Peninsula describes the landmass of current day Spain and Portugal and the people of Iberia were tribes of Pre-Celtic Iberians and Celts. For centuries they had traded with Phoenicians, Greeks and Carthaginians who established trading ports along the Eastern and Southern coast. Under the rule of local kings and chieftains, tribes such as the Bastetani and Edetani both fought and traded with one another.

In 237 BC, Hamilcar Barca, still smarting from the loss of Sicily to Rome in the 1st Punic war (264 to 241 BC), set about expanding Carthaginian control in Iberia through the subjugation of the fiercely independent tribes. Hamilcar gained control over strategic silver mines in the Sierra Morena and established the city Akra Lueka (modern day Alicante).

Hasdrubal the Fair succeeded Hamilcar Barca in 228 BC and expanded control through treaties rather than force. In 226 BC he signed the Ebro Treaty with Rome, which prevented Carthaginian expansion north of the Ebro River.

Hannibal succeeded Hasdrubal the Fair in 221 BC and quickly set about subjugating the Olcades and Vaccaei tribes south of the Ebro. By 219 BC, the course of the Iberian tribes was about to change profoundly. The oligarchy of the Greco-Iberian city of Saguntum, located 100 miles south of the Ebro, was split between pro-Roman and pro-Carthaginian factions. The more powerful pro-Roman faction called on Rome to be arbitrators in an internal matter and these arbitrators supported the execution of leading members of the city's pro-Carthaginian party. Simultaneously, Saguntum was engaged in disputes with neighbouring tribes and reportedly massacred Turdetani settlers.

Hannibal Barca could no longer ignore this powerful pro-Roman city in the center of the eastern Iberian seaboard and in 218 BC he laid siege to Saguntum. Lacking any advanced siege craft, Hannibal was forced to resort to a protracted 8-month assault against the heavily fortified city perched on the top of a steep-sided hill. Rome demanded the Carthaginians cease their attack on Saguntum and hand over Hannibal Barca. When Carthage refused, the Romans declared war and thus began the 2nd Punic War.

While Caros is a fictional character, the Bastetani were a powerful tribe located in southeast Iberia. The only deviation I have made in the sequence of historic events is the battle on the Tagus. This battle occurred in 220 BC, the year prior to the siege of Sagunt. I have set the battle during the siege to incorporate Hannibal's first major battlefield victory into the timeframe of the narrative. The exact location of the battle on the Tagus is uncertain, so I have located it near the little village of Peñalén in the Guadalajara province. Hannibal used the Tagus as a barrier and defeated the enemy much as I have described.

There was a minor rebellion during the siege caused by the high levies Hannibal demanded from the tribes. Leaving Maharbal in charge of the siege, Hannibal quelled the rebellion. I have replaced this minor rebellion with the battle on the Tagus.

Of the siege itself, Livy indicates that once the outer wall was breached, Hannibal employed siege towers and ballistae to reduce the defenders. I have left out the use of these siege weapons and included only battering rams. He was successful in undermining a large portion of the wall with pickaxes. According to history, the defenders fought with supreme valor and continued building new defenses to shore up the failing fortifications. When defeat became unavoidable, the wealthy rejected Hannibal's terms and attempted to destroy all their wealth in great fires. Hannibal had offered to allow them to leave and was prepared to grant the inhabitants land on which to build a new town. When the wealthy tried to deny him their riches, he ordered thousands of the citizens to be executed.

Being a mercenary army, it included warriors from many far-flung lands such as the Numidian horsemen who I describe as Masulians. Their correct name was Massylii. While stirrups were unknown in this era, the Massylii did not even use reins to control their mounts. They were truly at one with their horses which would follow their riders much like our pet dogs follow us.

As for deities, I have improvised based on the minimal archaeological evidence left from pre-Roman times. For the Iberians, I have based names on known gods and goddesses of the Gauls and Celts. As far as the sacrifices of maidens attributed to the high priest and priestess of Sagunt, this is entirely fictional.

The Iberian Lynx is referred to throughout the book. In the course of researching the fauna and flora of Spain, I discovered that these beautiful animals now only number about 300 individuals in the wild. In the time of Caros, these cats would have been prolific in the mountainous wilds of Iberia and would have made an impression on the psyche of the largely agrarian population.

AUTHOR'S NOTE

As of August 2019, I have released a further three Sons of Iberia titles since Warhorn was originally published in 2013. Thank you for choosing Warhorn and I hope that you enjoyed reading it as much as I enjoyed writing it. The Sons of Iberia series still has some way to go, after all, the 2nd Punic War lasted seventeen years and Carthaginian-backed resistance to Rome continued in the Cisalpine for a few years after Hannibal's defeat in Africa. In Hispania, the Romans got it very wrong and took two hundred years to subdue the Iberians. I have planned a further seven titles in the series.

You may have seen and read the first prequel to Sons of Iberia, Rise of the Spears, which I released in 2018. My thinking is that there are interesting backstories to many of the characters encountered in Sons of Iberia. The prequels are novellas that tell of these characters' lives before they enter Sons of Iberia. These are a great way for you to explore the backstory to the Second Punic War. I foresee at least twelve prequels, but there could be many more. The first, Rise of the Spears, centers on Dubgetious, a Bastetani warrior who makes an appearance in Gladius Winter, Sons of Iberia, Book 3. It also features Hamilcar Barca and his famous son, Hannibal.

For more about the Second Punic War, visit my website at www.jglennbauer.co.uk.

That is all from me until the next title. Oh, if there is a character whose backstory you would enjoy reading in a prequel, let me know via a message on any of my social media accounts or by emailing me at j.glennbauer@gmail.com.

MORE TITLES

Sons of Iberis Series
Battle Cloud
Gladius Winter
Howl of Blades

Prequel to Sons of Iberia
Rise of the Spears

Others
The Runeovex Secret
Von Steiner's Gold

Non-Fiction
Off-Grid Boaters. One couple's alternative nomad life on a 25-foot yoghurt pot

Printed in Great Britain
by Amazon